DOUGIE McHALE

The Island Between Us

VINCI BOOKS

Vinci Books

vinci-books.com

Published by Vinci Books Ltd in 2026

1

A CIP catalogue record for this book is available from the British Library.
Paperback ISBN: 9781036711238
The EU GPSR authorised representative is Logos Europe, 9 rue Nicolas
Poussion, 17000 La Rochelle, France contact@logoseurope.eu

Printed and bound in Great Britain by Clays Ltd, Elcograf S.p.A.

BY DOUGIE MCHALE

The Hellenic Collection

CHAPTER ONE

THE ENDING

Edinburgh 2007

'What are you saying? You've been living a lie. Is that what you're telling me?' Stuart glances at her accusingly.

Carissa, wrestling with emotion, is relieved to have finally told him after all these months of indecision, but frightened of the reaction it will evoke. 'I've tried. I really have. I wanted this to work. I wanted *us* to work.'

Stuart is sat opposite her as Carissa waits for her revelation to sink in. Sunlight streams through the bay window of their spacious ground-floor flat on Comiston Road, Morningside, catching a glass vase and casting an arched crimson streak of light across the wall just above Stuart's head. Carissa has never witnessed this before, and despite the gravity of her situation, it still catches her eye.

'You sound like you're trying to extract yourself from a business arrangement, not a relationship.' Stuart's voice raises a notch, and its sharpness pricks Carissa like the point of a knife.

'I'm trying to be honest with you. You know it hasn't been right for a long time.'

Stuart's cheek twitches involuntarily. 'I didn't see it coming, if that's what you mean.'

'There isn't a day that goes by that we don't argue.'

'All couples argue… disagree… It's healthy. That's normal.'

'They do, but not every day.'

'So, that's how we've been.'

'Come on, Stuart, this is supposed to be a two-way thing. You can't have been that numb to what was going on.'

'That's harsh, Carissa. Okay, I admit I haven't always been in the right headspace. Work has been intense lately, but it's my job, and it comes with the territory. I haven't been so detached that I hadn't noticed a change in you. You've not been yourself lately,' he improvised. 'If something's been troubling you, or not right, you have said nothing to me.'

'So, what is this I'm doing now? Stuart, I can't live like this anymore.'

'Like what? Has it been that bad? Have I been that bad? If I have, we can change.'

'I don't want *us* to change.'

'Then what do you want? I'm not getting this.'

Her head spins, her throat burns, and a hard knot seems wedged inside it. 'It's not just you. It's me,' she murmurs.

'Have you been that unhappy?' His words usher a response, but before she can reply, he injects, 'Do you love me?'

She glances at her hands. Her nails are digging into her

skirt, and although she can't see, she can feel the indentations on the skin of her thighs. 'Not in the way you want me to.'

Stuart frowns.

Carissa lets out a breath. 'People grow apart and end up wanting different things. It doesn't mean I've stopped caring about you.'

He looks at her with heavy brows. 'But you've stopped loving me.' He rubs his face. 'When?! At least let me know.'

She glances away from him. Then silence.

His gaze is steady, insistent. He exhales. 'It wasn't just yesterday, then.'

'It's not something that just happens. It's gradual.'

'That's very clinical; it sounds like a disease you can catch.'

She looks away.

'What did I do?' he asks.

'That's the point. We do nothing anymore. We both go to work, come home, go to work, come home.'

'Doesn't everyone? It's called life.'

'Not every single day, Stuart. We never go out. And on the few occasions I go out with friends, I'm hit with a barrage of questions and the same accusations. I feel like…'

'Like what?!'

She tries to summon the determination to finally say it. 'You're always saying, my friends think you're punching above your weight, and they think you aren't good enough for me. You've said I'm becoming paranoid. There's only one person in this room that applies to.'

'Really? It's not something I keep tabs on.'

Her hands tighten into a ball. 'You try to control everything I do. It's like you want to vet anyone that comes into my life, I feel suffocated.'

'There's someone else, isn't there? Someone at work?'

'No! Do you think I'd do something like that?'

'What am I supposed to think? I don't think I know you anymore.'

'I can't be the person you want me to be. I won't be that person anymore. I can't be. It's not me. It never has been.'

'What are you saying, Carissa, that you've been pretending all this time?'

She tries to breathe the tension from her chest. 'I've been trying to make it work. It's exhausting. I'm exhausted, and I can't do it anymore.'

'Maybe you just need some time. We could go on that holiday you're always talking about.'

She sighs. 'It takes something as drastic as this for you to agree to go on holiday. That sums us up, doesn't it? It's too late for that. A holiday will not make any difference. It won't change how I feel.'

'How can you do this? You're killing me.'

His words hit her hard, more than she expected. 'I'm sorry. The last thing I wanted to do was hurt you.'

He smirks. 'There's an irony in that.'

'I can't help how I feel. It's over. We're over, Stuart.'

'I'm wondering if we were ever together.'

'I've felt like this for months now,' she breathes.

'What if we give it some time? Forget the holiday idea. We can give it a month or two, what do you say?'

'It would only delay the inevitable.'

'So, there's no compromise? Out of the blue, you hit me with wanting us to finish. You've decided this without the slightest consideration of how this would make me feel. It's all about you, isn't it, Carissa? I'm wondering now if it always has been.'

'I've never said that.'

'You don't have to. The implication is very clear.'

'I'm not that cold-hearted. I still care about you, Stuart. How could I possibly have made this less painful for you? I couldn't.'

'What the hell does that mean?' Stuart splutters.

Carissa runs a hand through her hair. A voice at the back of her mind reminds her to tread carefully. 'This isn't easy for me.'

'We're back to how you feel again, Carissa; there's that common theme, isn't it?' With teeth clenched; Stuart spits the words: 'Fuck you, Carissa.'

The force of it jars her. An edge of rage has broken the surface of their civility, and she fears its trajectory. He's using his anger to defend himself, to protect himself. That's all this is, she tells herself. 'I think I should go now.'

She bends to pick up her handbag.

'Leave it!'

Her hand hovers and she glances at the living room door. 'I'm going to go now.'

'Where?' Stuart snaps.

'I've packed a bag.'

He rubs a hand over his face. 'You've what?'

Stuart's eyebrows knot in an incredulous frown. 'You've planned this.'

'I think it's best.'

Anger creases his face. 'So, you've been plotting behind my back.'

'It's not like that.'

He sneers. 'Have you told anyone, Carissa?'

'Only Kate. Who else was I going to tell? She's the only one who knows what I've been going through.' The second the words are out, she immediately regrets them.

'Obviously, because you never fucking told me. You've never been the same since you had that miscarriage.'

Carissa opens her mouth to reply, but no words come out. Stuart grins. 'Your silence says it all. It wasn't just you who was grieving; I lost it too, but you got all the attention. Your amazing friends rallied round, while I made the teas and coffees and put the biscuits out on our best saucers and let them get on with their grief counselling while I—'

'You! You went to the pub.'

'I felt an inconvenience. Anyway, they weren't there to ask me how I was coping; no, the quicker they could get you on your own, and me out of the way, the better. Kate has never liked me. She's always thought you could do so much better than spend your life with me. She's never hidden the fact that she doesn't like me. She's nothing but an interfering bitch.'

Carissa raises her hand, as if in doing so will deflect the accusation. 'I'm not doing this. We've gone over this countless times. It's not my fault you don't like my friends.' She looks at him, appalled. 'I can't believe you've just said that about me and the baby.'

'It wasn't a baby; it was a bloody miscarriage,' Stuart hisses.

Clarissa had been 19 weeks pregnant when she and Stuart went out with his family to celebrate his parents' 25th wedding anniversary at their favourite restaurant. That night, Carissa was sick, and the next morning the GP diagnosed food poisoning after she got an emergency appointment. She was told that the food poisoning could increase the risk of a miscarriage. The first signs appeared the following day. When the bleeding became heavy, the cramps and pain intensified. An ultrasound and blood tests confirmed the miscarriage.

Stuart's parents blamed themselves for insisting on having the meal at the restaurant they'd frequented for years. The issue, though unaddressed, loomed large.

Carissa stands and straightens her skirt. 'I'm going now.'

Stuart raises a hand, Carissa flinches, and then he lets it fall to his side. 'Just like that. You've planned this all along.'

A pressure rises behind her eyes. 'I think it's best I go.'

Stuart stares at the floor.

Carissa fights for air. 'Did you hear me, Stuart?'

'Yes. I heard you. There's someone, isn't there? You've been seeing someone. You have to be. I need to know.'

She takes a deep sigh. 'There's no one. Please don't do this.'

'I always wondered what it felt like when people said *their world was falling from under their feet*. I don't have to wonder about that anymore, do I?'

Every instinct urges her to leave. It unnerves her the way he continues to stare at the floor. 'I'll phone you in a few days' time to collect the rest of my things.'

'And what about all the other things that define us as a couple? This place, for example.'

Carissa hesitates. It feels like an opportunity to come to an agreement, soften the blow, and leave on a mutual understanding.

'There'll be time for that. I'll still pay my share of the rent for next month. It's best if I give you time to come to terms with this. It's a lot to take in.'

'Oh, I think I get the general gist of it. *Come to terms with it*, you say. I'm not sure I'll ever do that… but there's something I can do, something I can do, right now.'

She stares at him, confused, and then, unexpectedly, he stands and reaches for her.

CHAPTER TWO

THE BEGINNING OF SOMETHING NEW

Edinburgh 2007

They are sitting at her favourite cafe on the corner of Morningside Road. Opposite Carissa, her best friend Kate is dabbing crumbs of lemon sponge from her mouth with a napkin.

'Look at it like this,' Kate says. 'You've done the hard part – you've told him. At least you haven't got the baggage of being tied to a mortgage with him. That would bring another set of problems and headaches.'

'I said I'd still pay my share of next month's rent.'

'And he agreed? Of course he did.' Kate frowns. 'Why doesn't that surprise me? He was always money orientated. Carissa, you're not living there anymore. What are you thinking?'

'It's fine, Kate.' Carissa flicks a strand of hair from her face.

Sensing Carissa's hesitation, Kate screws her eyes

together. 'There's something else. Something you're not telling me. What is it, Carissa?'

'Nothing. It's fine, honestly.' Carissa shoots her an unconvincing glance as her stomach somersaults.

'Tell me. I've known you far too long to know when you're hiding something from me. What's happened?'

Carissa takes a deep breath. She tries to coax her muddled thoughts into a coherent sentence that can move the conversation from its current trajectory, but her eyes fill with tears and her fragile fortitude crumbles.

Kate raises a hand. 'Right, that's it. Tell me.'

'I tried to leave, but then he suddenly changed. He seemed angry. He… he forced himself on me.'

She shot Carissa a look that made her feel like a child. 'He what?! He raped you?'

'No.'

'If it's not consensual, then that's exactly what it is.'

'I got him off me before it went any further, and he sort of came to his senses.'

'Then it was attempted rape. That's what it was.'

'He was embarrassed. He couldn't apologise enough. He didn't know what had come over him. He asked me not to tell anyone.'

'Obviously, he would. Have you gone to the police? Did you report it?'

She swallows hard as a tumble of emotions wells inside her. She shakes her head. A panic rises in her chest. *Should she have done? While it didn't happen, the intent was there. No, it would only make things worse. She wants a clean break. No complications.*

Kate furrows her brow. 'So, you're just going to let him get away with it?'

'Get away with what? Nothing happened. He stopped.'

'Only because you made him stop. If it wasn't rape, it sure as hell was an assault.'

'It's finished. It's over. I don't want this hanging over me.'

'He just walks away,' Kate says, unable to quite comprehend what she has just heard.

Carissa's gaze shifts from Kate to the window, where condensation obscures the street outside. 'I've hurt him enough. I couldn't do that to him. I'm just relieved I've told him it's over.'

'You've told him, but does he actually understand it's finished?'

'What do you mean?'

'If he's capable of reacting like that, what else could he do?'

'What? Nothing he can do or say will make me change my mind. I told him, it's over.'

'Has he tried to contact you?'

'No. I said I'd phone him to organise when I could get the rest of my stuff.'

'Have you still got the key to the flat?'

Carissa nods.

Kate leans forward. 'Is there a time that he will not be in? I'm thinking of when he's at work. That's when you should go to the flat and get the rest of your things.'

'That would just make things worse between us.'

'You'd be protecting yourself. You can't take any chances. Let me go with you.' Kate tilts her head and, raising her eyebrows, says, 'Safety in numbers.'

'I'm not sure that's a good idea.'

'I'll take my car. You would struggle to get everything in yours, anyway. You could use that as an excuse if you want to? If it makes you feel any better about the whole thing?'

'I could, I suppose. If we used your car, I'd only have to make one trip.'

'Are your mum and dad okay with you staying with them? You can always bunk down on my settee until you get something permanent organised.'

'Thanks for the offer. My old room is still the same. They never changed it. My bed's still there, along with some old photographs I didn't take with me. After years of living away, it'll feel odd staying there, even with Mum and Dad, but I'm not staying too long.'

'What's the rush? You don't want to settle for any old flat, especially one that's below your expectations. You can still have standards. It's better to wait until something that suits you comes available.'

'I'm not intending to rent or buy.'

'What do you mean?'

'None of this has been a quick decision. For months now, I've been planning. Initially, I'd intended to stay. Edinburgh's a big city, but not that big. I need a clean break, and the possibility of knowing I could bump into Stuart at any time was a prospect I didn't want to entertain. So, I did a little research, looking at similar jobs to mine, did any offer relocation packages, and I went down one rabbit hole after another. Then, I came across the website of a girl who'd set herself up on the Greek island of Zakynthos. She offered walking and hiking tours. It was funded by an organisation called Trails of Greece, so I got in touch with them.'

'I've never heard of them,' Kate says, biting into her lemon sponge.

'They revive old footpaths and hiking trails by mapping, signposting and managing them. They offer walking groups.

It's amazing, really. Their current project has just begun. It's on an island called Skiathos. I looked it up. It's a gorgeous place, just a few miles off the mainland of Greece in the Aegean Sea.

'There's also the chance to teach yoga, personal wellbeing, and some fitness too. I thought, *What have I got to lose?* I love hill walking, trail walking, nature, and fitness. It sounded perfect. One thing led to another, and I was inquiring about how I could apply. They had an opportunity they thought might meet my needs – an initial three-month contract, with accommodation thrown in, working for them on Skiathos. They were holding interviews online and invited me to apply.'

'Wow, Carissa! This is so unlike you. You never told me.'

'I told no one, not even Stuart. I lived with the idea for about a week. By that time, I'd decided I couldn't carry on the way I was. It made me realise how stagnant my life had become and, most importantly, that I was no longer in love with Stuart. In a perverse way, the miscarriage was the catalyst that showed me we wanted different things out of our relationship, out of life, in fact.

'So, for the first time in my life, I made an intuitive decision and went onto their site, filled out the job application, and a week later, they offered me an initial interview. There was another one after that.'

'And…?'

Carissa takes a sip of her coffee. 'Well,' she says and sets down her cup with a smile. 'They offered me the job.'

Kate lets out a muffled scream. 'They never did.'

'I couldn't believe it. And then I thought, *What have I done?*'

'Have you accepted it?'

'I stewed it over for a few days. There was so much to

think about. I'd be leaving everything I'd known. Everything that made my life what it was – my family, my friends, my job.'

'It's not the other side of the world; it's Greece.' Kate gives Carissa a wilful smile. 'You took the job, and you didn't tell Stuart. He still doesn't know, does he?'

'No. It sounds terrible, doesn't it? But I think if I hadn't been offered it, I might not have gone through with leaving him. It made me realise I need to put myself first for a change. Does that make me a bad person?'

Kate raises a reassuring hand. 'Not at all. It makes you a strong person. You're what matters in all of this – your happiness, your sanity. It's a great opportunity to give you the time to work out what you really want. Life has offered you a door to open; walk through it and see where it leads you.'

Carissa chews the inside of her mouth. 'I should have told him.'

Kate shakes her head. 'Stuart doesn't own you, Carissa. He had every opportunity to make you happy, and he didn't. He screwed up.' She leans over and takes Carissa's hand. She gives it a light squeeze. 'Honey, I think it's wonderful. You're a beautiful person inside and out. If anyone deserves a chance to find something that makes them happy, it's you.'

'It doesn't feel like that right now.'

'Listen to me, he showed his true colours and, by doing so, he crossed a line. Did he think he could have you whenever he wanted? What was he trying to prove? You don't want anyone like that in your life.'

'But he's never done that before.'

'Once is enough.'

'He stopped when I asked.'

Kate furrows her brow. 'Only because you forced him to stop. What if there's a next time? It might have a different ending. He's broken the golden rule. There's no going back from that. How could you trust him?'

'I've no intention of going back to him. My mind's made up.'

'Good. So, when do you start this new job? It sounds like it'll be the perfect new start.'

Carissa tells Kate that she has already signed the job contract online. Initially for three months, with an extended option available if amenable to both parties.

'They'll also subsidise the rent and utility bills of an apartment in Skiathos Town, paying fifty percent of the monthly costs.

'It felt like ages waiting for the work permit to be processed. I had to have health insurance coverage for the duration of my stay and a certificate confirming the absence of a criminal record.'

"What a palaver. Do you have a start date?"

'In five weeks. May 15th. There're no flights from Edinburgh or Glasgow; Newcastle is the nearest airport that flies to Skiathos. Luckily, I managed to get a flight.'

'You're really going.'

'I am. Who would have believed it?'

'What does the job entail?'

'There's a weekly timetable of walking trails, yoga and wellbeing classes. The hours are seven in the morning to five in the afternoon, five days on and two days off.'

Kate smiles. 'It sounds perfect. And a place to stay, too. Ten-hour days though, how do you feel about that?'

'I'm used to working long days. It won't feel like work. I've been a health and fitness professional for ten years, I've run my own business, and not a single day has felt like work. I've enjoyed every minute. I'll be on a Greek island, doing what I love. What is there not to like about that?'

'Not much, I suppose. I don't want to put a dampener on things, but are you sure this company is the real deal? It's a long way to go to find out it's not what it says on the tin.'

'I've done my research. I wasn't going to jump in with two feet without being informed. They're a well-established and respected organisation within their field. Skiathos is well known as a hiking destination.

'Someone has been doing their homework. It's just that you hear these stories about people being ripped off or tied into contracts that are nothing short of slave labour.'

'It's nothing like that.'

'I know. I just had to ask. It sounds amazing.'

'And I appreciate your concern. I would have felt the same if it were you.'

'It's going to be great for you. Imagine having the whole of the island as your office.'

'I can't wait. There's an educational element to the job as well. I've to learn about the places on the routes that we'll come across – like churches, monasteries, watermills, oil presses – they're all part of Skiathos' culture and history.

'I've checked out a lot of sites online and social media groups about Skiathos. Some of the views on the island are breathtaking. And the beaches are just stunning.'

'It sounds amazing. You're already selling it.'

'If you love exploring and walking when on holiday, then Skiathos ticks all the right boxes. It's a small island but big in what it offers.'

'It's the perfect prescription for what you've been through.' Kate deposits the last of her lemon sponge into her mouth and, with a finger, gathers the crumbs into a neat pile on her plate. She gazes at Carissa. 'What about your business, your clients?'

'I've given them advanced warning I'm winding up the business.'

'Did they ask why?'

'I just said I had an offer I couldn't refuse, and it meant working abroad.'

'And no one enquired further.'

'I said it was for personal reasons. That shut down the conversation.'

'Good for you. You're doing the right thing. You know that, don't you? And if you ever get lonely, or need someone to talk to, remember I'm just at the end of the phone.'

'You'd be the first person I'd call.'

Kate smiles. 'I'd hope so.'

Just then, Carissa receives a text message from Stuart. It is his first contact since her bombshell announcement that she was leaving him.

She reads it.

He acted impulsively. He still can't decipher why he reacted the way he did. He has tried to make sense of it. That is not the person he is. He feels racked with guilt. He wants to meet her. He knows she won't change her mind. Stuart is ashamed and wants to put it right.

'I've just had a text from Stuart. He wants to see me.'

Kate is immediately suspicious. 'I hope you're going to tell him where to go?'

'I think he wants to apologise. He's struggling with it and ashamed of what he did and…'

'And so he should be. My God, what nerve he's got. Did he ask whether you reported it to the police?'

'No, he didn't.'

'Believe me, he will. This is what this is all about. He's

shit scared that the police are going to be knocking on his door and charging him, if not for attempted rape, then for an attempted assault.'

'I don't think that's his motive.'

'It was a text he sent you, Carissa. You can't decipher someone's intent from a text.'

'Is he harassing you? Because if he is, we can get the police onto him. You can block his number.'

'There's no need for that; that's like punishing him.'

'Well, at least block him from your Facebook account.'

'That's going too far, Kate. It's saying I want him out of my life entirely.'

'Don't you?'

'Not like that.'

'Then like what?'

'I just want our relationship to end… it has, but he's just not got that yet.'

'You're giving him hope. You're sending the wrong message. If he has no way of contacting you, he knows you want him out of your life for good.'

'What should I do about the text message?'

'Ignore it. Ignore him. It's finished.'

'I don't want us to end that way.'

'It would never end on good terms. Stuart is hurting. He'll be blaming you; that's for sure. He still doesn't get it, does he? He still can't work out, or see, that he's the issue here. It's typical. He's in denial.'

'To be fair, I'm also the issue – otherwise, I wouldn't have gone through with this. I've changed too.'

'Thank God you did.'

There is a long and strained silence.

'Carissa, are you okay?'

Carissa sighs with indecision. She can see Kate frowning. Her stomach is endeavouring to ram itself into her throat as she replies, 'I'm going to see him.'

'Jesus!'

Another silence follows.

Eventually Kate says, 'I'll go with you.'

Carissa considers this for a moment. 'No. It's best I do this on my own.'

CHAPTER THREE

TRAPPED

Edinburgh 2007

When Stuart opens the door to the flat, he is smiling. It is a wide smile. Carissa doesn't expect that reaction. It feels manufactured and for her benefit. This is not a good sign, she tells herself. Carissa returns his smile and wonders how she looks to him.

'Come in. You know where the sitting room is.'

Sarcasm as well.

They make their way to the sitting room, where she sits on the sofa and, to her relief, Stuart sits on the chair opposite. She places her handbag by her feet, and the sight of her mobile tucked next to her purse sends a rush of relief through her; the outside world is contactable if needed.

It feels odd sitting in the flat that was her home until a few days ago. She can still smell the vanilla-tinged fragrance of the plug-in air freshener she bought only a few weeks ago. A torrent of memories, both happy and sad, overwhelms her. It unsettles her.

Stuart sits cross-legged and places his clasped hands in his lap. There is an excruciating pause.

'Thanks for coming. I wasn't sure you would.'

'I'm here now.'

'You are, and I'm glad you came. It feels weird, you not being here. I've never spent a night on my own since we moved in.'

'Apart from that weekend I went to Ibiza on Anne's hen party.'

'Oh yeah! I forgot about that. That was when we first moved in, so that doesn't really count, does it?'

'I suppose not.'

'Are you staying at Kate's place?'

'No. She did offer, but I'm staying with Mum and Dad.'

'That'll feel strange.'

'It won't be for long.'

'You've already found a place to stay?'

Her back stiffens. 'Not yet.'

'But you're looking?'

'It's not a priority right now.' Carissa swallows the guilt which sweeps into her. Should she tell him about the job? About the move to Greece?

'Then what is?' The hint of bitterness is unmistakable.

'I haven't thought that far ahead.'

'That's not like you. You like to plan; you're organised and calculated. You've never made a decision without being forensic in your approach. I've never known you to follow an impulse. You've always had everything worked out to the letter.' He pauses, just for a moment, gauging her reaction and, whilst doing so, he rubs the back of his neck. 'So, why not this time?'

'This is different.'

'Is it? I don't see how. In fact, with something of such gravity, I would've thought you'd leave no stone unturned.'

'Maybe I'm changing. People do.'

Stuart cocks his head to one side. 'And sometimes not for the better.'

The pitch of his voice has tightened, and Carissa feels a ripple of alarm surge through her. Suddenly, she feels like a bird trapped in a cage. Around her, the room seems airless and constricting.

'And what about Kate?'

'What about her?'

'I'm sure she's got an opinion on all of this.'

'She's been supportive, if that's what you mean. She's a good friend.'

'Does she know you're here?'

Carissa nods.

'And does she know why I asked you to come?'

'I told her. She didn't want me to come.'

'I thought as much – she never did like me.'

Carissa fiddles with her hair and retorts, 'She's never said that to you.'

'She didn't have to. It was obvious.'

'I'm not getting into an argument with you; that's not why I'm here.'

'No, it's not. I could have text or phoned, but that didn't feel right; it didn't feel proper. I needed to see you so that it meant something.'

Carissa shifts her weight.

He continues. 'You know it was out of character. When have I ever done anything like that? The truth is, I don't know what came over me. I was in shock. I wasn't expecting to hear that four years of my life had just been chewed up and spat out like it meant nothing.'

'I'm sorry. What else can I say. We should have been happy. That's what it means to be a couple. But we weren't happy.'

Stuart eyes her suspiciously. 'You were the one who wasn't happy. I get that part.'

'And you were?'

He rubs his hand over the stubble on his chin. 'I thought we were. We've had our difficulties but always worked through them. Why can't this be one of them?'

Apprehension slithers in her stomach. The decision to return suddenly feels wrong.

This is a trap.

She swallows hard. 'It's too late for that. It's over. You're sorry for the way you reacted. You've done what you wanted to do, so now I'm—'

'I don't recall saying sorry,' he says casually. 'In fact, I'm going to be honest with you. I'm not sorry at all, and if I recall the situation correctly, you provoked me.'

Carissa raises her hand. 'Stuart, I'm uncomfortable with the way this is heading. We can sort this out.'

She hears him sigh.

His gaze unsettles her. 'I know we can,' she persists.

Stuart uncrosses his legs and slides to the edge of the chair. 'You see, Carissa, I don't believe that there isn't anyone else. There has to be – otherwise, why would you throw away all the years we've had together? It doesn't make sense to me.'

'There's no one. There never has been. Please understand, Stuart.' She evades his eyes. 'I'm doing this because I don't love you anymore.'

'Oh! So, love is a thing you can just turn off and on like a tap. Hot and cold. Cold and hot.'

'That's not what I mean… Stuart, I'm sorry.'

'Shut up!' he snarls the words, and suddenly, he is on his feet and the atmosphere between them changes abruptly. Carissa sweeps her bag from the floor and as she stands, before she knows it, he is so close to her, when he bends towards her, she can feel his breath on her face. She flinches as if he has stung her. He puts out his hand and curls a finger around her hair. He gives a violent pull, and Carissa lets out a scream.

Stuart smiles and drags his free hand through her hair. He scowls at her. 'I'm sorry. Did I hurt you?' He yanks on her hair again and whispers next to her ear, 'Oh! I'm sorry. Do you see how fickle and meaningless saying *sorry* can be? Just like you're not sorry for what you've done to me.'

'Stuart, please stop this. I want to leave,' she looks at him imploringly.

Three loud knocks sound, then a woman's voice resonates down the hall. Carissa can hear her name being called.

With long swoops of his hand, Stuart caresses Carissa's neck. His hand moves along her shoulders, down the incline of her waist, and deliberately, over the curve of her hip. And then, as quickly as it started, he releases her.

She pulls from him, pushes past him and whirls around. Striding down the hallway, she grabs the door handle and yanks it open. When the air hits her face, tears rise to the surface and relief floods her face as Kate rushes towards her with outstretched arms.

Kate appears from her kitchen with a glass of water and hands it to Carissa, who brings the glass to her lips and takes a trembling mouthful. Behind Kate, the stylish Georgian flats with their modern extensions and gardens shape Carissa's feeling of safety.

'It was a mistake. Why didn't I listen to you?' Carissa can hardly believe what has just happened.

Kate's face creases in concern. 'There's no point in beating yourself up about it. It's over now, and you're never going back. You don't have to see him again.'

Carissa takes a shuddering breath. 'I've never seen him like that.' Stuart's words enter her head like knives. 'That person, whoever it was, wasn't the Stuart I knew.'

'Then it's a good thing you found out now. Imagine if you were still with him and that's how he behaved. You've had a lucky escape.'

She shudders. 'I can't believe he would react like that. His eyes were dark. What have I done to him?'

'Don't you even think like that! The guy's a psychopath, Carissa. He's showing his true colours. From now on, you're having nothing to do with him. Block his number from your phone. I'll go around to the flat tomorrow and collect the rest of your things.'

'You can't go on your own.'

'I won't. I'll ask Mark to go with me.'

'Your neighbour?'

'He won't mind, especially when I tell him what's happened.'

'Please don't. I've been embarrassed enough.'

'Okay, I won't. I'll just say I'm doing you a favour. Mark won't mind.'

'Thanks. I don't know what I'd do without you.'

Kate grins. 'How are you going to manage in Skiathos, then?'

. . .

The past few months have been difficult; her thoughts all spun in a knot. Now, she has overcome her self-doubt and realised she can't continue living the way she has. She has extracted herself from that daily torment and feels energised. Carissa needs this. She needs to start afresh.

It fills her with anticipation and excitement.

It has been a day since Kate and Mark collected her clothes and belongings from the flat. Stuart wasn't home. Upon leaving, they locked the front door and posted Carissa's key through the letterbox. A final statement. She hopes Stuart will accept this. It is over.

She sets her coffee down on the table and rubs at the tension in her neck just as her mobile lights up and vibrates. She sees Stuart's name illuminated on the screen; it's a shock, like a blow to the abdomen. With short, shallow breaths, she reaches for the phone and then retracts her hand. 'You're not doing this anymore. Goodbye, Stuart.'

CHAPTER FOUR

WALKING ON AIR

Skiathos 2007

Carissa exits the diminutive arrivals lounge, dragging her suitcase into the blaring sunlight. She squints as she fishes her sunglasses from her shoulder bag, puts them on, and the outside world sharpens into view. In front of her, several taxis line a designated area, already busy with accommodating the new arrivals. Carissa wanders to the end of the queue, where a driver, a stout, tall man with silver swept-back hair, has just finished loading the boot of his taxi.

He beams at her and says in English, 'I'll take your case; there is space for one more.' And before she can reply, he is swinging her luggage into the boot beside another two cases. Carissa raises her sunglasses and peers into the taxi. Two individuals already occupy the taxi, much to her alarm. Confused, she confronts the taxi driver.

'There's already someone in your taxi.'

'There are only nineteen taxis on the entire island. If

you want to wait all day, you can stay here, or you can come with me,' he says, his words held a practised ease, familiar and routine and probably she thinks, spoken to every potential customer.

Carissa hesitates before opening the door, slipping her sunglasses over her head. The seated woman looks at her with wide eyes and is about to object when Carissa apologises, 'I'm sorry, I know this is your taxi, but the driver said it's okay.' To her relief, the woman accepts this with a shrug, and Carissa slides into the seat, still feeling self-conscious after her unconventional introduction.

The driver is soon behind the wheel, and within minutes, they have left the small airport and are heading through the narrow roads of Skiathos Town.

As her husband chats to the driver, the woman tells Carissa that this is their first visit to Skiathos, and she has always wanted to visit the church that is the wedding scene in her favourite film of all time, *Mama Mia*.

'Have you been before?' she asks Carissa in a broad Yorkshire accent.

'No. This is my first time on Skiathos.'

'Is it far to the *Mama Mia* church?' she is now asking the driver as Carissa takes in her first views of the town.

'You have to get a boat to Skopelos. There are many to choose from in the old port.'

Carissa can sense the woman's confusion.

'Skopelos? Where's that?'

'It is the next island. It takes just over an hour to get there.'

'Oh! I thought it was here on Skiathos,' she says, disappointed.

'Don't worry. There are many boats to choose from.

Some also go to Alonissos. This is another island. Very nice.'

'I hate boats. They make me sick.'

'I saw on Facebook they're playing the movie at an outdoor cinema on the main street in town. You can always watch the film again, love,' the husband says over his shoulder.

'I could do, but I've come this far, it would be a shame not to see the real thing. What do you think, Steve?'

'I'll take a bucket with me then, shall I love?' He laughs.

Carissa turns and gazes out of the window, smiling to herself.

Soon, the taxi stops, and the couple say their goodbyes, wishing Carissa a pleasant holiday. She hasn't told them she is here to work. As the taxi sets off again, Carissa settles into her seat, happy to be alone and give the view of the town her full attention.

Within minutes, the driver announces they have arrived.

'We are here. This place is called Plakes. It is one of the oldest neighbourhoods in Skiathos Town. Very pretty.'

She pays the fare, seeks directions, and it is not until he has driven off that she realises he has charged two full fares: one for the couple, and one for her, instead of one for the distance. Another advantage to only having nineteen taxis on the entire island, she smiles.

She wanders the decorative stone path, dragging her suitcase behind her, past a church, where a few old men sit in the shade of several trees.

Following the driver's instructions, at the bakery, Carissa takes a right. Wandering along a narrow lane, she checks the door number of each whitewashed facade, all with sun-bleached wooden shutters. Opposite, she is delighted to see an unobstructed view of the sea, where verdant cliffs slide into its turquoise, translucent waters. Finally, she stops at the corresponding number she was given, and a warm liquid sensation melts within her.

She was told that the key to her apartment was under the purple bougainvillea pot at the bottom of the white steps leading up to her new temporary home. The bougainvillea is striking against the white of the wall, its petals the deepest hue of purple she has ever seen.

Once she has hauled her case up the steps, she inserts the key into the lock, praying for it to turn in her hand, and to her relief it does so with an affirming click.

She steps over the threshold with trepidation, hoping the photographs of the accommodation sent to her by email are an accurate reflection of the interior. She needn't have worried. Although the apartment is basic, she can see it is functional and well looked after, with the fresh scent of rose in the air and a tiled floor that gleams spotlessly clean.

She inspects the small kitchen, fitted with all the mod cons one would expect. Next, the bathroom, then the sitting room. It is perfect, tastefully decorated, blending the modern with the traditional, and she nods her head in approval.

As she opens the apartment shutters, the view takes her breath away.

She will never get used to this, she tells herself, as she looks across the bay towards rolling hills, their lush green slopes blending seamlessly into golden sand and aquamarine water, where several sailboats float serenely. To top it all off, a small balcony is set with two chairs, a table, and a row of plants in terracotta pots.

She checks her watch and tries to stifle a yawn, but it gets the better of her. She has been awake since five o'clock that morning.

Carissa unpacks and, once she has hung her clothes in the small compact wardrobe and laid out her toiletries in the bathroom, she is ready to find a place to eat lunch, the overpriced sandwich and shortbread on the flight now a distant memory.

Opening the fridge, she is pleasantly surprised to see milk, bottled water, a packet of cheese, and a box of eggs. She checks, and she assumes someone bought them for her arrival since they are all in date. A cheese omelette or lunch out?

She steps outside, adjusting her sunglasses to soften the sun's glare off the whitewashed walls of charming houses lining the narrow lane, which she hopes will lead to her lunch.

The descent into the main area is steep in places, but breathtaking; flowers and vases line her path, interspersed with cascading vines and ostentatious plants in a riot of vibrant colour. Cascading bougainvillea tumbles over balconies, as if bejewelling them for a festivity she has not been invited to.

Shops tuck into every corner: boutiques selling hand-made sandals, clothing, and olive oil soaps, local crafts, jewellery and souvenirs. Interspersed among them are tavernas and cafés with tables spilling out onto the cobble-stones, often shaded by awnings and trailing vines.

At the harbour's edge, the lanes open to an attractive waterfront promenade, and beyond, pine-covered hills rise above the town.

Lunch at the old port is perfect: Gemista — rice-stuffed tomatoes and peppers with feta — and a bottle of water, followed by tea. The spot is ideal for watching locals and tourists alike stroll by, where yachts bob beside pleasure boats offering '*Mama Mia*' trips to the neighbouring islands of Skopelos and Alonissos.

Much to Carissa's amusement, she chuckles as the woman who'd arrived by taxi with her is already eyeing the *Mama Mia* tour boat vendors and their prices along the harbour promenade.

She checks on Google Maps for the Trails of Greece office and is pleased it is only a ten-minute walk away. She decides she will introduce herself before her first day of work tomorrow.

Carissa meanders along the street where, on one side, the tables of restaurants and bars are filling with people looking for lunch and, to her right, boats of various shapes and sizes, sit still in the calm waters of the New Port. She finds the office – a five-minute walk away, just opposite the bus terminal, which, like everything on the island, is smaller than usual, really just a bus stop, Carissa thinks.

The door to the office is already open as Carissa approaches and walks inside.

Two desks hold individual computers and a telephone. Several filing cabinets and a photocopier make up the otherwise sparse office space. A man's gaze shifts upward from the screen, and he smiles. 'Can I help you?' he asks in perfect English.

Carissa takes in the large map of Skiathos on the wall behind him. 'I hope so. My name's Carissa. I'm going to be working here tomorrow.'

He slides his chair backwards and stands, offering her his hand. 'Hello, Carissa. I'm Dimitrios. When did you arrive?'

'Today, less than two hours ago,' she tells him, feeling his hand in hers.

'You're staying at the apartment.'

'I am. It's perfect, and the view is amazing.'

Dimitrios smiles. 'It is, isn't it?'

He is of medium height, with thick black hair swept back over his brow, classic Greek features: smooth olive skin, a stubbled chin, straight nose, and incandescent, penetrating eyes. He is a few years older than Carissa and speaks fluent English.

'I thought I'd see where your office was, to save me time tomorrow, but found it quite easily.'

'It would be hard to get lost in town; we're not the biggest.'

'But very picturesque. I love it already.'

'While you're here, you can pick up your uniform. Well, I say uniform, but it's just four polo tops, four pairs of knee-length shorts and a waterproof jacket. It does rain sometimes.' He lifts a bundle wrapped in clear cellophane and hands it to her. 'I hope you don't mind bottle green?'

'It's fine.'

'Were you asked for your measurements? It's a bit late now if they're the wrong size.'

'I was.'

'Good. That's saved an awkward moment.'

There is silence. 'Would you like a drink – water, a coffee perhaps?'

'I'm fine. I've just had some lunch.'

'Well then, you start at seven. I'll meet you here. There's just another two of us, Evangelia and Athena. You'll meet them tomorrow. I'll give you an induction, and then we can do the paperwork, and then you can accompany me on the first trail of the day, which starts at ten o'clock.'

'That sounds great.'

'Do you have any questions?'

'Not that I can think of. I've gone over the material the company sent me.'

'If you think of any, don't hesitate to ask me tomorrow.'

The phone rings.

'I'd better get that.'

'Sure. See you tomorrow.'

He turns and picks up the phone. 'Yia sas.'

Outside, Carissa smiles to herself. If she had any doubts, they have just dissipated, and she feels she is walking on air.

CHAPTER FIVE

CONTENTMENT

Skiathos 2007

Her days fall into a rhythm: after being supervised on several hikes, Clarissa begins leading her own trail groups along ravines, hillsides, mountains and gorges, beside streams that trickle alongside olive groves and vineyards. Her favourite is taking yoga classes at sunrise on the beach.

She navigates the town, its lanes and decorative stone paths memorised, where vibrant purple and red hues drape whitewashed houses in a breathtaking and graceful manner. Sea-blue shutters and wood-grained doors adorn them, where each turn reveals tempting shops, tavernas, and restaurants.

Carissa buys her weekly groceries at the small supermarket, just a few hundred yards from her apartment.

She sometimes enjoys a meal at one of the town's many restaurants, perhaps overlooking the harbour or sitting outside in a narrow lane or square off Papadiamanti Street, Skiathos Town's vibrant main thoroughfare, named after the famed Greek writer Alexandros Papadiamantis.

Colourful shops, designer boutiques, banks, cafes, and tavernas define the town's commercial hub.

Already, she has her favourite places to eat: La Cucina di Maria, in Trion Lerarhon Square, an Italian restaurant, owned and run by the delectable Maria and her family, who are all Greek, the food delicious and definitely Italian. Then there is Taverna Alexandros, a typical Greek taverna with live, laid-back and seductive Greek music played by two accomplished musicians and singers. Taverna Manavaki is fast becoming one of her favourites too.

She's beginning to settle into the slow pace of life, a far cry from her hectic life in Edinburgh. It has been four weeks since she arrived, and she's made friends with Evangelia and Athena. They have been welcoming, always happy to help her navigate the computerised office systems and answer any work-related questions or her constant enquires about understanding the cost of living, getting a Greek SIM card, opening a bank account, investing in a health insurance plan, and how to organise her bills. She feels exhausted trying to get to grips with what she needs to know.

Before she left, Carissa spent her days with Stuart, anticipating. A look. A slammed door. The subtle withdrawal of kindness that always came before the inevitable storm of words. She survived, shrinking from life.

The scars and memories remain, but they are passing through her, and in their place, something else is growing.

There is a change in her. Carissa can feel its gentle stir most days. She is content. That's what she would call it, and it enshrines her.

It's a loosening. A stillness.

Mornings bring it during her yoga class on the beach. Quietly like the sea, when waves soften, pulsing with their soft rhythm on the sand, as sunlight touches the horizon and the sky is contemplating its theatre of colour, it is present. It's in the church bells chiming, and the scent of warm bread from the bakers along from her apartment. It's in the distant bleating of goats on a hillside during her daily walking trails, and in the Greek words, *kalimera, efcharistó*, forming on her lips, each a small step, an assertion towards belonging here, on this island.

It cradles her in the evenings too, as she sits on the narrow balcony of her apartment watching the sky perform its ancient ritual. The colours bleed across the horizon, and like honey spreading through her chest, she is discovering what it means to *be*. It lives inside her, this thing she calls *contentment*, growing stronger and affirming, at the end of each day.

They speak little at first. A nod. A soft smile if their eyes meet. Offerings of coffee in the morning. No expectations. They sit without the urgency to fill the air with words; this silence feels like its own conversation.

Over the weeks, they offer small pieces of themselves. Dimitrios asks about Edinburgh and tells her how he'd love to visit one day and asks if it is as cold as they say. He teaches her Greek words and phrases. She tells him about her job, her friends and family back in Edinburgh. She doesn't tell him everything, not yet. But she feels like she could and that she might, one day.

There's a quietness about him, a space that feels safe. And then, one morning when Evangelia and Athena are out on an early morning walking trail, he asks her to look at a report and as he hands it to her, his fingers brush against hers, barely a touch at all, yet long enough for something inside her to stir.

Something is happening; something is developing between them. She knows he feels it too.

CHAPTER SIX

RETURNING

Skiathos 2007

Evangelia leaps up from her desk. 'Are you all right, Carissa?' We were about to send out a search party. You didn't answer our calls.'

'I'm sorry. I'll just get a drink of water first.'

'What's happened?' Athena asks, concerned.

She gulps some water, and wiping her mouth with the back of her hand, she gasps. 'I was about thirty minutes into the walk when we were passing a house where I often see an old man in his garden. The house is on its own and quite isolated. He wasn't there – well, he was, but I didn't see him. I could hear his dog barking, and it sounded quite frantic. I've never heard his dog bark before. As we got closer, one of the group thought they could see what looked like someone lying on the ground. It was the old man. He'd collapsed.'

'That's dreadful.' Athena says.

'Is he dead?' Evangelia burst out.

'No, thankfully. He was unconscious. I thought I might have to do CPR, but luckily, he had a pulse. We put him in the recovery position and kept him as comfortable as we could. By the time the ambulance arrived, he still had a pulse. They took over after that. The poor dog was left on its own. I noticed a flap in the door, so it could get in and out of the house.'

'Never mind the dog. You poor thing,' Evangelia says, gently touching Carissa's arm.

'I should have phoned. Sorry. I forgot what the protocol is when something like this happens.'

'Don't worry. Is everyone in the group okay?'

'Yeah. I've just left them. We carried on with the walk; they seemed to still enjoy it.'

'There's nothing to worry about, then. We'll go over the protocol tomorrow.' Athena draws a breath. 'I've worked here for three years and nothing like that has happened.'

'Just my luck, then.'

'Put it down to experience.'

'Last year, Dimitrios was out on the Eikonistria Monastery trail.' Evangelia points to the location on the map. 'An eight-kilometre one, when one of his group fell and twisted their ankle. Nasty, but a freak accident. That's why we're insured.'

Athena leans forward. 'Get yourself home; we'll finish up around here. Relax, have a glass of wine, and we'll see you tomorrow.'

'Are you sure? I'm fine, really.'

'I'm pulling rank.'

Carissa is walking through her apartment. Her temple aches as she clears away that morning's breakfast dishes, which she hadn't had time to wash because she'd slept through the alarm.

For someone of his age, the old man still had thick hair, even if it had turned white. She wonders what it must be like living on your own at his age, your nearest neighbour a few hundred yards away.

She walks out onto the balcony and stands with her hands on the railings. Below her, three cats lie stretched out in the shade. Carissa doesn't know if they belong to anyone, or if they are strays, like the cats that gather at and forage through the refuge bins near the cemetery, but these cats look well fed and cared for. She noticed bowls of food placed along the lane and saw the cats eating from them. Carissa has given them names, Socks – because of the white fur that stops halfway up the legs, Patch – the black mark over an eye and Boss – because, well, he just looks like one and acts like it and the others seem to know it too.

She can't get the old man out of her mind. She won't settle until she knows he is well. And then there's the dog. What if he has to go to the hospital? What hospital! The nearest one is on the mainland. What would happen to the dog? Who would feed it? It had been a shock and panic not knowing whether he was alive or dead. Her mind replayed her actions – constantly checking his pulse, watching for the rise and fall of his chest, awaiting the ambulance, and then watching them carry him away.

Was it a stroke? What life would he have? How could he stay on his own? Did he have a family? She hoped so.

Carissa goes back inside, the coolness and shade a relief from the glare of the sun. She presses her teeth into her lip. Carissa has decided. She will return to the house.

CHAPTER SEVEN

THOMAS

Skiathos 2007

Resting her hand on the wooden gate, she is struck by the aesthetic appeal of the substantial garden with its winding stone path edged with lavender, and dry limestone wall that delineates the space. A cluster of gnarled, thick-trunked olive trees with silvery-green leaves populates the bottom of the garden. Towards the house, lemon, orange, and fig trees, heavy with vibrant fruits, add colour and a pleasing fragrance to the tepid air, which is already rich with the aromas of rosemary, thyme, sage, and oregano, which flourish before her. Flamboyant bougainvillea in vivid magenta, purple, and red cascades over the garden wall and pergola, shading the front of the house beneath its vibrant canopy.

Geraniums flourish in terracotta pots, while jasmine and honeysuckle climb the trellises. Here and there, at pleasing intervals, lavender, oleander, and daisies bloom in abundance, whilst in the vegetable garden, tomatoes, peppers, aubergines, and courgettes thrive. When last here, she didn't take in the garden nor the house. In fact, when she thinks of it now, all she can recall is the feeling of dread that erupted inside her when she discovered the old man lying prone on the ground, his dog sitting next to him. Its bark alerted her that something was not quite right.

Today, the dog is dozing on the veranda. It lifts its head from its outstretched paws and regards her with heavy eyes.

The old man is bent over, working a spade into the ground and turning the earth. Carissa observes him. He places a hand on his lower back and stretches. Under shirt-sleeves rolled to the elbow, bronzed, wrinkled skin is patched with brown liver spots that dot his hands and forearms.

'Can I help you?' he asks, in a posh English accent.

Carissa raises her hand and waves. It's a welcome relief to discover the old man is not Greek. She hadn't expected this and had been fretting about how she was going to explain her presence. 'I was just admiring your garden. It's beautiful.'

The old man wipes his brow under the rim of his hat.

'I do my best; it's always been a passion of mine, but the old back and the creaking knees seem to complain more and more these days.' He leans on the spade with both hands. 'Is there something I can do for you?'

'Sorry. I should have introduced myself. I was the one who found you the other day.' He looks much better than when she last saw him, she thinks. His colour has returned.

His face lights up. 'It was you. Wasn't it? You phoned the ambulance. How fortunate you discovered me.'

'It was luck. I was passing at the time. It was your dog that got my attention. It was barking, and that's when I saw you.'

'You're a lifesaver. Who knows what would have

happened if you hadn't found me.' He is walking towards her now. 'I can thank you properly. Please come in. We can take a seat up at the house.'

As they walk, he asks, 'What's your name?'

'Carissa.'

'That's not a name I was expecting.'

'You weren't?' she says, momentarily confused.

'I didn't mean to be rude. What I actually meant was, it's a Greek name, and given your nice Scottish accent…'

'Oh! I see. It was my grandmother's name. Her mother was Greek.'

'Ah! That explains it. It's a lovely name. I'm Thomas.'

'Pleased to meet you… again, Thomas.'

Thomas grins. 'Under better circumstances this time. I can't remember the first time we met, but I was told a nice young woman found me and phoned for an ambulance. How can I ever thank you?'

'I did nothing out of the ordinary; anyone passing would have done the same.'

'Well, yes. You'd like to think they would.'

They reach the house and the shade of the pergola. 'Please take a seat. Get yourself out of the sun; it's frightfully hot today.'

They sit together. Thomas sinks into a chair and groans. 'I think I've overdone it today. That's what I get for trying to prove a point to myself.'

'Are you sure you're okay?'

'I'll be as right as rain in a moment or two.'

'You're not the only one who's surprised. I wasn't expecting to hear your English accent.'

'Of course you weren't. You thought I was Greek, which is understandable, but as you can see and hear, I'm one hundred percent English. Sorry, where are my manners? I haven't offered you anything to drink. What would you like? I've got orange juice, water, coffee, or tea, if that's your tipple. It's technically afternoon now, so you can have a wine if you'd prefer?'

'I'm fine. I've got a bottle of water with me,' she lifts the bottle in her hand to show him. 'How are you feeling? You're looking much better since I last saw you.'

'I am. Much better because of you. Thank you.'

'I'm just glad I found you. If it weren't for your dog barking, I would have just walked by. I'd seen your dog a few times when I passed your house on my walks, and it was always calm and lying in the shade, but not that day. I knew there was something wrong, something different about it. It seemed agitated, and I'd never heard it bark until then.'

'I don't know how long I would have been lying there, and in the sun, too.'

Carissa strokes the dog's head, which has positioned itself between them. 'And what's your name?'

'This is Daisy.'

'Nice to meet you again, Daisy. How old is she?'

'Daisy's an old lady now. She's ten. A touch of arthritis, but apart from that, she's doing remarkably well for her age.'

'I've seen you tending to your garden; you're not doing too badly yourself.'

'I've always tried to keep active. It's a lifelong habit of mine.'

'And a good one.'

'I've seen you walking through the olive groves and heading up to the monastery with a group of people in tow.'

'I work for a company that does walks along the trails, as well as a bit of yoga and wellbeing, that kind of thing.'

'So, you live here on Skiathos?'

'I do.' She smiles and takes a sip of water, relaxing now in Thomas's company.

'For how long?'

'About eight weeks now. I came here to work.'

'And how's the job going?'

'I love it. Who wouldn't? In Edinburgh, where I'm from, summer lasts a week if we're lucky. Here, the weather's gorgeous, and I get to walk around this beautiful island, meet different people, and indulge in my passion for fitness. I work for a company called Trails of Greece.'

'It sounds wonderful. If I were a few years younger, I'd join you on one of your walks. I miss just being able to get up and head off on a walk. I used to do it every day. Even before I had Daisy. It was a daily routine. Now, I take the car into town once a week for shopping, have a coffee and then head home again. It's nice to chat with people, but at my age, most of my friends are dead or can't even remember what they had for breakfast that morning.'

Thomas smiles. 'It's nice to sit in the garden with someone other than Daisy. She's adorable, but not much of a conversationalist.'

He takes off his hat, which reveals a mop of thick silver hair.

'You were still wearing that hat when I found you.'

'I always wear it when I'm out in the garden. It protects my head from the sun. You should get one, especially during the summer months, as the sun can be fierce.'

'When on my walks, I wear a baseball cap. It's mandatory to wear one. Company policy.'

'That's good to hear.'

'How are you feeling now?'

'I'm fine. Luckily, I didn't break any bones. The doctor

in Skiathos Town wanted me to go to the mainland to get further checks. He said my blood pressure had dropped, and that's why I fainted. He also asked about my heart. Was I having chest pain at the time? Did I feel unwell, clammy, sweating? He wants to make sure I haven't had a heart attack. I've been taking medication for my heart for years. Beta blockers and statins, they're called. Anyway, he has adjusted the dose of the one that lowers my blood pressure, and I've felt fine ever since.'

She looks at him with intent. 'That is good, but don't you think you should take the doctor's advice and go to the hospital to get further tests?'

'Taking a ferry and then getting to the hospital and back again would take more than a day. Who would look after Daisy? I couldn't leave her on her own.'

'She could stay with me. It wouldn't be a problem.'

'That's kind of you, but like I told the doctor, I feel better now, and at my age that's a blessing. There's no need for me to go to the hospital. I'm fine.'

Time to change the subject, she thinks. There's a book sitting on the small table in front of her. She nods towards it. 'What's that your reading?'

Thomas pats the book with his hand. '*The Struggle for Greece.* I've read it several times over the years, but I like to dip into it now and again.'

'Is it fiction?'

'No. It's a historical account of a certain time in the history of Greece, 1941 to 1949, the German occupation and the story of the resistance that followed.'

'Oh, I see.'

He raises an eyebrow. 'Not your thing, then?'

'I like history. But when I read, it's generally contemporary women's fiction I like.'

'I don't think I've read one of them.'

'Reading is like music; everyone has their own tastes.'

'As it should be. Imagine what kind of world it would be if we all liked the same things.'

'Quite boring, I'd imagine.'

'Exactly. That's the good thing about history; those of us who are interested in it have their own time periods that appeal to us. It's a broad church. That's why you get those who specialise in certain periods of history or events and countries.'

'Have you always been interested in Greek history?' Carissa asks.

'When I was younger, I read classical Greek at university. That's when my fascination with this country really began.'

'Wow! That sounds very highbrow,' Carissa says, pleasantly surprised. 'What university did you go to?'

'I was educated at Heathfield and Eton. I read classics at Oxford – a double first. I was awarded a research fellowship. It was a long time ago.'

'And after that?' she asks eagerly.

'My big interest was Frankish castles in Greece. So, I travelled throughout Greece as much as possible, trying to visit as many castles as I could before the outbreak of war, the Second World War, which by that time was imminent.'

'That must have been frightening, being in a foreign country when the world was about to implode.'

'It didn't feel like that. In some ways, Greece was a new experience, but it didn't feel a foreign country to me. Even then, I felt a connection. I could speak the language well, I had studied the history and the classics, it felt very natural to be there.'

'Were you still in Greece when war broke out?'

'I was in Athens when I heard that war had been declared on Germany. I was walking through Plaka at the foot of the Acropolis when, from a café, I heard Chamberlain, the then prime minister, announce on a radio that Britain was at war with Germany and my worst fears were recognised.'

Her eyes widened. 'What did you do?'

'I returned home to England, where I enlisted in the Royal Artillery. Later, because of my academic background, and I could speak Greek fluently, I moved to the British Military Mission to the Greek Army as an intelligence officer, interpreting at meetings, translating communiques and charting wireless traffic. I was perfectly placed.'

'It must have been a frightening time,' she says softly. 'I can't imagine what it would have been like.'

Thomas tilts his head. 'It had its moments.'

Carissa leans forward. 'I know many veterans don't like to talk about it… but if *you* want to, I'd love to hear it, the war, *your* war, sometime,' her tone is cautious but sincere.

'Surely you don't want to listen to an old man's ramblings.'

'Ramblings!' Carissa's brow lifts. 'You lived history. Because of people like you, I'm able to live the life I choose. You *gave* us that choice.'

He looked at her, surprised by the conviction in her voice. 'It's nice to know that's how you feel.'

'It is.'

'Thank you. That means a lot.'

'I mean it. My great-grandad fought in the war. He didn't speak about what happened, but Remembrance Day was always an emotional time for him. He expressed it in his own way.'

Thomas nods knowingly. He takes a deep breath. 'This

is my favourite time of day, when the light begins to soften, and the shadows stretch long into the garden.'

'It's so peaceful.'

'It's perfection.'

They sit silently.

'Thank you for what you did; it was kind of you. Most people would have just walked past. I'm so grateful.'

'As I said, I've passed this way on my walks and often see you and Daisy in the garden, and when I saw how distressed she was that day, well, my gut instinct told me something wasn't right.'

'Always listen to your instinct; it's something I've followed since my army days. It's a good job you did.'

Carissa pets Daisy one last time before she stands.

Thomas eases himself from his chair. 'I'm sure I'll see a lot more of you.'

Carissa looks at him, unsure about what he means.

'On your walks. I'll look out for you when I'm in the garden.'

'Oh! Of course,' she smiles.

Thomas walks her to the garden gate, and Carissa compliments him on his garden.

'I do my best. I'm not as agile as I used to be, but age is just a number, isn't it? I'm determined to be active as long as I can.'

'It's a good mindset to have. If you don't mind me asking, Thomas, how old are you?'

'I'm eighty-seven.'

'Wow! I would never have guessed that. You look great.'

'Thank you. I don't always feel great.'

'How old were you in the war?'

'When I was in Greece, I was twenty-three.'

Carissa rubs her hand over the grain of the gate as a

thought suddenly occurs to her, but she hesitates, feeling the moment has passed.

Thomas knows she wants to ask him. He helps her out.

'I can recall it as vividly as if it were yesterday.'

'You can?'

'As clear as day.'

'Maybe I could come back another time.'

'Whenever's best. You're the busy one.'

'That would be up to you.'

'I'm not going anywhere.' With raised eyebrows, he places his hand over his heart and grimaces comically. 'I hope I'm not.'

Carissa chuckles, 'You shouldn't tempt fate.'

'At my age, fate is just around the corner.' Thomas straightens his back. 'You're welcome to come by anytime.'

'I wouldn't want to impose.'

'Believe me, you're not. I don't get many visitors these days.' He tilts his head and watches her. 'We could start where I left off, about the war. If you want?'

Carissa smiles. 'I'd like that.'

Thomas nods in agreement. 'Me too.'

Carissa can see he is thinking to himself.

'Oh! Before I forget to ask…' He grins. 'Do you like tea?'

CHAPTER EIGHT

FIRST MEMORIES

Skiathos 2007

The next day, she wanders into the office. Dimitrios is just making a coffee and looks up.

'Morning, Carissa. Would you like a coffee?'

'A cup of tea would be nice, thanks.'

'I forgot. You're a tea person.'

'I've never got used to the taste of coffee. It's too bitter for me.' She reaches her desk and perches on its edge.

'I was just looking at your schedule for today; you're busy,' Dimitrios says, dumping a tea bag into a mug.

'Just the way I like it.'

'It's nice to see you're settling in. I've heard nothing but good things about you. That's what comes with experience. You'd think you'd been working here for years.'

'Really. That's nice to know.'

Dimitrios hands her the mug of tea. She reaches and takes it from him.

'And the apartment, you've settled in there too?'

'It's perfect. More than that, actually. You hear these stories about accommodation not living up to the photos online, which, if I'm honest, was a worry, but it does.' She smiles, 'I can't believe the view.'

'You struck lucky there, but really, if you've got an unobstructed view of the sea it's going to be special, especially here in Skiathos.'

'That's what attracted me to the job in the first place – the walking trails through the countryside, the yoga classes on the beach and the outdoor fitness classes. It sounded the perfect job. I'm loving it. I'm just grateful this opportunity came my way.'

'That's good to hear. And you're doing a great job. Your references were exceptional, but you can't buy the experience you have. And that's only half of it; you need to be a good communicator and a people person, and you've definitely got those skills. Believe me, we're lucky to have you.'

'Oh, thank you.' She feels her cheeks blush.

'It can't be easy starting a new job in a new country. It's a big change. It's admirable. And the way you dealt with that situation with the old man. It's a wonder you're still here. Honestly, that was a one-off. I hope it hasn't put you off.'

'No. Not at all. I'm just glad the ambulance came as quickly as it did,' she said dismissively.

'Evangelia said the old guy recovered from his ordeal, which was good to hear.'

'I've visited him. His name is Thomas. We had a nice chat. He's lovely and English too, would you believe?'

'Oh! And he's still well?'

'Thankfully, he is. He mentioned something about

having low blood pressure and the doctor wanting him to go to the mainland for further investigations, but he's not keen.'

'He should go.'

'That's what I told him. He was worried about who would look after his dog if he went. I wouldn't mind; she's an old thing. She's called Daisy. She wouldn't be any problem.'

'He might not get a second chance the next time.'

She wonders about this fleetingly. It had crossed her mind. 'Yeah, I got the feeling he was hiding something; maybe it's more serious than he was letting on. I'm glad I went. In fact, I'm going back to see him.'

Dimitrios raises his eyebrows. 'You are?'

Carissa explained all about her visit, how Thomas had told her about his background when he was younger, and that she was intrigued and looking forward to learning about Greece during World War Two from someone who had been there. 'I find it all quite fascinating.'

'Has he lived in Greece since the war?'

'I don't know. I feel he's led a colourful life.'

'He must have a good memory; I can't remember what I did yesterday,' Dimitrios says, as if confessing.

She looked at him, smiling. 'I don't believe that. You'd never be able to run this place!'

'Have you seen my desk? It's full of Post-it notes and lists. Although, in saying that, I can still remember some things I did when I was a child.'

She feels intrigued. 'What's your first memory?'

Dimitrios looks thoughtful. 'My first memory! I must have been three or four. Struggling to push open the heavy wooden door of my grandmother's house. I've never forgotten how entering her house always felt like a warm embrace that continued to wrap itself around me for years after. Grandmother's house always smelled of something warm, usually a pot of stifado simmering on the stove. You'd catch the scent from halfway down her stone path. The whole house was filled with the smell of cooking. I'd push a stool over to the pot and stand on it, peering at the source of this wonderful smell. I was fascinated by its rich dark, wine-dark fragrance, the tender, soft chunks of beef, braised for hours where small pearl caramelised onions bobbed and mingled with tomatoes; it seemed to seep into the walls around me.

'Grandmother allowed me, under her watchful eye, of course, to stir the pot with her wooden spoon worn smooth by countless family gatherings. The steam rising from the heavy pot perfumed the kitchen air as if it were incense. As time moved on, I watched as the aroma deepened and mellowed, becoming richer as it bubbled in the old pot.

'The house seemed to breathe it in, another memory to join the countless others that had soaked into those walls. It wasn't just food; it was the smell of love and of tradition passed down through generations. It was the smell of home.'

'That's beautiful. It makes me want to try… what was it called?

'Stifado. '

'Yes. I must try it.'

'It's a slow-cooked beef stew; it takes time to cook, but it's worth it. It can't be hurried; it's like a good wine; there's an art to getting it just right. Skill and patience are vital parts of the ingredients.'

'That's quite a promise for a stew.'

His eyes widened. 'Oh, no. Oh… No. It's not just a stew! You can't say that, not in my family.'

She couldn't help but laugh. Before she could say anything else, Dimitrios continued. It's not just a stew! First, the beef. It has to be cut into big, proud pieces, seasoned, then dredged lightly in flour. Not too much, just enough to make it hug the sauce later.

'And then?'

'You brown it, of course. Always brown it! You want a golden crust. My grandmother would always tell us, that's where the flavour hides.'

'So basically, so far you're describing a British stew.'

'Haha! Maybe, but wait! Now comes the part my—'

'Your grandmother,' Carissa interrupted him with a smile.

Dimitrios grinned at her. 'She always called this part the heart. The pearl onions – lots of them. You score them like this,' – he mimes an 'X', as if he is cutting with a knife. 'But they have to be left whole, sweetening everything with time. Then, the tomatoes get added – ripe, red, and full. They have to be grated. Then more onions, this time, blended onions and garlic. They melt into the sauce.'

Carissa raises an eyebrow. 'You Greeks really like onions.'

'As grandmother would say, onions build the soul of the dish. Add the sugar, salt, and pepper. And then, the spices: a cinnamon stick for warmth, whole peppercorns, rosemary, bay leaves… and the secret?'

Carissa leans in. 'What?'

'Cedar wood. Small pieces,'

'Really! I've never heard of cooking with cedar.'

'Then pour in, not just any wine, Gratsi red wine. This one is soft, rich, full of body. It makes the cinnamon sing and the onions dance.'

'You're very poetic about your ingredients. What would your grandmother say about that?' she asks, amused.

'To her, she cooked out of love, so I think she would have approved.'

'So, then you stir it all together?'

'No! Never stir! You shake the pot gently. Stirring breaks the onions. It needs to come together on its own.'

Carissa smiles. 'As well as being poetic, there's a scientific element to it.'

'You can't separate the two. It goes in the oven, covered, at high heat. When it bubbles, you lower it and let it cook slowly, two and a half to three hours. Then, for the last bit, you uncover it, so it thickens and darkens.

'And then… it's ready to eat?

'With wine. Always with wine. You sip the wine, take a bite, and everything is tender, rich. The meat should fall apart, the onions should taste sweet, and the spices…'

'If it tastes half as good as you make it sound, it would still be amazing.'

'My problem is, I've never tasted a stifado that comes anywhere near my grandmother's. Even when my mother makes it. Your turn now. What's your first memory?'

'Nothing like yours.' It takes a moment for her brain to kick into gear. 'It was when my brother was born, and Mum and Dad brought him home. I would have just turned three. My gran had stayed over, and I'd just woken and had breakfast. Mum said I was a big sister now. I didn't know what that meant, but I distinctly remember not wanting to be a big sister. Mum stood in the hallway with this bundle wrapped in a white shawl. She looked tired. Dad was standing beside her with his arm around her shoulder and a beaming smile. Mum bent down and asked me to come closer, and inside the wrapping was this tiny thing swaddled in blue that looked like one of my baby dolls. I asked Mum, where did he come from, and is she allowed to take him back? He made a little noise – a small squeak – and everyone laughed. I didn't. I just watched, trying to understand why my world had changed without anyone asking me first.' Carissa hesitated, and then reflected, 'It's quite a fitting metaphor for my life today.'

CHAPTER NINE

THE BIRTHPLACE OF DEMOCRACY AND OTHER SUFFERINGS

Skiathos 2007

'So, you're telling me I don't have the brainpower to take in all of that important information you've obviously got stored in your big head.' Carissa is smiling at Thomas as he pours tea from a teapot into her cup.

Thomas, acknowledging her sarcasm, tilts his head and considers her. He thinks for a moment, wondering how to put it to her.

He takes his cup in his hand and sits back in his chair, smiling over his teacup. 'That's not what I was implying. I was merely insinuating I could give you the condensed version or a more detailed version of events, that's all. It's up to you. What would you prefer?'

Carissa frowns. 'Hmm. What's the difference?'

'The condensed version is like a clapped-out old car compared to one with detail, which I'd describe as the Rolls Royce.'

She shifts in her chair. 'Well, you're the expert. If I'm going to learn about Greece during World War Two, it has to be the Rolls Royce version,' she raises a small smile, waiting for his reaction.

Thomas nods. 'Good choice. Well then, since we've cleared that up, shall we begin?'

'From the start?'

'There's no better place.'

'I don't just want a history lesson; I'd like to know about your experience during the war. Would that be okay?'

'I'd be cheating you if I didn't,' Thomas tells her.

'Good,' Carissa says satisfied.

Thomas doesn't need much encouragement. He takes a breath. 'It all began on the 28th of October 1940, the Greek leader Metaxas received an Italian ultimatum demanding the surrender of Greece and accusing it of intensifying its support of the British armed forces. Metaxas rejected the ultimatum, and Greek popular sentiment agreed. The ultimatum came from Mussolini.'

Carissa nods. 'I've heard of Mussolini.'

'He's better known than Metaxas. Italy invaded, and Greece entered the war. Britain had made promises to support countries facing German aggression, and the Italians were on the German side. Churchill… he knew full well our military support would be limited. However, by the time the British Military Mission arrived, the Greeks, much to Britain's surprise, had already driven Italy back at the Albanian front.'

He sips his tea; the cup shaking in his hand.

'Churchill offered to send ground troops, but Metaxas refused. He feared provoking Germany. And then, out of the blue, Metaxas died suddenly, and his successor accepted the offer. It turned out that the "British support" was mostly Commonwealth troops. Germany came to Italy's aid and in less than three weeks, Greece was occupied.'

Carissa's eyes widen. 'That fast?'

'Brutally fast,' Thomas says. 'My unit was in Crete – an island the British hoped would become a strategic stronghold. From there, we thought we might launch raids, even bomb the Romanian oil fields the Germans depended on.'

He shakes his head.

'Those hopes were dashed when the Germans launched a massive airborne assault. They bombed Crete relentlessly. We fought, and so did the Cretans, but it wasn't enough. The island fell.'

He stalls and bites the inside of his mouth and looks away. Whatever it is, Carissa can see it's a painful subject or memory, maybe both, but she feels uncomfortable with Thomas's reaction, so she doesn't enquire further.

'I'm sorry. Even after all this time, some memories grab me unexpectedly.'

He pauses and composes himself. 'The people... they resisted. Civilians armed themselves with whatever they could find. Knives, hunting rifles, old sabres. Their defiance became a symbol of Greek courage.

'We lost Crete. And not long after that, the Germans had full control: mainland Greece, the islands, the ports. Everything.'

Carissa's eyes arch interrogatively. 'And you were on Crete. What happened to you?'

'We were lucky. We were evacuated. I was transferred to a training facility near Haifa,' he said. 'That's in modern-day Israel. It had been set up by the Special Operations Executive. The SOE.'

Carissa cranes her head. 'I've heard of them.'

Thomas nods. 'Their job was to support and incite resistance in occupied Europe. I was part of a team training Greek operatives. It was a thankless job, frustrating work. Many of the Greeks had no military training. Brave, yes. But bravery isn't enough. We needed trained fighters. And for real success inside Greece, we needed Allied officers in the country, clandestinely involved.'

He looks down at his hands; his fingers curl as if he is holding the memories.

'I was eventually moved to SOE Middle East Headquarters in Cairo,' he continues. 'That's when things shifted for me. My war took on a different meaning and purpose.'

Thomas looks at her, eyes softening. 'We're both out of tea.' He reaches for the teapot and refills their cups.

'I'm afraid I know little about the war,' she admits, the words coming out in a breath. 'Especially not Greece's part in it. Honestly… I haven't got a clue.'

The admission mortifies Carissa, given what Thomas had just told her. To her relief, Thomas is gracious when he speaks.

'And why should you?' he says with a smile. 'Not everyone has to be interested in history. I studied it at university: Greek classics, the language, the people and their history. It shaped everything that followed. It defined my involvement in the war. It's why I ended up in Greece in the first place.'

Carissa feels herself leaning in, intrigued, drawn by the threads of his story. 'What was Greece like at that time?' she asks. 'It must have been very different from today.'

Thomas shifts forward in his seat. 'It was nothing like what you see now. It wasn't a developed country, not like Britain or Germany. Greece was politically fractured, economically weak, and deeply rural. Outside of Athens, especially in the countryside and the mountains, the economy was mostly agricultural, and even that was outdated, people working tiny plots of land using tools from another century.'

Carissa imagines hillsides dotted with olive trees and small stone houses, the kind she has hiked past on Skiathos.

'When Metaxas came to power, he modelled his regime on fascist governments like Hitler's. He cracked down on opposition – especially communists. Censorship, prison camps… it was a hard regime.'

Carissa's brows furrow. 'But I thought Greece was the birthplace of democracy?'

Thomas gives a half-smile, one that doesn't quite reach his eyes. 'And that's the great irony, isn't it? Its legacy didn't protect it from history's cruelties. When the Italians and then the Germans came, that old sense of national identity began to awaken – but it came through suffering.'

'I didn't realise Greece was occupied too,' she says apologetically.

'They were,' Thomas says quietly. 'The Germans installed a Greek puppet government.'

Thomas scratches his creased brow. 'I'm sorry. I've been ranting on like a maniac. I must be boring you half to death.'

'You're not. Honestly. I find it fascinating.'

'Don't be polite, especially on my account.'

'I wasn't.' She glances at her watch. 'But I need to get going though. I've got a walking trail in forty minutes.'

'I don't want to keep you and make you late.'

'You're not,' she says simply. 'I can see talking about the war means a lot to you.'

'It helps me remember. The old brain cells are getting duller by the day.'

'Have you ever written about your time in the war? Some people keep journals or diaries.'

'No. There have been lots of books and research done on that period of Greek history. Maybe I could have contributed something to it. I was too busy being an academic. Now, there's only me and old Daisy.'

Carissa clears her throat. 'If you ever wrote about your time in the war, I would definitely read it.' Her smile is full of admiration. 'There can't be many people who are still alive who have such personal experience about that time, especially the war in Greece.'

'There have been a few who've written extensively about it. If you're interested, there are books out there that have documented personal accounts. The trouble is getting a hold of them. Not all are available in bookstores.'

'What about Amazon?'

'Because they're not in print, the prices are grossly inflated. Although you can still get good condition second-hand books. Chris Woodhouse's books are still in print,' he says brightly. 'That's the one I was reading the other day. He's written extensively about it. His writings are a well-regarded authority on Greece. In good times and bad, he always had the interests of Greece and its people at heart. He shaped the history of Greece. His role was that critical. His contribution was fundamental to the country we see today.'

Sadness clouds his eyes, and his gaze slides away from her. 'I recently found out he'd died. That's why I reread his book again. There can't be many of us left, if any.'

CHAPTER TEN

ACRONYMS AND A HISTORY LESSON

Skiathos 2007

Over the next few weeks, Carissa continues to visit Thomas, who details the German occupation of Greece with zest. The process transforms him. It transfers him to a past he rarely can visit or discuss. As he depicts events and circumstances, Carissa becomes more aware that it is a kind of therapy for him. His eyes reflect an animated sheen, and at other times, they cloud with a sadness and despair that is so tangible, Carissa feels she can reach out and touch his sorrow.

This, she understands, transcends past recollection. He is being pulled into his past, a time he experienced and lived through. This is not just the telling of Greece's historical past; it is also the recollections of raw, lived experience; as she soon comes to realise, this is Thomas's story. He tells the event as if it happened yesterday, constantly replaying in his mind.

It fascinates her how time runs away from them and

how quickly she becomes enthralled and engrossed in Thomas's words, Thomas's world. It becomes clear, and somewhat surprising to Carissa, how emotive the experience leaves her.

They always sit outside in the pergola's shade. It has become his habit to have a pot of tea, and two cups and saucers placed on the small table in front of him. After Carissa is seated, he pours the tea, and often enquires about her day.

'You don't look your usual self today, Carissa. You look… pensive, troubled even. Is everything okay?'

'It's nothing for you to worry about, Thomas. I can deal with it.'

'Well, that hasn't put my mind at rest. Do you want to expand on that?' he encourages her. 'Or you can just tell me to mind my own business. I won't be offended.'

She feels lightheaded as another wave of nausea washes over her.

Her face exhibits a pallor that speaks to Thomas of either sickness or exhaustion. 'I'm no doctor, but you don't look well, either. You've gone a terrible colour. Shall I get you some water?'

She waves away his concern with a raised hand. 'I'm fine.' She speaks through a surge of nausea. 'I'm fine. I just need a minute.'

'Very well.'

Daisy ambles towards her and brushes against her skin, the dog's fur soft against Carissa's leg.

Carissa is forced to take in great gulps of air, her chest heaves, her skin hot and clammy, to her alarm, she jumps to her feet, her hand clamped over her mouth, as she runs to the garden wall and leaning over it, retches several times.

She returns sheepishly, wiping her chin with her fingers. She smooths her hair and ties it up with a clasp.

'Here, clean yourself up.' Thomas gives her a handful of wipes and places a bottle of water on the table in front of her.

'Thank you.' Carissa wipes her chin and around her mouth, mortified and embarrassed. She takes a gulp of the water. 'I'll be fine now. I feel much better.'

Thomas studies her, and Carissa can see, by the tightening of his eyes, she hasn't convinced him.

Thomas rubs his chin.

Carissa sighs. 'The truth is, I think I saw something, someone yesterday, who I wasn't expecting to see here in Skiathos.'

'Who?'

'I'm not sure if it was him. In fact, I feel stupid even talking about it.'

'Well, going on your recent performance, it was enough to make you feel unwell… scared even?'

'It was just a second. I caught this person looking at me, well us, my walking group, as we were returning from a trail. He was quite a distance away, but he reminded me of someone. I was distracted by a question one of the group asked, and when I looked again, he was gone.'

'Who was he?'

'I'm probably just being oversensitive. It can't have been him.'

'And who is *him*?'

Reliving the experience and talking about it has unbalanced her. Her heart pounds against her chest, and blood throbs in her temple.

'My ex-partner, Stuart.'

'You think you saw him?'

'He was a good distance away. It was probably just a coincidence – someone who looked like him. They say we all have a double.'

'Even so, it's worried you. Is there a reason why it would?'

'It's complicated.' Carissa takes a breath. She's worried Thomas. He is due an explanation.

When she's finished, she's annoyed with herself as tears brim in her eyes. Worse still, she can see it has unsettled Thomas.

'And you think this Stuart, this excuse of a man, has followed you to Skiathos.'

'I can't be sure. It was probably nothing – an overreaction on my part. Now that I'm thinking about it, he was too far away for me to really see. It was probably nothing. I feel stupid just talking about it.'

'It was enough to make you stressed and anxious. People are not sick for no reason. You're either ill or worried to death.'

'I feel fine now,' she says, avoiding a defining answer to Thomas's reasoning.

'Is it safe for you to be alone?'

She shifts in her chair. 'I don't even know if it was him. To be honest, I'm probably blowing this out of proportion. Can we just begin now?'

'Under the circumstances, I think it's better if we leave it for today and reconvene another time. What do you say, Carissa?'

'Not at all. I'm here now, so let's get started. I've been looking forward to this. I always do.'

Thomas stares at her. 'It might be a better idea to wait. You've obviously suffered a shock.'

'No, Thomas. We'll carry on as normal,' Carissa persists.

He leans back in his chair and considers her. 'Very well then, if you say so. Shall we begin?'

Carissa nods and takes a sip of tea, savouring its taste.

'I thought about this the other day. My only experience of war, was in the '90s in the former Yugoslavia – between the Serbs, the Croats and the Bosnians. Who would have thought something like that could have happened in modern Europe? It was shocking seeing those scenes of emaciated people. It reminded me of the concentration camps.'

He gathers his thoughts, and checks on her complexion.

'Most countries under occupation suffer. Unfortunately, it's the nature of war. Take Greece, it suffered terribly. Not just from war, but from how systematically the Germans dismantled what little infrastructure the country had. They drained its resources: food, goods, fuel… all diverted to Germany. Greece lost over half of its merchant fleet. What remained was under Allied control, leaving the country cut off from trade. No ships, therefore, no income.'

Carissa's brow furrows as she leans forward, pulled in by the gravity of his tone.

'Inflation spiralled,' Thomas continues. 'Prices were a thousand times higher than they had been before the war. Wages rose barely a hundredfold. That meant the black market, where most food could be found, was out of reach for almost everyone.' He shakes his head. 'Fuel shortages compounded the hardship. Unemployment increased dramatically. In urban areas, particularly in Athens and Piraeus, there was no bread at all. It led to widespread starvation, and soon, half a million people relied on food kitchens just to survive. People died from the cold and hunger, particularly the vulnerable: children, the elderly, and war veterans.'

'That's dreadful.'

'And it was,' Thomas says. 'Famine swept through not just the cities, but the villages too. The countryside may have had fields, but it wasn't immune. One in ten children lived past the first month. Starvation, disease… they stalked every family.'

Carissa folds her arms across her chest and sadly shakes her head.

Then, with a shift in his voice, a flicker of energy, Thomas leans in, his eyes wide. 'But that suffering… it lit something in people. A fire. The occupation was cruel, but it didn't break them. If anything, it steeled them.'

Carissa's eyes light up. 'What do you mean?'

'The cities sparked first. Political awareness was stronger there. Protests began – pulling down Nazi flags, civil disobedience. Symbolic, yes, but at the same time powerful.'

'Good. I'm glad to hear it.'

Thomas grins. 'It wasn't all grand gestures and torch-lit speeches. Some groups carried out sabotage, others gathered intelligence.'

He sits straighter now, his words picking up pace. 'The Communist-led bands were better organised and larger; they absorbed or eliminated many of the smaller ones.'

'They were fighting the Germans and Italians *and* each other?' She looks at him incredulously.

Thomas sighs. 'It's the Greek way. Passion, politics, division. And yet, a common enemy can do remarkable things. Graffiti began appearing, patriotic slogans. And there was one story, famous now, of a young guard who wrapped himself in the Greek flag and jumped from the Acropolis rather than serve under the Germans.'

Carissa gasps. 'He jumped!'

Thomas's eyebrows rise. 'He became a symbol. A martyr. That kind of courage fed the resistance like fuel.

'Around the same time, EDES – The National Republican Greek League – was founded. Anti-monarchist, right-leaning. They were led by Colonel Zervas.'

Thomas feels a burst of emotion – a physical assault of sights and sounds from a memory that shifts inside him. He pushes back his wide-brimmed hat and looking into his eyes, Carissa can see another time reflected within them.

Thomas smiles. 'Zervas got British support too and he became a prominent figure.'

Carissa, still trying to keep up, takes a breath. 'And the Communists?'

'Ah,' Thomas says, sitting back. 'The biggest player. The KKE, the Communist Party, founded the other big player, EAM, the National Liberation Front.' Thomas spoke more slowly. 'Their goal? Resist the occupation and then hold free elections. On paper, it sounded wonderful. In practice… well, they were highly organised. Ruthlessly so.' He pauses. 'They had layers: urban leadership, rural administration, workers' councils, youth wings. They controlled entire communities. They even collected taxes.'

Carissa's eyes widen. 'That sounds more than just resistance.'

'Exactly. They weren't just fighting. They were governing. In '42, they formed ELAS, the National Popular Liberation Army, which was their military wing. By mid '42, ELAS and EDES were the two major guerrilla forces. Both with British backing. Both resisted the Axis, and both had substantial influence over Greek society. To make matters interesting, not all ELAS members were as keen on communism or staunch in their beliefs, and likewise, it was the same on the republican side: Zervas's men had their flaws too, which often resulted in the tragedy of Greeks fighting Greeks.'

Carissa leans forward; her hands wrap around her cup. 'All of this… it's incredible. I had no idea Greece's role was so complicated,' she says, sounding embarrassed.

'Have you heard of Churchill?' his eyes quiz her. 'You *have* heard of *him*?'

'Of course. My knowledge of history isn't that bad. He was a general, right?'

Thomas flinches.

'Just kidding. I know he was the prime minister at the time, and he always smoked huge cigars. In every photo I've seen of him, he had a cigar in his hand or one clamped in his mouth.'

Thomas smiles. 'Yes. He liked his cigars. I suppose nowadays you'd call that, his trademark.' Thomas leans forward. 'Greece isn't often mentioned alongside France or Poland. But it mattered. Churchill knew that. That's why British officers were sent to coordinate the *andartes*.'

Carrissa is momentarily confused.

'The resistance fighters,' Thomas tells her.

She stares at him. 'Ah! I see. And the British were there too!'

'One of those officers… was Brigadier Eddie Myers, head of the British Military Mission; another, was a young major who would later become Colonel Chris Woodhouse.'

'That's the guy whose book you were reading when I first came to visit you.'

'That's right.'

'You knew him?'

He smiles warmly. 'We knew each other rather well.'

'That's amazing.'

Thomas nods. 'All these years later, I can still remember every name. There were Eddie Myers and Chris Woodhouse, Themie Marinos, Denys Hamson, Nat Barker, Inder Gill, John Cook, Arthur Edmonds, Tom Barnes, Len Wilmot.'

With bated breath, Carissa waited to hear what he would say next.

'It was a time that's never left me. There hasn't been a day that I haven't thought about it. They were dropped into Greece in the fall of '42 for what was at the time, a "one-shot" operation.' Thomas gives a little knowing smile. 'And that's where my story in all of this begins… because I was there too.'

CHAPTER ELEVEN

HARLING

Combined General Headquarters, Cairo 1942

The old overhead fan squeaked like a rusty wheel, doing little to ease the stifling heat in the windowless Combined General Headquarters in Cairo.

'Just two more weeks, and I'm out of here,' Brigadier Eddie Myers said, loosening his tie and switching on his desk fan. 'It can't come soon enough. I haven't done a thing since Haifa – three months of sitting at this desk.'

Thomas took two cigarettes from a packet and handed one to Eddie. He offered him a light and lit his own as the end glowed red with a soft crackle before he inhaled deeply, welcoming the burn over his throat.

Thomas sank into a chair opposite Eddie. 'Speaking of which, I met Paddy Fermor the other day and Nick Hammond. You know Nick. I'm sure the two of you met in Haifa.'

'We did. I asked him what was an archaeologist doing training Greeks? Surely, they knew about the Acropolis?'

Eddie laughed. 'He knew I was pulling his leg. I remember he had a decent sense of humour.'

'We all needed one of them. And still do,' he added.

'Exactly, he said it certainly wasn't for his expertise at shooting a rifle, but because he could speak Greek. He spoke it like a local, much like yourself.'

'He was playing himself down. He was a good shot, better than most of the Greeks we were there to train. I had serious doubts about sending them back to Greece; most were of poor quality military-wise.'

'Unfortunately, they don't have the luxury of time.' Eddie took a drag of his cigarette. 'Did Nick go to Crete with you?'

'No. I've not seen him since Haifa. With any luck, he'll be back home.'

Just then, a tall officer craned his head around the open door. He removed his hat, which covered oiled hair pressed into a side pattern, and, scratching his dark, pencilled moustache, grinned. 'I hope I'm not interrupting anything that might be of national importance.'

'Well, look who it is, Lieutenant Colonel Hamilton. Come in. It's been a while. What are you doing here? We were just talking about our days in Haifa.'

'Ah, the Middle East Staff College. I can't say I remember it with fond memories. It's been six months since I left.'

Hamilton extended his hand, and Eddie shook it enthusiastically.

'You know Major Thomas Wilson.'

'I do.' Hamilton and Thomas shook hands. 'Good to see you again, Thomas. Well, if this isn't a stroke of luck. I've got rather a confidential matter I'd like to run past you, Eddie.'

Thomas rose from his chair. 'I'll leave you to it, sir.'

Hamilton raised his hand. 'Sit Thomas. I'd like you to hear this too. Two heads are better than one and all that.'

'That sounds rather intriguing. Please take a seat.' Eddie flicked his cigarette into the ashtray on the desk.

Hamilton sat opposite and crossed his legs. 'I'm on the staff of SOE now, and to cut to the chase, I need to know who is best qualified to get parachute-trained sapper officers to jump into Greece and blow up a bridge. It's really a viaduct, I suppose, but what's the difference? Since you, Eddie, are training the first RE contingent of Airborne troops here in the Middle East, I immediately thought of you.'

'They haven't started their training yet, and to date, no one has been allocated. In fact, there isn't even a pool of parachute-trained sapper officers in the Middle East you can choose from. There's no one apart from the active SAS. They're under the command of Lieutenant Colonel David Stirling. They're in the North African desert, raiding aerodromes and installations.'

Hamilton took out a handkerchief from his pocket and dabbed at his brow. 'Can it get any hotter? What I'd give for an English winter right now!'

Eddie stubbed out his cigarette. 'I'm not sure how I can be of help.'

Hamilton pointed to the badge on Eddie's uniform and grinned. 'Forgive me if I'm incorrect, but that badge would presume you're a parachutist, would it not?'

'Ah, I see,' Eddie rubbed the stubble on his chin. 'It does. If the truth be known, I'm not what you'd call a proper parachutist.'

'But you're wearing the badge. Surely, you've done it before.'

'I have, but only in my spare time when I was the senior instructor at the Combined Operations School on the Suez Canal and I'd been cajoled into it by SAS training instructors. It wasn't anything serious or official at the time.'

'But you jumped out of a plane with a parachute?'

'Well, after doing one jump, I thought, why not. I would only need to do another four jumps to enable me to wear the parachute badge. So, I did all the jumps, – but I've done none since,' he added.

'That doesn't matter.'

'I see where you're going here. Look, Hamilton, I'm just completing my seventh year in the Middle East, and I'm going home in two weeks' time, which I'm rather looking forward to.'

Hamilton waved his hand dismissively.

Eddie's brows furrowed. 'My knowledge of Greece comprises spending a few hours in Athens. I'm not what you'd describe as an expert on the country. And anyway, I don't speak the language.'

Hamilton glanced at Thomas. 'But he does.'

Thomas shifted in his chair uncomfortably.

Hamilton's eyes widened. 'I realise the timing's not perfect, but when is it? There've been discussions at a high level, and your name came up as the perfect man for the job. All agreed, you're the chap we're looking for,' Hamilton said. 'Look, Eddie, how would you like to be in command of this show? It's crucial to our needs in the region.'

'What's the timescale?'

'I knew I could massage that curiosity of yours.'

'That wasn't a statement of intent.'

'Of course not. You'd be back within a few weeks, and then you can leave this Goddamn heat behind you and return to the shores of England on the crest of a wave. What do you say?'

Eddie stubbed out his cigarette. He sighed. 'I'm going to have to say no. Another time, maybe, when I wasn't close to going home, my answer would be different, but there it is. I've been here too long. I can't wait to see the back of the Middle East. And anyway, what you're looking for is not my expertise; I'm just a regular soldier.'

'Precisely. A regular soldier. That's exactly what we're looking for. That's what this operation is calling out for. We need a trained staff officer who can influence the *andarte* leaders and consolidate a collaborative assault.'

'Are you serious?'

'I am. I've never been more serious.'

'And you're convinced I'm the right man for the job?'

'Yes, I am, and it's not just me, I'd like to remind you.'

'The decision isn't entirely mine to make. I'd have to ask my boss, Admiral Maund.'

'And where is his office?'

'Next door.'

'Then, there's no time like the present.' Hamilton rose from his chair. 'Shall we?' He turned to Thomas. 'And is Admiral Maund your boss too?'

'He is.'

'Then, Thomas, you'll be part of our discussion as well.'

Thomas paced the floor, straining to hear the conversation that could change the course of his war. Hamilton had been cagey about revealing any concrete details about the proposed mission, and all Thomas knew was that it was in Greece and involved an attack that depended on the efforts of a joint operation with the Greek resistance. The Greek resistance? Thomas didn't even know there was one. He had heard of minor assaults on Axis forces in

Greece, but these were sporadic attacks, and to his knowledge, not organised by a militarised resistance organisation.

As Eddie emerged from Admiral Maund's office, Hamilton proclaimed with an air of confidence, 'Well, at least we know where we stand now.'

Thomas grilled Eddie with a glance.

'The Admiral is of the opinion, it's my decision to make. He thinks I'm just the chap for the job. It's beginning to sound like a conspiracy. If I agree to this, you're coming too, Thomas.'

Thomas thought if Hamilton could smile any wider, his ears would split. 'We have one other officer who is proficient in speaking Greek.' Hamilton turned to Eddie. 'Major Chris Woodhouse. Do you know him?'

'I can't say we've met.'

'He's already spent time in Crete, and it's already been decided he'll be second-in-command. His command of the language is impeccable. However, it makes sense to have more than one on the ground that can converse with the Greeks, and you, Thomas, fit the bill perfectly.'

Eddie rubbed his brow, and Thomas could tell he was forming a decision. 'If I'm needed and there's no one else for the job, I should accept.'

Hamilton tilted his head. 'Can I take that as a yes, then?'

'I'll take the job, but it's up to you, Hamilton, to make it happen.'

'Good man. I'll get the permission from my commanding officer, who'll see the Chief of Staff about it. It shouldn't take more than a day to get sorted.'

'This should be a job for volunteers and not an order from above,' Eddie reminded Hamilton.

'I know that, Eddie, but it will happen. You've been personally selected.'

'And what about Thomas? He hasn't.'

'He has now.'

'Time is of the essence. For the next week or two, the weather is perfect; after that, we'd have to postpone the operation until the next moon, and that doesn't suit our objectives. I'll know tomorrow if I've got the permission for you and Thomas to go. Once it's been cleared, you'll both be briefed.'

Two days later, Eddie and Thomas were trailing an officer in a short-sleeved shirt through the warren of corridors at SOE headquarters, housed in a weathered colonial building in Cairo.

Large ceiling fans spun lazily overhead, doing little to dispel the persistent heat that seeped through the shuttered windows.

Maps of North Africa, the Mediterranean, and the Middle East, their corners curled and yellowed, covered the walls with detailed troop movements and strategic positions marked by coloured pins, small flags and hurried pencilled notes that crowded the margins.

Typewriters tapped and clicked incessantly in the rooms off the corridors.

They entered an office where Hamilton was sitting behind a heavy mahogany desk. He arranged some paper-work, requesting them to be seated. From an open window, a warm breeze drifted over Thomas's face as he followed Eddie's lead and sat opposite Hamilton.

Amongst an array of files and reports, Thomas noted a photograph of family back in England.

On a side table, the steady crackle of a radio vied with the sounds of military vehicles on the street below and the distant call to prayer from a nearby mosque.

Hamilton unfolded a creased map and laid it flat on his desk with a deliberate hand.

'Eddie, Thomas. Thanks for coming,' he began, his voice clipped and purposeful, 'I'll come straight to the point.'

He gestured to the map with the end of his pen.

'Our air operations out of Malta and our submarine activities along Greece's western coast have forced the Germans to depend almost entirely on the Balkan railway line for supply transport to their ports in Greece, at Salonika and Piraeus.'

He traced the route of the railway with the pen.

'It's a single-line, standard-gauge track,' he said. 'It runs down the coastline south of Salonika here, crosses the Thessaly plains, then snakes through the mountains of Roumeli and Attica before terminating at Piraeus. Because of enemy air cover from their island bases, we've found direct strikes against the port itself damned difficult.

'In a nutshell, it's imperative we make it difficult for the Jerries to be successful in bringing supplies by sea to their bases along the North African coast, and this railway line is key to their success.'

'So the rail line is the jugular,' Eddie said.

'Precisely,' Hamilton replied, tapping the desk with his pen to punctuate the point. 'Cut it, and we choke Rommel's supplies to North Africa. It's essential to their campaign, and therefore to ours.'

He leaned over the map again.

'In the Roumeli region, we've identified three major viaducts: Gorgopotamos, Asopos, and Papadia. All lie within nine miles of each other, on the northeastern fringe of the Giona mountains. Bring down any of them, and we'll stop the trains getting to the port of Piraeus for weeks, possibly months.'

He paused, glancing up. 'It will take around a tonne of explosives – which means three aircraft for the drop. That's just the beginning. Getting it to the target, under cover, through the mountainous terrain – that's going to be the real challenge.'

Thomas leaned forward. 'Do we know what we're up against? What about the defences on the ground?'

'Italians,' Hamilton replied. 'Our latest intelligence estimates around one to two hundred troops guarding each bridge.'

He flipped open a file on his desk.

'We're in contact by wireless with Greek agents in Athens. Our main asset is a Greek naval officer operating under the codename Prometheus. He's got solid connections with several mountain-based *andarte* bands. We've supported them before, airdropped small arms and explosives. They've used them effectively in sabotage operations and raids against isolated Italian units.'

Hamilton's brow creased.

'But there's a problem. Prometheus's wireless isn't strong enough to reach us directly. Everything has to be relayed through a station in Turkey. Regrettably, that's caused delays – weeks, in some cases.'

He looked up, his expression serious.

'We informed Prometheus of the need to blow up one of the viaducts and asked if the *andartes* would help. We promised to supply the explosives and funds. Prometheus replied eventually. It took more than a fortnight. He said the drop, if it was going ahead, had to occur between

September 28th and October 3rd. That's the window we're working with.'

Hamilton returned to the map and tapped two spots in quick succession.

'As far as we know, there are two main *andarte* forces in the region. One led by Seferiades, commands two to three hundred men. The other, more formidable, is under a Colonel Zervas, a former Greek army colonel, who commands around twelve hundred men.' Hamilton allowed himself the briefest smile. 'That intelligence sealed our decision to green-light the operation, which we're now calling – *Harling*.'

'And how will we know we're being dropped in the right area?' Eddie asked.

'Seferiades' men will mark the drop zone with bonfires arranged in a cross. As for Zervas's group – well, it's less clear cut; there's a snag, I'm afraid. Prometheus's coordinates were partially corrupted. It's a bugger, I know.

'We've checked the maps for any name resembling the group of corrupt letters in Prometheus's message, and we think we've found the location. Our best assessment places it at a village near a mountain called Timfristos in Central Greece, about thirty miles northwest of Giona. We believe Zervas has relocated there, but unfortunately, time constraints prevent us from confirming this through Prometheus.'

Hamilton scratched his chin.

'Three Liberator aircraft will be used to drop the explosives, stores and men. Your force will comprise twelve men, nine officers and three wireless operators.'

He met Eddie's gaze.

'You'll lead the operation, Eddie. Colonel Woodhouse will be your second-in-command. You'll all be wearing

British uniforms. Once you're on the ground, you're to join up with the respective *andarte* forces for the assault. After the operation, you'll be evacuated from the west coast of Greece by submarine, apart from Woodhouse and two wireless operators. It's part of a longer-term plan. They'll help coordinate further sabotage and maintain SOE presence in the region.

'It's crucial to get the *andarte* commanders onboard as soon as possible.' Hamilton's face creased into a frown. 'Time is of the essence, gentlemen. You deploy in four days. I realise this leaves precious little time for preparation, but operational necessity dictates our timeline.'

He returned to his chair, reached for a silver cigarette case on his desk, lit one, and drew deeply.

He rubbed his chin. 'The *andarte* bands are independent. Their cooperation is delicate, but essential, and not guaranteed. This is precisely why Colonel Woodhouse's role is so vital – his excellent command of Greek and diplomatic skills will be essential in managing these relationships. Also, Thomas, you too speak like a native, we'll be counting on you to manage communications between yourselves and the *andartes*.'

'How the hell do we move a tonne of explosives through the mountains and under enemy eyes?' Eddie asked.

Hamilton took a deep draw of his cigarette. 'It'll be a feat, there's no getting away from it. But it must be done. That's why timing is everything. We don't have the luxury of waiting.'

Hamilton stubbed out his cigarette in a silver ashtray and fixed them both with a resolute gaze.

'It's tight, I know. I won't pretend it'll be easy. But the strategic impact of this could be enormous. Rommel's lifeline depends on those rails. Cut them, and we may very well turn the tide in the Mediterranean.'

Eddie looked at Hamilton's desk, where a pile of files sat. 'There's Woodhouse, Thomas and myself; how far forward are you in recruiting the others?'

'We've already chosen a Major John Cook; he's a commando officer.' Hamilton's eyes brightened as he sat forward in his chair. 'We've earmarked a group of fourteen men. All have volunteered and are up for it. We've had to be on our toes with this one. Most are already at the Parachute Training School next to the Suez Canal.'

Eddie raised his eyebrows. 'They're just learning to jump?'

'I'm afraid so. They've never parachuted out of a plane before. There're a good bunch though, a solid group of men. They learn quickly.'

'I hope so.'

'Well, I'm sure there'll be a lot for you both to do. You'll get all the help you need. I suspect you'll want to know the situation in Greece and make plans. Woodhouse is already assessing the volunteers. You'll both need to get down there and cast an eye over them too. You'll have the final say on personnel selection, of course, and full support for your preparation requirements.' Hamilton stood and came around the desk. He extended his hand, which both Thomas and Eddie shook.

'Good luck. You know what's at stake. I'll tell Woodhouse you're on your way.'

Thomas and Eddie spent the following two days in the offices of SOE studying maps of the region, drawings, and plans of the viaducts.

They sought the advice of an officer from the Royal New Zealand Engineers and by the end of the day had planned a demolition plan for each individual viaduct.

The next day, they drove down to the Parachute Training School and, after meeting with Chris Woodhouse and bringing him up to speed with their plans, they set about assessing the volunteers.

All had two days of preliminary training behind them and had completed their first parachute drop. The first and only night jump was set for midnight. Eddie and Thomas joined them, and to everyone's relief, the jump was a success.

Eddie, Thomas, Chris, and Major John Cook discussed the qualities of each volunteer; Chris's opinion held significant weight, given his two-day observation period. Regardless, the three radio operators would still go, each in their own plane. Second-lieutenant Marinos would be present too, as he and Chris were designated to remain after the operation finished. Given their shared background in Greek and explosive training, Captains Hamson and Barker, both needed, were given a spot. Three more individuals were chosen from a group of five, including two captains from the Royal New Zealand Engineers and one lieutenant from the Royal Engineers. In case of an unforeseen circumstance, they put the remaining two on standby.

The only remaining detail was assigning personnel to the three aircraft; once this was done, the men received their mission briefing.

That night, Thomas lay on top of his bed. He tried to read but his thoughts tumbled one after the other, stealing his concentration. He cast the book onto the bedside table.

Thomas swung his feet from the bed and sat with his head in his hands. The familiar loud pulse announced itself like a bass drum in his temple, his hand trembled slightly, and beads of sweat breached his pores. He wiped his forehead with the back of his hand. He waited and screwed his eyes shut. Thomas sighed heavily, rubbing both eyes with the heels of his hands, and the images came, just as he knew they would. They always did. Torturing him, baiting him.

On the night of their departure, at an aerodrome in the Canal Zone, they changed out of their desert uniforms and pulled on thick winter battledress clothes. The members of the party each received leather money-belts, and they distributed several hundred gold sovereigns equally. In the heat of the Egyptian night, the men sweltered as they ate a last meal in the RAF Mess before pulling on thick overalls and their parachute harnesses. As well as explosives, they were taking rifles, light automatics, ammunition, and hand grenades for the *andartes*, clothing and food. They packed their stores into metal canisters. Each of the three aircraft held twelve containers, with three canisters apiece, loaded into the bomb bays. They would drop their wireless sets and the batteries attached to the parachutes.

As dusk fell, sweltering and perspiring in their layers of clothes, they made their way over to the waiting aircraft. A final brief had already been given after their meal, and all that remained was for each party to head to its allocated Liberator.

They waited as one engine, then another, fired into life, the blazing exhausts jetting blue flames in the fading light.

Once given the signal, each party entered their respective aircraft through a small opening underneath the fuselage of the airplane. It was a poignant moment, as each man knew this was the way they would also exit the aeroplane.

Thomas's party crowded into the cockpit as instructed, keeping as much weight as possible off the tail of the aircraft during take-off. Each airplane would take off at fifteen-minute intervals. Thomas's was the first to go. Once airborne, they scrambled along the gangway, passed the containers on the bomb bays, and, removing their harnesses and overalls, set about making themselves as comfortable as possible for the rest of the five-hour flight.

Each man retreated into his thoughts, or attempted to sleep amidst the rumble of the engines, ignoring any conversation. Two hours into the flight, the entire aircraft shuddered as the engines roared and it banked sharply, evading several sporadic bursts of flak rising from an island off their flank. An hour later, below them, Eddie pointed out the undulating and chiselled mountains of Greece silhouetted in the moonlight.

Thomas glanced at his watch. Eddie rose to his feet and crept to the cockpit. When he returned, he informed the rest that they would be over the dropping ground in around twenty minutes and ordered everyone to prepare for their jumps. After hours of tedious boredom, they stretched and rubbed their limbs. Once everyone was dressed and ready, Eddie communicated with the pilot using a set of headphones. They sat in stony silence as the aircraft circled. By now, there was an open hole in the fuselage floor where the men would exit. Eddie beckoned Thomas over to him, where he had been peering out of a small window.

'I can see several bonfires scattered about,' Eddie raised his voice above the ever-increasing level of noise. 'But I don't see any in the shape of a cross. Take a look over at the hole; you might see more land from there.'

Thomas nodded. The dispatcher disengaged Thomas's parachute from the static line, and he crept over to the opening in the fuselage floor. He crouched and strained his eyes to get a better view. The darkness concealed tiny yellow flickers, but no cross emerged.

They circled for several minutes more and then headed westwards towards Timfristos. Still, no fire emerged. They made their way to the west coast of Greece, circling at intervals, then turning back, they flew over the Giona area again, circling several times.

After a further fifteen minutes, the pilot summoned Eddie to the cockpit.

'I'm not seeing any signals on the ground that we were expecting to find. I have no other option but to return to Cairo, as we were instructed, Sir.'

Bitterly frustrated, Eddie conceded and returned to the others to convey the pilot's decision.

Disappointed, they shed their parachute harnesses, wrapped themselves in blankets to escape the cold, and succumbed to sleep.

As dawn crept over the Egyptian horizon, the aeroplane landed where their journey had begun eleven hours earlier. As they disembarked, an RAF officer met them and informed them that one other aircraft had already returned for the same reason.

During breakfast at the station mess, the third aircraft returned. They would be delayed for a further twenty-four hours.

They drove back to Cairo, Thomas sleeping most of that day. Should the next drop fail, there would be a three-week delay, dependent upon cloud cover and a clear moon, with mission cancellation as a possibility. The team decided that if there was no signal, John Cook's aircraft would drop his party near Mount Giona and, if safe, they would light red flares to guide the other two parties.

The three parties returned to the aerodrome, airborne once more and reaching Greece, they were soon over Mount Giona. They identified several bonfires, but frustratingly none that resembled a cross. Then, just as the aeroplane reached a flat valley, Thomas picked out three bonfires.

'What do you think, Eddie?' Thomas asked.

'I'm not going back this time.'

Eddie contacted the pilot via the telephone, then faced his crew. 'Prepare to drop. It's on. Let's go.'

Activity swirled as each man poised to drop, their static lines securing them. The pilot circled the drop zone and brought the aeroplane as low as he could above the deep valleys and mountain summits.

As the aircraft shuddered, the men anticipated the jump with intensity. Thomas had the dissociative feeling of watching himself prepare to do something that every nerve and survival instinct was warning him against.

He watched as Eddie disappeared through the opening in the fuselage, as if the blackness swallowed him.

Thomas's rapid breath quickened his racing heart, a metallic taste coating his dry mouth; sweat slicked his palms as excitement, heightened awareness, pure electric terror, and exhilaration all tangled together. As he crouched above the opening, time dilated, it distorted, it stretched and compressed – seconds felt like hours. And then calmness descended upon him, a clarity that came with his full acceptance and commitment to what was about to come.

He received the signal, and a push sent him falling fast into darkness.

The change was immediate, with an arctic blast of air that caught his breath, like rushing wind. The dramatic shift in air pressure slammed into him, as the wind resistance created a cushion of air that felt almost solid against his body. The line between self and surroundings temporarily dissolved in the darkness as he stared into, and plunged through, blackness. Disoriented and deprived of visual anchors, he battled between a primal fear and a determination to be in control.

He pulled the ripcord and deployed the parachute. There was a sudden deceleration and shift. The roar of his fall gave way to an abrupt and surreal silence, evoking a strange sense of solitude – a dreamlike sensation, almost transcendent – as the rush of freefall softened to a gentle descent beneath the vast canopy above him.

He felt his heartbeat, the expansion of his lungs, the slight shake in his hands, the pressure of the harness, and his muscles tensing and releasing. Above him, the moonlight reflected off clouds in the vast darkness and the limited visibility around him.

The world below him revealed itself, showcasing rugged mountains and steep valleys that dominated the landscape. Thomas peered through the thin cloud cover, trying to detect the valley with a triangle of fires. To his dismay, both eluded him. To his right, he spotted several parachutes – containers with their stores dangling below the canopies. Eddie should be under him with the other duo leaping directly after him, but there was no sight of them. Thomas shouted out; no one replied. He took out a torch from his overalls pocket and shone it on his parachute. If anyone was above him, they would surely see the torch light up the parachute. He shouted again but was met with nothing but the wind and the drone of the Liberators' engines fading from him.

He deposited the torch back in his overall pocket and raised himself on his arms to get a clear view of what was below him.

The wind had propelled him above the mountains and across valleys at a considerable rate, much further from his intended landing area. He estimated over a mile at least. He could determine roughly where he was about to land. With only a few hundred feet to go, the landscape was covered with a carpet of shrubs. At least his landing would be smooth. And then, as he descended further, to his alarm, what looked like undergrowth became clearer with each passing second. Below him, a vast forest of pine trees stretched out endlessly. His eyes darted along the dense canopy of treetops, frantically searching for a gap. Even if there were one, he doubted if he could manoeuvre towards it.

The ground suddenly rushed towards him with alarming speed, the wind like thunder in his ears. He pulled on the straps trying to adjust his trajectory. The treetops were getting larger and closer, faster than he'd expected.

He tensed every inch of his body, despite his training that advised in such circumstances to loosen every limb. He clenched his feet together, his knees bent, his forearms crossed in front of his eyes to protect his face, his elbows tucked close to reduce snagging. Straight and streamlined, he reminded himself with bated breath.

Then, he hit the dense layer of branches, the impact violent and chaotic, sending shockwaves through him. The smaller wispy outer branches snapped around him, whipping him with sharp stings in a rapid-fire series of snaps and cracks. His head jolted from side to side, striking a thick branch. His helmet absorbed most of the impact. He fell like a battering ram through the tree, cursing every collision, the tree grabbing at him in all directions.

Thick limbs violently hampered his deceleration, halting in brutal stops and starts. The parachute started to catch and tangle, jerking Thomas as it wrapped around branches, and eventually collapsing.

Within seconds of the impact, Thomas was sitting on the ground. Around him, lay a chaotic maze of leaves and branches. Tree sap and bits of bark covered him as the potent smell of broken pine needles and fresh sap filled the air.

He moved each arm and leg with caution. Miraculously, he hadn't broken anything.

Thomas had fallen onto a steep slope. Impulsively, he freed himself from his harness and tumbled downwards only to collide with a tree trunk that stopped his descent.

Above the sound of the wind hissing through the trees, he detected the sonorous pulse of the Liberator's engines, the aircraft now heading home. Thomas pulled a flare from a pocket of his overalls, lit it and threw it towards the top of the trees. He lit another three, throwing them in quick succession. He waited. Nothing but the wind met his ears. He blew his whistle and shouted, again and again. The silence was a blow. He stood, and peering through the darkness, his eyes raked the valley below for a replying signal. He waited, searching with hopeful eyes. But he was lost.

Ominous mountains and unfathomable valleys, draped in a concealing cloak of darkness, covered the world he had entered. The silence was haunting, the diminishing wind only adding to the effect. He felt diminutive, his surroundings oppressive in their sheer scale and the excruciating ache inside him. This was desolation.

CHAPTER TWELVE

THIS OPENING OF THE HEART

Skiathos 2007

After finishing a song from his traditional bouzouki music repertoire and between drags on his cigarette or mouthfuls of coffee, the musician routinely smiles at her. At first, Carissa returns his smiles with her own but becomes concerned and thinks he is being too friendly with the attention he is giving her.

'Is everything okay? You seem worried,' Dimitrios asks, sipping his wine, as they sit outside at a table for two, under the evening sky.

She leans across the table. 'The old guy, when he's not singing or playing a song, he keeps smiling at me. I thought he was just being nice, friendly at first, and doing it to everyone…'

Dimitrios shakes his head and sighs. 'He's my uncle. I'm sorry, I'll have a word with him.'

Carissa feels embarrassed. 'He is? Oh!'

'He's always asking if I've found someone special yet. His words, not mine.'

Carissa gives him a mischievous smile. 'Don't worry. I think that's cute.'

She asked Dimitrios for restaurant recommendations; he gave her a few, then spontaneously offered to take her to one.

To her own surprise, she agreed. They opted to eat at Taverna Alexandros. She didn't want to tell him she'd already eaten there and dull his praise for its exceptional Greek cuisine. She'd enjoyed a meal there a few weeks previously and was more than happy to return.

'That's the problem of living on a small island that has only one town where most of the population live; everyone knows everyone's business.'

'It's a refreshing change from Edinburgh.'

'You didn't enjoy living in Edinburgh?'

'It's a big city, busy and noisy. Believe me, this place is paradise in comparison. People smile here without a reason. I like the intimate feel of the island. It doesn't feel over-crowded.'

'Population-wise, there's around five and a half thousand, I think, but that increases during the holiday season.'

'That's just the size of a village back home.'

'We're not the biggest; Skiathos is really quite small; twelve kilometres long and six kilometres wide.'

'What's that in miles?' She asks, brushing crumbs into a small pile from the pita bread they've just shared.

'Around seven miles long and roughly four miles wide.'

'I knew it wasn't big but didn't appreciate how small it really was. That doesn't detract from how beautiful it is. I love the walking trails. That's what attracted me to come here. The countryside is just gorgeous, and the views around the top of the island are amazing.'

'She might be a small lady, but Skiathos packs a punch, that's for sure.'

They speak some more. He asks if she feels settled, compliments her on her professionalism and tells her he has heard nothing but good things from people who have been on her walks or attended her classes, all praising her with enthusiasm.

Dimitrios is open with her and mentions his divorce, his past life in Athens and his temporary need to stay at his parents' until he finds somewhere suitable to buy on the island.

She tells him she likes the fact that the job was educational. She is loving learning about Skiathos, its history, traditions and culture, as well as its place and influence in today's Greece. The flower and plant life are remarkable, she enthuses. 'I've never seen so many butterflies. Their colours are beautiful.'

She wonders whether she should tell him about Stuart and her miscarriage. Was she ready to share such personal details – the trauma it brought and her grief?

'Do you like to read?' she asks instead.

'I do, but not as often as I'd like.'

'What's your favourite book? It has to be one you've read more than once?' Carissa asked.

'I don't think I've read a book more than once. What about you?'

'Oh! Lots of books. There are plenty of authors I like, and it's always an event when their latest book is published. I have to buy it and read it in a day or two.'

'I could never read a book that quickly; I take ages to read one. Who's your favourite author?'

'There are so many, but Anita Shreve is my all-time favourite. I don't even need to know what the title of her new book is; I'll just buy it. I just love the way she writes about human emotion and connection. The detail and intricacy of her characters make them jump off the page as if they are in the room with you as you read. She's a beautiful storyteller. It was my gran who introduced me to her work. Have you heard of her?'

'No. Sorry. I'm more into thrillers.'

'Her novels have deeply driven characters that focus on their interior world. They're introspective and immersing. What I like about her books is that she often places them in the same setting, the New England coast in America. They're rich in vivid sensory details that create a sense of place. I like that about them.'

'I can tell. So, what's your favourite book?'

'Fortune's Rocks.'

'Anita Shreve?'

'Of course.'

'How many times have you read it?'

'Let me see… four, no, five times. It has almost been an extension of my arm,' she laughs.

'You have a wonderful laugh.'

'I've never been told that before.' She feels herself blushing. It has been a long time since she enjoyed such attention.

'Tell me what the book is about. What you like about it.'

'Initially, I felt obliged to read it because my gran had given it to me and recommended it. It was the first time I had read a book by Anita Shreve. It surprised me. Shreve's writing was gorgeous, even though the premise was quite shocking; it was brave of Shreve to write.'

'You've got me interested now.'

The waiter brings their main meals, chicken souvlaki and meatballs in tomato sauce.

'This looks good,' Carissa says and tries a piece of chicken. 'Delicious.'

Dimitrios smiles. 'Tell me about the book.'

She wipes the side of her mouth with a napkin. 'It's set in eighteen ninety-nine.'

He raises an eyebrow. 'Historical fiction.'

'Aha. The main character, Olympia, is just fifteen when the story starts. She's intellectual, curious, and on the cusp of womanhood when she arrives at her family's summer home. She's from a wealthy, proper Boston family, and she ends up falling into this wildly inappropriate relationship with a much older man, a married doctor. He's forty-one, and a close friend of her parents. Despite the age difference, Olympia and Haskell — that's the doctor — can't help themselves and begin a passionate and illicit affair. The romance is intense and laden with consequences. Their affair is soon discovered, leading to scandal and disgrace.'

'That sounds… complicated and slightly uncomfortable. You said she was only fifteen years old?'

'I know. It's uncomfortable to read, but Shreve doesn't romanticise it. It shows how much the relationship scars Olympia. She's pregnant and there's a huge scandal, and she's essentially exiled from her family, her social circle and is sent to a convent to give birth in secrecy. Her baby is immediately taken from her and placed for adoption without her consent.

'Olympia is devastated, and this loss becomes the defining moment of her young life. Her family basically erased the whole thing as if it had never happened. You feel her isolation, her grief. Throughout the story, Olympia remains haunted by the child she lost.'

'That's heavy.'

Carissa pierces a piece of chicken with her fork. 'It *is*. But it's also beautiful because of what happens as the story develops. What I love about it is that it shows Olympia's resilience and growth. She finds her voice and independence in a time when women had very few choices. Despite incredible hardship, she refuses to be defeated. Slowly, she rebuilds herself, refusing to be ruined by shame, and channelling her grief into tenacity. Olympia goes on to advocate for women who shared her experience. She becomes involved in social reform, fights for the rights of unwed mothers and opens a shelter and maternity home for them in Fortune's Rocks. Her work is groundbreaking and progressive, giving dignity back to these young women.

'Years later, she begins the search for her son, and it's painful. The reunion is climactic and emotionally charged, pushing the boundaries of identity, love, and redemption. She meets Haskell again, but she's not the young woman he knew, and their reunion is revisited with the intricacies and consequences that time and maturity bring.'

'Not just a love story gone wrong?'

'It's much more than that, much more. It explores forbidden love and all its consequences, female autonomy, motherhood and loss, social reform and justice, class and gender roles in the 1900s America. But the centre of the novel is really about coming-of-age and identity and having the strength and capability of reinventing yourself.'

'You really connected with her?'

'It's one of those books that bury themselves inside you. You feel it resonate long after you've read it.'

'I might have to read it after that. Have you ever thought of reviewing books? You really brought it to life?'

'No. I wouldn't be able to comment like that about any

other book. It's my favourite book of all time. I've read it countless times; if I didn't have an idea what it was about by now, I'd be worried,' she concludes, with a gentle laugh.

Dimitrios fills their glasses with more wine. 'It was just a thought.'

She lifts her glass to her lips and smiles. 'And a nice one at that.'

After their meal, they wander through the narrow lanes, which get busier when they approach a taverna or restaurant, where waiters politely suggest menus, 'Take a table, my mother makes all the meals. The best on Skiathos.' Dimitrios pats his stomach suggesting they've already eaten, and are always met with, 'Come back tomorrow.' At times, Dimitrios will chat to someone he knows and introduces Carissa as a friend, and not a colleague, which she discerns with thoughtful interest.

What surprises her most is the simplicity of it. He doesn't ask or try to pry from her what she is not ready to give. How his gaze never lingers too long. He is content to let her unfold like a flower, when she is ready.

'I need to think about getting back. I've got an early start tomorrow,' Carissa says.

'Yoga on the beach at sunrise.' He smiles. 'It's a hard life.'

'And then two trails after that,' Carissa reminds him, with a chuckle.

He walks her to her apartment, and they stop with the view of the bay receding from them, as the hood of night covers the sky in pinprick stars.

'You didn't have to walk back with me.'

'I know.'

'Well, I'm here now.' She hesitates. 'I'll see you tomorrow.'

'You will. Good night then.'

'Goodnight, Dimitrios, and thank you; it's been lovely.'

God! He wants to kiss her, but he worries about her response.

She is about to turn from him and walk up the stairs when he resolves on a compromise. Dimitrios brushes her arm and kisses her on the cheek, tantalisingly close to her. He can see the blue flecks in her eyes and reluctantly draws back. He wants so much to feel the touch and brush of her lips; it takes an effort to resist. Then he sees it caught in her smile, a fleeting expression of wanting more, and a warmth explodes in his chest. Before he knows it, she is halfway up the stairs and reaching the door. She hovers before turning to him, raising her hand in a final goodnight. She steps up to the door, turns the key in the lock, pushes the door and then she is gone, the silence swallowing him.

That evening, Dimitrios is sitting outside a bar by the old port, indifferent to the world around him.

He wasn't looking for this. This wasn't supposed to happen. Yet, it has.

He asks himself: Is this real? Or am I looking for distraction? Could this be another mistake? It has only been three months since the divorce. Is that long enough? I should know if I'm ready, but how can I really know something like that?

I can't shake off the thought; am I allowed to feel this way when it may be too soon given my past?

What if I'm just saying the right things, what she wants to hear, and then I disappoint her?

Can I open myself like the pages of a book and let Carissa read my story, while the words still feel raw on the page?

I'm just learning to pick up the pieces of the past, but what if the pieces are too complicated to fit together again, or worst still, I'm not rebuilding my life at all, just standing in the ruins and trying blindly to find the fallen pieces?

It's a feeling he knows all too well.

Yet, she stirs his curiosity. She intrigues him. She brings a quietness to his mind, a reprieve to the hurt, to the failings of his marriage, a peace he hasn't known in months.

It shows itself in the small things about her. He feels a rousing of joy when their eyes meet. He feels a rush of protectiveness when she shares intimate details. He feels a sense of awe, even after the carnage of his divorce, that he has found a way towards someone, towards something new.

It terrifies him, but it also feels beautiful that Carissa has shown him he can feel deeply again, of risking again, and of starting something that feels wonderful. Yet it stirs a deeper reaction – a longing to want more.

The idea of joy, laughter, and intimacy whispers the promise of a future he could never have imagined just months ago. And it scares him more than anything, because he is letting it grow; he is letting himself *want* again.

A warmth he hasn't felt for an age glows inside his chest; he can't recall the last time he felt this way.

It has caught him off guard, this opening of the heart.

CHAPTER THIRTEEN

ARRIVING

Mainland Greece 1942

It occurred to Thomas that he had two options: return to where he had landed and wait until dawn or continue to search for the others in the dark. Then, the decision was taken out of his hands. Coming from further down the valley, he heard sheep bleating and the unmistakable sound of a man's voice.

He scrambled up the embankment he had fallen down and yanked as much of the parachute as he could from the pine branches, cutting it free in the sections he could reach with his knife. He wrapped his pack in the remains of the parachute canvas and hid it under a bush.

Thomas started his descent, placing each foot with caution in front of the other, the gradient at such an angle that it increased his momentum, and he skidded and fell several times. He stopped at intervals, straining to hear the sheep. With each passing minute, to his satisfaction, they sounded closer. After around twenty minutes, he came to what was the bottom of the valley and calculated he must have slid and tumbled down at least a thousand feet.

Thomas heard a man's voice, then another. To his relief, both were speaking Greek and not Italian or German. He imagined they were likely shepherds and perhaps had seen the aircraft and parachutes. He peered through the thicket of trees in front of him and caught sight of two men sitting next to a small fire. The men had fallen silent, their voices replaced by the soft crackle of their fire. He used the trunk of a pine tree for cover and undid the clip of his revolver holster. He called out in Greek. 'Hello! I'm English,' which was met with a disturbing silence, echoing his anxiety.

From his position, he could tell they weren't wearing uniforms, and neither had a rifle or a small arm. Assured that his earlier suspicions – that they were neither German nor Italian – were correct, Thomas broke his cover and, with a hand on his revolver, walked cautiously towards the clearing where the two men now stood.

'I'm English,' Thomas repeated.

The two men fidgeted. Thomas removed his hand from the revolver, now convinced they were both shepherds. 'I'm a British soldier. I'm trying to find the others in my group.' He pointed towards the top of the valley. 'I landed up there. The wind blew me off course.'

'You speak Greek,' one shepherd said, astounded.

'I do.'

'We heard your planes.'

'Did you see where the others landed?' Thomas asked hopefully.

'No. I didn't see any parachutes.'

'I need to find them.'

'It would be better if you waited until morning. It will

get light in about three hours. You're welcome to sit with us and warm yourself by the fire.'

Thomas nodded. 'Thank you.'

The heat from the flames fanned over Thomas's face as he sat with the shepherds. He struggled to keep his eyes from closing and in his exhaustion said, 'In the morning, I'll return to where I landed. It would be better to start from there. I need to locate my pack and supplies.'

'There's a path you can take. It's much better than the way you came down. We'll come with you. It's easy to lose your way.'

'I'd appreciated that, thank you. My name is Thomas.'

The shepherd smiled. 'I'm Ioannis and this is Giorgos.'

'Thomas, it's time to go.' Thomas awoke to Ioannis shaking him by the shoulder and offering him a small portion of olives. Thomas savoured his meagre breakfast, and as the first rays of light embellished the sky in soft tones of violet and plum, Ioannis and Giorgos led the way along a narrow dirt path.

The ascent was less perilous than his hazardous descent the night before, but all the same, his thighs and calves burned as the path was steep, and at times, they had to navigate over rocks and thick shrubs.

After half an hour of hard climbing, they arrived at the area Thomas had recognised from the night before. In a large pine tree, shreds of canvas from his parachute remained caught and tangled in its branches.

Thomas located his pack, and just then, to his wonderment, Eddie Myers appeared.

'Am I glad to see you,' Eddie smiled. 'I've been wandering about all night.'

'Where did you land?'

'About a quarter of a mile away. Have you seen any traces of the others?'

'No, not yet. It's just me and these two. They're shepherds – friendly, and familiar with the area. They've already been helpful, and I'm certain they'll help us find the others. I take it you have seen none of the canisters with our stores.'

'Unfortunately, no. I'm pretty sure Wilmot, the wireless operator, landed not too far from me. He jumped just after me, and I saw a sight of him most of the way down. I've had no sight of Denys. If these chaps are agreeable, why don't you take one and I'll go with the other and see if we can locate Wilmot and Denys. We can meet back here in two hours' time.'

During their search, Thomas and Ioannis encountered an individual from a village within the valley; this individual had viewed the aircraft during the prior evening and sought to discover what it discharged. It transpired he was from a village called Karoutes, about a mile from their present location and some ten miles south of the point where they should have dropped. Thomas breathed a sigh of relief; he discovered the village contained no Italians or Germans, and the closest garrison town, which housed a battalion, was an hour's walk away.

The villager returned with them to the meeting point, where Thomas was delighted to find Wilmot and Denys with Eddie, along with their kit, the wireless set and batteries.

The villager stated he would seek aid in Karoutes from a former army officer.

Eddie deduced that, considering the wind direction when they had dropped, the lighter parachutes carrying the stores would have blown further up the mountainside.

'It's going to take a few days to recover them all. It's too late in the day for that. We'll wait and learn what this army officer can give us concerning help. In the meantime, we'll rest up here.'

Later in the day, the villager arrived with some food: goat's cheese, brown bread, and two bottles of local wine and the army officer.

The officer's name was Katsimbas. He was unexpectedly young, polite and eager to help in any way he could.

'It's not a good idea for you and your men to return with me to the village. With the Italian garrison so near, I'd be placing the entire village in danger. It's a risk I can't take. There's a place near the village, it's safe and out of the way and easier to bring you food. I could show you where it is?'

Thomas translated for Eddie. Eddie agreed to this and within the hour, Katsimbas had escorted the group half a mile down the valley to an area that was well hidden.

He returned later that night with bread, cheese, and black olives and, to everyone's gratitude, more wine.

'I've got some good news for you. An *andarte* called Karalivanos, and his band of men, have arrived on the other side of the valley. He wants to meet you. I'll take you to meet with him in the morning, if you're agreeable?'

Once Thomas had translated, Eddie raised his eyebrows. 'Good. This Karalivanos was a name we were given. It was hoped we would meet in the Giona area.'

'We know this man,' Thomas informed Katsimbas.

'That is good then.'

'It is. Our intelligence estimates he has over a hundred men.'

Katsimbas shrugged. 'I wouldn't know about that. We'll have to leave early. We should start on our way in the half-light of dawn. I'll return then.'

That night, after finishing their meal, they slept in their parachutes, together again since they had left the safe skies of Egypt and parachuted into the unknown.

Katsimbas returned the following morning with three villagers. With their personal equipment, wireless set and batteries packed, they carried it all into the valley, across a road and traversed up a steep rocky path on the opposite side.

After half an hour, they came to a clearing in the trees where there stood a small, thickset man in a grubby black Evzone uniform. Around his waist and slung over his two shoulders, he wore three bandoliers packed with ammunition. Several knives with exquisitely engraved handles jutted from his waist. He raised his rifle in a welcoming gesture and smiled a toothless grin as he shook each British soldier by the hand. They followed him along a track and, turning a corner, met four similarly dressed men.

Thomas eyed the group of *andartes* and wondered, given their appearance, if they were efficient in military matters. They looked a ramshackle bunch. One wore tattered army trousers – possibly Greek, Thomas thought – a threadbare winter overcoat with holes at the elbows and laceless boots epitomised the collective appearance. One of the *andartes* with a red fez on his head and a tommy gun in hand stepped forward.

'I am Karalivanos, the *Capitanos* of this fine band of men.'

Thomas explained they had arrived the previous night by aeroplane and wanted to get in touch with the *andarte* bands of the area.

'We're happy to help the British.'

'That's good to hear. Tell me,' Thomas glanced around. 'Where are the rest of your men?'

'You're looking at them.'

'There're only five of you.'

'What is he saying?' Eddie asked.

Thomas turned to Eddie. 'This is all the men he has.'

'That's disappointing.' Eddie rubbed his chin. 'Tell him we need to retrieve our stores, which we believe are spread over a large area on the mountain slopes on the opposite side of the valley. We'd be grateful for his help, especially since our wireless was damaged by the drop from the aeroplane and its spare parts are lying somewhere in a canister on the mountain opposite.'

Karalivanos heartily agreed, adding he would enlist the help of villagers. Before he left, Karalivanos designated a small plateau as an ideal position to set up a temporary headquarters because of its unobstructed view of the valley and all approaches below, and its suitability for a bonfire. He then left to organise the search for the stores and returned that evening with nothing found, but assured Eddie that villagers were combing every inch of the mountainside.

The next morning, with newfound enthusiasm, he left with four of his men, leaving one behind. Throughout the rest of the day, only one mule, overloaded with two canisters filled with hand grenades and demolition equipment, trudged towards the plateau guided by a villager.

'We need to have a serious word with Karalivanos. At this rate, it's going to take weeks to get all our supplies back.' Eddie confided in Thomas.

That evening, Eddie and Thomas spoke with Karalivanos.

'It's a problem,' Karalivanos agreed. 'As soon as the villagers find a canister, they're hiding it to collect later for themselves. I've instructed my men to take a firmer approach in this matter.'

'We don't want to scare the villagers off; we need their help, but, there're not helping with matters,' Thomas told him. 'Isn't there a middle ground we can adopt?'

Karalivanos smiled. 'Sometimes, punishment is the only option available and the only course of action that will get the desired results, but in this case, there is another way.'

'And what would that be?' Thomas asked.

'Tomorrow morning, I will bring you the village president.'

The village president was a slightly built man in his late fifties, with thinning silver hair and a thick moustache that curled at each end towards the sky. He shifted on his feet, his fingers fidgeting at his side. He blinked repeatedly. Beside him stood two Greek policemen, their eyes darting from side to side as they took in the ammunition belts wrapped around Karalivanos's men.

With Thomas translating, Eddie clarified that it was of the utmost importance that their stores were recovered and returned to them as soon as possible. Their purpose in being in Greece depended upon it. He gave the frightened men in front of him a hard stare.

The village president rubbed his temple. 'I will do all I can. I promise you.'

Karalivanos grabbed a policeman by the arm. 'You're a disgrace to your family, to your village, and to Greece. You're puppets of the Italians, whose blood money you accept.' With a flash of steel, he had a knife to the police-man's throat, whose eyes bulged in terror. With swift slashes, he cut every button off the policeman's tunic.

He turned to Eddie with a wide grin. 'I'll keep these two pieces of shit as hostages until all the canisters are returned.' Then, staring into the policeman's terrified eyes, he warned. 'If the stores do not arrive within the next twenty-four hours, the next thing I'll cut will be your throat.' Karalivanos waved his knife menacingly at the other policeman. 'And yours too.'

The village president's panicked eyes pleaded with Eddie. 'I need to speak with you in private.'

Thomas beckoned him forward, and when they were out of earshot of the others, the village president stared at Eddie's boots as he spoke. 'I want to help, believe me I do, but I've been put in an impossible situation with you turning up like this. There's no doubt the Italian garrison will already know there have been supplies dropped from an aeroplane three nights ago. Unless I report back to them concerning this, it's inevitable they will send a patrol to the village to find out for themselves. If the Italians find any trace of your supplies, I will be arrested. I don't want you here. You are placing the villagers and me in danger.'

Thomas translated the village president's concerns.

Eddie stroked his chin while gazing at the village president. 'Tell him we can't leave until we've collected all our stores and hidden them in a safe place. At this moment in time, we need each other and the villagers to cooperate in helping us achieve this.'

The village president hesitated and nodded. 'I'll do all I can to get your stores collected. Give me forty-eight hours.'

Eddie smiled. It was a bold statement. 'If he can do this, tell him we'll move from his village, and he can report back to the Italians that they found just a few parachutes with stores, but no men were with them.'

The village president concentrated as Thomas relayed

Eddie's guarantee to him. He extended his hand and as Eddie shook it, the village president said convincingly, 'It will be done. I promise.'

Later that day, six mule loads of canisters housing ammunition, arms, explosives and clothing arrived on the plateau. Upon opening them, there was disappointment that there was no canister containing food.

'There's still more out there. I saw a canister being dropped that hasn't arrived yet,' Thomas said.

Eddie agreed. 'It could have been dropped from one of the other planes. I'm hopeful it's been collected by one of the other two groups, and if so, they can't be that far off. They must be in the area.'

As the deadline approached, only a few more canisters were returned. The village president was adamant that there was no more to be found.

'I'm running out of time. I have to go to the Italian garrison tomorrow and report something, anything that will stop them from coming to the village. You have to leave now.'

Eddie had estimated they already had the required amount of explosives to demolish at least one bridge. It wasn't ideal, but it meant they could continue with their mission.

They agreed to head in a north-westerly direction toward the original landing point, ten miles away. It was here they hoped to find Seferiades and the band of *andartes* of several hundred men.

They hid the equipment and stores they didn't need at that time and the following morning, just as the sun had tinged the sky with its light, they loaded three mules with the wireless set, batteries, and clothing. They set off with Karalivanos and his men.

The grey sky constantly poured with heavy rain that soaked them to the skin. They walked, heads bowed, along stony pathways that cleaved a passage over the mountains and through forests of thick pines and firs. In the evening, Karalivanos's men expertly constructed two wigwam-shaped shelters with a single small entrance from broken fir branches. Inside, the bracken-covered floor was dry, and for the first time that day they escaped the unremitting rain.

Yorgo, one of the *andartes*, disappeared into the trees, reappearing an hour later with a live sheep across his back, like it was the most natural thing to do.

'Dinner has arrived,' Karalivanos bellowed, and within minutes the creature's throat was cut, then skilfully skinned and a portion of its body roasted on an open fire.

Yorgo placed the kidney, heart and liver into the sheep's gut, wound it around a stick and cooked it over the fire. Thomas collected water from a stream and, with portions of bread, they settled down to eat their meal.

'I think I might have got the wireless to work, Sir,' Sergeant Wilmot announced with a mouthful of meat.

'Excellent news,' Eddie remarked. 'There's a piece of open ground quite near. We'll try it out there.'

With full bellies, they scrambled onto the open ground, and once the aerial was in position, they waited in great expectation as Wilmot tapped out his communications. Ten minutes passed, half an hour went by, and after an hour of fruitless endeavour, they called it a night and tried again first thing in the morning.

As the sun rose and bathed the trees in silver light, their communications, once again, stubbornly remained unan-swered. Dejected, they dismantled the wireless and aerial, and packed the mules before setting off northwest towards Mount Giona.

Disappointed, with his clothes still damp, Thomas consoled himself. At least the rain had stopped, and the sun now shone in the first cloudless sky since their arrival.

The improved weather didn't last. A few hours into their journey, oily, opaque clouds rolled in over the mountains and unleashed a thunderous rush of rain that saturated their already sodden jackets and clothes.

Up ahead, through the greying mist, a shepherd with his flock of sheep emerged like an apparition. Karalivanos conversed with him and, turning to face Eddie with an ear-splitting grin, informed him that on the other side of the next mountain was a party of British soldiers.

'Can we trust him?' Eddie asked Karalivanos.

'Under the threat of my knife cutting him from ear to ear, he's sworn on the Holy Bible he's telling the truth. He knows I will find him if he's lying.'

'Very well, then. At last, the tide is turning. This is wonderful news. What do you say, Thomas?'

'The mules are slowing us, but we can send someone to go ahead.'

Karalivanos agreed. 'We'll be spending the night not far from here. One of my men can go as well, and they can return and report back what they find.'

Denys, accompanied by one of Karalivanos's men, departed.

That night, while they were huddled around their camp-fire to keep warm, Denys brought back the uplifting news that he had found Chris Woodhouse's group of men on a plateau known as Prophet Elias.

'When we got there, Chris had already left to visit a contact in a nearby village. He plans to return tomorrow.

The good thing is, they've retrieved all their stores and placed them in a nearby cave.'

Eddie breathed a sigh of relief. 'We'll head out first thing in the morning and join them.'

Later, one of Karalivanos's men escorted a stranger into their encampment. He was in his mid-fifties, with a walrus moustache and slight in build. He wore a hat on his head, his clothes were worn, and one boot had hardly any sole left. He held an old musket in his hand and a rusting revolver in his belt.

'He was found passing nearby. I know his face. I've seen him around this area before,' Karalavanos said, gesturing for the newcomer to sit by the fire.

The man welcomed a cigarette and, fixing it between his teeth, he puffed on it, inhaling deeply. He warmed his hands by the fire and then took off his hat, his hair thin and grey.

Initially reserved, he became less tense as the evening progressed. He spoke broken English with an American accent. He was known as 'Barba Niko,' but his name was Nikolaos Beis.

Eddie gazed at Thomas for confirmation.

'It means, Uncle Niko.'

Barba Niko explained he had moved to America in his early forties but had returned just before the start of the war. He had visited the village of Koukouvista. When he mentioned this, both Eddie and Thomas looked at one another in surprise. This village was close to where they were meant to have been dropped.

Barba Niko continued. 'Italian soldiers arrived a few days ago and took all the males of the village who were over sixteen years of age. There was a lawyer among them, a man named Seferiades.'

Thomas raised a brow. 'That's not good.'

'Who is this lawyer?' Karalavanos asked.

Eddie hadn't divulged the reason they were in Greece, only telling Karalavanos their aim was to meet with other *andarte* bands within the Giona area and enlist them in sabotage operations.

'It explains why there were no signals. The Italians must have been warned. Seferiades was our contact.'

'I don't know why you British soldiers are here in Greece, but I will help you in any way I can if you will have me,' Barba Niko said. 'I know these mountains; my boots are worn out from walking their trails. I see the comings and goings. I know when to be seen and when not to be seen. I saw your fire; that's why I let your sentry see me.'

Thomas raised an eyebrow, unconvinced. Eddie viewed Barba Niko, perceiving something beyond the vagrant appearance. He thought for a moment.

'Very well. In the morning, you can accompany us to join the others.'

The next morning, they set off at dawn and, after a two-hour hike, they scaled over a rocky ridge to find a large plateau spread out below, that Thomas estimated to be around a thousand yards in diameter. He placed his field glasses to his eye and, scanning the area, caught sight of a tent constructed of parachutes. He grinned. 'We've found them.'

They scrambled down the stony trail and were soon heartily welcomed.

Thomas and Eddie were shown the cave being used to store the containers and supplies. The entrance was small, but once inside, it opened into a large space of around five feet in height and twenty feet square.

Good,' Eddie said confidently. 'There'll be enough room for the drop of extra stores tonight.'

The wireless operator, Sergeant Chittis, confirmed they too couldn't contact Cairo, so the two reunited wireless operators attempted to get at least one set to work, while the others set about collecting firewood to light as bonfire signals.

That night, snow and rain hammered down. Karalivanos's men took it in turns to make sure the fires burned as well as they could, while the others sheltered in a makeshift tent as droplets of rain, like a showerhead, trickled on heads and shoulders. The *andartes* told stories and bemoaned the wretched weather, ill-prepared with their boots that leaked in the rain and snow, their clothes offering meagre protection to the cold and wind. Given their predicament, Thomas admired their hardened mentality. Most seemed happy, and they laughed a lot among themselves. They kept up their spirits by telling each other how smart they would look in uniforms, fitted and watertight boots, with plenty of coffee to drink and English cigarettes to smoke when the plane eventually came.

As the hood of night covered the cloud-thick sky, a plane circled and droned overhead. They hastily restocked the fires, which glowed bright orange and red. Emerging from the clouds, spurts of flame burst from the exhausts of the Liberator's engines before becoming obscured and dissolving into the murky night sky.

'They haven't seen us. Damn this weather,' Eddie spat into the rain and wind.

Then, the clouds swirled and parted, and from an opening, the Liberator appeared. It had turned and was engaged in a second run when it released several parachutes to a wave of exhilaration among the group below. The parachutes drifted, vanishing over the plateau's distant edge, carried by the wind. On the aircraft's second run, the wind carried the remaining parachutes in a similar direction. Thomas flashed a signal with his torch, which was reciprocated with an acknowledgment from the aircraft, and it melted into the darkness, the drone of its engines receding as if swallowed by the constant whistle of wind.

The group's uplifted spirits were drained upon their return as they saw their collapsed makeshift tent, whipping and fluttering in the wind's fury. The decision was made to move into the cave. It was dry, sheltered and hidden. They lit some candles from their stores, and the soft glow created an intimate, church-like atmosphere, enhanced by the low vaulted ceiling and flickering shadows. Eddie took this as an omen.

At dawn, the sun's rays seeped through the narrow entrance of the cave and lit a silver path of light along the floor of the cave. They set out to retrieve their stores and, about a mile from the cave, found them dispersed over an expansive area on the side of a steep hillside.

The containers were too heavy to move, and the terrain unsuitable for the mules, so they set about emptying the canisters from the containers. The task was backbreaking work. They continued throughout the day, and by nightfall, only a small number of canisters had been moved to the plateau, where they could then be transported by mule to be stored in the cave.

'At this rate, it's going to take a week to move all the canisters,' Eddie complained before instructing Karalivanos to send some of his men into a nearby village to acquire more mules. That evening they returned, and the number of mules doubled. For the next few days, Karalivanos sent two of his men to the village to collect food. On one of these days they returned with the news that a party of Italian troops had arrived.

'It seems the Italians heard a plane dropped stores over the area close to the village. The villagers warned the Italians would send out scouting parties tomorrow. They want you to leave the area as they fear if you are discovered they will suffer reprisals,' Karalivanos warned Eddie.

Thomas translated.

Eddie's brows knitted. 'Tell him we need to collect all of our stores. They'll be needed. If we can't take them with us, then we need to make sure they're well hidden,' Eddie insisted.

Karalivanos frowned. 'You promised there would be food in the containers and so far, there's been none. My men are not happy with the situation. With the Italians now in the village, it's too dangerous to go there and get food. It's only a matter of days, maybe even hours, before the Italians discover the cave, your stores, and you. I suggest you travel with me to the mountains of Panassus, two days southeast from here. It will be safer there.'

'That doesn't suit our needs,' Eddie said forthrightly. 'We need to go in the opposite direction.'

'Then you go without me. There's no time to argue. The Italians will come anytime now.'

As Thomas translated, Eddie searched his face and listened, hoping for anything he could fix his hopes to. Events had moved fast and dictated a decision.

Barba Niko had been listening with interest. He approached them and, rubbing the stubble on his chin, said, 'I can help you in this matter.'

'Go on,' Eddie invited.

'I know of a cave near a village called Stromni. It's big enough for all your stores and will be a good place to stay.

I'm well known around there. I believe the villagers will help, and we shouldn't have any problems getting food. No problems.'

Eddie glanced at Chris. 'What do you think, Chris? Can we trust him?'

'I don't think we have a choice. He may have just given us a way to get out of this.'

Eddie turned his head. 'Thomas, what do you say?'

'I'm with Chris.'

'Good. That's it settled then.' Eddie turned his attention to Karalivanos. 'Thomas, tell him we've decided to go to the village of Stromni, where there's a cave that meets our needs. If he's intent on not coming with us, I'd like to thank him for his help so far and I wish him and his men well.'

Karalivanos held out his hand for Eddie to shake. Given the current circumstances, Eddie knew it was just a mere formality. Chris, a born skilled negotiator, persuaded Karalivanos to leave two of his men to help prepare for the journey ahead.

'We need to act fast,' Eddie said, emboldened by new purpose. 'We'll post sentries, and Barba Niko and Karalivanos's men can get as many mules from the nearby villages that we know don't have Italians in them. We can't risk all of us going together, there are too many of us; we'd be easily seen. It's better to split into two groups; that way, it evens the odds one of us will make it to Stromni.'

The next day, a villager arrived and warned that the Italians were planning to send out a party that day to sweep through the area where they were camped.

With this news, it became imperative for the first group to move out as soon as possible. Barba Niko acquired another six mules. A new sense of urgency grabbed them in its vice-like grip, and a flurry of activity ensued.

Later that day, Thomas and Barba Niko left with the first group with four laden mules. The second group, including Eddie and Chris and the two Karalivanos's men, stayed behind. They would follow the next day at dawn, guided by Barba Niko's detailed directions.

With nervous fingers trained on the triggers of rifles, the sentries remained vigilant with a new sense of purpose.

CHAPTER FOURTEEN

LOYALTY AND OTHER VIRTUES

Skiathos 2007

Thomas pours some tea, and Carissa cradles the cup in both hands as she sinks back into her chair. 'I've been giving this a lot of thought, but I still can't imagine what it must have been like. You were in a strange country. You must have felt like an alien visiting another world. It's incredible; you were virtually my age.'

There is a brief silence. Thomas pauses and looks at her. 'When we parachuted into Greece, into the mountains, it really felt we were stepping back in time. It was a simpler age, where devastation and poverty existed side by side. The modern world had no bearing on the inhabitants of the villages. There were very few roads, only mule tracks. On a summer's day we could travel twenty-five miles, but on a bad winter's day, we'd be lucky to achieve five.'

'Was it that remote everywhere?'

'No – this was the heart of Greece, but to those in Athens, it may as well have been another country. We travelled through many villages. The houses were built from stone; most had two floors, the ground floor housing animals: the family goats and mule. They were often built close together, between stone paths. They collected water from springs that ran off the hills. There was no sanitation. In winter, it could get bitterly cold, and the weather could be extreme too. You don't associate Greece with snow, but in the mountains, in winter, I'd never seen snow like it.'

'They must have felt forgotten.'

'They were. The villagers were poor, coarse, and uncomplicated. The women kept everything together. The men liked to think it was them, smoking cigarettes in the *kafenion*, debating politics. But the women did the actual work – they ran the homes, tended animals, and raised the children.'

Carissa smirks. 'Some things never change.'

Thomas hears the wryness in her voice. 'They were the backbone then, as they are now.'

'But what about schools? Weren't there teachers?'

'There were, but many schools had closed during the occupation. The teachers either joined the army during the Albanian conflict, then after that, if they survived, they joined the resistance – or they were executed, as warnings and reprisals. Literacy was low. Most kids didn't even know what lay beyond their village, let alone the rest of Greece.'

'And what did people do to survive?'

'For many, it was a struggle just to stay alive. Their standard of living was dreadful. Some turned to the Red Cross; others to the black market. The young men joined the *andartes*. The lucky ones fled Greece altogether. But for most, survival was a daily burden. When the winters were harsh and food was scarce, people died.'

Carissa tries to digest this. 'That sounds medieval. Like something from centuries ago – not the 1940s.'

'In some ways, it was. Villages were self-contained. They grew wheat and maize with wooden ploughs. Some families had a few goats, which gave them milk and cheese, and they could make thick blankets and clothes from the wool. Eggs, chicken, meat, wine, and ouzo were luxuries. It was a fragile balance. In winter, when the snows are heavy, and the country is at war, eventually things turn bad, people start to die.'

'Carissa's voice drops. 'That's… horrific.'

Thomas's jaw tightens. 'I saw it. The old, sick, and young died first, and then, as it got worse, everyone died.'

'I can't imagine that.'

'There were other kinds of suffering too. I've lost count of the times I saw thick plumes of smoke twist into the sky. I can still feel the dragging in my stomach, knowing that farmhouses and villages were being erased with a mechanical efficiency that had no room for sympathy or empathy. The *andartes* just moved further into the hills.'

'And the villagers?'

'They were left at the mercy of the Germans, of which there was a short supply. Those who didn't stay, left their homes and took with them what little possessions they could carry, moving further into the hills.'

It takes Carissa a moment to register this. 'It must have been dreadful, constantly living like that.'

'I witnessed it many times. The sounds that have always stayed with me were the constant tinkle of the bells of goats being herded and moved, and the wailing of babies and crying children.' He shakes his head at the memory.

She reaches across the table and touches his hand gently. 'I'm so sorry, Thomas.'

He nods, swallowing hard.

'You must have felt helpless.'

He takes a moment before he speaks. 'We would do what we could, which was usually very little and ineffective. We often blew holes in the roads that led to the villages. This only delayed the inevitable as the Germans repaired the holes and advanced at ease. The Germans shot anyone who ran. Animals too. In one village, they locked people in the church – then burned everything else.'

Carissa shakes her head sadly. 'God!'

'It was mostly SS troops. They moved with mechanical cruelty. Greece was burning. The Germans believed that destroying villages would crush the resistance. Starve them into submission. The Germans wanted to show that the *andartes* didn't offer protection or safety and that they were powerless to stop the Germans doing whatever they wanted. Starvation is an effective weapon, and by burning villages and crops and killing their animals, they hoped to crush the resistance.'

Carissa's eyes widen. 'But didn't the resistance bring this suffering on the villagers? I mean… weren't they putting them at risk?'

'What transpired was the opposite. Villagers moved their grain and animals into the hills, and when the Germans had moved through, they returned to their burnt-out homes. But they didn't blame the *andartes*, at least not aloud. Their hatred was reserved for the ones doing the killing.'

Carissa shifts uncomfortably in her seat. 'It's incredible to think after all they went through they could still think that way.'

Thomas stiffens his shoulders. 'It was the peasant, the

villager, the everyday Greek who bore the cost, and many paid for that loyalty with their lives.'

CHAPTER FIFTEEN

RECONNAISSANCE

Mainland Greece 1942

The terrain was difficult. The mountain tracks dissolved into shale and stone and treacherous rocks that were demanding and challenging. In places, the ground climbed and seemed to evaporate into the mist. The bitter cold stung his exposed skin, burning Thomas's face in icy blasts and blurring his sight as his hooded eyes watered, straining to gauge depth and distance. The concentration needed to avoid tripping on a cumbersome rock was exhausting, and as they climbed, each step fatigued every muscle in his body. Dark clouds hung over the crown of mountains, depositing a constant deluge of rain – heavy, then easing into a drizzle – coating everything in a soggy layer of damp.

They travelled at a laborious pace; the mules laboured under the weight of their load, the climb gruelling and strenuous. One mule halted and refused to budge. Barba Niko placed his hands on its rear end and with force, attempted to persuade the mule to continue walking. The mule shook its head and refused to move, bellowing out a mocking and whining noise. Thomas checked its hooves and ran his hands down its legs. 'There doesn't seem to be anything physically wrong with it. I think it's had enough for the time being.'

'What are we going to do?' Barba Nico asked.

'Eddie and Chris's group will pass this way in a few hours, so we'll tie it to a tree. First, we'll take what we need from its pack. Hopefully they'll see the mule when they pass this way.'

They continued, and through driving rain crossed the main range of Giona, where they descended for two hours, arriving at a hut on the periphery of a small village.

They tied up the mules and removed their stores, placing them in the hut. The hut was a welcome respite from the wind and rain. Thomas removed his boots and socks and inspected the damage. With a fingertip, he touched the bubbled skin of several blisters on the pads and heels of his feet and pressed the pockets of fluid. He knew bursting them risked the prospect of infection, and that was not an option. He didn't have the time or energy to rummage through their stores and locate their medical supplies for a plaster, so he put on another layer of socks, they would have the dual purpose of trying to keep the cold from his feet and protect the blisters.

The rain stopped, and they made a small fire. Barba Niko told Thomas that one villager owed him a favour and upon entering the village he soon returned, leading a goat and a mule tied to a rope.

Within minutes, the unfortunate goat's throat was cut, skilfully skinned by Barba Niko's hand, skewered and roasting above the fire.

The meat was tough and needed a lot of chewing. Thomas cared little for its taste. However, it being their first meal since leaving that morning, he gratefully filled his stomach.

After the meal, Thomas sauntered over to where he could get an unobstructed view of the village. An olive grove descended into a small depression where a stone wall crumbled in places and ran along its length. Most of the houses were two-storey, stone-built constructions. The bell tower of a church rose above the rooftops. Dwellings flanked both margins of the main road, which transformed into a muddy pathway because of the rain, forming the village's sole entrance and exit.

Thomas felt a sudden exhaustion overcome him. He could hear the chatter of conversation emit from the men sitting around the fire. He envied them. As he stood, he looked out over the sodden rooftops. His eyes felt heavy with fatigue. His breathing stuttered in his chest. He waited.

In quiet moments like these, the details surfaced with cruel clarity.

The stone path leading to the door. The jasmine vine growing up the wall that had just flowered.

He remembered the young woman had a dusting of flour on her cheek, the smell of yeast and olive oil drifting from the kitchen, her daughter's missing front tooth and the sound of its soft whistle when she spoke.

The guilt lived and prowled in these details: the sheet of paper on the kitchen table, sandals by the door, one strap mended with strong thread, the sound of the mother's bracelets jingling as she ushered the children inside and a cup on the windowsill, still half-full, that would shatter moments later.

Thomas opened his eyes; he inhaled deeply, keeping the nausea at bay.

The next morning, they awoke to a watery sun and a light covering of cloud. The men washed in a stream, had a breakfast of bread and olives accompanied by mountain water, and set off on the final stage towards Barba Niko's cave.

An hour's climb from Stromni, on a wooded mountain-side at the foot of a rocky escarpment, they reached the cave. It opened onto a small area of ground, where densely packed fir trees concealed it from the opposite side of the valley. It was a vast improvement on their previous cave and large enough to accommodate their stores and for the group to set up camp.

The next day, Eddie and Chris's group arrived with the abandoned mule in tow. Everyone felt aged and weary but uplifted by a surge of relief that they were together again.

That afternoon, Barba Niko, having entered the village to collect pots and pans and gain news of any Italian movements in the near vicinity, returned with a young Greek man who had been asking about the location of a party of British soldiers.

Eddie was cautious in his approach, fearful that the Greek could be a spy and working for the Italians. Barba Niko thought it a risk worth taking, given if the Greek was a spy, he would remain captive; if he was not, he may have valuable information to tell.

Eddie led the interrogation, with Thomas interpreting. It became apparent that the Greek knew names and details only someone with prior in-depth knowledge of the Harling operation would know. After that, the atmosphere changed from a wary vigilance to the concentrated application of open questions to gain information.

The Greek's name was Yiannis. He was a *runner* for the agent Prometheus in Athens.

'Prometheus received a signal from Cairo confirming that the three groups had been dropped. Given the radio silence that followed, SOE instructed Prometheus to make contact, and so he sent me to find out if you were safe or had been captured by the Italians. If I made contact, I was to ask how far the operation had advanced, in terms of a suitable target being identified and the progress in contacting the identified resistance leaders. He also wanted to know if you needed anything?'

'We need to know how we can get in touch with Zervas and the other *andartes* in the region.'

Yiannis nodded.

'Also, we need new boots and socks.'

'I can get these on the black market; a few gold sovereigns will see to it.'

'Good,' Eddie said. 'Get Prometheus to signal to Cairo that eight of us are safe and well. Worryingly, there's been no word from the other party. If they had been dropped, we don't know where they are. We've heard rumours of their whereabouts, but when we send local villagers to enquire about them, it's turned out to be just rumours. It's strange; I'm convinced that some stores we collected had come from the other aircraft that they were in. If this is the case, it seems they may have been captured while hiding, or, dare I say, they never made it at all. Tell Prometheus we have four hundred pounds of explosives and accessories. I've estimated this would be just enough for the demolition of one bridge. Also, we've got sixteen Stens, a lot of ammunition to go with them and fifty hand grenades.

'I will relay this information to Prometheus when I get back to Athens. It'll take me at least ten days to return.'

Barba Nikos hovered out of earshot of the interrogation. He paced backwards and forwards, sucking on a cigarette, glancing towards the three men deep in conversation.

Finally, upon seeing Eddie handing over gold sovereigns, Barba Niko concluded the conversation had ended and approached them.

'When I was in the village, I heard some villagers talk about Italian soldiers setting up camp on the opposite side of the valley, not two miles from where we are. I met the president of the village, whom I know well. He told me about another Italian force that was camped further down the valley.'

'How far?' Eddie asked.

'He reckons about three miles away. He's also heard from a shepherd who came down from Giona that Italians were marching towards Stromni from Karoutes.'

Eddie and Thomas exchanged glances. Thomas scratched his chin. 'We're being surrounded.'

'It appears so. Niko, how far are the bridges from here?'

'A day's walk.'

'Jesus! We're so close.' Eddie sighed. 'We don't have an option. We'll have to move further from the targets.'

'This is why I need to speak with you. I have a solution.'

'Then out with it, man, don't keep it to yourself.'

'There's a place only an hour's walk away. It's well concealed. Even if the Italians passed that way, they wouldn't find us. I can take you there. You can see for yourself.'

Eddie ran his hand through his hair. 'What do you think, Thomas?'

'I think Barba Niko has come to the rescue, again.'

Anticipating an imminent Italian advance, they awoke at dawn and, fearing discovery of their explosives and extra arms, buried them in the nearby forest.

Thomas's eyes felt heavy with fatigue, the night bringing its usual rotation of haunting images and film-like sequences that denied both his mind rest and his body sleep. At midday, in a drizzle of rain, Thomas, Eddie, and Barba Niko set off along the side of the valley, following a narrow track winding up through dense woodland. The forest was still, the dripping of rain whispering in the trees above them.

Half an hour into their journey, with Barba Niko leading, he raised a hand and pointed through the trees across the valley towards a mountain pathway opposite. A few hundred yards away, a column of Italians led laden mules moving in the opposite direction. Barba Niko placed a finger on his lips and gestured for them to continue. They proceeded in silence, trudging through the ceaseless forest as the track wound upward through the trees and into a subsidiary valley, which placed a considerable distance between them and the Italians.

Thomas's eyes strained at the constant flow of woodland. Branches closed in like arms reaching out, fingers sliding along their bodies, while they focused on placing one foot in front of the other, their hearing riveted to the faintest sound that might betray the presence of Italians.

Then, to his surprise, they descended into a dell only fifty yards in diameter. The feeling of being cut off from the world they had inhabited with its constant threats of discovery was immediate, as they wandered into a welcoming oasis of shelter and calm that silenced the wind around them.

They erected tents fashioned from the parachutes brought with other supplies, including pots and pans Barba Niko had acquired from sympathetic villagers.

The next day, Barba Niko returned to the cave, and the others arrived at their new camp with news that no one had reported any Italian movements.

They wasted no time in erecting the wireless station three hundred feet above them on a rocky outcrop and began attempts to contact Cairo.

While waiting for Prometheus's runner to return, it was decided to conduct a reconnaissance of the railway viaducts. With the intelligence and information available during the planning stages, Eddie was convinced they could succeed best at the Gorgopotamos viaduct. Getting on-site validation was essential.

Barba Niko knew of an ex-sergeant of the Greek army, Stefanos Pistolis, who lived in Stromni and upon contact, Stefanos agreed to act as a guide. They decided Thomas would lead a small reconnaissance party.

Thomas, Denys Hamson, and their guide, Stefanos, headed down to the village of Stromni, which they reached just as dusk fell.

Stefanos entered the village, while Thomas and Denys sheltered in a dilapidated barn. He returned with three mufti overcoats. They wore them to conceal their uniforms and hurried through the village to Stefanos's modest home.

Simplicity and functionality defined the space with thick stone walls to keep the warmth in and small windows to keep the heat circulating in the winter and the heat out during the hot summer months. The main room served a myriad of functions: kitchen, dining area, and a gathering space.

Handwoven rugs in geometric patterns covered packed earth and the rough stone floor.

Above Thomas, exposed wooden beams darkened by years of smoke crossed the low ceiling, hanging with drying herbs and garlic braids. Blackened cooking pots hung from iron hooks, where the stone around the fireplace bore the stains of the still-lingering smoke and the cooking of countless meals.

A heavy wooden table, worn smooth by generations of use and surrounded by simple mismatched chairs, dominated the room. This was where Stefanos directed them to sit. Behind them, a cabinet stood in a corner, beside shelving that supported clay pots, copper cooking vessels, and an assortment of glass bottles.

Oil lamps and candles cast long pools of shadows and warm light across the walls adorned with religious icons.

Thomas felt awkward and intrusive as a bean soup simmered in a pot. Stefanos's wife smiled hesitantly as Thomas met her eyes. He noted the strong features of her face as she ladled the soup into bowls, accompanied by a chunk of homemade bread, darker and denser than usual because of the scarcity of refined flour.

She placed a plate in the middle of the table, with a small portion of cheese, crumbly and pungent, made from the milk of the family's goat, and olives preserved from the previous year's harvest.

'Thank you. This is kind of you.'

Her eyes were awash with surprise that Thomas spoke Greek. It was a look he was becoming accustomed to.

She held his eyes this time. 'It is the least we can do.'

Thomas felt a quiet elation sitting as a guest in this

modest house enriched with a tapestry of aromas as the earthy bean scent of the soup mingled with the faint smokiness from the hearth fire. It generated a heartened atmosphere of contentment despite the daily hardships of occupation and war.

'Do you have children, Stefanos?' Denys asked, stirring his soup with a spoon.

'I have a boy and a girl. They should be fast asleep in bed, but they are at this very minute sitting at the top of the stairs and peering through the banister spokes. Off to bed, you two.'

Thomas glanced, observing two children vanish toward a bedroom above the stairs.

The memories sharpened over time, striking in fragments and cutting deeper with each recollection.

His guilt lived in the details.

The precise angle of the mother's grateful nod. The way her headscarf caught the morning light. He could see their faces. The girl's dark hair and large soft eyes. He remembered the flutter of her dress as she ran inside the house; the doll bouncing as it dangled from her clutch. He recalled the sound of her feet padding on the stone floor.

The girl's last words, 'You are a soldier; you will keep us safe,' accompanied the creak of the door as it closed for the last time.

The tearing sound sliced through the air. The ground shook, and debris rained down on his head, bursting in detonations of noise and colour.

'Are you okay, Thomas?' Denys asked nervously.

The words yanked him back. Thomas felt a hot stinging in his eyes and a tremor in his hand. His dry mouth swallowed the words as he attempted to answer. He coughed and looked down at the table, rubbing his head. He hesitated under their gaze and was aware Denys was watching for his response.

Mustering the words, he said, 'I'm fine. Just tired, that's all.'

At ten p.m., Stefanos smiled and kissed his wife's forehead. He reassured her he would return as soon as he could. Thomas and Denys thanked her for her hospitality and the delicious soup, and reluctantly left the warmth of the house.

They proceeded with haste towards the viaducts. On their way, they picked and ate ripe apples, rivulets of juice running down their forearms.

An hour before dawn, they reached high ground with the Papadia viaduct in sight. They settled in overgrown shrubbery that offered a suitable point to rest, and tried to get some sleep.

As the sun rose, and with the aid of his field glasses, Thomas had a perfect view of the viaduct and surrounding area. Surrounded by open and rolling hills, the sparse covering of trees and the guard posts that covered all approaches deflated his optimism. To launch a credible assault, they would need a considerable number of *andartes*, given the Italians' strong guard on the viaduct.

Thomas gave a last sweep of the terrain and viaduct.

'We'd need an army to deal with that number of Italians, especially as there's little cover to launch a surprise attack.'

Denys seemed reluctant but admitted it. 'Several hundred, at least.' He pushed his cap back off his forehead. 'That's just the first; two to go. It can't get any worse.'

'There was movement on the road above us during the night; several trucks passed. It'll get busier now. Time to move,' Thomas urged.

They headed northwest toward the Aspos viaduct. It took an hour of difficult walking through undergrowth and trackless terrain before they finally reached a suitable view-point several hundred feet above the viaduct. A river flooded under the structure, entering a narrow and precipi-tous gorge between cliff-like mountains on both sides.

They rested and ate a small meal of bread, goat's cheese, and olives that Stefanos had brought.

'I think we need to get lower,' Thomas said.

They descended a short distance down the gorge, the uneven ground making it difficult underfoot to maintain balance and coordination. Several times, one or the other fell onto their behinds and slid before breaking their descent. Further onward, they reached a lofty waterfall.

They rested for a while, and Thomas consulted the maps they had brought. He muttered to himself as he traced his fingertip along the geography. He muttered some more. The flat valley below the viaduct made an assault most unlikely and hindered the placing of explosives on the vulnerable areas of the viaduct.

'The land is flat and open all the way along here,' Stefanos pointed to the area of the map he was referring to.

Thomas pressed his field glasses to his eyes and scanned the area again, biting his bottom lip.

'What are you thinking?' Denys asked.

'The terrain looks a bastard,' Thomas said bleakly.

'My thoughts exactly.'

'It's not what we had in mind. Eddie wouldn't like it. It's not without a lot of risk, and we need to get men in position to fix the explosives to the viaduct. Our objective is to cut the railway line anywhere and anyhow. That's the bottom line. But I know Eddie, and he wouldn't take the risks we face here. I can't think of any plan that would render this a success, yet failure's not an option. Its effects would be far-reaching, not only to the morale of us all, but on our future dealings with the *andartes* and what we might have to ask of them.' He lowered his binoculars and gave Denys a meaningful look. 'Only one to go.'

When they reached the Gorgopotamos viaduct, Stefanos left to contact a friend at the railway junction of Leianokladi to gain information on the number of Italians guarding the viaduct.

Their view was restricted, and venturing further was sought with danger; therefore, they remained hidden during daylight hours.

'How are you holding up, Denys?' Thomas asked.

'Every inch of me aches. I think I've run a marathon.'

'We've probably walked one, that's for sure. Stefanos hasn't slept in the last twenty-four hours. And now he's off again. These Greeks' fortitude is outstanding. I wonder if we British would have the same resilience if Hitler breached the Channel?'

'I'd like to think so.'

Concealed by foliage, they could still view the bridge.

Thomas could observe several key areas of the viaduct but not the exact number of guardhouses or Italians guarding the bridge. He identified two pillboxes at the bridge ends. From where the river below flowed, he could see a barbed wire fence surrounding the base of the viaduct.

Just before dusk, Stefanos returned, his eyes wide, panic creasing his face.

Thomas gripped his arm to keep him still and quiet. 'Stefanos, calm down.'

'On my way back, I was stopped by Italian guards. I can't believe I was so careless.' He shrank in front of them, embarrassed. 'They asked me what I was doing? Where was I going, and what was my name? They fired their questions at me like bullets.' Stefanos scowled, then shook his head ruefully.

'Slow down, Stefanos. The main thing is they didn't detain you. They let you go,' Thomas reminded him.

'Were you followed?' Denys asked.

'I don't think so, though I can't be sure of it. We must move quickly now. They told me no one could come within a mile of the railway after dusk. Every local knows this.'

'That would be enough to raise their suspicions,' Denys warned.

'I told them my mother was sick. She was not expected to live beyond the next day. She lived in the village close to mine. I was visiting her, saying my last goodbyes, and returning home. I lost track of time. I didn't realise how late it was.'

'That must have done the trick. We need to move fast.'

Exhausted and hungry, they scrambled upwards along the hard ground of shale and then through thick under-growth and vegetation.

Eventually, panting and muscles sore, Thomas announced, 'This looks like a good place to rest. We need to light a fire before we freeze to death. It won't be seen from the railway.'

'Are you sure?' A sudden feeling of panic seized Stefanos.

'Without it, we won't see tomorrow's sunrise.'

'More like tomorrow's pissing rain.' Denys complained.

They ate the last of their food and settled down to sleep. Even with the fire burning, the cold seeped through their clothes, and they spent an uncomfortable night huddled around the fire, falling in and out of sleep.

They rose before dawn, sore and tired, and once again climbed upwards. Eventually, after keeping on the move for two hours, they found a path that led along the edge of the mountain. After travelling with relative ease on the path, a state of panic grabbed Stefanos.

'It's too dangerous to keep on this path. The Italians will use it. I'm sure of it.'

'It's a chance worth taking,' Denys said.

'No! It's not safe. We need to get off this path.'

Denys glared sideways at Thomas.

'He's hardly slept in two days, and unlike us, he hasn't rested. Cut him some slack, Denys. We'll follow his lead.'

They left the path and trudged through the forest that carpeted the mountainside. Before long, Stefanos stopped and surveyed the dense thicket of trees in front of him.

'Why have we stopped?' Denys asked.

'We're heading in the right direction, but I can't be sure if we need to veer to the left or carry on the way we're going.'

'We're lost. Fucking hell. I knew we should have kept to the track. You're supposed to be a guide and know where we're going.'

'That's enough, Denys. You're not helping matters,' Thomas scowled.

Stefanos scratched his head. 'It's this way. I'm sure of it; Stromni is not too far from here. We should reach it before it gets dark.'

'Good.' Thomas shot a glance at Denys. 'We'll take a short break and rest up.'

They sat on a crop of rocks, and Thomas shared out cigarettes. Denys removed a boot and pulled the sock so that he could inspect his foot. 'The skin on my heels is red raw and my toes are numb with this bloody cold.'

'Once we get to Stromni, we'll rest there for the night,' Thomas said. He removed a gold sovereign from his leather belt and offered it to Stefanos. 'For you. You've risked your life coming with us, and your knowledge of the countryside and your contacts have been invaluable. We wouldn't have got this far without you. I'm immensely grateful.'

Stefanos pushed Thomas's hand away from him. 'I don't need your money. I'm doing this because it's my duty as a Greek and a patriot.'

'I'm sorry if I've offended you, Stefanos. I wanted to give you this as a token of our appreciation of what you've done for us, that's all. Don't see this as being paid for your services; it's not that at all. Think of it as a gesture of our appreciation and respect for you.'

Stefanos shifted awkwardly. Thomas extended his arm again, and this time, the gesture altered Stefanos's reaction.

'Very well. I accept it with gratitude.'

They trudged on and reached the outskirts of Stromni as daylight faded. Not knowing if the Italians were there, as a precaution they settled in a barn Stefanos knew on the periphery of the village.

The following morning, as Thomas and Denys awoke, Stefanos returned from the village with breakfast. To their ravenous eyes, it looked a feast: ten eggs, a fresh loaf of bread, a slab of goat's cheese and a handful of olives.

They ate like a pack of ravaging dogs. Stefanos informed them that when in the village, he had learnt the Italians had packed up their camp and were no longer in the district.

'The day just keeps getting better,' Thomas smiled, wiping his mouth with the back of his hand.

Nourished and inspired by Stefanos's news, they climbed towards the cave with renewed determination.

Joyful cheers and warm handshakes welcomed them back.

Eddie and Chris were eager to hear the outcome of the reconnaissance. Once Thomas had briefed them, both agreed the Gorgopotamos viaduct was the easiest of the three to attempt a demolition.

'If we can enlist the help of the *andartes*, I think it's achievable,' Thomas said confidently.

Eddie nodded, his mind heavy in thought. 'There's only one thing that's still troubling me, and it needs to be clarified. We need confirmation of the details about the Italian garrison and its defence.'

'On our journey back, I thought about that too. Stefanos told me he had a cousin, a schoolmaster called Costa Pistolis, who lived in a town called Lamia. Unfortunately, it's occupied by the Italians. This cousin stays with Stefanos occasionally in Stromni. Apparently, his cousin Costa has a friend who stays only a few hundred yards from the viaduct. This friend will, without trouble to himself, be able to answer our questions regarding the details we need to know. As luck would have it, Costa is coming to stay with Stefanos tomorrow. Stefanos vouches for him. He said he is reliable and would be happy to assist us. Stefanos said he would swear on a Bible that Costa could be taken into our confidence.'

'Stefanos has certainly proven he can be trusted,' Chris agreed.

'Then, tell Stefanos that his cousin is vital to the

progression of our mission. We'll need the information within the week.'

Underfoot, the icy ground crackled. Thomas smoked a cigarette and watched the sun emerge above the milky horizon, as pastel and crimson rinsed the sky. His stomach churned. He stamped his feet and wriggled his fingers; the air chilled his face like icy breath shifting across it. He tried to gather his thoughts while rubbing the chill from his face.

Thomas inhaled the smoke of his cigarette as if it were his last breath. He sensed someone beside him and turned.

'You can't sleep either,' Chris said, his face now covered in a swathe of carrot stubble.

Thomas's hand stroked his own well-established beard. 'I've always been an early riser.'

How could he explain the ghosts that kept him awake?

He took another long drag. Did Chris notice his expression alter, just a notch? Thomas was aware of it. It always did. He couldn't control it.

'I've seen my fair share of sunrises too. When I was a child, my father always told me, early to bed, early to rise. Never waste a day by sleeping beyond six thirty in the morning. It was his mantra.'

'Was it good advice?'

'It trained me to appreciate structure and routine in my day. Not much call for that at the moment, I'm afraid.'

'It's a peculiar existence we find ourselves in, that's for sure.'

'It could be worse,' Chris said cheerfully.

'Are you always this optimistic in the morning?'

'I'd like to think it carries on through the day too.'

'It does. You're like a fine wine, Chris. Your optimism

continues gracefully; it leaves a lasting impression and a refined experience.'

'I've never been compared to wine before. I think it's a compliment.'

'It is. We're lucky to have you. You know this country and the people. You have an intimate knowledge of their psyche, of what it really means to be Greek. Not the Athenians, but the inhabitants of these mountains – they are a different race of Greeks altogether.'

'You've studied the classics. Your Greek is excellent too,' Chris reminded him.

Thomas ran his fingers through his hair; it felt grimy to the touch. He would wash in the stream that morning. 'Eddie trusts your advice implicitly, not just on matters of the Greeks, but on this type of warfare. It's not what he's used to. He values your advice, and even when you disagree with him, his loyalty never sways. Then there's your stamina. You're like a mountain goat the way you can outrun everyone over this treacherous landscape.'

'I've never been referred to as a goat before. Two firsts in a day and I've not even had breakfast,' Chris said, embarrassed and gratified simultaneously.

Thomas took a breath. 'It's all true.'

Chris glanced at him, his eyes reading Thomas's face. 'Look, Thomas, don't take this the wrong way, but I'm asking you this as a friend… is everything alright?'

'I'm fine. Why do you ask?'

'It's just that… sometimes, I've seen you retreat into yourself. I've noticed times when you take yourself away and sit alone with your thoughts. There's nothing wrong with that, Christ, we all need to do it. But sometimes, without knowing it, our veil can slip just for a moment. That's not a bad thing, Thomas. What I'm getting at is that it might help to share it, just for once, whatever it may be.'

In front of them, a bird rose into the sky. The flutter of its wings hit Thomas, and he blinked several times.

He cleared his throat. Trying to find the right words – essential, in just one sentence, to capture the totality of what had crippled him. Was he ready for this? Could he lay bare his vulnerabilities, such debilitation?

'Like I said, I'm fine. There's nothing to worry about. I'm still the soldier I've always been. That hasn't changed.'

Chris laid a gentle hand on Thomas's shoulder. 'I never doubted it.'

CHAPTER SIXTEEN

HER SANCTUARY EXPOSED

Skiathos 2007

The night air is warm as if it still carries the heat of the Aegean sun long melted into the horizon. The salt-tinged breeze rises from the old port, mingling with the fusion of oregano, garlic, and rosemary, where wafts of grilled fish, meat, and fresh bread drift from tavernas. Carissa makes her way along the flagstone lanes, worn smooth by generations of footsteps, that wind between the weathered blues and greens of wooden shutters framing small windows of whitewashed houses. Trailing vines spill from hidden courtyards, and voices float from open windows. Showy bougainvillea blossoms in flushes of purple and magenta, trained over stonewalls, wooden balconies and decorative gates in spectacular curtains of colour that wing toward her apartment. She steadies herself on a steep incline, uneven beneath her feet, as the resonant peel of the church bell marks the time from the pocket-sized square just ahead.

Her feet throb from the day's long walk, but it's the satisfying ache of achievement that comes from completing
another arduous walking trail to Evangelistria Monastery.
Dimitrios's mother had insisted she take home leftover
stifado once Dimitrios told her Carissa wanted to taste the
dish, and the container presses against her side like an
endorsement of acceptance.

For the first time in months, Carissa feels valued and
useful. It has taken time for her to feel confident in her new
job; she has settled into its routines and absorbed the new
learning it demands of her, bolstering her confidence and
sense of accomplishment in her role. She has even managed
conversations in broken Greek with the locals.

There is a definite shift. Day by day, the weight she
felt pressing on her is lifting. She has searched for how
best to describe it and realises she is learning to become
satisfied.

At the narrow steps leading to her apartment, she
fumbles in her bag and fishes out her keys. She can hear the
gentle lapping of waves in the bay below as Patch the cat,
who has adopted Carissa's doorstep as his evening haunt,
winds around her ankles, purring contentedly as Carissa
bends to scratch behind his ears.

'Kalispera, Patch,' she murmurs, as Patch slumps onto
his back and Carissa obliges by rubbing his stomach.

Her fingers finally close around her keys, and she
straightens, her thoughts already wandering towards the
pleasure of a hot shower, the stifado she is eager to taste,
and perhaps a few pages of the Greek phrase book she's
been studying.

She thought it odd at first. The folded piece of paper lay
centred on her doormat, a stone fastening it to the ground.
She thinks, puzzled, so far, no one she knows in the village

has left her a note as a means of communication. Those who know her would either phone or visit.

She bends to retrieve the note and opens its perfect, crisp fold. The keys slide from her fingers, clattering around her feet as the handwriting screams at her. Careful and neat lettering, precise spacing between the words, flawless compared to her own hurried scrawl. The way the 'a's are formed, the slight leftward slant, this swirling handwriting has composed shopping lists, birthday cards, anniversary notes, reminders fixed to the refrigerator. The images swamp her with their visceral clarity.

Carissa, I hope you're taking care of yourself. This isn't Edinburgh.
You think you know these people, but they're not your friends.
No one knows you like I do.
The work at 'Trails of Greece' looks demanding.
I like the look of the restaurants you've been eating in; they look nice; I need to try them.
I just want you to know you're in my thoughts. Always. S.

He has found her. But it was worse than that – he's been watching her. The reference to her work. Stuart knows where she works. He knew when to deliver the note. He knew she was not at home. Most shocking of all, he knows where she lives and he is here in Skiathos. A sickly feeling of worry grips her throat.

When did he arrive? How long has he been watching her? Days? Weeks? Has he been here all along, waiting, calculating the right moment to act?

Carissa's eyes dart along the narrow lane, sweeping doorways and balconies, the perfect hiding places. Is he staying at a hotel? Has he rented a room somewhere close by? Is he watching her right now?

Every sound amplifies around her: the distant music from a taverna, the nearby hum of a scooter, her own ragged breathing. Her haven, her refuge, her beautiful island, is now compromised. Violated.

Her keys shake in her hand. Fumbling with the lock, it feels an eternity before it clicks open. Once inside, she locks the door and leans against its surface, breathing hard.

She forces herself to unfold the note again. The tone attuned: concerned rather than threatening, loving rather than possessive. To anyone reading the note, it would seem like a worried partner checking in. But she knows Stuart. She knows what lies behind every chosen word.

No one knows you like I do. He is reminding her he knows her intimately – every weakness, every thread of insecurity, every worry and fear.

The work at 'Trails of Greece' looks demanding. Confirming he knows where she works, that he's been following her.

I like the look of the restaurants you've been eating in; they look nice; I need to try them. He wants her to know he has been watching her. Monitoring her every movement. He is close by.

I just want you to know you're in my thoughts. Always. S. Intimidation swathed in warm affection. The assurance that this will never end.

The signature – just an *S.* Intimacy wrapped in casual familiarity. As if their separation is temporary and easily fixed.

She is unsteady on her feet and slumps onto the sofa. A lucid panic rattles her. She needs to call the police. What will she tell them? That her ex-boyfriend has left her a polite note. She fears his handwriting.

Behind her panic and the dread, the embers of a fire are asserting themselves. Her stomach boils with a fledgling anger. She looks down at her hands. Her fists are curled into a ball.

She has grown into this small apartment; it has become a home. It has gathered all her belongings in its comforting embrace, and now she feels trapped behind its walls. He threatens to take it from her.

She checks again that she has locked the door, then she closes the curtains, and turns on the small lamp. She sits on the couch and stares at the note. Beneath the surface concern, beneath the modulated tone of loving worry, Stuart is telling her something very clear:

I have found you. I'm watching you. I know everything about you in your new life. And this will never end.

Sleep does not visit her. She lies in bed staring at the ceiling, turning onto her side, then shuffling onto her back again. Her thoughts tumbling over one another, her mind in constant flux. The air presses against her, hot and uncomfortable. She has kept the windows closed, but her ears still strain to pick up every creak of her apartment settling, every distant sound from the street below. Carissa gives up the pretence, unwinding herself from the sheet. She staggers from the bedroom and, scuffing her bare feet on the floor, goes into the kitchen. She makes tea, turns on the small lamp and sinks into the sofa, soft yellow light pooling around her.

Carissa can't settle. She walks over to the window. She can see the neighbouring houses, their shuttered windows dark and blank, the narrow lane empty and still.

Her thoughts sprint ahead of her. Why has he come? Why in God's name did he feel the need to contact her? His note has changed everything – the space that should have been her sanctuary now exposes her.

CHAPTER SEVENTEEN

MOMENT OF ARRIVAL

Mainland Greece 1942

Costa returned within the week with details that included the numbers and location of the Italians, their emplacements and specifics pertaining to the barbed-wire fence which encased the piers of the viaduct. The information concluded with what they had already known, giving Eddie the confidence to commit to an attack on the Gorgopotamos bridge.

'All we need now is the support of the *andartes.*'

Two days later, Prometheus's runner returned from Athens, not only with the new boots and socks he had promised but with news about Zervas.

'He's still in the Valtos area, northeast of Arta.'

'So, he is where we thought he was all this time. How far is that from where we are now?' Eddie asked.

'Four, maybe six days on foot, depending on the weather.'

'That doesn't give us much time to get a message to

him. He needs to reach us before the next full moon. If I sent you with one of my men, would you be able to reach Zervas?'

The runner nodded. 'It's possible.'

'I'll go.' Chris volunteered.

'I'd hoped you would. If anyone can get Zervas and his men to agree to help us, it's you.'

The next day, Chris and the runner departed. Eddie had to rely on the bare minimum of explosives that they already had in their possession. It was not ideal. Since they had now contacted Cairo from their wireless sets positioned on high ground, Eddie sent an urgent message requesting the drop of explosives and gave the coordinates of a suitable area close to their camp. Before they received confirmation, the wireless set died on them. The two operators concluded they needed spare parts to get it functional again. This was an impossible situation. With no way of knowing if the message had reached Cairo, for the next six nights they waited at the aligned dropping point. The aircraft did not come.

Undeterred, Eddie and his men continued with their preparations and the established routines of keeping their camp functional. They chopped wood for their fire. They set about warming the explosives by hand and pressing the separate sticks into prepared wooden moulds, made to fit the charges into the cross-sections of the steel pier legs of the Gorgopotamos viaduct. It was laborious work but satisfying, taking several days to get through the four hundred pounds of explosives.

They constructed a wooden model of the steel piers and, day and night while blindfolded, practised fixing the charges and fuse until they completed each attempt successfully. They acquired sawn strips of timber from a nearby woodcutter and tied the demolition charges to them so they could transport them on the backs of mules, disassemble them near the bridge, and fix them quickly. Then, they prepared the subsidiary charges for cutting the railway line. All knew, but no one expressed their thoughts, that if Chris did not secure the support of and return with the *andarte* bands, it would all be in vain.

The moon had already passed its first quarter, and now an anxious wait hung over the camp in anticipation of Chris's return.

The villagers of Stromni could not risk the Italians discovering British soldiers within their village. The villagers agreed to supply food if the soldiers stayed near their cave, which was an hour's walk away. Barba Niko collected the food, and on some days the villagers themselves would visit. They were generous beyond measure: brown bread and potatoes, apples, a variety of nuts, and olives. The soldiers got meat by compensating shepherds with gold sovereigns for a sheep taken from their flock.

Baba Niko proved to be an adequate cook, wasting nothing and adapting his knowledge to substituting mountain herbs for tea when the tea supplies ran out. The men used the nearby stream for drinking water and washing utensils. Further downstream, they bathed and once a week, an old woman from the village washed their clothes.

They set up parachutes among the trees in front of the cave's mouth to protect them from the wind and to conceal their fires at night as much as possible. Inside the cave, each man had a bed covered with brushwood and bracken. They enjoyed the warmth of the additional blankets supplied by the villagers, and wore their parachute overalls at night for extra warmth.

At the end of each day, they gathered around the log

fire at the mouth of the cave and watched with keen eyes, Barba Niko prepare and cook that night's meal. Once they'd devoured their food, they sat around the burning embers and listened to Barba Niko recite embellished and fanciful stories. At times, Barba Niko would proclaim, 'Tonight, we will hold the examinations,' and test the others in what Greek they had learned.

Late one night, while still waiting for Chris's return, the village priest of Stromni arrived at the cave, insisting on speaking with Eddie, as he had an important and confidential message to pass on to him. The priest spoke excellent English, allowing Eddie to converse with him without the need to painstakingly translate every word. The priest had piercing brown eyes, a thick long beard which obscured his upper lip and fell onto his chest. Eddie estimated his age, possibly mid-thirties to early forties.

Eddie offered him tea, but he refused. Instead, he lit a small pipe and puffed on it satisfyingly.

'I have some important news.'

'Go on.'

'One of your officers who was travelling westwards has met with several British soldiers. They are making their way to you. They are expected to be with you tomorrow and are travelling with a band of *andartes* belonging to Aris Veloukhiotis.'

'What was the name of the officer who sent them to us?'

'His name is Chris.'

Thomas smiled.

'You don't believe me?' The priest looked puzzled.

'I believe you. I just had to make sure. Your news brings me happiness and relief. Thank you.'

The following afternoon, just as the priest said, John Cook and the rest of the party arrived at the cave with nothing but the clothes they wore, accompanied by a band of twenty-five *andartes*.

After being warmly greeted, John informed them, 'That second night when we flew from Cairo, we failed to see any fires. The pilot was adamant that he couldn't let us drop because of the poor cloud cover. He agreed to drop our containers of stores near Mount Giona and then, regrettably, we flew back to Cairo. I'd never been so disappointed.'

'You must have been over the area when our aircraft was looking for signals further west, then left before we arrived back from Giona before our drop. It makes sense now,' Eddie said.

'What does?' John asked.

'That you dropped your stores exactly where we landed. We found them, but obviously not you. It spurred several theories of what might have become of you.'

'It was a nightmare. We had a further two attempts at being dropped, but each time we had to head back because of the weather. Then, when I was thinking we'd never get here, we were finally dropped two weeks ago in the Karpenisi valley. It was a surprise to me why there, but there we were, floating down towards the outskirts of an Italian garrison town being welcomed by considerable mortar and small arms' fire. It was a miracle we all survived unscathed. We hid in the bushes, evading an Italian search. I thought it best that, to avoid capture, we split up and scampered out of there.

'I was pretty sure the Italians had found all our containers, including, to my horror, new plans of the railway viaducts, which, God knows why, were packed in one container. I consoled myself by hoping an idiot Italian had found them without realising their importance.

'For the next few days, we individually sought refuge in villages or isolated cottages with friendly families. Finally, we got in touch with one another and, as luck would have it, we came across a band of *andartes*. They took us to their commanding officer, Aris. Once he was reassured that we were British, we were looked after rather well.

'I informed Aris that he should contact you immediately. It was only later that I learned he feigned ignorance of your whereabouts, knowing you were only two or three days' ride away to the east. You see, he wanted to take us on what I could only describe as a publicity tour towards Agrinion, which I learnt was in the opposite direction.'

Eddie frowned. 'That explains why he's ignored all my requests to meet with him.'

'You know of Aris?'

Eddie nodded. 'I'd heard he was an *andarte* leader and in the area. He went under the name of Aris Veloukhiotis. Subsequently, we discovered his real name was Athanasios Klaras, a Communist who fought in the Spanish Civil War. His name was on every villager's lips. I tried to contact him frequently but failed each time, my messages unanswered. It looks like now, after what you've just told me, he was doing his best to avoid us.'

'How did Chris know where you were?' Thomas asked.

'Only by pure luck. Chris had passed close to us on his journey to find Zervas and was told by a priest that a group of British soldiers were nearby. Chris sent a message that gave me your location. Learning of this, Aris sheepishly sent us off to meet with you, escorted by twenty-five of his *andartes*.'

Eddie smiled. 'We're ready. We've decided on the Gorgopotamos viaduct. All we need now is at least fifty *andartes* to conduct the assault. That should be enough to give the Italians a fight. Tom Barnes will lead the main demolition party. We estimate it'll take up to four hours to complete a successful demolition. We need to take out the Italian defences on both ends of the viaduct before we blow it up, and cut the railway line on both ends a good distance away to prevent reinforcements from reaching us from the Italian garrison. They have an armoured troop train that will carry troops from their garrison towards the bridge once the fighting begins. We need to neutralise it. Now that you're here, John, you'll lead the party that will carry this out, along with Themie and Nat and at least fifteen *andartes*.'

John nodded. 'At last, we've got something to get our teeth into.'

The *andartes'* leader, who escorted John, was not much older than twenty. He was a surprising figure with dishevelled hair, called Giannis, who went under the pseudonym of Nikiphoros. He carried a German automatic rifle. His band displayed an assortment of rifles – Greek, German, Italian, and also two Italian Breda light automatics. They dressed poorly, and some wore goatskin shoes instead of boots. There was not a distinguishable uniform amongst them; however, a few wore a cap, on the front of which was embroidered four Greek letters: ELAS.

Giannis's eyes lit up when he saw the rifles and pistols in the camp.

'Rifles and tommy guns are needed, but what we need most is ammunition; without bullets, such things are of no use. You can't drive trucks without fuel.'

He told Thomas that most of their operations involved ambushes and rear actions. He spoke with an air of confidence, believing that with enough arms and ammunition, they could defeat the Germans.

Thomas's mind conjured several words when speaking with Giannis. He had an air of modesty and sincerity about him. As they spoke more, Thomas detected noble attributes that he admired. Giannis spoke with a sense of pride and a trace of valour, but also with an undeniable obstinacy about him.

'What made you become an *andarte*?'

'It wasn't a career choice,' Giannis smiled sarcastically. 'When your country is invaded, what other choice do you have? First the Italians, the Bulgarians, and the Germans, the Security Battalions, and the black marketeers. They have all brought suffering and death to Greece and its people. The Germans burn villages, kill men, women, and children, and our animals. They destroy and rape. Then there is the homegrown enemy – those that collaborate with the enemy for money and profit. They all have blood on their hands.'

'Who would you have rule the country?'

'The worker. The common people, of course. It will be our time. In the mountains, we are in free Greece. After this war, all of Greece will be free of the old politicians,' he said with a conviction that burned in his eyes. 'The people will demand it. A popular democratic government, run by the people and for the people.'

'But what does that actually mean in practice? What is a popular democracy? Don't you think that sounds rather vague?'

'Exactly what it says: the common man will rule the country.'

And that was that. Giannis didn't possess an in-depth comprehension or a well-developed understanding of the policies that were sought by those who wished to rule after the war finished. What Thomas saw clearly was that Giannis possessed a vigour and burning idealism that expressed his patriotic duty to become an *andarte* and rid his country of those that had invaded it.

When Thomas asked what the letters on Giannis's cap stood for, he stuck out his chest and replied, 'The National Popular Liberation Army.'

Thomas enquired further. What was this army? How strong was it? And who controlled it? Giannis could not give him concise and informed answers.

However, it was established that Aris led two to three hundred armed *andartes* of ELAS, who organised in bands of about twenty-five each, dispersed throughout the mountains of Roumeli. Giannis knew there were people in Athens who controlled ELAS. He knew other bands of the organisation were also in the Greek mountains. It became clear; he knew only that.

The village priest arrived from Stromni with a wide smile that even his substantial beard could not hide, with news that a runner had brought word that Chris would reach the cave the next day. Not only did this subside Eddie's worries, but the priest also added, a considerable force of over a hundred *andartes* accompanied him consisting of Zervas's and Aris's men.

The following night, when the camp slumbered in sleep, Chris eventually appeared, tired but jubilant.

'Thank God, you made it back,' Eddie said, rubbing the sleep from his eyes. He had missed Chris's air of containment and his reserved and calm demeanour. It had been a long fourteen days.

'Half a day behind me, Zervas is approaching with fifty of his men, and following him on the same route is Aris with more than that number,' Chris informed Eddie. 'By tomorrow night, both should have reached the village of Mavrolithari, two hours from here. I've come ahead of them with Zervas's adjutant, Captain Michalli, as I didn't want to be late.'

Eddie glanced at his watch. 'You've been away for fourteen days, travelled on foot across the mountains of Greece and back again. It's quarter past midnight. You're fifteen minutes late.'

'Not according to Greenwich time. I'm early. I've got three quarters of an hour in hand.'

Chris gave a slight grin, and with that, they both laughed and welcomed each other in a wholehearted handshake.

The next morning after much-needed sleep, Chris recounted his journey.

'It was arduous and slow at times. I'd no way of knowing if I was going to come across friendly *andartes* or enemy troops wherever I went. During the daylight hours, I had to go around villages. Once, when it was almost dark, I took the chance of entering a village only to find that the Italians were occupying it. I was forced frequently to make wide, unprepared detours, and in doing so, I'd estimate, I must have walked over two hundred miles since leaving and returning to Stromni.'

'Your achievement is amazing,' Eddie said.

Thomas nodded. 'I can't imagine what that must have been like, out there on your own without knowing who was friend or foe.'

'I was lucky. While over the Pindus Mountains, I met a priest in a village called Velota who told me Aris Veloukhiotis, another *andarte* commander, was nearby and had found four British parachutists. I believed this had to be the third group that had landed on the outskirts of Karpenisi. I wrote John a letter, telling him where to find us in Giona and asking him to join us, and I requested Aris meet me when I returned. The priest had it delivered to Aris. When I gave the priest the letter, he wrote on the envelope, ELAS, and it seemed an effective strategy as John and his men joined you forthwith.

'At the meeting place in Valtos, which Prometheus's runner gave us, I was met by Captain Michalli. Zervas was bang in the middle of what could only be described as a successful battle against several hundred Italian troops, the commander of which was negotiating terms of a with-drawal as I was about to meet Zervas. Zervas's reception was very welcoming and warmly enthusiastic. He kissed me on both cheeks and proclaimed, *Kalos irthes aggelos kalon idiseon*, which means, "Welcome, angel of good tidings." He then told me; *You're our saviour. Evangelos will be your name in the Greek mountains*. Once I'd clarified our presence in Greece and our mission, he agreed straightaway to help. The next day we set out eastwards with a hundred and fifty of his men.

'We rested overnight in a village called Viniani, where I was told Aris was in a neighbouring village. With my persuasion, both Zervas and Aris exchanged letters, and it was agreed that the two should meet to discuss their involve-ment in assisting the British officers who were now amongst them in the mountains. It was a friendly affair. There was a dance in the square. Both sets of *andartes*, Zervas's and Aris's men, mixed pleasantly together. Zervas convinced Aris to assist us, to the strength of a hundred men.'

Zervas arrived the next day and went straight to the

cave. Standing barely five and a half feet tall, his round stature emitted a vibrant presence and confidence that filled the cave when he entered. It instinctively drew Eddie to him, making him instantly at ease in his presence.

As introductions proceeded, Thomas noted how the exuberance in Zervas's deep-set hazel eyes contrasted with the stern set of his heavy black beard, streaked with distinguished silver, which covered his cheeks and chin like a wild thicket yet could not hide the expressiveness of his features. Zervas removed his khaki-coloured cap, exposing a generous crop of salt-and-pepper hair, and greeted Eddie and Thomas with a kiss on both cheeks, which they willingly returned. The underlying warmth that softened Zervas's features struck Thomas, and his deep, melodious laugh, which Thomas was soon to discover, often erupted from him.

Eddie informed Zervas of the task ahead, the details of the three viaducts and the proposed plan for the assault, the resources at hand, and the demolition. 'You'll have all of my men at your disposal, and I would be happy to act as your chief of staff.' Zervas smiled 'This is a good plan, well thought out, and it covers the aspects needed for a successful operation.'

'I'm glad it meets with your approval.'

'There's only one thing omitted.'

'What's that?'

'It would be pertinent for us to offer Aris joint command of the operation, given he is supplying most of the men needed for our success.'

'That's a fair point, Zervas, but it eludes me to see how the three of us can lead the same operation.'

Poised between a thoughtful pursing of his lips and the beginning of a smile, Zervas said, 'I will be the one in command, but we will agree on what needs to be agreed in advance.'

Eddie gave a knowing nod.

Over mountain herb tea and bread fried in olive oil, Zervas suggested that instead of living in a cave, Eddie and his men would be welcome to join him in Mavrolithari, where they could enjoy the luxury of warm beds.

The next day, they awoke to the spectacular sight of the mountain slopes, with their copious covering of fir trees, swathed in a dense coat of brilliant snow.

With a train of twenty mules, packed with equipment, stores, and arms, they left their cave with hearts full of sentiment but in high spirits at the promise of comfortable lodgings insulated by walls and a roof instead of rock.

A watery sun clung to the expanse of cobalt sky, doing little to warm the refrigerating air that stole each breath.

Thomas tried to keep his mind off the numbness that plagued his fingers and toes by counting the tops of endless fir trees, knowing that when night came, a warm bed awaited him.

Eddie went over his plan with Zervas and Aris. The full moon of the next few nights gave them the advantage.

Once satisfied with the plans, Aris and Zervas sent out a small reconnaissance party with the leaders of the attacking groups to gauge the lay of the land and to identify routes for the final approach to the viaduct.

At last, the purpose of their being in Greece was finally before them. Everything they had gone through so far had led to this moment of arrival and unknown consequences.

CHAPTER EIGHTEEN

THROUGH HIM COMES SOMETHING WONDERFUL

Skiathos 2007

'Jesus Christ,' Dimitrios says, troubled and trying to comprehend the awful reality of the situation. 'This Stuart. What's he doing here? He's trying to traumatise you. It's sick. He's sick.'

'He's being very calculating. There's nothing in his note that would give anyone concern if they read it. It would have the opposite effect, but I can read between the lines. This is Stuart. It's what he does.'

'What do you think he'll do next?'

'I don't know. Whatever it is, it'll be planned, thought out. He hasn't come all this way to be reckless.'

'Does he think that by doing this, you'll go back to him?'

'It's over. I told him.'

'He's not listening, then. He can't hide for long. Do you have a photograph of him?'

Carissa checks her phone. 'I've still got lots. I thought

about deleting them, but erasing that part of my life doesn't mean I'm free of him, as last night shows.'

Carissa had thought about not going into work, but she didn't want to change her daily routine. It would have felt like giving in, and she was determined not to give him the satisfaction that he was in control. She had considered asking Dimitrios to the apartment, but given that Stuart was watching her, she didn't want to involve Dimitrios in this charade, so eventually, she went to work that morning. And then she realised he would know about Dimitrios too.

Reading the note felt like a disembowelment, the life she was making for herself, her newfound aspirations ripped and tossed from her, scattered to the wind like rubbish.

'Here's one.'

She holds up her phone. Dimitrios bends his head and stares at Stuart, scrutinising his face, his eyes, the composition of the man looking back at him out of the screen.

'He knows where you live, where you work. Does he think he'll grind you into compliance? The man has a problem.'

Carissa's shoulders give a small shrug. 'I don't know. I don't know what to think.' She fiddles with a loose hem on her dress.

In her life with Stuart, he had always been protective of her. Always asking her, where was she going when out with friends, who was she going with, and when she would she be back. At first, she thought of this as Stuart's way of caring for her, and showing concern for her wellbeing. As time passed, this changed. He became more demanding, his questions increasingly stifling, and his language more assertive – until he was trying to control what she could and could not do, and who she could and could not see. The odd thing was, now that she can see it from a distance,

Carissa admitted Stuart had been right: she knew it to be truthful, her friends never liked him, for they could see him for what he really was.

Kate comes to mind, and she remembers how much she misses her, especially when facing such situations, knowing she could always count on her.

'Where are Evangelia and Athena?' Carissa asks.

'They're both out this morning.'

'I'd appreciate if you didn't tell them about this. Not just yet anyway.'

'Of course.'

The urge to hold her seizes Dimitrios. For once, he doesn't listen to the voice in his head that has told him to take things slow; instead; he puts it in the corner of his mind and moves towards her. Carissa shifts on her feet but holds his gaze. Dimitrios reaches out and rests his hands on each arm. He wants to immerse himself in her. In this moment, she is remarkable to him; she is a wonder that has entered his life and turned it upside down, and he hesitates then, but moves through it and bends to her face. He trails his fingers along her spine and then circles her with his arms. Carissa closes her eyes and opens her mouth, stretching her fingers along his back. Gently, he kisses her. It is a gracious meeting of lips, but not enough. Her taste arousing the currents of passion flexing beneath him, demanding to break the surface. Pulling her closer, their kiss becomes deeper and searching, until there is a loosening in her, a freeing of tension, a fleeting sense of relief that spills shimmers in her eyes before spilling into tears.

He tastes their bitter saltiness as they moisten his lips. She tries to speak, but he brings his fingers to her lips. She searches his eyes, and something wonderful settles in her chest. With him, she feels safe, and inside, she smiles at the thought.

CHAPTER NINETEEN

ENDINGS AND NEW BEGINNINGS

Mainland Greece 1942

In silence, the mules and men walked in single file on a winding, narrow track, through low-lying cloud that hugged the mountain. A mile from the Gorgopotamos viaduct and three thousand feet above it, they ate a meal of cold meat and bread accompanied by icy water. Some had flasks of ouzo that the villagers of Mavrolithari had given them, to warm their bodies and souls on their trek through the damp clinging mist and drizzle of rain and snow. To conceal their anonymity, even this far from their target, no fires were to be lit and talking was discouraged. They sat in huddled groups shielding from the cold, and as darkness fell, a ghostly mist encased them, and the hood of night covered the sky.

They made final inspections, confirming the last adjustments to the explosives were correctly made and secure on the eight mules that carried them. Thomas and Chris mingled amongst the *andartes*, confirming there were no misunderstandings around the orders of engagement and their roles.

They began their final approach. The group that was to disable the railway had the furthest to travel, so they led the way, carrying explosives and wire cutters to cut the telephone wires beside the railway track a mile south of the viaduct. Behind them, with the same number of men, the second group followed to cut the railway to the north.

Behind them, a group of around forty men, comprising both Zervas's and Aris's *andartes*, would attack the south end and behind them, another band of Zervas's men were instructed to attack the north end of the viaduct. Following behind, a reserve of thirty *andartes*, led by Thomas and then Eddie, Chris, and Zervas, who were to be known as 'Joint Headquarters'. Last, the demolition party led, by Tom Barnes, with eight *andartes* each leading a mule.

When they reached the area where they had to cross to the other side of the valley, Chris was stunned to learn this was not Aris and Zervas's aim.

Eddie's jaw dropped. 'It's what we agreed.'

Zervas stroked his beard. 'I feel it would serve us better to have kept our headquarters and the reserve on the near side of the valley. Aris agrees with me. I thought you knew this?'

'Does it look like I knew this? Jesus, this is not the time for such discussions. I thought we made it clear, or did I just imagine it?'

'I translated your instructions word for word,' Thomas reminded Eddie.

'We don't have time for this. What do you think, Chris?'

'The demolition lads will have to cross to the other side. They need to get a clear approach to the steel spans. It means we can't give them cover or tell them when to advance to the viaduct to fix the charges.'

'This doesn't serve our purpose. Can't you see that.'

'The explosives can be fixed by your men, and they will have the protection of my men, who will be with them,' Zervas said. 'They can advance to the viaduct when we signal them to do so.'

'With a torch, I presume,' Eddie said incredulously. Eddie turned to Tom Barnes, the demolition engineer. 'Once the signal is given, I'll come and join you from the other side of the valley.'

Tom raised an eyebrow. 'It won't be easy; you'll have to cross the river, and it doesn't look happy.'

'I don't think we have the time to argue the point or the choice,' he said grimly.

'I'll go with them,' Thomas said. 'If I remember, you told me in Cairo, you couldn't swim. I don't fancy your chances if you lose your balance and fall into the river.'

Eddie bit his lip. Thomas was right. He couldn't take a chance. The operation was better served by his staying at Joint Headquarters.

'I'll put my second in command, Komninos Pyromaglou in charge of the reserve,' Zervas offered.

Eddie grimaced. 'Once this end of the viaduct is in our control, I'll give you the all-clear signal. You'd better get on your way. Good luck.'

Thomas nodded. 'Same to you, Sir.'

With only the reserve force, Eddie, Chris, Zervas, and Aris waited in silence. Around them, the curtain of mist dissipated, and the full moon appeared as if it had brushed the clouds aside, lighting the surrounding countryside in a muted silver glow.

With only a few minutes to zero hour, Zervas, Aris,

Chris, and Eddie crawled like lizards to within a hundred and fifty yards of the viaduct and then advanced at a more hastily pace towards a crest of a sloping ridge and gazed over the edge. Eddie surveyed the ravine through his field glasses. The river cut through the mountain pass; its waters flowing over rocks and stones. Even from their elevated position and distance, the constant rush wailed like thunder. The bridge loomed against the night sky, its concrete pillars stark white in the moonlight. It was an incredible sight. The structure seemed to grow in magnitude since their daylight reconnaissance. The air hung heavy with nerves and anticipation as a train rumbled along the track, its rhythmic clatter resounding throughout the ravine.

'There goes the last train to cross that bridge for a while,' Chris said.

'Let's hope so,' Eddie agreed.

Zervas checked his watch. He pursed his lips. They waited another fourteen minutes, lying prone on the ground, the smell of pine resin mixed with the cold and sodden earth underneath.

No one spoke, but they all knew each other's thoughts. The silence unnerved them.

Eddie peered through his field glasses. 'Something's gone wrong,' he whispered, his voice barely audible. He lowered the field glasses, his face grim. He turned to face Chris, his anticipation feeding his fear. 'All the parties must be late, lost in the dark.'

'They've been over the charts and maps a hundred times; they know that terrain with their eyes closed.'

Then, from both the south and north end, mayhem erupted with the deafening crack of rifles, the metallic ping of ricocheting bullets and the rapid staccato of automatic machine gun fire, echoing and amplifying throughout the ravine in a resonating and disorientating cacophony.

Muzzle flashes illuminated the darkness in strobing bursts, and tracers like slow-moving fireflies streaked the air against intermittent blasts and flashes from grenades.

The gunfire continued. Ten... fifteen... twenty anxious minutes passed.

Zervas cried, 'At this rate, we'll run out of ammunition.'

Eddie turned to Chris. 'What did he say?'

Chris translated Zervas's concern.

The fighting abruptly ceased, punctuated only by sporadic rifle cracks and machine-gun bursts.

A wide-eyed *andarte* scrambled towards them, bringing news that some of the group at the north end had been pushed back.

From the south end of the bridge, fire raged heavily, interspersed with cheering.

'It sounds like they're getting the job done. We need to shore up this end,' Eddie instructed.

They committed the entire reserve, tasking Komninos Pyromaglou, Zervas's second in command, to lead the renewed attack on the north end.

Once they departed, within minutes, a brace of renewed and rapid firing began. Time protracted and Zervas paced, ringing his hands and peering through his field glasses. In quick succession, he rattled off his worries.

Chris translated. 'He's convinced we've been betrayed and that the Italians knew we were coming and strengthened their numbers. He's going to fire the withdrawal flare in the next ten minutes if the north end of the bridge is not captured. He wants the pistol now.'

'Who has it?' Eddie asked.

'I don't,' Chris replied.

'Jesus! Where is it then?'

'Komninos had it.'

Eddie, scanning the bridge, considered Chris's words. It bought them some time.

Chris read Eddie's thoughts. 'I'll get it from Komninos.'

'When you do, keep it. Don't let anyone set it off. Bring it back to me.'

Chris nodded and set off.

Ten anxious minutes later, he returned with the pistol, the flare intact and with encouraging news. 'Komninos is confident the north end of the bridge will be in our hands soon.'

Just then, loud cheering rose from the south end of the bridge, followed by a white flare.

Eddie smiled; his relief echoed in the cries of joy from the others. They had captured the far end.

The steel piers were at that end. Eddie turned to the others. 'We need to get Tom and his men started on those piers.'

Eddie scrambled down to a point where he could take in the opposite side of the valley where Tom, Thomas and the rest of his men lay in wait. He flashed his torch and yelled. 'Go in, Tom! The south end of the bridge is in our hands. Go in! I'll join you as soon as I can.'

In quick succession, several flashes of white light answered him.

The demolition group began their descent, leading the mules and their load of explosives, each step crushing snow beneath their boots. The youngest of the *andartes*, a boy of sixteen, held his gun in trembling hands, jumping as though each snap of a twig sounded like a gunshot in his ears.

Noticing his nervousness, Thomas came up beside him. 'First time?' he whispered in Greek.

The young *andarte* nodded, embarrassed, but surprised Thomas had spoken to him in his own language.

'What's your name?'

'Andreas.'

'The fear is normal,' Thomas said. 'If it keeps you alert, Andreas, it'll keep you alive.'

Andreas nodded, but his eyes blazed with fright.

As they neared the riverbank, the fighting raged on, gunfire and grenades splitting the night air above them. The cold bit into Thomas's bones as they waded through the river, the water rushing against his legs, each step a negotiation between slippery stones, sharp rocks and the current's relentless push. The water surged to mid-thigh, numbing his legs until they felt like foreign objects. Beside him, Tom Barnes moved with purpose, his breathing controlled and shallow.

'Andreas, keep your eyes on the water,' Thomas bellowed, his voice barely audible over the water's constant rush.

Andreas nodded, fighting the urge to look up at the bridge looming above him. Thomas glanced at the underside of the bridge, revealing rust stains bleeding from the steel reinforcements within the concrete.

Thomas waded through the water, each breath thunderous in his ears.

'Hold on to those mules,' Thomas bellowed. 'We don't want a dead mule floating down the river with explosives on its back.'

An *andarte* smirked, 'Even the Italians will notice that.' His words brought an outburst of nervous laughter from the rest of the group.

At last, to their relief, they reached the other side and set to work cutting the wire fence that surrounded the viaduct.

They passed through the gap, pushing through the tall grass at the foot of the viaduct.

A few *andartes* began securing the mules, while the others unloaded the crates of explosives. Thomas followed Tom and pressed himself against the first pillar, grateful for the momentary stability. Tom was already unpacking the explosives, his hands moving with practised efficiency despite the cold.

'Fuck!'

Thomas gazed at Tom. 'What is it?'

'We thought the cross sections of the legs of the piers were L shaped, they're not. They're fucking U-shaped.'

'And that's a problem?'

'The L-shaped charges are about as much good as a chocolate fireguard.'

'That's a problem. What can we do?'

'Get everyone together, we'll have to dismantle all the charges and repack the explosives by hand into the vertical U-shaped girders.'

'That's going to delay us.'

'We don't have a choice, Thomas.'

They worked stealthily as gunfire and explosives raged above them.

Thomas instructed the *andartes* where to place the explosives, and within the hour they were ready.

'Hold this,' Tom murmured, passing Thomas a length of wire. Above them, the bridge creaked, distinct and menacing.

The *andartes* settled into position, training their rifles on the bridge above that continued to crack and pop with the distinctive sounds of automatic fire.

Thomas's tongue stuck to the roof of his mouth, and as

he took a swig from his water canister, the ammunition belt across his shoulder felt reassuringly heavy.

'Not long now,' Tom breathed, his words passing through the group like a current.

Tom was now working faster. One was giving him trouble, the wires refusing to stay connected in the damp and cold air.

'Steady,' he muttered, more to himself than to Thomas. Sweat beaded on his forehead despite the cold, rolling down to sting his eyes. He blinked it away, focusing on the delicate connection.

As he watched Tom, Thomas's world had narrowed to the sound of his own breathing and the metallic scrape of Tom's tools against the detonator. Time seemed to stretch and compress together.

Gunshots continued above, the sound violently physical. 'Seven minutes on the timer,' Tom said, his voice suddenly loud in Thomas's ear. 'Move, now!'

They splashed toward the opposite bank, abandoning stealth for speed. The water dragged at Thomas's legs, every step a battle.

The sharp smell of cordite drifted down towards them, mingling with the river scent. Above them, Komninos and his men had opened with everything they had, creating a wall of sound. Italian voices shouted blindly, high-pitched with alarm and confusion.

A bullet struck the water several feet from Thomas, the impact surprisingly gentle – just a *plunk* followed by a small splash. Then another, closer. The third struck a rock near his head, fragments of stone stinging his cheek. The abstract notion of danger crystallised into a desperate, animal terror.

Someone had spotted them!

Tom stumbled, going down on one knee in the water. Thomas grabbed Tom's shoulder, hauling him upright with strength he didn't know he possessed. A beholden glance stretched over Tom's face.

Fear altered into a strange, detached clarity. Thomas's body reacted without conscious thought, responding to threats before his mind had processed them.

At last, they reached the bank, and clawed their way up the snow-covered slope, boots finding purchase on exposed roots. The earth felt ridiculously solid after the unstable riverbed. Thomas's legs burned, pushed by adrenaline and necessity.

A grenade exploded somewhere above them. Tom shouted something, the words indistinct but the urgency clear. They scrambled toward the rendezvous point, staying low among the scrubby vegetation. Another blast overhead froze them in place. Tom blew his whistle, a shrill sound that reverberated around the gorge. The signal sent those on the bridge scrambling for cover.

An unnerving silence prevailed, punctuated only by subsiding gunfire. The Italian's return fire ceased ominously. They were retreating, sensing something coming.

'Timer?' Thomas demanded.

Tom glanced at his watch. 'Two minutes.'

They huddled together, counting seconds that stretched like hours. Thomas's heart rate slowed for the first time since entering the water. The immediate danger passed. In its place came a bone-deep exhaustion and the delayed recognition of dozens of minor injuries – scratches, bruises, a twisted ankle that would swell impressively by morning.

Thomas pressed his face into the dirt, with the smell of resin and damp earth filling his nostrils and pine needles pricking his cheek.

The last few seconds compelled him to lift his head and look in the explosion's direction. Their struggle in getting there merited seeing it. When it came, it rumbled through the ground before he heard it – a deep, subterranean growl followed by a sound like the end of the world. The air itself seemed to compress and expand. Thomas's eyes fixed on one of the seventy-foot steel spans and the exhilarating sight of it lifting into the air and then dropping into the gorge in twisting, breaking metal. He covered his head as debris rained down around them, stone and dust gushing through the air.

The sudden, absolute silence that followed soon broke with the burst of gunfire and heavy explosions from the north end of the bridge.

Tom shouted over the gunfire. 'The Italian reinforce-ments from their garrison must be arriving. I hope our lads have cut the railway line.'

Thomas knew the train would bring a substantial force, and as it stood, the lads on the bridge didn't have the manpower or ammunition to stave them off.

Just then, Denys Hamson scurried into the shallow depression Thomas and Tom had taken cover in. His breath came in gasps as he spoke. 'I've just seen Eddie. He was on the other side of the river. I told him it's going to take at least another forty minutes to bring down the other steel pier and span and to finish the job. He told me to be as quick as we could. The train from Lamia has stopped, and our boys are engaging with the enemy on the train. Zervas is only prepared to give it another ten minutes and then he's going to fire the withdrawal signal.'

Thomas grimaced. 'That's not long enough.'

'Eddie has told Chris to hold Zervas off for twenty

minutes. That's if our boys can keep the Italians on the train at bay.'

Tom nodded an acknowledgment and patted Thomas on the shoulder, and grinned. 'Let's get to it, then. We've got a bridge to blow.'

The enemy advance sounded imminent, explosions and gunfire increasing at an alarming rate as Tom finally gave the order to withdraw to cover. It had taken fifteen minutes when the sound of Tom's whistle shrieked through the ravine for the second time that night, just as a green flare burst over the bridge, announcing the withdrawal signal.

'Good timing,' Thomas shouted over the gunfire.

A second vast explosion ripped through the ravine and bellowed over the bridge.

'You know the drill, Thomas. They've fired the withdrawal flare; we need to move out. It's done.' Tom said, looking at Thomas with something like wonder.

'I'll catch up with you.'

'What do you mean?' He stared at Thomas. 'You're not going to do what I think you are…'

'We've not come all this way to walk away now.'

'There's no time to inspect the damage. We need to make our way back to the meeting point. We've got a mile of hard walking ahead of us.'

'We need eyes on the damage. I need to see it. Withdraw yourself and your men as agreed. I'll be right behind you.'

'What if you don't come back? What will I tell the others?'

'I'd be dead, so it wouldn't matter what you told them.'

'You're a mad bastard, Thomas.'

Thomas's face broke into a smile. 'It takes one to know one.'

Behind them, the gunfire slackened as Tom's men executed their withdrawal. Denys appeared beside Tom.

'Where's Thomas? I thought he was with you.'

'He's inspecting the state of play.' It was the chirpiest response Tom could think of to say.

Thomas rubbed his eyes. The familiar state overcame him: leaden and weightless, his exhaustion grappling with adrenaline, the fragmented impressions visiting him: her dark hair. Her large soft eyes. The flutter of her dress. Her last words, *'You are a soldier; you will keep us safe.'*

Then, she took him by surprise. For the first time, she deviated from the fragmented images of her visitations and spoke to him.

'You are still alive.' Her voice was gentle.

He didn't answer. Instead, he just nodded, surprised to discover it was true. The realisation came with no triumph, no relief, only a hollow, exhausted acceptance that would not diminish.

He abandoned his rifle on the bank, stumbling down towards the river. He lurched into the water and hung his head in its charging flow. It froze every pore, but not his thoughts.

He hauled himself onto the bank and lay facing the blackened sky, which moments before had boomed and lit up in explosive light, like fireworks. Her words continued to press against his skull. They uncurled in him. *'You are still alive.'*

He felt them like a weight in his chest, next to his heart. Something without a name. Something that would never fade away.

. . .

The light in his eyes had returned as Thomas stared at the outcome of their work, executed less than an hour ago. He took off his cap and removed a wet cigarette packet from his breast pocket. A damp tidemark stretched along the white of the cigarette that he lit.

In his head, he could still hear the explosions, where rocks and earth fell around him, as he stood motionless in the eerie and disconcerting silence around him.

The second explosion had cut and distorted the two already fallen spans, where smoke rose in lazy spirals, but to his dismay, the charges on the second pier had only cut two of the four legs, and the pier and spans remained intact. He consoled himself; they had still achieved what they set out to do. The damage would sever the railway line to Athens for six to twelve weeks. Eddie would be pleased.

He began the long trek back to the meeting point. Clambering through the dense thicket, Thomas finally emerged into open and rocky moorland. Here, the footing proved easier; despite bone-deep exhaustion and a peculiar weightlessness, Thomas progressed swiftly. Soon, he came across the pathway he had descended a few hours earlier in the pitch blackness. He remembered thinking, would he retrace his steps after the assault? He was alive and keenly aware of the squelch of snow under his boots, the stiffening cold that clung to his uniform, and his body's protestations of extreme fatigue, having been on the move since four the previous morning with a morsel of rations to stave off hunger.

Further ahead, a line of exhausted *andartes* leading the mules now emptied of their loads, trekked upwards along the pathway, leaving behind a collage of footprints in the thick snow that clung to the slopes of Mount Oiti.

The sun rose fully, catching distant snow-capped peaks

in a crown of scarlet and gold. The light transformed the landscape in the quiet aftermath of the world reasserting itself after the chaos of the night before.

At the edge of a dense and formidable pine forest, Thomas finally reached the others, where most of the *andartes* and British had already gathered. Eddie and Chris were congratulating Zervas and Aris on the success of the assault when Tom Barnes sided up to Thomas.

'You decided to join us, after all.'

'Good to see you too, Tom.'

'Well?' Tom asked expectantly.

'The second explosion only cut two of the four legs. The pier and spans remained intact, I'm afraid.'

'Still a good night's work, given the circumstances.'

'And we met our objective. The Jerries won't be using that rail track and visiting Athens for some time.'

They hiked the remaining thousand feet of Mount Oiti and then, evading the prospect of being sighted by Italian aircraft, trudged into the thick forest firs where a dense mist descended around them.

That afternoon, they finally reached the forest huts where the dependable Barba Niko had prepared a hot meal and several warm, crackling fires.

Later, as Thomas was eating with the others around a fire, Andreas approached, wringing his hands. Thomas offered him a seat. He noticed Andreas had lost the sole of one of his boots and the colour had drained from his face.

'You made it back,' Andreas said shyly.

Thomas nodded. 'I did. Does that surprise you?'

'I just...' Andreas stammered. 'I didn't think I'd see you again.'

'Well, it really is me.' Thomas gave a wry smile. 'If I were wounded, you could be like doubting Thomas and stick your finger in my wound. Luckily, for the both of us, I'm not.'

'Some of the men who were with the demolition team said you stayed behind instead of returning with them. Someone said it was a mad thing to do, as the place would swarm with Italians once we withdrew.'

'They were right,' Thomas smiled. 'I'm pleased to see you made it back too, Andreas.'

He nodded.

Thomas took a bite of bread and swallowed. 'I heard your group neutralised the pillboxes. That was crucial to our success.'

The words landed like sharp needles on Andreas's skin. 'We did. Grenades were thrown into them, and we were told to mop up those who weren't killed. They ran out like frightened rabbits.' His voice choked up, heat rushing to his face. 'I think I shot one of them.'

'The first time is always the worst.' Thomas leaned into Andreas. 'Not because it gets any easier, but because you learn what to expect. If you don't kill them first, they'll certainly kill you. Death becomes… familiar.'

Andreas considered this. 'Does that make it better or worse?'

Thomas gave him a sidelong glance. 'That depends.'

'On what?' His voice was a whisper.

'On who you are. Do you know who you are, Andreas?'

Andreas fell silent, grappling with the question and his answer.

Thomas patted him on the shoulder. 'Amongst your fellow *andartes*, and in these mountains, you'll soon find out, but first, you need a new pair of boots.'

That night, the *andartes* danced in a circle and sang songs and hymns. The following day, in triumph, Eddie,

Chris, and Thomas, along with Zervas and his *andartes*, returned to Mavrolithari.

The next day, they prepared to move off. Zervas was travelling back to Valtos, a journey of eight days, and Chris, following the instructions from Cairo, would remain in Greece with Zervas. Eddie and the rest of the party were to be evacuated by submarine. They would accompany Zervas as far as Valtos.

Their wireless set was still inoperable. Eddie sent a runner to Athens to ask Prometheus to inform Cairo the operation had met its objectives, and to communicate the date and precise rendezvous point for the submarine: the west coast of Greece, around five miles south of Parga, on one of four nights between 22nd and 25th December. He also requested a supplies drop of boots, clothing, and arms, with a case of whisky for Zervas to be dropped in Valtos on Zervas's return.

Aris would remain in the Roumeli area as he had 'certain matters' that needed his immediate attention. When Eddie informed Aris that he intended to recommend him and Zervas for a decoration, Aris was adamant; it wasn't a medal he needed but boots for his men. He did, however, accept a gift of two hundred and fifty gold sovereigns.

Eddie and Chris attempted to persuade Zervas and Aris to join forces and unify the *andarte* movement, but their efforts were to no avail. They soon discovered they were now entangled in the complex web and politics of the resistance and that their approach towards a Greek should be through the heart and not the head.

'What about you, Barba Niko? What will you do now?' Eddie asked.

'I will return to my family. They need me.'

'I've always wondered why you've rendered yourself so completely to helping us, the British?'

Barba Niko smiled. 'God told me from heaven that the English were coming, and I knew it was my duty to serve them.'

'We will be forever indebted to you. I will recommend you for a special decoration.'

Tears lined Barba Niko's eyes. 'I would do it all again if asked to.'

'That has never been in doubt.' Eddie told him. 'Your family needs you now, and I release you into their embrace.'

Thomas said his own farewell to Barba Niko, and it was with a heavy heart they took their leave, letting him return to his family, setting their sights on their own journey home.

Their passage was not without its dangers. Early on, they had to change course and find shelter in a small mountain village to avoid a column of Italian troops that had marched north from Agrinion to capture them.

They had to be alert to enemy aircraft, but only on one occasion were they forced to take cover, and only once did they have to cross a main road, which they did at dawn, avoiding Italian convoys that supplied their garrisons at Karpenisi.

Each night, they stopped in a planned village along the route. Even though the inhabitants were deprived of basic amenities and lived day to day, they were always generous and welcoming.

They learnt that in that region of Roumeli, villages were being frequently visited and sometimes billeted by small bands of ELAS *andartes* under Aris's control and influence.

They also heard of a political organisation called, National Liberation Front, frequently referred to as EAM, which as far as they could surmise, was the leading civilian organisation to which the armed *andarte* bands of ELAS gave their loyalty.

It was during their nightly stays in the villages, and through conversations with the educated Greeks they met, that a clearer picture began to emerge. Most were reluctant to share their knowledge or even speak of EAM or ELAS, but the fragments they offered revealed more about the dynamics that had led to the formation of the two main resistance movements. With a coordinated effort by Thomas and Chris interpreting, they could piece together, like a multilayered jigsaw, the historical background and present-day situation on the ground.

A lawyer from Athens, Mikis Papandreou, had returned from Athens to his family's village and joined the resistance like many educated men before him. He spoke perfect English and was willing to aid the British soldiers in their request to discuss the formation of the resistance.

'When did resistance begin?' Eddie asked, sharing a bitter coffee with Mikis, as Thomas and Chris listened on.

'The day the Italians and Germans first invaded. It's never stopped since Athens was occupied. Within months, many Greek organisations were born out of the occupation. As well as Athens, it spread to places like Epirus, Macedonia, Thessaly, and the Peloponnese.

'Could you tell me more about EDES?' Eddie asked.

'As far as I'm aware, they were a political organisation at their inception, but also one of the first major resistance groups to take up arms with Zervas's campaign in the mountains.

'If you don't know already, he's a hard-lined republican;

the monarchy and communism play no part in his vision of a future Greece. EDES's goal is the founding of a republic. It wasn't until the British offered him their support that Zervas eventually took to the mountains.'

'And EAM, what can you tell me about them?' Eddie asked.

Mikis cleared his throat. 'In Athens, when I was there, I saw EAM leaflets denouncing the occupation. I remember reading an article in the *Rizospastis*, EAM's daily newspaper, calling for the resistance to take up arms and follow the example of Crete and Macedonia. That's when the first armed units were formed and the Greek People's Liberation Army – ELAS. Soon after, they announced they too were taking up arms.'

'How did the Germans react to this?'

He hissed a sigh through his teeth. 'As they always do, by executing those caught for subversive activities. Athens erupted with speeches, resistance, strikes, and bureaucratic slowdowns. Graffiti appeared on walls and buildings denouncing the Germans. Commonwealth and British soldiers also sought refuge in Athens then. Many families took them into their homes, placing themselves at great risk and cost. Athens was destitute. Everyone relied on the black market to feed themselves and their families.

'Such personal sacrifice typifies the Greek people's will to resist the occupation. It comes at a terrible cost. The reprisals are devastating and brutal.'

'Politically, what's it like in Athens?'

Mikis's voice sharpened. 'Most of Greece's political leaders and most of the population are not in favour of the monarchy returning from exile. Most people blame King George for the Metaxas dictatorship and the defeat of Greece by the Axis. Those who came to power after

Metaxas don't fare any better in people's assessments. The monarchy and the exiled government of Tsourdes don't represent Greece. They're viewed with disdain, especially the government, with sympathisers and supporters of the Metaxas regime in its ranks. It's an insult to the people to have Metaxas ministers in the Greek cabinet.'

Eddie nodded. 'I can see the difficulty with that.'

Mikis took a deep breath. 'It doesn't help that the British government remains steadfast in its support of a king and a government in exile that most Greeks don't support.'

Eddie sat back. 'Thank you, Mikis. You've been a tremendous help. You've given us a clear picture of the events and the current situation.'

Eddie, Chris, and Thomas found it inconceivable that the intelligence they received was wholly inadequate. Cairo was incompetent in their lack of knowledge of Greek resistance in the mountains. They were dumbfounded that the briefings about the operation did not mention, comprehensively or fleetingly, the intricacies of the Greek resistance regarding EAM, the largest and best organised resistant group, or ELAS, its military arm, nor the communist party KKE and its role in the formation and dominance of both groups. Given that the Special Operations Executive were aware of these organisations and of their political persuasions, it was a conundrum they failed to make sense of. It was only after their arrival in the mountains of Greece that they heard about and discovered the existence of these organisations.

They didn't know the Greeks they should have worked with and were unaware of the situation in the Greek mountains. SOE in Cairo, the Middle East Command and the Greek government in London, ignored, or at best, scarcely understood the political aspects of the Greek Resistance Movement.

When any of Zervas's officers mentioned EAM, they referred to them as 'the Communists'. There was no effort on Zervas's part or his officers to hide their dislike and distrust of EAM's political goals.

It was becoming increasingly obvious that ELAS's and EDES's political differences formed a major obstacle to united action.

It took eight days to reach Zervas's mountain base in Valtos, the small village of Mavrolithari. Eddie's message, sent by runner to Prometheus in Athens, requesting a submarine to evacuate them, still hadn't received an answer. There was still the possibility that Cairo had not received the message. It was a risk worth taking. They estimated it would take twelve days to travel to the meeting point, and Zervas offered twelve *andartes* to escort them. Two wireless operators, who were staying behind with Chris, would attempt to repair the wireless set.

On the day they left for the submarine, Chris joined Zervas, who set out on a recruiting tour.

Their route took Thomas and the others through a region where it was not unusual to see Greek Gendarmerie and Italian troops in villages and no *andarte* presence in the countryside.

The further west they travelled, the more they avoided being seen in the daytime. In the late afternoon, an *andarte* would enter a village and arrange accommodation, picking the smallest and most rundown house as it would be less likely to be visited at night by Greeks or Italians. The whole of the party crammed into these houses, ate the meagre amount of food the owner could supply and left again early in the morning.

When, finally, they reached the rendezvous point, exhausted and hungry, they rested up in a dilapidated shepherd shelter a mile from the shore. At night, they crossed a stretch of moorland and, reaching a beach, signalled out to sea. At dawn, they moved back to their hideout and slept during the day. An *andarte* entered a nearby village to gain some food and received several small loaves of bread from the village priest. Three days passed with no sighting of the submarine. Each day, the daily generous contributions of the priest kept their hunger at bay. On the fourth evening, they were ready to depart the beach following another unsuccessful signal attempt, when the priest arrived alongside another man. He introduced himself as a runner whom Chris had sent. He handed Eddie a note, which he read out to the rest of the group.

I was dropped a new wireless set and received a message from Cairo saying that they will not be sending a submarine. New instructions are being sent in the safe hands of a Captain Bill Jordan, who will be dropped by plane within the next few days.

Within twenty minutes of receiving the message, they packed their kits into their rucksacks and, bitterly disheartened, began the return journey back to Valtos. Night after night they trudged on, traversing steep and stony goat tracks, drenched to the skin as rain and wind hampered their progress. They rested during the day and moved at night, avoiding villages and open countryside.

When they finally reached Zervas's base at Megalohari, their bodies exhausted, with blood-stained and blistered feet, and crippled with constant hunger they were greeted by cheerful voices of the wireless operators: Chris, and Captain Bill Jordan, who had arrived a few days previously armed with a bulging instruction-filled envelope that signalled for the days, weeks and months to come, their feet would be firmly planted in Greece. They were not returning home.

News often travelled late, by word of mouth and written notes. That night, they received a message delivered by one of Zervas's men.

After reading the note, Eddie folded the piece of paper and then scrunched it in his hands. For a second, he closed his eyes and then, clearing his throat, he looked at the men around him.

'I'm afraid I've got some dreadful news.' He hesitated. 'There's no easy way of saying this. The day after our successful operation at the Gorgopotamos bridge, the Italians took fifteen male villagers to the bottom of the gorge, just under the bridge. They sat them down, and then shot each one of them. It was a reprisal execution. They were sending a message.' The colour drained from his face. 'Was there anything we could have done?'

Silence filled the void that waited for an answer. Chris's face twitched; his eyes glazed. Finally resigned, his words choking him, he blinked. 'What could we have done?'

Thomas noticed the subtle shift, the first hints of deep blue along the horizon penetrating the inky darkness of the night. Gradually, it lightened, moving over a palate of navy to cobalt, then a soft azure stretching higher in the sky.

He had witnessed the sun's approach many times, each dawn experienced anew, as if it were the first. It was a constant source of amazement that never failed to catch his breath.

Thomas peered intently, as the horizon glowed in warm amber fanning outwards, coating the edge of the sky in pale shades of apricot, then peach, then, intensifying, it seized him with vibrant gold and with a fiery orange that announced the sun's imminent arrival.

He stood. Waiting. Anticipating. Then, within seconds, the full orb breached the horizon in a perfect circle that pulsed with energy, casting its light over wispy clouds, their edges rimmed with liquid gold.

He thought the mountains around him stood like dark, majestic sentinels as they lit up in a warm alpenglow, stressing every ridge and contour in a dramatic play of light and shadow.

In such moments, he devoured the gift of being alive.

Then, Thomas heard someone approaching. He turned. Chris strode towards him.

'Catching the sunrise again.'

When Chris came alongside him, Thomas noticed a faint strain in Chris's eyes. 'It seems to have become a habit of yours, too.'

Chris swept his eyes across the horizon. 'It looks amazing, doesn't it? It's marvellous, really, when you think about it. The sun will appear every day without fail. It will slide above the horizon and paint the sky in its palette of colours, even when we are long gone. It will create such masterpieces every day and into infinity.' He blinked and then looked at his feet. 'Death, on the other hand, is final. Those poor men. I can't imagine what their mothers, their wives... and children must be going through.'

Thomas's throat tightened. He swallowed. He couldn't find the words; instead, he took a long breath that lifted his shoulders. Suddenly, he could feel the young girl's eyes upon him. He pushed her from his mind, slamming the door.

Chris pulled his jacket closer around him and shuffled his feet. 'Before we flew from Egypt, in fact, just as we were heading onto the plane, a ladybird settled on me. I told myself everything would turn out right if the ladybird was still there when I arrived in Greece. When I landed, in my harness, there was the ladybird still inside, even after our long journey from Cairo and falling all that way to the ground. It sounds silly, I know, but it was like a sign that everything would turn out right. I kept it as long as I could.'

Thomas considered this. 'I heard Eddie's read his new orders. Is everything going to turn out right now that we're actually staying?'

'He's shared them with me if that's what you mean. He's going to gather the men later this morning and inform them of SOE's new instructions. He won't keep anyone here any longer than necessary. No one volunteered to stay past the operation except myself, Themie, Wilmots, and Philips? For those that still want to leave, he'll arrange it with SOE as soon as is practical.' He raised his eyebrows. 'What about you, Thomas?'

He felt Chris's eyes on him but didn't move his from the sunrise. 'Like you, Chris, I'm in it for the long run.'

That morning, Eddie gathered his men and informed them of their new orders from SOE.

He lit a cigarette and took a lungful of smoke, observing the dejection on the faces before him; his expression lost some of its composure. He took another long drag of his cigarette before addressing them.

'As you all know, I received a long message from SOE.

I've spent most of last night poring over the details, and I'm now in a position to make you aware of its content.

We've been asked to stay on in Greece.'

A groundswell of restless unease stirred through the men. He gave them time to digest this before he held up his hand. 'I'd like you to know that, like you all, I'm bitterly disappointed with this request.' He rubbed his temple. 'I know that most of you volunteered under the understanding that as soon as we had reached our objectives and cut the railway line with the demolition of the bridge, every effort would be made to evacuate you off Greece. There's no one here more upset than I am about having to take that long, hard and arduous journey to the coast only to turn back and retrace our footsteps.' He gave the men time to take this in.

'I can see amongst your faces there's little heart amongst you all to undertake a new mission which will prolong your time in Greece.

'Last night, I decided I would only keep those who were keen to stay on. For those of you who want to leave, I'll do all that is in my power to get you evacuated.

'I've been asked by SOE in Cairo to take command in coordinating and developing further activities of the *andartes*. It looks like we're going to have many more days in Greece together.'

Eddie then instructed his officers on the situation they had found themselves in. He explained it was obvious SOE in Cairo knew nothing of the strength and organisational structure of the *andartes*. Even with their agents in Athens and communications with *andarte* bands in the field through runners and by wireless with the Middle East, SOE was in the dark about the political differences in the Greek Resistance Movement. The Greek government in exile in

London knew no more than SOE and the Middle East Command.

That night, an aircraft dropped stores and an additional wireless operator. Eddie sent requests by wireless for more ammunition and arms.

A few days later, a new directive came over the air from SOE Cairo.

Once the message was deciphered, Eddie gathered Thomas and Chris around the table where he had rolled out several maps.

'Gentlemen, I've received a new directive from Cairo. What I'm about to tell you is classified, and it comes from the highest level.

'We're about to play our part in one of the biggest deceptions of the war. Hitler is to be made to believe that the British are preparing to invade Greece. We're not. Once the Germans are driven out of Tunisia, our lads are moving to capture Sicily, then into Italy itself. But first, we need to make the bastards think it's all about Greece.

'Simultaneously, the Middle East Command will launch an attack on the Dodecanese to weaken the "iron ring" blocking access to Southern Greece. This could potentially lead to an assault on the mainland. The main goal is to divert German and Italian forces from Southern Italy and from Russia towards the Balkans. Stretch the Axi. It's expected German troops and aircraft will start shifting south into Greece by June, especially to back up or replace the Italians in the Aegean and Dodecanese.'

'So, we're standing by for orders. What exactly are we supposed to do?' Chris asked.

'Our task, from this moment on, will be to train and equip and arm the *andartes* throughout Greece as soon as is practically possible. Build them up to whatever level the SOE can support.'

'Are there specific areas they want us to concentrate on?' Chris asked.

Eddie nodded. 'The Peloponnese, Attica, and the Southern Pindus. I've to inform them which areas we can effectively control. SOE will supply Area Commanders to those areas I feel we wouldn't be able to efficiently cover.'

Eddie halted, seemingly in contemplation, then continued. 'In the short-term, our task is to ready the *andartes* at any moment for sabotaging communications, should it be needed in support of our Allied strategy. At the moment, we've been asked to employ the *andartes* in using sabotage, mainly of the railway lines.'

'We'll need a lot of firepower,' Thomas said.

Eddie arched an eyebrow. 'We will. To this end, SOE will equip us with arms, ammunition and explosives during the next three months and distribute these in accordance with our plans. There will be eight sorties in March, twelve in April, sixteen in May and June and thereafter.

'Not every sortie will be successful,' Chris warned.

Eddie nodded thoughtfully. 'That's true. We just have to pray there'll be enough that will be dropped.'

Eddie's jaw tightened. 'Depending on events in Europe, it's possible the target date for the invasion of Sicily may change, but to this end, we'll be kept informed.'

Eddie took a deep breath. 'Well, Thomas, Chris, we have what will be a difficult job in front of us. It's going to take a good few months to amass the required firepower and the extra personnel we'll need. There's also the question of the men waiting to be evacuated. This now changes that.'

Eddie assembled the men and informed them of their

new orders. He stressed that it was now crucial to the war effort that each man stay in Greece.

'I'm not going to order you to stay, but it's my hope you will all want to, and do your very best until we get the job done.'

Each man, one after the other, volunteered to play his part.

That night, in faint candlelight, which framed their faces in soft gold, Eddie and his officers conferred over large-scale maps of Greece. They divided the mountainous regions into four areas, each region under the command of a lieutenant-colonel.

Eddie gestured towards each area on the map. 'Tom will be in charge of Epirus, Arthur in Roumeli, Nick in Macedonia and Sheppard in Olympus.'

Thomas scratched his chin. 'That still leaves the Peloponnese.'

Eddie scrutinised the map. He thought briefly. 'You're right. We need someone in the Peloponnese. Also, we'll need more officers and wireless sets. There are still a lot of different bands of *andartes* without British influence amongst them. That needs to be fixed.'

Just then, a runner arrived. 'I've urgent news.'

'You speak English. Good. What is it?' Eddie asked.

'Saraphis, Kostopoulos and all their officers have been taken prisoner by ELAS forces under the command of a bandleader named Kapralos.'

Eddie's face darkened. 'Jesus! That's all we need.'

'Some deserted from ELAS. They were executed,' the runner reported. 'The others who refused to join ELAS were disarmed and ordered to return to their villages. I spoke with one of Kostopoulos' officers and several survivors.'

'It's true, then.'

The runner nodded grimly. 'Every word, sir.'

Eddie turned to his staff. 'I've heard reports about this ELAS force – about two to three hundred men under this Kapralos. They've been attacking EDES bands under Zervas's command, right in his territory.' He slammed his fist on the table. 'This is a flagrant attack on him, tantamount to starting a civil war in the mountains.'

'But if Zervas's forces outnumber Kapralos…' Thomas thought out loud.

'That doesn't matter,' Eddie said. 'Any fighting between them would severely set back the resistance movement and possibly interfere with our plans for widespread sabotage.

I've had an intense exchange of telegrams with Cairo,' Eddie explained. 'Regarding both our short-term military interests and Greece's long-term political future, we need to take the firmest possible line, not only to prevent civil war but to bring ELAS into the fold to assist us militarily.'

'Will Zervas retaliate?' Chris asked.

'He won't declare full and open conflict against EAM without Allied backing,' Eddie assured him. 'And Cairo has approved my "National Bands" policy as not only preferable but feasible.'

'The document is ready,' Chris said, placing papers on the table.

Eddie laid his hand on the papers. 'This is simple, really. I'll demand all bands sign this to qualify for material support from the Allies. By signing, they'll be bound to allow all bands, EDES or ELAS, to exist side by side in the mountains and carry out operations against the enemy according to Middle East Command's instructions, delivered through me or my officers.'

'And in return?' Thomas asked.

'In return, they'll receive arms, ammunition, and other essentials from the Allies, as far as our means allow,' Eddie explained. 'Zervas already has a copy, which I expect him to sign. Kapralos and all other band leaders will need to sign it as well.'

Eddie focused his attention on the maps again. 'I keep hearing about this Kapralos. He seems to take the law into his own hands and is judge and jury in the villages in Thessaly. We need to meet him as soon as possible and sort this mess out before it escalates out of control. We need a presence on the plains of southern Thessaly. Someone who won't need to rely on an interpreter. Things get lost in translation at times. That can't happen.'

He looked up, his eyes level and steady. 'Would you like to get out of the mountains, Thomas?'

'Thessaly?'

'It's what I'm thinking.'

'But I'm not a lieutenant-colonel.'

'Then, I'll make you one.'

CHAPTER TWENTY

REVEALING TRUTH AND MIRACLES

Skiathos 2007

They take a seat at Las Ramblas, an artisan coffee house situated beside the road that skirts the town. Dimitrios orders an espresso and Carissa a tea. Heat radiates from the road as they sit outside under a parasol. They agreed that Stuart's recent appearance wouldn't hold Carissa hostage, and she would continue her life as normal – a compromised normality.

It had been two days since Carissa had found the note and, in that time, there had been no more contact from Stuart. This uneased Carissa, prolonging the inevitable. Was that his plan? To make her suffer under the constant expectation, the gruelling hypervigilance, scrutinising every face, on every street and every lane and every doorway? Every window felt like an eye, every shadow like a hiding place. Places that once evoked the beauty of the town were now sullied and defiled, regarded with suspicion and fear as potential opportunities for Stuart to conceal himself and follow her. The exhaustive recognition that he wanted her to suffer was tangible.

She has decided that not telling Dimitrios would be disastrous. She stirs her tea, the ritual of it helping to prepare her, ease her into it. 'There's something I need to tell you. I want to tell you. It will make sense of this whole nightmare.' She meets his eyes. 'I had a miscarriage. Last year. That's when it started, really.'

This startles him. 'I'm sorry.'

'You don't have to be sorry; I'm not looking for your sympathy.'

Dimitrios looks away with awkward eyes.

She takes a breath, time to recalibrate. 'But *I* should be sorry,' she added in a small, remorseful voice. 'That wasn't called for.'

'It was understandable. I can still see it affects you.'

'It wasn't deserved.' She takes a breath. 'I think about what might have been, you know, if…' she falters and looks away, her eyes glazing with tears, '…if I'd had the baby. How different my life would have been. It's hard to think about that. I continually find myself thinking about the milestones that never were. You know, what she would have looked like, what she would be doing, her first steps, her first words.'

'You said, *her*.'

'I know. It's weird, but it's always *her*. I even thought of a name but stopped myself.'

Dimitrios has noticed there are moments when her eyes hold pockets of sadness, and this is one of them. 'It's difficult to grieve on your own, especially when there's someone else involved who is emotionally detached. It becomes harder. You need space to grieve, and there are no time limits on that.'

She smiles. 'You have a lovely way with words.'

'Not always.'

'Stuart became everything I feared. He found it hard to talk about how the miscarriage made him feel. You see, he always talked about having children. He was an only child. The thought of children… I don't know, would make up for that. He didn't have the best upbringing. His parents were strict in their approach to parenting. He was never good at expressing his emotions. He had his own unresolved trauma, let's just say that. As time went on, he became more…' She searched for the right words. 'He became emotionally detached. I wanted to talk about how I was feeling; he just wanted to lock it away. You can't go on like that without something or someone breaking. We ended up sleeping apart. He slept on the couch most nights. There was nothing intimate about us, not physically or emotionally. I thought I could bury my worries under routine. Keep everything the same, go back to my normal life, work, see friends, be the person I was before. Change nothing.

'Stuart became more distant, irritable and increasingly volatile.

'My home became a prison; each day felt like a sentence. The suppression became overwhelming.'

Dimitrios moves his coffee cup in his hand. 'I came back to Skiathos after I split up with my wife. We were married for three years. One of them was happy; the other two years, not so much. We're both happily divorced now. It's funny; I thought I loved her, but you never really know a person until you live with them. The mistake we made was getting married. We should have lived together first. Luckily there were no children involved, just possessions and a house.'

'I thought I knew Stuart, but that was just a caricature

of the Stuart he wanted me to believe was him. The real one, the real Stuart, was always just below the surface, and he occasionally showed himself. The problem was that *occasionally* became a daily occurrence, it became normality. There was a voice inside me that kept reminding me, *I don't know who we are anymore*. I kept pushing it away until eventually, that voice grew louder, so loud, I couldn't ignore it any longer. That was when the threat of violence was at its worst. He could manage it, but he scared me. It was only a matter of time until he'd cross the line.'

'Did he ever…'

'No, he came close… once.'

He reaches out and places his hand on hers. She feels the gentle weight of it, like a comforter.

'I realise now I can own my past without letting it define me. When I told you about the book, Fortune's Rocks, afterwards, I was struck by how much Olympia's life reflected my own. And I thought more about Olympia's resilience… it made me think about how I tried to hide into myself after the hurt of the miscarriage and the wreckage that Stuart and I had become. And how much strength it takes to engage in the world again. I know what it feels like to lose something and to have to decide who I was going to be on the other side of it.

'There's a change in me. The hills, the sea, this island – it's gradually helping. I feel stronger within myself. I lost myself, but I've finally found who I was, who I am, and I'm holding on to her this time.' When she stops talking, she feels she's been speaking for an age.

'I'm glad you're holding on to her. I like her too, and I wouldn't want her to change.'

'You say that, but you don't know me, not really.'

'I know you've changed me. It shocks me how much…

how much… I love you. There it is. It's out in the open now, between us.'

Carissa lowers her eyes. She wasn't expecting that. His honesty strikes her; his words lift her heart. Reaching over, she takes his hand. 'Do you believe in miracles, Dimitrios?'

'Miracles?'

'Yes, you're my miracle. I've no idea how I would have coped with this without you.'

She looks perplexed.

'What is it?' he asks, a shadow of worry crossing his face.

'Do you think love just exists in the mind… in our heads?'

'No. It fills the heart.'

'Is that enough?'

He lightly squeezes her hand. 'We're in this together. I won't let him harm you.'

'Coming to Skiathos has never felt like running away; it feels like I've arrived. Stuart has not jeopardised that. He's made me realise I can love again. You're right; love concerns the heart. It consumes it. Stuart never understood that.'

Dimitrios draws a breath. 'We have the luxury of time. I'll wait for you. Whenever you're ready, I'll still be here, but first, we must deal with… him.'

CHAPTER TWENTY-ONE

THESSALY

Mainland Greece 1943

Over the next few days, Thomas prepared to leave the group of men he had shared so much with.

'I'll miss our sunrises,' Chris told Thomas as they shook hands.

'I've been thinking about that ladybird of yours and found myself looking for one of my own.'

'You don't need a ladybird to keep you safe, Thomas. You've proven many times you're capable of what's expected; that's why Eddie's chosen you. You're the best man for the job.'

'I hope I can repay his trust.'

'Trust is earned, and you've earned his trust many times, Thomas. I know we'll share a few more sunrises together.'

Thomas's eyes dropped to their hands and returned to Chris's eyes. He smiled. 'Until the next sunrise, then.'

. . .

Thomas, along with an *andarte* guide and James Hammond, a wireless operator, packed their stores onto two mules and set off early the next morning, travelling in the half-darkness.

Fanis Nakos was only twenty years old but told Thomas it felt he had already spent a lifetime serving the *andarte* cause. He was one of Aris's men who had left to assist Eddie in whatever manner he saw fit. Since Fanis had grown up in a village at the foot of the mountains on the southwest edge of the plains of Thessaly, he volunteered to be Thomas's guide.

When the breathtaking splendour of impeccable light and the violet flush of the lingering dawn finally announced the sun, it reminded Thomas of his sunrises with Chris with a melancholy that pounded his chest, so at odds with the peaceful serenity of the dawn

The weather was changing. A deep blue replaced the pale, bright-grey sky, so rich that Thomas could hardly imagine it ever raining again or feeling the wind brand his face with its bitter burn. A new, intense light had established itself, forcing Thomas to cover his eyes with the shade of a hand, as it immersed the land and sky in its glow.

They pushed on through trails carved out over decades by a thousand heavy footprints and burdened mules carrying goods. They covered fifteen, twenty miles a day, trudging over flat, and at times uneven, paths and rested the mules once or twice a day depending on their progress. Each evening as the molten sun slid beyond the horizon, they set up camp, sheltered by protective, shaded firs and soothed by the crackle of a fire that warmed them from the chill of the night.

They ate their supper, food brought with their provisions, and huddled around the fire, resting enervated limbs.

'There are limited patrols in this area. We should be safe to continue to travel to Porta in daylight hours,' Fanis said as he drank coffee.

'The village we're going to – do you know it well?' Thomas asked.

'It's not far from my home. Compared with most villages, Porta is large. Kapralos and his men have been billeted there for several weeks now. When we get there, we'll once again have the luxury of a warm bed and a roof over our heads.'

'Do you know this Kapralos?' Thomas asked.

'Only by reputation. He's feared and respected by his men in equal measure. That gives you a sense of the man. I've been told he hands out his own interpretation of justice and punishment, and it doesn't always follow the party line.'

'And is EAM aware of this?'

'They often turned a blind eye if it achieved the desired results.'

'Has it always been like this?'

'In the early days, it was similar too.'

'What do you mean?'

Fanis's eyes gleamed in the orange glow of the firelight. 'When we first infiltrated the countryside and mountains, most people were hesitant to risk their family's and village's safety for us. We were viewed as outsiders. We needed to build ties, trust, and support in these communities in order to gain reliable information, food, and, importantly, recruits.'

'And how did you do that?' Thomas asked.

'By offering the only currency we knew. We hunted

bandits, thieves, and collaborators. Such actions made the villages safe places once more.

'It put us in a position of strength and built an aura of approval from many, especially the youth who joined us.'

Fanis's eyes narrowed. 'At that time, Italian soldiers were responsible for theft, rape, violence, looting houses and torturing veterans who were suspected of hiding weapons and ammunition. The Greek state in the mountains was non-existent. There was no work, shops were looted and livestock stolen from farms. The government had failed to stop the famine and its consequences.

'In rural communities, there was a lack of law and order and an indifference to the state. It was in communities like these that villagers asked for our help in return for their support and allegiance to ELAS.'

'So, you obliged?'

'We suppressed criminality in the villages and the threat of the bandit gangs, if that's what you mean. It expanded our rule and ELAS's influence. Traitors and collaborators were also targeted, given beatings, lashed, branded, some even tortured and executed. Women who had sexual relationships with occupying troops were collaborators. Their punishment was harsh.'

His eyes were despairing, guilt and shame eclipsing their depths. 'I've seen women get their hair shorn, branded with knives and irons, even tortured and executed. The cruelty and brutality earned respect, but others saw our actions as no different from those we set out to punish.

He dropped his gaze. 'Most of the beatings and executions were conducted in the village square, attended by hundreds of onlookers. Bodies were left exposed in public areas with explanatory notes pinned to them, as a deterrent to others. It created fear and distrust. There were undoubtedly victims who were innocent, and that didn't always endear us to the villages' support, but the brutality they witnessed convinced most to comply in fear of being next.'

Thomas's eyebrows furrowed. 'Did you take part in any of this, Fanis?'

Fanis knew Thomas was watching his response. 'New recruits were expected to prove their worth. You could only hide for so long, and then your time would come to show your loyalty, your grit. I've not always been proud of the things I've done, but it's expected and needed.'

Fanis looked wistful. 'Carrying a gun changes men, and boys who think they're men. It gives them a sense of power over others, a self-confidence, a psychological boost that's not always used in the correct manner. In the hands of some, it has been used for personal gain, to the detriment of the very people they swore to protect.'

'What attracted you to enlist in ELAS?'

Fanis ran a hand over his beard. 'At first, I distributed leaflets to places like shops, houses, wherever I could. It was dangerous work, but it filled me with the belief that I was playing my part in the struggle against the occupation.

'Like many young men, I was determined to take up arms. It was a matter of honour, my patriotic duty to accept the hardships that would follow, and if need be, to stand as one against all the odds.'

Something in his face altered. 'It was difficult leaving my family. I didn't know what the future held. I'd be lying if I said I didn't have doubts. Like others, I was worried about reprisals to my family, or that I'd become like a bandit myself.'

Thomas raised an eyebrow, fixing Fanis with a curious stare. 'Were you recruited?'

'There were eight of us from my village. A family friend

had joined several months earlier. He was my intermediary and vouched for me. We travelled in pairs, with a sack each that contained our clothes, and we kept a few hundred yards apart. We didn't want to attract attention in the villages we passed through. We hid in a safe house for two days, where we were given a gun and some bullets before setting off again, but this time at night. We walked for a whole day, climbing higher into the mountains, resting at a monastery, enjoying our first proper meal and sleeping in a proper bed. It was there that we discovered that the ammunition we had been given was of the wrong type and calibre for our rifles. In the morning, we climbed higher into the mountains and finally met our band of thirty men, of whom only twelve had rifles.

'We took an oath of allegiance, swore on the Bible and took a new name and identity. I was no longer a civilian. I was now a fighter for freedom, who belonged to his brothers in arms. It was an incredible feeling. I felt like I could touch the sun. I belonged to a new family. With my new name and uniform I was given, it felt like a baptism. It was the new me.'

Fanis ran his hand over his beard. Thomas observed the gesture as a habit, a pacifier.

Fanis continued. 'It surprised me where other recruits came from. Some came from the towns and cities; their political views were well advanced and developed compared to most of us from the villages. Ideology was their main influence, the struggle for social change and a society based on socialist principles. Some called themselves Marxists. I'd no idea what that meant.' Fanis looked at Thomas. 'I do now. I understand such an ideology and have come to believe in the importance of equality and justice.'

'Worthwhile virtues to hold,' Thomas agreed. 'What about the others, like yourself?'

'In my first few days, I became friendly with men not too dissimilar to myself: Spiros and his brother Giorgos from a nearby village, and their cousin Nikolas. Amongst us there was a schoolteacher, several shepherds, a farmer and another, Thanasis, who was described by some as being a local gangster.'

'A diverse group of men. Did any of them know what they were signing up for?'

'No,' Fanis said, with conviction. 'We were ill-prepared for life in the mountains and quickly learned about the hardships we were expected to endure. The first few weeks were our real baptism. It came as a shock that not all the villages we visited were willing to assist us,' Fanis sighed. 'At first, we struggled with living outdoors when the weather was bad, the food and getting used to the lack of medicine and medical supplies. For most of us, this was our first time away from our homes and villages. We'd never been more than a few miles from our villages. The mountains were a strange and different world from the one we were used to. I'd never had to kill and then cook an animal, or know what herbs were poisonous or which ones could be eaten.'

He spoke in a measured tone. 'We quickly noticed which shepherds we could trust and which we couldn't. Sometimes, the ones we thought we could trust could easily turn and become our enemies. It was vital that we kept good relationships with the shepherds. They were the ones who knew the mountains like no other, every passage, fountain and cave that offered shelter. We often sought refuge and shelter in their huts, and they shared their food with us. Some were our eyes and ears, and they shared the intelligence they had gathered, advised us on how to survive in the open, how to avoid being tracked, how to live off the land, march at night as if it were daylight, and what were the best paths and hideaways. In return, we offered them protection from rustlers and villagers who were unfriendly towards them.'

He stared into the fire, and it crackled and popped in reply. 'We'd heard stories from other bands that shepherds had poisoned men, so we always made them drink and eat first before we did. At night, if we went into villages for provisions, we always asked for more food than we needed to give the illusion our numbers were more than they actually were.'

He scratched below his chin. 'At times, we went without food; we were hungry and wanted for the basic comforts of life, but what bore into my bones was the isolation; the loneliness and boredom. Life in the mountains was harsh. We spent long weeks without engaging the enemy, marching for days and nights on the meagre, ever-dwindling food we had left. When we entered a village, we were often met with suspicion and fear. We learned how to treat wounds, where to find edible herbs, suitable shelter and how to avoid enemy patrols.

'There were a lot of defections among the various bands. If it was known that one band had more food and guns than another, if they were stronger and could protect your family, that was a better prospect.'

'Is that why you're now with Aris?'

Fanis looked affronted. 'Our band joined with him, as did many others. Together we're stronger.'

As they spoke, James meticulously checked the wireless, transmitter, and batteries. He looked up from his work. 'He's talking a lot, but I don't understand a single word he's saying.'

'All you need to do is concentrate on getting a voice to come out of that wireless and understand their words.' Thomas turned to Fanis. 'It must have been hard at first and still is, I imagine.'

Fanis fixed him with a stare. 'We talk a lot about the lives we've left behind, our homes, our families; some even have wives and children.

'When I first joined, I had to prove myself to the more experienced fighters, who saw us new recruits as weak and like children. We had to be like them, become warriors. We took up smoking, grew beards and walked with the bravado of machismo and a rough character. There was no other choice if you wanted to survive.'

There was a pause. Fanis thought for a moment. 'I've become closer to nature, the trees, the earth; it's like I've become one with it. I've learnt to find the easiest passage through the mountains, to know the difference between the distant sound of a herd of animals or a nearby village. I can travel on walks through the night with the moon as my light and the shrubs and trees and land as my signposts. I can deal with the hunger and the marches. I'm now more agile and firmer; my steps are more purposeful. It becomes instinctive,' he said with certainty. 'Even in battle, I'm different. I'm more mature. I've grown physically, and in my thoughts and actions. I can look adversity in the eye and be confident in my responses. I know what it's like to see someone die, to kill and to suffer. I'm different from how I was when I first arrived in the mountains. I've grown over the months and years. Nothing can move me anymore. I've gone through a rite of passage. Reputations can only be made and sustained through pain, hardship and staring down fear with the face of courage.'

He gazed at Thomas and James, and then he burst into

a jovial, undulating, and wonderful laugh. Thomas's eyes grew wide in disbelief, his face a picture of surprise, but the sound was marvellous, infectious.

Thomas was getting the measure of the man sitting next to him. This proved comforting in its way. They were putting their safety, their lives in his hands. Thomas saw something in Fanis, a reflection of himself, perhaps. He found he was laughing too.

The next day, they reached the outskirts of a small village just as it was getting dark. The houses were stone-built, with thick, uneven walls, designed to keep warmth in during long winters. Heavy, curved clay tiles covered the roofs, the windows small and shuttered with wooden planks that rattled in the wind. Thomas counted twenty-one two-storey stone houses and one main track that ran the village length.

Fanis left Thomas and James to find them a bed for the night, just as the rain began. He appeared ten minutes later. Thomas didn't have to ask; disappointment sketched across Fanis's face.

'There's a building of sorts just up there, outside the village perimeter.' Fanis gestured with a hand.

When they reached the building, tied up the mules and went inside. With the use of their flashlights, they could see it was nothing but a simple stable and already occupied. A mule considered its visitors with disinterest, its snout deep inside a bucket.

'Bloody hell! It stinks in here, and that thing is covered in fleas,' James moaned, scratching his head.

'Well, you've two choices,' Thomas said. 'You either spend the night outside and get soaked, or sleep in here with the mule. I know what I'll be doing.'

James pulled his collar close to his throat and moved as far from the mule as he could. 'Either way, I'm not going to get much sleep.'

The stable was too small for the two mules, so they unloaded and moved their supplies inside.

At dawn, a man arrived from the village with bread, cheese and goat's milk.

'Did you sleep well?' the man enquired.

'Just a few bites, but I'll live,' Thomas smiled. 'Thank you for breakfast.'

'It was safer to sleep in the stable in case the Germans or security battalions visited the village. It would have been easier for you to evade capture, and we wouldn't have been under suspicion. No one would be arrested, and our homes would not be set on fire.'

'I understand. I'm just grateful for the roof over our heads.'

'At least it's stopped raining.'

'Thankfully, it has.'

That morning, they were met by ten *andartes* who were to escort them to Kapralos's headquarters at Porta.

It struck Thomas how young some of their escorts were, still in their teens, while others, slightly older, wore beards. One, Thomas assumed was their superior as he spoke with an air of authority. He introduced himself as Stathis Ioannidis. Thomas later discovered that Stathis was well-educated and hoped to emigrate to the United States after the war.

'How far is it to your headquarters?' Thomas asked him.

'It would normally take around five hours if we were walking without supplies and the weather was good.' He pointed to the mules loaded with provisions and equipment. 'Some paths are steep. The mules are used to such terrain, but it'll take at least eight hours if we don't have any setbacks.'

'Good. I want to speak with Kapralos once we arrive.'

'He's not in Porta. He's on a tour visiting villages and towns, recruiting fresh blood.'

Thomas tried not to show his frustration, but the acid tone of his voice gave him away. 'When will he be back?'

'Tomorrow, or the day after, possibly later.'

'He knows I'm coming?'

'He does, but he also has other business, day-to-day affairs that need his attention in the villages.'

'I see.' Thomas knew this referred to the ELAS-run courts, where Kapralos was the proprietary judge and jury.

When they arrived in Porta, Thomas was keen to contact Eddie. He requested Stathis's assistance, who guided them to a small clearing overlooking Porta, above the houses and buildings. After they secured the antenna and established the wireless set and battery connections, James proceeded to make contact, and they waited with bated breath. After several failed attempts, the mood among them became sombre. Thomas lit a cigarette to disguise his anguish and offered one to Stathis. It was only when Thomas stubbed it out that, to his delight, a faint voice emerged from the constant static and crackle.

'Thank God for that. I thought we would never get through,' James said, offering the mouthpiece to Thomas.

Thomas confirmed they had arrived safely at Porta and would begin their objectives as planned. He sought confirmation that the drop of supplies, explosives, ammunition and arms, as well as gold sovereigns would occur on schedule. This was confirmed just as the connection was lost.

Stathis nodded. 'As a form of currency, the drachma is virtually obsolete; it's worthless. When we get to Porta, you'll see what I mean. Drachma notes are used for toilet paper. It's good you have gold sovereigns. The price of one gold sovereign is worth around fifty million drachmas.

'People exchange goods for other goods. We have all become experts in bartering and negotiating how many cigarettes an egg is worth.'

'What about those who have nothing to exchange?'

'They go hungry. Their families will starve.'

They arrived at Porta, the *andarte's* headquarters, and were shown to a house where a family lived, the mother and father welcoming them with nervous smiles.

'It's only for tonight,' Stathis told Thomas. 'You have been allocated a house in the village, but…' He averted his eyes. 'The occupant is recently deceased. He is being buried tomorrow, so still needs the house for one more night. Kapralos didn't think you'd want to share it with him.'

They stepped through a wooden door and entered the low-ceilinged and dim interior. Thomas scanned the room that functioned as the kitchen, dining area, and living space. The smell of cooking, wood-smoke and a radiant warmth from a stone fireplace greeted them, along with the apprehensive glances of their hosts. Thomas wondered if they had been forced to accept them for the night or if, unlikely as it seemed, they had voluntarily agreed to share their home with strangers, especially British ones, knowing the risks such a decision could bring.

A heavy wooden table with a few mismatched chairs dominated the floor space. Simple functional cabinets and shelves held dishes, clay water jugs and copper cooking vessels stained and blackened with use.

The earthiness of the stone walls, the mix of dirt and stone underfoot, the faint mustiness of stored clothing and blankets, and the slight sourness of goat's cheese blended into a layered, distinctive scent. During the day, Thomas imagined shafts of daylight entering the small windows, now covered with wooden shutters, whereas at night, the only illumination came from the fire and a small oil lamp.

In a corner, Thomas noticed a low, wooden platform covered with woven blankets and a thin mattress that a young boy and girl sat on top of, hesitantly eyeing them.

Thomas clenched his jaw, his heart jolting as though someone had struck it.

He plunged his hand into his pocket and felt a length of fabric entwine through his fingers. He took a sharp intake of breath and turned his head away.

'You are a soldier; you will keep us safe.'

He pushed his hand through his hair.

'You are still alive,' the voice accused him.

He clasped his hands together to stifle their tremor.

In an instant, the fire sucked the air from the room, suffocating him, his stomach twisting.

Every fibre in his body urged him, begged him to run and escape, to be anywhere but inside this house.

He felt an insistent tug on his arm.

James leaned close to him. 'Thomas! Are you okay? You look ill.'

Thomas flinched.

It was the warmth of the fire, not the scorching and burning flames…

A dog barked outside, not shells pulverising walls…

The fire's heat and wood-smoke stung his eyes, not dust or smoke…

James's voice roused him, drawing him upwards, and he surfaced from the shadows, returning to the living.

A tight smile played on Thomas's lips; he hoped his hosts hadn't noticed his turn. 'I'm fine. I'm fine. I think I might be coming down with something; that's all. Nothing to worry about.'

James's nod lacked conviction.

The father insisted they give up their beds, but when Thomas found out they all slept in the one room on the second floor, he told him this would not be necessary.

They were offered eggs, clumps of bread, goat's cheese, and warm goat's milk for their supper, and they ate them wholeheartedly while warming themselves by the fire.

In gratitude, Thomas offered the father a small packet of ersatz coffee and a packet of Chelsea cigarettes, which the father was eager to smoke.

That night, as the family slept upstairs, Thomas and James wrapped themselves in blankets and lay on the floor. James fell asleep instantly. The fire had dwindled to glowing embers, casting elongated shadows across the worn stone floor. Around Thomas, the darkness clung to the edges of the simple furniture, obscuring any detail with its heaviness.

He tried to shelter in the blackness behind his eyelids, but the images were always insistent, playing like a movie reel, filling his head with colour and sound; a microcosm of detail that prowled every corner of his broken mind.

Thomas exhaled a long, dejected breath that crushed his chest with its weight. Then he rose and sat beside the fire, staring into its dying embers. He looked up to see a faint strip of light appear and fade at the top of the stairs, as a door gently opened and closed again. The father's bare feet padded towards Thomas, and he emerged from the darkness with a knowing smile. He pulled a stool towards the fire and sank onto it. It was then that Thomas noticed two small glasses and a bottle in his hand. The father poured a thimbleful of tsipouro into the two glasses.

He offered one to Thomas. 'Yamas.'

Thomas accepted it with a thankful nod and raised the glass. 'Yamas.'

He savoured the burn over his throat.

The father leaned forward, the stool creaking slightly as he added a small piece of kindling to the fire.

Both men sat huddled close to the growing warmth, their voices kept to hushed whispers that wouldn't carry far.

'I am Thimios.'

'Thomas.'

Thimios nodded.

'I didn't get a chance to properly thank you for allowing us to stay.'

'It is I who should thank you. It can't be easy coming to a foreign country and doing what you do without being part of an army that is not already here.'

'It's different, I'll give you that. This is not my first time in Greece,' Thomas explained how he had visited before the war and before that his studies in the classics.

'I've never met anyone who has been to a university; there's not much call for it around here.' Thimios grinned.

Thomas tried to smile, but his head still spun with the images he'd failed to dispel. Instead, he asked, 'What do you want to do after the war has finished?'

Thimios leaned forward, his weathered hands clasped together. His eyes drifted toward the small doorway leading to where his wife and the children slept. 'The children, they are my grandchildren. You must have wondered about that?'

'I just thought you had your children later in life.'

'I'm forty-eight. I'm still able to be of use in the fight for our country, but my grandchildren need a home; they need to feel safe and be looked after.'

Thimios stood and Thomas watched him move towards

the cabinet, returning with a framed photograph. Thimios sank onto the stool and held the frame near to the embers of the fire to show a young couple.

'My son on his wedding day.'

Thomas felt an indescribable pang knowing how this conversation would unfold. 'He looks so happy.'

'He was. We all were.'

'His wife is pretty.'

'Yes, she was.'

The past tense, Thomas thought.

'They were both killed, shot. About a year ago, along with twelve others, as a reprisal for a train being blown up on a railway line not far from here.'

This information threw him. 'I can't imagine how that must feel. I'm so sorry. I don't know what to say.'

'You don't have to say anything.'

Thomas knew words were futile. He took another sip of the tsipouro that warmed a path through his chest but failed to reach the knot in his stomach.

Thomas shifted slightly, his hand moving to touch the ribbon in his pocket. He stared at the fire.

Fragmented pieces, flashing pictures, on, off, on again.

The girl's high-pitched whistle through the gap in her front teeth. The flutter of her dress as she skipped inside. The look of absolute trust when she turned to look at him, as the door creaked and closed for the last time.

'Thomas.' Thimios watched him, concerned and thoughtful. 'You seem troubled.'

'Sorry, I was miles away,' Thomas said, deflecting.

'Memories can be comforting but also painful.'

'Something like that.' He finds himself unable to maintain the pretence. 'Seeing the children brought back…' His chest tightened. 'Sometimes, we make promises we can't always keep.' It wasn't a lie. He was a man bearing his own ghosts while beholding another's grief.

Thimios's expression doesn't change. 'We all know the risks.'

Thomas met his eyes. 'It doesn't sit easily with me, asking you to open your home to us.'

'I'm not that naïve. I know the risks, as does my wife. We understand what might come, but it's a choice I'm prepared to make. Everyone has sacrificed something in this war. The trick is believing that such a sacrifice will eventually be worth it.'

'Does that make it any easier?'

'No. But it makes it possible to continue.'

Thomas nods, grateful for the absolution he doesn't deserve. He desperately wants to tell Thimios about what happened, about how he wakes breathless and covered in sweat from dreams that visit him each night. He wants to confess that each new house he enters, each new family that shelters him, becomes another weight of guilt.

'Your Greek is excellent.' Thimios smiled. 'You learned it before the war?'

Thomas nodded, grateful for the momentary shift. 'At university. When studying Greek classics.'

'How old are you, Thomas?'

'I'm twenty-three.'

'My son was twenty-three.' Thimios stared into the fire. 'I never imagined my grandchildren would grow up in such times. Before all this, I had such different dreams for them.' He clasped his hands together. 'I would like them to attend school where they could learn to read and write and maybe one day go to a university in a city like Athens. Maria, my daughter, she's bright. Education is a passport out of the mountains, to make a decent and good life, where she can blossom and become a doctor or a lawyer. This is what I would hope for her, but in Greece it is the men that enjoy such occupations. Are there women doctors and lawyers in England?'

'Women go to university. These days it's not the norm, but I think it'll change; people will expect more and strive to achieve what wasn't possible before the war.'

'My grandson, even at his young age, is always making things. He likes to know how things work and is constantly asking questions. Maybe one day he too will go to university and become an engineer.'

'Wouldn't you like them to work closer to hand and stay in Porta?'

'Part of me would want that, but I know if they stayed here their lives wouldn't improve. They need to leave and experience life in the cities where there are more opportunities to improve their lives.'

'Is there a school here?'

'There was. The teacher died along with my son and his wife.'

A silence stretched between them, comfortable yet charged with an unspoken tension.

'I dream my grandchildren will grow without knowing hunger or fear. They'll sleep every night without wondering if soldiers will break down their door.' He gestured to the house around them. 'This house, like every other around here, has stood for generations. My great-grandfather built it with his own hands. I dream that my family and friends will gather here again for Easter, that we'll roast lamb and dance until dawn, that we'll be able to argue about politics without fear.'

Thomas felt reassured by Thimios's thoughtful demeanour, and said confidently, 'It will happen.'

Thimios gave a tired smile. 'It must. Otherwise, what are we fighting for?' He stared at Thomas. 'My niece Selena, she aspired to be a teacher before the war. Now she runs messages for the *andartes*.' Pride and concern fused in his expression. 'After the war, if she wants to, she should be a teacher, or if she wishes, she should marry and have children who I hope will grow up knowing only peace.'

'She sounds courageous.' Thomas smiled.

'She is, but she's doing what must be done. Starvation is an effective weapon, and by burning crops, villages, and killing animals, the Germans hope to crush the resistance.'

'Is there resentment towards the *andartes*?'

'It's the Germans – and before them the Italians – we hate. They are the ones responsible for the killing and destruction. The *andartes* are thought of differently. It's true, some may blame them, but never out loud. It's my experience that the majority do not. It is the everyday Greeks who suffer for the resistance, and many have paid for that loyalty with their lives.'

He reached for the bottle of tsipouro, pouring them each another drink. 'Before the war, we argued about everything – politics, religion, whose olives made the best oil. Now we are united in learning to survive.' He raised his glass slightly. 'After the war, I hope we can argue again about unimportant matters. That's my dream – a return to the luxury of trivial concerns.'

'To trivial concerns,' Thomas said, raising his glass.

As they sipped the strong spirit, Thimios added almost as an afterthought, 'And you, Thomas. What do you dream of after the war?'

'I've got several options, I suppose. I could work in academia. Lecture, write research papers, maybe write a book or two. A quiet and contained life.'

Thimios raised his glass. 'To a contained life, then.'

Thomas too, raised his glass and smiled. He couldn't disagree with that.

Stathis arrived the next morning and took Thomas and James to their new accommodation, the unfortunate previous occupant having moved to the church in the square to prepare for his funeral.

Unlike Thimios's home, this house enjoyed two upstairs bedrooms, and a small plot of land to its rear. The dimly lit room, illuminated only by an oil lamp, revealed a worn wooden floor, a few carved chairs, and a simple table.

When inspecting the wardrobes on the second floor, James found one room still contained the clothes of the deceased man, which Thomas said might work to their advantage at some point if the need to disguise themselves as villagers ever arose.

Their first visitor was Fanis, who Thomas thought had come to say his farewells before his return trip to Aris's headquarters. However, it seemed Aris had other plans for Fanis. A runner had arrived that morning informing Fanis of new orders. He was to stay in Porta and gather information on Kapralos's activities that may contravene ELAS's command, and its principles and protocols with civilians. The order from EAM headquarters in Athens necessitated Aris's immediate action.

'So, I'm to stay for the time being in Porta. Aris has asked, in order to create a smokescreen with the matter at hand, that I continue to act as your guide. The runner will return to Aris today with your answer.'

'I see no reason why not. In fact, the situation could benefit us as well. I would like eyes and ears on Kapralos myself, especially in matters we discuss, and agreements made. You can stay in this house with us; it's being our base while we remain in Porta.'

That afternoon, Thomas took a walk through the streets and environs of Porta. It felt strange being out in the open without the need to be vigilant. This was *andarte* Greece.

He walked among tightly clustered stone houses with terracotta tile roofs, built close together for protection against both harsh mountain weather and potential raids. The homes were constructed of local stone, with thick walls for insulation against winter cold and summer heat. The windows were small, especially on north-facing walls, probably to conserve heat, Thomas thought. Many of the houses had external staircases leading to the upper floors, with the ground floors being used for storage or keeping animals during the harsh winter months.

As he continued through the village, he soon became aware he was the centre of attention, as villagers came out to meet him, curious why a British officer was walking through their streets. Villagers greeted him with enthusiastic handshakes. One villager explained they had not seen a British officer since the British withdrew from Greece in 1941.

The clean air of the mountains was just a memory, as wood smoke from cooking fires hung in the air, mixing with boiling chickpeas, lentils, wild greens, bread made with whatever quality of grain could be obtained, and the occasional whiff of tobacco.

A labyrinthine network of narrow streets and winding paths swept out in all directions like cobblestone capillaries congregating around a central square with a simple Byzantine-style church and bell tower as its focal point. Nearby were the abandoned schoolhouse, several shops, and a small municipal building that swarmed with attending *andartes* noisily coming and going in various sized groups. Thomas had stumbled upon Kapralos's headquarters.

As he approached, the crowd of *andartes*, noting his distinctive uniform, parted and let him through under a flurry of curious stares.

He entered the building, the air inside dense with the smell of cigarettes and unwashed bodies. Along a narrow hallway in one room, several men stood huddled over maps spread over a large wooden table.

Stathis looked up, and recognising Thomas, struggled to hide his surprise. 'Lieutenant-Colonel!'

'Thomas will do just fine.'

'I thought you'd be settling into your new accommodation.'

'I like to get the lay of the land when I'm in a new location.'

Something caught his eye. The men around the table were all standing, except one, who sat on a chair, cross-legged, smoking a cigar. He placed his cigar in an ashtray, stood up and strode across the room.

'Lieutenant-Colonel. It's a pleasure to meet you. We've all heard about your heroics at the Gorgopotamos bridge. A magnificent victory.'

The man stretched out his hand. When Thomas shook it, the hand felt like sandpaper, the handshake strong and firm, as the man smiled widely, his yellow teeth in stark contrast to the full dark beard that fell to his chest. He had a thick thatch of black hair and deep walnut eyes.

'Forgive me. I've not introduced myself. I'm Kapralos.'

'Thomas.'

'I presume your accommodation is to your liking?'

'It is. Thank you.'

'Excellent. Welcome to my headquarters. My men have been billeted in this village for some time now. You'll find it an agreeable place to stay. Do you plan to stay long?'

'As long as is necessary.'

'Then we should get down to the details of your visit.'

Just then, a woman entered the room and pushed her way through the group of men. Kapralos's face burst into a wide smile. 'Selena, how are you today?'

'I'm well, thank you.'

Thomas's eyes slid to the woman. Her gaze travelled the room before settling on Thomas. Thomas took her in: the loose auburn hair that fell over slender shoulders, her oval eyes, dark and penetrating. His heart did a peculiar little sputter that knocked him off guard.

'And what have you got for me today?'

She raised her eyebrows.

'You can speak in front of the Lieutenant-Colonel. In fact, let us go upstairs; it'll be better if we speak up there.'

They climbed a tight staircase and then entered a room overlooking the square.

'Now that spring has arrived, there has been an increase in German patrols. Several trainloads of equipment and arms have also been sighted, and several larger towns are now in German and Italian hands.'

Kapralos nodded and gave a calm smile. He seemed pleased. 'As always, your information is helpful.' He turned to Thomas. 'It seems the Germans and Italians are preparing to move further into the plains of Thessaly. It's not unexpected. Over the winter they dug in; nothing moves when the snows come. Now, it will be different.'

'How do you know these things?' Thomas asked Selena.

Selena turned to Thomas. 'I have eyes and ears in many places.'

'Such as?'

'It's none of your business where I get my information from.'

'I think you'll find it is my business. Your eyes and ears and the information they gain are very much of interest to me. This is something you'll learn and learn quickly, if you know what's good for you.'

'I won't take orders from him.'

Kapralos raised a hand. 'Selena, he is my guest, and the uniform he wears means our enemy is his enemy too.'

'That may be so, but I will not betray the trust that others put in me, not for you, or for him, or the uniform he wears.' She fixed him with a stare, her eyes burning with contempt.

'My uncle spoke highly of you. For the life of me, I cannot see why.' And with that, she turned on her heels and strode briskly out of the room.

'Are all Greek women like this?' Thomas asked, half-amused but also disarmed.

Kapralos waved a dismissive hand. 'Fortunately, no, they're not.'

Thomas went to the window, viewing the square. As if feeling his stare, Selena looked up at him, her face clouded.

'That's good to know.'

'Underneath that armour there is a heart. I've seen it seldom, but it's there.'

After a moment, Thomas said, 'I'll get straight to the point. We know you've arrested Saraphis and his officers. You need to tell me where they are and release them.'

Kapralos exhaled loudly. 'I couldn't, even if I wanted to.

They've been sent to Roumeli, where they will be tried as collaborators to the enemy.'

Thomas wanted to know who authorised this.

'Karayioryis, the leader of EAM in Central Greece. I'm expecting him any day now.'

'And do you have evidence that supports your claim?'

'I do.'

'Then, tell me, or show me this evidence.'

'I can provide indisputable documentary evidence that Saraphis has been in contact with the Italians in Trikkala.'

'You expect me to believe this without seeing any proof.'

'It matters not to me whether you do or do not, but I will provide you with the documentation once Karayioryis arrives.'

Thomas eyed Kapralos. 'There's another concern I need to ask you about.'

Kapralos shrugged. 'Go on.'

'Your threats against Zervas are unwarranted and damaging to the resistance's efforts against our common enemy.'

'What do you expect me to do? Zervas is hiding Saraphis's men; they are collaborators. He's showing his true colours. I've heard Zervas has now changed his tune and favours the return of the King without asking the people first.'

'On that matter, you're mistaken. Zervas isn't sheltering these men you presume are traitors. In fact, they've returned to reform their bands in the Northen Pindus. I've also heard you've taken their arms, which now leaves them at a disadvantage.' Before Kapralos could protest, Thomas sighed. 'There's a far bigger game at play here. Middle East Command will soon begin increasing aircraft sorties to supply arms to the *andartes* but I guarantee you this: neither you nor any ELAS band will get so much as a sniff of those weapons and supplies if they attack Zervas or any other group operating in the mountains. Do I make myself clear?'

Kapralos grunted.

'There'll be a drop of arms and supplies in the next few days. I'd be grateful if you could lend me some of your men.'

'I will see to it. Stathis will also accompany you.'

Kapralos watched Thomas slip his hand inside his jacket and pull out a copy of the Military Agreement, setting it on the table. 'I would be happy to ask Middle East Command to supply you with weapons if, first, you return the weapons you took from Saraphis's men and sign this agreement and abide by it.'

Kapralos considered the demands and sighed. 'Some of Saraphis's men have willingly joined our ranks. Those who didn't were disarmed and sent back to their villages. Their guns have been distributed among my own men. Even if I wanted to, I couldn't take these weapons off them; it would be seen as a personal insult against each man who bore them. I will, however, read this Military Agreement of yours.'

Thomas narrowed his eyes. 'As you can see, it's written in Greek, so there should be no misunderstanding on your part.'

Kapralos examined the document. When he finished, he scratched his neck. 'There's nothing unreasonable in this.'

'Good, I'm glad we agree on something. Then, you'll sign it?'

'Ah! I said I agreed with it, but that's not to say I can sign it.'

A frown pulled at Thomas's eyebrows. 'Why not?'

'I need Aris's permission to do so. I take my orders from him.'

Thomas felt a rush of scorn for Kapralos but kept it at bay. 'He's not the one responsible for attacking Zervas's men; you are. Aris has told us it's you and you alone who are responsible for these offences. It's a disgrace.'

Kapralos rubbed his beard. 'Given the current situation and his immediate arrival, I'd need Karayioryis's authority to do so, and that means he too will have to agree with this Military Agreement.' There was a thoughtful silence. 'However, I'm prepared to abide by its principles.'

'And what does that mean?'

'If what you say about Zervas not sheltering any of Saraphis's men is true, I'll issue orders tomorrow morning to withdraw my bands from the areas adjoining Zervas.'

'Good.'

'Despite that, your preferential treatment of Zervas over ELAS in terms of material support is confusing to me. As I see it, all the supplies end up going to Zervas and not us, not ELAS. You even have your headquarters with Zervas; your officers are there. Why haven't we seen you before now? You must admit, it doesn't look good.'

Thomas's forehead wrinkled. 'Very well.'

Thomas briefed Kapralos on the events since the Gorgopotamos operation. The plan for only Chris and Themie to stay in Greece, with everyone else evacuating by submarine. He described their journey to the coast, the despatch of a liaison officer and supplies to Aris at the earliest opportunity, and their intention to launch a sabotage campaign across central Greece. He hoped it would be enough to persuade Kapralos of the actual truth of the matter. It seemed to have worked. Kapralos reassured Thomas that Saraphis's trial could not begin until several days after Karayioryis had arrived, to give him time to go over the documented evidence. This relieved Thomas's concerns for Saraphis's immediate safety, with the added benefit of knowing the opportunity would soon present itself with a leading figure of EAM to sign the Military Agreement.

It was a time of caution, and a time of waiting, and in the mountains and plains of Greece, time stretched at its own pace.

That evening, Thomas sent a radio message to Eddie explaining the situation with Kapralos, his satisfaction that Saraphis's immediate safety was secure, and finally, he would take full advantage of the opportunity to get Karayioryis to sign the Military Agreement.

James had gone to bed. Thomas's hands clenched around his cup as he brought it to his mouth and savoured the dark, strong coffee.

Fanis, with a resolute expression, told him that his education expanded after several months of living as an *andarte*. All his life, Fanis had never travelled five miles beyond his village. He knew nothing of the world, but now, every day, he experienced a new way of life, and his eyes continued to feast upon magnificent sights. He was still mesmerised by the mountains' heavenly majesty, the vivid and glorious colours of the landscape, and the strange and new customs of a country even now, though his own country was still foreign to him.

A small frown furrowed his forehead. 'Growing up in my village, I wasn't allowed to sit in the village café, drink or smoke, or play cards in front of my elders. It was expected that I'd follow in my father's footsteps and become a farmer.

Now I can smoke, grow a beard, curse, and speak my mind. I have a mission and ethos. I protect, I have a political mind, I am a fighter but also lead by example.'

He emphasised that education was the difference. 'We must guide and inform the common peasant and villager about our national struggle, about the holiness and justness of our calling. We're brave and courageous, but that means nothing without moral and personal honour. Sadly, there are many in our ranks who raid flocks, barns, and houses to show their manliness, gamble, get drunk, to endorse a reputation of being above and superior to those we've sworn an oath to protect.'

He informed Thomas that they marched at night and, to acquire food, they could request a sheep or two from a shepherd to feed his protectors.

'If that sheep has to be taken by threat, it's done with as little force as possible. If a village refuses to give us food and provisions when asked, a little persuasion is justified as we need food in order to protect those that we're requesting it from.'

He emphasised they lacked clothes, weapons, and medical supplies. 'Look around you. What do you see? A cobbled-together army of shoeless, rag-draped soldiers with their military breeches and the shirts their mothers made. We all have bits of British uniforms and captured Italian breeches and jackets, boots with holes and rifles and equipment that any museum would house. We have knives, captured Italian carbines, British and Greek rifles, and even nineteenth-century Turkish muskets.'

He recounted that in the winter months; thirty-two men suffered from frostbite and three died. Then there was the bronchitis, colds, malaria, and rheumatic fever. 'And that's not even mentioning the lice that crawl over us like a second layer of skin. We boil our clothes when we can, but it makes no difference; the lice return with a vengeance.'

Fanis voiced it was better to get shot and be killed than suffer a wound. 'Our medical provisions are pitiful. It's not uncommon for us to dress the wounds ourselves or rely on villagers for treatment.

'We can go through long periods of inactivity and then it's the boredom, the cold, the hunger, and disease that is the enemy, not the Germans. We can go from numbing monotony and very little action to suddenly being involved in intensive fighting, long marches with little sleep, food, and water, and at the mercy of the elements.'

He calculated he must have walked over eight hundred kilometres and stayed in over thirty villages and, if lucky, was given a bed for the night, but not all villages were as welcoming. They needed food, shelter and provisions and fodder for their pack animals. Even when they offered to pay, their money was not always wanted.

Fanis said that in the early days, they mainly engaged the enemy in small-scale ambushes, involving around thirty men. They brought the fight to the enemy using hit-and-run tactics, knowledge of the terrain, and their ability to move quickly with little to slow them down, and local help from villagers. It was through such engagement that they learned how to take cover, dress wounds in the field, and maintain equipment.

'It trained our senses,' he said. 'I would be lying if I said it didn't bring worry and also fear, but it was also exhilarating. I was never more acutely alive than in such moments. The thunder of machine guns, mortars and rifles sharpens the senses. It's a beautiful thing to conquer death because in doing so, as fighters, we also, in those moments, conquer life. You become hardened to the spectacle of death and regret the bullet you used but feel no remorse for the man you killed. In such moments, your mind becomes blind to suffering and death.

'We know the fate of our comrades who are taken prisoner by the Germans. They're tortured, and then, when the information is extracted or not, their fate is always the same – they're executed. We're more humane; we just kill them.'

'It's not always so,' Thomas corrected him. 'I've seen the end results of the orders given out by ELAS officers and local *kapetanios*. Axis soldiers, collaborationist militiamen, gendarmes and civilian collaborators all tortured. I've seen their mutilated and desecrated corpses.' He clenched his jaw. 'Once, I saw several bodies. The *andartes* had hacked off their balls and placed them in the mouths of their severed heads.'

Fanis shrugged. 'It's official ELAS policy to shoot any prisoner once information has been got. I've seen fellow *andartes* gain revenge for the death of a family member or comrade. My personal feelings may differ, but such things will not stop. The killing of prisoners is all too common. If only their level of political education were more widespread in our ranks – there seems to be more of an allegiance to killing than to ideology.'

'And that worries you?' Thomas asked.

He pulled a small booklet from his jacket pocket. Thomas glanced at the title, *O Antartis tou EAM-ELAS*.

'It's a how-to guide for aspiring *andarte* commanders. It contains subjects such as command and morale, tactics, and dealings with civilians. Most importantly, it emphasises what is of utmost importance and that is for each *andarte* to have the understanding of what he is fighting for, to foster an ideological determination through political education and a faith that leads to self-sacrifice for the holiness of our struggle. We are ready to die whenever our struggle demands it.

'No one can prepare you for what it's like; no level of training is ever going to come close to it. When it comes to war, you can try to imagine it, but imagining something and then experiencing it are two completely different things, two separate states of being. Of all people, you should know this, Thomas.'

Thomas nodded agreement. 'There were those that believed you needed an inner belief, a moral standpoint… king and country, democracy, defending a way of life, in order to acclimatise to the nature of war. These are the concepts they believe are worth dying for.

'There were others who would say war is just confusion, noise, disruption, and if experienced enough, you become immune to them all.'

'What about you, Thomas? Where do you stand on the matter?'

Surprised by the question, Thomas said, 'Patriotism was the common faith, and if you believed in its value, if you believed in it enough, it would save you. Unfortunately, war demands more than that.

'The common man in the street doesn't start wars; others do, with their beliefs, moral values, ideologies, hatred, and prejudice. He either survives them or dies in them. Others start wars, evil starts war, and death ends them.'

Thomas felt Fanis's eyes on him.

'What about the belief that you and I are doing the right thing?'

Thomas shrugged. 'For Greece, it's simple. It's about morality and the sovereignty of being a country. It calls for bravery and courage. I've seen bravery and courage. In war, these are not things that can be taught. They're qualities that are learned. Unfortunately, the currency of war is death. Unless you've witnessed death, it's difficult to contemplate the brutality and finality of war. Seeing a man torn to pieces by a shell or witnessing the mess to a head a bullet can inflict is a horror beyond comprehension and moral philosophy, especially when these things involve innocent civilians and children.'

Impulsively, his fingers traced the piece of ribbon in his pocket, and the familiar wave of guilt gushed through him.

'It can be brutal, uncompromising and personal.'

By now, the fire had burned to embers. The darkness was heavy and obscure, clinging to the edges of the furniture and walls.

Fanis regarded him questioningly. 'In days like these, Thomas, we all have our demons.'

CHAPTER TWENTY-TWO

DISPELLING SHADOWS

Skiathos 2007

Carissa stands at the old port, watching the sun spark on the pellucid water, where fish glide between the moored boats and pleasure craft. Dimitrios gestures towards a white and blue fishing boat, its paint fading in patches. 'It looks old, but the deck and inside are spotlessly clean, and she glides through the water like a dream.'

'Are you sure your uncle doesn't mind?' she asks.

'I told him we'd be gentle with the old lady; it's his pride and joy. You need a change of air and to get away for a while,' he says as he helps her aboard. Skopelos is just what you need.'

'The *Mama Mia* Island?'

'It's been there a long time before that film,' Dimitrios grins.

The thought of Stuart's shadow not being a constant

threat and the idea of the open sea is like a door swinging wide inside Carissa's chest.

They motor out of the old port, the island shrinking behind them, the pine-clad hills giving way to open sea. The engine's hum settles into a rhythm as the boat cuts across the gentle swell, gulls accompanying them, catching pockets of air and gliding in graceful flight alongside the boat.

'How long will it take to get there?'

'Just over an hour and we can stay as long as you like.'

The closer they come to Skopelos, the more it looks like a painting – clusters of whitewashed houses, topped in terracotta tiles, spilling down the hillside, their shutters painted sky-blue and earthly green and brown. Narrow lanes criss-cross between them, where bright bursts of bougainvillea climb walls and archways.

When they berth, it feels as if the world has adopted a placid and softer pace. As they ascend a lane, the brilliant whitewashed walls on either side are so close that they have to walk one behind the other. A cat watches them from a doorway as its tail flicks lazily at them.

'It's beautiful here,' Carissa gasps, brushing her fingertips over a plastered wall warm from the sun.

They don't rush, and soon they stop to look at a small church, its courtyard shaded by a single tree. The smell of cooking hangs in the air, reminding Carissa how hungry she is. As they wander, they come across trees stretching above a garden wall, their branches heavy with ripe lemons. Carissa feels the sun on her skin loosening the tension of the last few weeks.

The scent of charred fish from the grill pulls them towards a taverna tucked into a corner of the port. They take a table under a vine-covered trellis where boats sway in front of them as if they have fallen asleep. The waiter brings plates of grilled sardines, lemon wedges, and a salad gleaming with olive oil.

'You're quiet,' Carissa says as she picks at the salad.

Dimitrios takes a sip of water. 'There's something I want to tell you. It's been playing on my mind for some time now.'

Her stomach tightens. 'Alright.'

Dimitrios's eyes are forlorn, guilt and shame shading their depths. 'When I was married... as you do, I thought it would last forever. It didn't. What I'm trying to say is, it left its mark. I think for a while, I grieved for the life I thought I was going to have, if that's the right word.

'I came back to Skiathos to leave behind everything that reminded me of that time. Then, you appeared in my life. I felt caught between the past and the present. I wasn't looking for this; I wasn't ready. I didn't want to give myself fully to someone again, something that could fall apart again.'

She gazes at him, as though trying to fathom where this is going. 'What are you saying, Dimitrios?'

'I'm saying,' he tells her, 'Even with him here − especially with him here − my feelings can't be denied.' He reaches across the table and takes her hand. 'If you walked away from me and never came back, I know what that would do to me; it would kill me... Maybe it took him being here for me to see how much you mean to me.'

She feels oddly betrayed, and she can hardly breathe. 'You're with me because of Stuart?'

Dimitrios shakes his head, his hand tightening around hers. 'No. It's not like that. That's not what I'm saying.'

She frowns as she thinks. 'Then what *are* you saying?'

'I want to be with you, not because he wants to take you away from me, but because I love you.'

'You're sure?' She feels his fingers warm around hers.

Exasperated and relieved, he tells her, 'Carissa, listen to me. I've never been surer about anything in my life. I'm telling you this because I don't want there to be any secrets between us.'

There is a brief silence between them.

'Then, what's her name?'

He looks at her confused.

'Your ex-wife.'

'Oh! Savina.'

'It's a nice name.'

'In the end, that was all that was nice about her.'

As the boat carried them back, Skiathos came back into view – its familiar outline no longer just a place; already, it felt like home to her. Somewhere between what they'd been and what they were becoming, Carissa realised Stuart's shadow might still follow them, but it no longer defined them or stood between them.

CHAPTER TWENTY-THREE

AN ILLUSTRATION OF BEAUTY

Mainland Greece 1942

Thomas made it his business to speak with as many *andarte* officers and leaders that passed through the town. He made the British policy clear: their willingness to arm every band who would fight the common enemy and not Greek against Greek.

Many asked the same question. 'Then why does not Zervas publish his political aims? How can we trust such a man?'

Thomas was at pains to emphasise Zervas had agreed to forsake all notions of politics in favour of joining up with all the varying factions and organisations that made up the *andarte* bands.

Thomas also spoke with people who were not members of the *andarte* organisations. They had a different take on things.

Many desired Zervas's presence in Thessaly, fearing

EAM and ELAS, with some predicting that a liberated Greece would allow for true political freedom after the war.

After one particular meeting with a group of villagers, Thomas sat outside a café to clear his head and enjoy the sun's warmth when he noticed Selena walking by.

She turned her head away from him.

He took a deep breath. 'Selena, how are you?'

She shrugged. 'I was fine, but my mood has suddenly changed.'

'Let me buy you a coffee or some lunch; it's the least I can do after the other day,' Thomas said, lightening the atmosphere with a change of subject.

'I'm not hungry.'

'A drink? It's my way of offering an apology.'

'And if I won't accept your apology.'

'A truce then? Life's too short to hold grudges. I'm trying to be nice.' She intrigued him, and he couldn't take his eyes off her.

Her eyes moved towards him. 'You weren't very polite the last time we talked.'

He had rattled her again. 'You're right. I wasn't, and I need to make that right. If you'll give me the chance.'

She smiled weakly, but it was a smile. He'd broken the ice between them, and even if she continued to walk by him, he'd take that as a win, a small one, but he could work on it. He didn't know what to expect from her, but he needed to find out.

She narrowed her eyes, contemplating her decision.

'Very well. I'll have a coffee,' she said as she slipped into the chair opposite.

He breathes a small breath of victory. 'Are you sure you won't have lunch? I was just about to order some food. It's been a while since I've been able to eat in a café.' Thomas smiled. 'There's not much call for it in the mountains.'

'I can't imagine there is.'

He took out a cigarette packet from his pocket and, extracting a cigarette, offered it to her.

She raised a hand. 'I don't smoke.'

'Do you mind if I do?'

She shrugged. 'You can do what you like.'

Thomas lit a cigarette.

When a waiter appeared, he ordered a coffee and an omelette.

His eyes scanned her face. 'Your uncle Thimios told me you want to be a teacher after the war.'

'He did, did he? Why was I the subject of your conversation?'

Thomas shrugged. 'I can't remember. I must have asked him about his family.'

She folded her arms. 'That was my train of thought before we were occupied, when we had a future; now I'm not so sure.'

'Teaching is a noble profession. After the war, there'll be a need to teach children to write and read.'

'There will be, but a lot must change. We can't just go back to how things were. There would be no future if that were the case.'

'Then it needs people like you to make that future happen.'

'What do you know about me? You don't know me, just as I don't know you.'

'You're right, I don't.' His forehead furrowed. 'It was insensitive of me to even assume that. I'm sorry.'

She seemed to relax a little. 'I think I need to make an apology too.'

'Then, in my book, that makes us even. Maybe we can start again?'

The waiter brought coffee and Thomas's omelette.

'You haven't always been in the army. What did you do before the war?'

He put out his cigarette. 'It feels like another life. I did what most young men of my kind were expected to do; I went to university.'

'What did you study?'

'Greek classics.'

'So, you've always had an interest in Greece?'

'I suppose I have.'

'I haven't met many non-Greeks who can speak our language as well as you.'

'It was a requirement for the job.'

'Coming here?'

He nodded.

'You had no desire to be a soldier… an officer.'

'It wasn't part of the plan. No.'

'Yet, here you are. You must be good at it. You're all on your own without the protection of your comrades.'

'I follow orders. It's as simple as that.'

'Did you do anything before you went to university?'

'I had a privileged upbringing. My life was mapped out for me in that regard. There was no expectation of earning a living until after my education.'

'Your life… it could almost be like you lived on a different planet. Such is the difference between us. I always wanted to visit Athens; it too is a completely different world from this one. To walk down a street with palatial buildings that people live in; to have an abundance of shops and restaurants and theatres was a dream of mine.'

'It doesn't have to be a dream. One day, you'll be able to go to Athens, even live there and train to be a teacher.'

'Dreams don't come true. This is real. This is life. Until we are free from occupation, dreaming is also the enemy. It blurs your focus with its false prophecies and takes your eye off what is real, even if that reality is hell.'

'There can always be optimism, even in the face of such adversity.'

'You're fortunate. Your upbringing allows you to think in this way. Everyone has lost someone in this war, be that a life, a loved one, a child, their health or even their mind. Suffering consumes the air we breathe; it permeates everything; it suffocates some and crushes others, yet there are those that use it as a strength; it empowers them. It fuels extraordinary acts. Some risk their families for complete strangers, putting them in danger for the safety of others. Some leave behind the only life they have known, family, friends, for an existence in the mountains that cannot promise they will live to see another day. Even seemingly insignificant acts of resistance, repeated endlessly, become incredibly powerful, ultimately achieving remarkable things.'

'Together you are stronger.'

'Yes, we are.'

'That's what I've been trying to get over to Kapralos and the others. Leave the politics for another day; by fighting amongst themselves, they're doing the job of the Italians and the Germans. Unless they work together, there won't be a free Greece.'

'You mean unless we do what the British demand.'

She couldn't look at him. His discernment scoured her with anger, not because she disagreed with him; she knew his words spoke the truth.

'You're annoyed with me. It seems I'm making a habit of it. I apologise. I'm sorry.'

'Don't be. You're right. Greece should come first, nothing else. But sadly, it won't.'

Selena ran her hand through her hair. There was something about him. He was not like other men, the men she knew. When he looked at her, she was not just a woman; she was more than that, and she liked the way it made her feel.

'You haven't touched your coffee.'

'And you've eaten all your lunch. That's it in a nutshell, isn't it?' Selena said.

She regretted it instantly.

Just then, Stathis appeared from Kapralos's headquarters with two other *andartes*. He glared at Selena as he passed her. Thomas noticed Stathis's grimace. Stathis was barely disguising his contempt as he mumbled incoherently.

'What was that all about?' Thomas asked.

'It was for my benefit. I think he disapproves of us sitting together.'

Across from them, a crowd was gathering. Two young men, no more than sixteen years of age, both stripped to the waist, faced each other, as vociferous voices of encouragement rose from the circle that now formed around them. It distracted Thomas from enquiring further about Stathis.

'What's going on?' Thomas asked, alarmed.

'Don't worry. It's a wrestling competition. Several ELAS bands arrived a few days ago.'

'Then it's just harmless sport.'

'It is. But it also has another function. It's a way for the wrestlers to prove their masculinity, through physical prowess and courage in front of the other men.'

'Is there a hidden reason behind everything an *andarte* does?'

Selena smiled. 'It's a way for new recruits to show their fighting skills; it's also about acceptance. The winner will be viewed differently by his fellow *andartes*. He will no longer be a boy; he will be viewed as a man. He will have earned respect among his fellow men, and that is everything. These wrestling competitions between ELAS bands are common practice. They are encouraged. It builds comradeship and togetherness. It also breaks the monotony and boredom of being in a place like this.'

The euphoria that rose from the onlookers reminded Thomas of the boxing matches he watched when at university. 'It's certainly stirring a reaction from the audience.'

Selena's eyes sparkled as she watched the wrestling match. He could no longer hear the elation of the crowd as his eyes drifted over her face. She was beautiful. He wanted to know her more intimately. Even if it was just for the short time his work in the town allowed. He didn't want to be known as a stranger to her.

She turned to look at him as a loud cheer rose for the victor. 'Wasn't that enthralling?'

Thomas caught her eye. 'Yes, it was.'

That night, he lay awake as the house slept, the candle burning low, soon to die in its holder. Its diminishing orange light cast flickering shadows on the wall, accentuating a crack in the cream-coloured surface that stretched in front of him like the winding curves and jagged turns of a river.

He raised his eyes from the wall and across the ceiling. His mind raced. Selena's words were like notes from a piano played on her voice, creating chords that formed sentences, each a captivating symphony that enveloped and flooded him with its melody. He wanted more. He needed more, like an audience demanding an encore.

This shouldn't have happened, yet it did – despite its improbability – and it filled him with dread. Still, he couldn't suppress his smile or thoughts of her. His heart had been empty for a long time; he'd forgotten what it felt like to beat with possibility and desire.

The following morning, as he walked, he moved briskly and found Selena was never far from his thoughts. He marvelled at how extraordinary this made him feel. The sharp tang of goats and sheep grew stronger, reminding him of the shepherds and mountain trails that were, until recently, ever-present realities in his world. And as in that world, in his new existence the distinctive earthliness of wild herbs drifted from the nearby slopes, sweetened by the scent of blossoming fruit trees and wildflowers, with undertones of pine and cypress from the surrounding forests.

A breeze ruffled the trees; its warmth was a welcome relief after the months of snow, rain, and cold wind. Thomas was heading to the square, able to walk in just a shirt and luxuriate in the simple pleasure of rolling his sleeves up his arms. The houses had opened their shutters and doors lay ajar, where women sat outside, peeling and chopping potatoes and cabbage, and catching up on village gossip. *Andartes* milled around or sat in groups, displaying their weapons like trophies. Thomas could feel their eyes on him.

He walked with a watchfulness, a constant vigilance, alert to the possibility that around him his world could change in an instant – the sky and air raining horror and death, the ground cracking and shaking beneath his feet. He looked up towards the sky and instinctively checked the ribbon was still in his pocket.

Ahead, others sat outside the café, smoking and talking around tables, taking advantage of the welcome change in the weather.

Several children, barefooted, kicked and threw a ball, their shrieks of joy startling him.

'You are a soldier; you will keep us safe.'

His head pounded, and his heart raced. He swallowed back the anguish that gripped his throat. And then he saw her. The look that greeted him was warm and calming, like the sun on his face. Her hair was lit from behind as she looked up at him, the surface of her cheeks high and dramatic.

He stood before her, not wanting to sit until invited, his eyes skipping the tops of her shoulders.

'Thomas, or should I call you by your rank?' she teased him.

He loved the way his name rolled off her tongue.

'Everyone calls me Thomas.'

'Then, Thomas it is. Are you going to stand there all day… Thomas?'

He pulled out a chair and sat opposite her. 'Back at headquarters, no one uses their rank; we just use our first names, or the name we like to be known as.'

'What do you mean? Is it like the *andartes*, they change their names when they join up to fight?'

'No, it's not like that. People often shorten their names.

'Instead of Thomas. I could call myself Tom, Tommy, and if I were Scottish, I could be called Tam.'

Selena smiled. 'I prefer Thomas.'

'I do, too.'

'You look tired. When did you last have a proper sleep?'

'I'm not a good sleeper.'

'Too many bad dreams?'

'I've enough nightmares to deal with when I'm awake, never mind when I'm asleep.'

'Your eyes tell a different story.'

'They do?'

'How long have you been in Greece?'

'A few months now.'

'It must be difficult, living the way you've done, in the mountains and forests, relying on the charity of others and not knowing if one is a friend or foe, constantly alert with the threat of being discovered.'

'We did, for a while. In the beginning, food and shelter were scares. It wasn't all bad. When supplies were dropped, it felt we lived like kings for a few days.'

She raised an eyebrow. 'I was told you lived in a cave. In the middle of winter too.'

Thomas reminisced with a grin. 'That's right. In the hills, the winter was harsh. I've never seen snow like it.'

He hesitated and swallowed his words. He'd like nothing better than to tell her about the past few months like any normal person would do, but he could not indulge in such carefree conversation. Thomas hated the restrictions placed upon him, especially because of the feelings that had surfaced. They had taken him by surprise. He had only known her a few days, yet every time they met, his heart raced, and he had to stop himself from reaching out to touch her hair, to trace a finger along her cheek and satisfy his longing to brush her lips with his own.

He looked down at his hands.

'Are you feeling okay, Thomas?' She looked at him over

her coffee and could see anxiety etched in the creases of his brow. 'You look sad.'

He forced a smile. 'It's been a difficult few days, and I'm afraid there's probably more to come.' He hated lying to her about how he felt, but at least there was some truth in his words.

He attempted to change the flow of their conversation. 'Do ELAS enjoy the support of the villages and towns in Thessaly?'

'There are obviously those that do, but not everyone. On the surface it may be so, but in private, people speak their minds without the threat of violence or intimidation.'

'That seems to be a common theme I've been hearing.'

'Allegiances vary, there're those who support Zervas and republicanism, and others who are the royalists.'

'When we first arrived, we knew nothing about Greek politics in the mountains. Underneath the veneer of EAM, there's a communist agenda. That much is clear, and they're waiting out their time. The Republicans and royalists are waiting too. The British will have a part to play, and no doubt use their influence by force if necessary to steer it to meet their political agenda. The future for Greece is uncertain, but what is certain is that there will be more bloodshed before there's a lasting peace.'

She looked thoughtful. 'Sadly, I think you're right. Will you still be here to see it through?'

'I don't know, but what is certain is there're no winners in a civil war; everyone loses something.' He regarded her carefully. 'What about you, Selena? Who has your heart? The communists, the republicans, or the royalists?'

She looked down at her hands and then, lifting her eyes to him, she said, 'You do. You've been taking it piece by piece.'

His breath caught in his chest, dazed by her wholly unexpected response. He opened his mouth as if to speak, but she had stolen his words. The effect she had on him was extraordinary.

Her face broke into a smile, and he thought it the most astonishing illustration of beauty he had ever seen.

CHAPTER TWENTY-FOUR

WATCHING

Skiathos 2007

As she reaches the last step to her apartment, the drone of a scooter, somewhere in the warren of alleyways behind her, punctures the silence around. The last few days have been uneventful, and she's lapsed into the comforting thought that maybe the worst has happened. Until her eyes snag the perfectly folded sheet of paper weighed down by a pebble against her door.

A tide of panic crashes over her, and she freezes, startled. He could almost be standing in front of her.

Carissa's first thought is to crumple the note without reading it.

A contempt for the words he'd written would feel a sort of victory, erasing his presence from her. But she knows she won't.

The pull is too strong.

She will confront it.

She will confront him.

Carissa bends and swipes the note from under the pebble that scuttles beneath the iron railing and tumbles towards the ground below.

Once inside her apartment, she sits back on the sofa, shuts her eyes, and takes a deep breath before opening them again. She forces them to fall upon the distinctive handwriting.

She doesn't see the words at first, just the formation, the spacing, the slant, curves, and size of each individual letter.

The script flows across the page in deliberate and confident sweeping strokes. It suggests someone who is enjoying the writing, taking pleasure from it, his style elegant, a far cry from her own hurried scrawl.

Yet there's something hurried about certain words that pop like neon lights: *new friend* and *getting on well*, where he seems to have applied more pressure to the pen.

She tries to steady her racing heart and give the note her full attention.

I saw you the other day with him at that trendy place where all the young people seem to go. You looked more than just friends. It didn't take you long, did it? There was a strained look about you. Are you getting enough sleep? I hope so.

Do you remember when you had the flu and couldn't leave the flat, and I made you ginger tea every morning and looked after you. That was love. You used to see it too. I wish you still did.
I wouldn't still feel this way if it wasn't real. I know you feel this way too. Stop pretending. You made me better. And then you left.
What does that make me now?
You said you felt safest when I held your hand. You used those exact words once, outside the Christmas market near George Street.
Remember?

I think about that moment every time I imagine you with him. Do you hold his hand the same way? Does he even notice?
I always did.
The blue dress you wore looked beautiful on you. It's the one I bought you for your last birthday, remember? I'm glad you still wear it. You were so happy that day. That's all I want — for you to be happy. You can only be happy with me. Deep down you know that.

You are always in my thoughts. S.

He was there. Somewhere. Watching.

The note shakes in her hand. She can't hold it a second longer and lets it drop, fluttering to the floor.

The blue dress. It is a simple sundress, cornflower blue with tiny white flowers embroidered around the neckline. He had bought it for her twenty-seventh birthday, along with matching sandals.

She remembers the birthday dinner at Gaucho, in St Andrew Square in Edinburgh, how pleased he'd been with his choice, how he'd watched her face as she opened each carefully wrapped box. She'd felt loved, understood, cherished. How the memory now curdles in her stomach.

Her hands shake so badly, she can hardly hold the phone.

'There's another note!'

She is relieved to hear Dimitrios' voice.

'I'm coming over.'

When Dimitrios arrives, Carissa rushes to him. Her breath catches in her throat. 'Stuart's been watching us. He saw us at Las Ramblas. He probably saw you coming here too. God! I feel like he's suffocating me.' She massages her temple with her fingers, as if doing so will erase him from her thoughts. 'What if he's taken photographs of us together? Just thinking about it makes my skin crawl.'

'This is what he wants. He wants you to feel this way. In his own sick mind, he's punishing you and probably enjoying it.' Dimitrios looks around the room. 'Where's the note?'

She gestures towards the table and slumps onto the sofa. A thought strikes her. 'What if he never leaves? Does he think that because of this I'll go back with him to Edinburgh, and we can start again, like none of this has happened?

Dimitrios lifts his eyes from the note and turns to Carissa. 'He knows exactly what he's doing. On the surface, he's concerned about you, but he's chipping away at you. There's a threatening tone, and that's what he's really doing; that's his purpose. He's intimidating you. He's trying to show his possessiveness was really just affection.

'It's disguised as heartbreak, but it's a guilt trip. He's trying to pressure you into contacting him. He's waiting his time.'

Carissa drags her fingertips through her hair. 'For what?' A feeling of helplessness overtakes her. 'He knows where I live. He's been standing outside my front door, posting his bloody notes like a psycho postman.'

'I don't know. I wish I did. He'll show us soon enough. He can't hide forever. No one's that invisible, especially here.' Dimitrios sits beside her. He keeps his voice steady. 'Let's print some copies of that photo of him you showed me, get a few copies made, and hand it out. I know a lot of restaurant owners and hotel managers. We can make him visible. We need to find out where he's staying. Turn the tables. Confront him. Fight back.'

'Yes. We could do that. I'm tired of being the victim. Let's give him some of his own medicine.'

'We need to find out where he's staying first.'

She places her finger against her forehead.

'Are you alright?'

'The start of a headache. I haven't drunk enough water today.' Carissa swallows. She can barely move, scarcely breathe. She clasps her hands together. 'I don't want to be alone tonight.'

He cups her face between both palms and lightly kisses her forehead. 'I'll stay as long as you want.'

Her eyes glance up at his, and she holds them there. She lifts her hand and brushes a fingertip against his wrist.

'Stay the night.'

He bends towards her, resting his forehead on hers. 'If that's what you want.'

She nods, her head still between his hands.

He draws in a long breath. 'I'll sleep here, then. On the sofa.'

She hesitates. 'That's not what I meant.'

Her words steal his breath for a moment. 'That's what I'd hoped. Are you sure?'

'Completely.'

Incapable of controlling himself, his mouth finds hers, and she makes no effort to release herself from him.

CHAPTER TWENTY-FIVE

CAUGHT IN THE WEIGHT OF WORDS

Mainland Greece 1942

I n the black attire common among the village's elderly women, she tended to a garden behind a stone house, her back curved, but despite her age, her movements were decisive. There was something about her meticulous attention to each plant that lured him in, like a moth to a flame.

She heard his boots scuff the dirt as he walked towards her.

'Good morning. You've got a lot of vegetables in there. I'm impressed,' Thomas offered as he placed a hand on the wall that bordered a small and tidy garden.

She tilted her head a little, acknowledging his command of Greek. 'I've had a lot of practice. I enjoy it too, and it stops the bones from seizing up.' The fragmented veins on her cheeks spread out like red ink. 'Are you a gardener yourself?'

'I wouldn't call myself that, no. I know my carrots from

my courgettes, but that's about it. You move like a woman half your age.'

'I could take that as a compliment, but you don't know how old I am.'

'My mother always told me it was rude to ask a woman her age.'

'Especially one so old?'

'Now you're mixing my words.'

'I'm sorry.' She gave him a gleaming sideways look and tilted her head in a quizzical half-smile. 'If you must know, I'm eighty-two.'

'I'd never have thought that.'

'In fact, I'll be eighty-three in two days' time.'

'Happy birthday when it comes.'

'I see by your uniform, you're British.'

Thomas nodded.

'I noticed you when you first arrived. My eyes are not as sharp as they used to be, but, being in my garden most days, there's not much I miss.'

'I suppose not.'

'It's like reading a newspaper, if we had any. I get to keep up with all the comings and goings in the village. People pass by and we chat. It's important to talk with people, you know. At my age, most of my friends have permanently left the village, and not by the road out of here, if you know what I mean.'

Thomas smiled. 'I do.'

'It's good for the soul and the mind to talk to others. There's not a day that goes by that I've not spoken with someone. Being lonely would be like an illness to me. It's not in my nature to be sick.'

'Do you have family in the village?'

'Not anymore. I've been a widow for twenty years. My

children left when they were old enough to do so. Don't get me wrong; they visit when they can. I have six grandchildren, and three great-grandchildren.'

She spoke while continuing to tend to her garden. 'One of my grandsons was like you; he was a soldier. He fought the Italians in Albania. I tried not to have favourites, but he was mine. I had a lot to do with him when he was younger. His mother wasn't well.' She pointed at her head. 'She had to go to hospital and…well, she spent more time in hospital than with her son. And his father – he was a waste of space, a drunk, and a thief. He left to find work in the towns and never returned. Good riddance, was all I could say. He wasn't missed. He probably drank himself into an early grave.'

'So, you brought up your grandchild on your own?'

'Like he was my son.'

'Where is he now?'

'When he didn't return, I was told he'd died. They called it a hero's death. I'd rather he were alive and with me today than being called a hero and cold in the ground. For a year, I did nothing but grieve. I let my garden die. I stopped making bread. I spoke hardly to anyone. In some ways, I thought the pain I was going through honoured his death.'

'I'm sorry.'

'I blamed myself. I'd let him down. I was the one who had looked after him from when he was a boy, and as a man, when he went to the army, I could no longer be there for him. It ate at me. It ruptured me. My pain was my punishment.'

Her words swarmed towards him.

Thomas looked away. He swallowed and took a deep breath, his throat tightening. The memories surged forward:

the girl's red dress, the boy's cap, the mother's grateful smile, the girl's words, '*You are a soldier; you will keep us safe.*'

She straightened slowly, wiping earth from her hands. 'But guilt without purpose is like sprinkling salt in the soil; nothing will grow from it, it will remain arid, only the weeds will prevail.'

She took a few steps forward and cocked her head. 'Are you alright?'

He plunged a hand into his pocket; the soft material soothed over his fingers as he traced the piece of ribbon.

Thomas's stomach churned. He hesitated, considering how to answer. 'Your words reminded me of someone, some other place,' he said without thinking.

She reached out and touched his arm, her gesture so maternal it felt like she had wrapped a blanket around him.

With a crease between her eyebrows, she said, 'You carry something; I can see that. I can also see how you try to protect yourself from it.'

There was a glow about her that was dismantling the barricades he'd built around himself. Thomas gasped between breaths.

She regarded him. 'When it rains, water always falls from the mountains; you can't stop it. What has happened, whatever it was, cannot be undone.'

Thomas kneaded his fingers into his bloodshot eyes. Embarrassed with himself, he pressed his tears away.

'I'm sorry,' he said, startled by his reaction. 'I don't normally do this. I just feel this incredible guilt. It crushes me every day.'

She considered him with eyes that seemed to read every line on his face. 'Whatever makes you feel this – your guilt, your shame, whatever it is – it can become something else, but only if you let it.'

'What do you mean?'

She turned back to her garden. 'Look around you. My garden grows again. Not because I forgot my grandson, but because I learned to use my grief. I can't eat all the vegetables that grow here. Each vegetable, each herb that I grow, feeds others in the village. Each flower that sprouts in colour honours my grandson's memory not with pain, but with life. The dead don't need our suffering, but the living need us,' she said softly.

Her words assailed him like physical blows, crumbling his internally constructed walls, and he realised he was shaking. His knees weakened. He slumped onto the low stone wall of the garden and took the ribbon from his pocket, wrapping it around his hand. He pressed it against his lips. The old woman continued tending her garden, giving him space while remaining present. Thomas watched her, and as he rubbed his hand against his jaw, his breath came easier. He thought of the young girl's most precious possession, her doll, and he stared at the ribbon in his hand, the ribbon he needed to touch, to keep safe. He thought of how she trusted him. Could he honour that trust, just as the old woman had found a way to honour her grandson? He pressed the ribbon to his chest, the ache wrenching his heart.

Several days passed, and still Thomas received no news of Karayioryis's arrival. One morning after breakfast, Thomas's patience ran out.

'I can't wait another day longer,' he said, extinguishing his cigarette with forceful stabs into the ashtray.

James slurped his coffee. 'What are you going to do?'

'Visit Kapralos unannounced and settle this matter once and for all.'

'Do you want me to come with you?'

'No, make sure we have radio contact with Eddie on my return. If I can't get a satisfactory explanation from Kapralos regarding this whole charade, then decisive action needs to be considered. I'll need to update Eddie.'

With purposeful strides, Thomas reached the square, and as he moved through the usual assembly of *andartes*, he detected a change in their mood. Instead of their usual relaxed demeanour, a distinctive air of activity and watchfulness swarmed around them.

Someone escorted him into Kapralos's headquarters and showed him to the upstairs room. Kapralos, sucking on his customary cigar, stretched out his hand in greeting.

'Thomas, we were just talking about you.'

Standing next to Kapralos, a man in civilian clothes, with a bushy beard and dusty shoes smiled at him.

'Karayioryis has just arrived this morning; I was about to send someone to get you.'

Karayioryis shook Thomas's hand with a firm grip. 'I'm sorry it has taken me so long to get here. The vehicle I was travelling in broke down, and I had to continue the rest of my journey on foot. After hearing of your arrival, I was eager to get here as soon as I could.'

'It's good to see you,' Thomas said.

'Let's sit.' Kapralos motioned to several cups and a pot sitting on a table. 'Some coffee?'

'Not for me,' Thomas said, hearing a clock ticking in the room that fuelled his impatience to discuss the Saraphis situation.

Karayioryis raised his hand, suggesting an apology, which his tone of voice confirmed. 'I understand you're eager to get this business with Saraphis sorted out, as am I. It's an unfortunate situation.'

'And one that's wholly misinformed.' Thomas voiced his indignation at the unacceptable activities and behaviour of ELAS in the Northern Pindus and the disarmament of *andarte* bands loyal to the Allies – an act he stressed was an insult to GHQ, Middle East. He demanded to know on what authority they had acted and why Saraphis and his officers were still being held prisoner. He warned Karayioryis that he would report his answers to Cairo, and all the Allies would publish the facts. Thomas would recommend to Cairo that all supplies to and contact with EAM and ELAS should be halted until they had made reprisals.

Karayioryis's face grew hard. 'Is it not a fact that Zervas has received preferential treatment from the British? He's been bribed with British gold to take to the mountains. His ultimate aim is to become a military dictator of Greece, just like that pig Metaxas before him.' Karayioryis went on, accusing the British of supporting the exiled Greek government and the King of Greece, both recently arrived back in the Middle East from London. He blamed Britain for supporting the King, whom he branded as a traitor with his involvement in setting up the Metaxas dictatorship.

Thomas countered Karayioryis's allegations by detailing why the British Mission was in the mountains of Greece, its impartiality and its objectives.

He told Karayioryis that the British now knew that communists dominated the Central Committee of EAM and to confirm this, he named two. He emphasised that Cairo expected the immediate cessation of threats towards Zervas, and that the *andarte* bands concentrate their efforts against the real enemy. Thomas recommended stopping stores from reaching any ELAS bands until they signed the

Military Agreement, which he presented to Karayioryis. Thomas reinforced that the British's final condition for supporting ELAS was their signature on the document before him and their firm observance of it.

It was a gamble.

Thomas knew that securing the involvement of EAM and ELAS in the planned anti-German sabotage in Thessaly required him to win Karayioryis's confidence and trust.

Karayioryis read through the document, stopping only once to take a gulp of coffee. 'Personally, I have no objections to the Agreement in principle; however, I have an issue with British Liaison Officers having a controlling influence over what is solely a matter for Greeks, namely, Greek Resistance.'

'I don't have the authority to alter the Agreement; only Middle East Command can do that.'

'Likewise, even if I wanted to, I can't agree to this without the authority of the Central Committee in Athens. I don't need to tell you, a runner will take two weeks to return from Athens with their answer.'

A sigh escaped Thomas's lips as he fought to control his mounting frustration at what was now the standard response. He felt a headache coming on.

Thomas wondered if he was ever going to progress in the search for an agreement, and then Karayioryis added, 'Let me assure you, since my arrival, I've painstakingly gone over the documented evidence that has been provided, and I'm satisfied this whole affair can come to a satisfactory conclusion. As you know, Saraphis, Kostopoulos and four other officers have been sent to Aris's headquarters in Roumeli to await their trial. In my capacity as a lawyer, which was my profession before the occupation, I'll be advocating for their release and their freedom to do as they please.' He glanced at Kapralos, who was red with embarrassment. 'It has been an unfortunate and grave mistake, for which there will be severe admonishments.'

The colour drained from Kapralos's face.

Thomas's frustration at the lack of signatures to the Agreement and his pleasure in seeing Kapralos squirm with unease, jerked him in different directions. 'I can't tell you how much this has derailed our plans and intentions, but the release of Saraphis and his officers is excellent news.'

Karayioryis lit a cigarette and plucked away a shred of tobacco from his lip. 'Will you be coming with me to Roumeli for the trial?'

'I won't, but my superior, Brigadier Eddie Myers, will be, once I've informed him of Saraphis's pending release.'

'Then, I'll look forward to meeting him.'

When Thomas returned to the cottage, his uplifted mood was about to be deflated.

'I can't lie, Thomas,' Fanis said, his lips screwed into a tight line on his face, 'there's talk among the men concerning your closeness to Selena.'

'What kind of talk?'

'They feel it will bring them bad luck.'

'That's nonsense,' Thomas frowned.

'Amongst the *andartes*, there's an entrenched set of rituals, practices and beliefs, certain taboos that are rife amongst the men that are used to predict fate and prevent bad luck.'

'Such as?'

'Well, one of these is the belief that abstaining from having sex with a woman will help them avoid being killed in combat. If they do not, then the Grim Reaper will find them with a bullet.'

'Really!' Thomas rolled his eyes.

'I know of a man who exchanged the gun he was issued with for another gun once he learned the previous owner had been killed over a sexual affair with a woman.'

'That's ridiculous. Superstitious nonsense.'

'That may be so, but among the men it's not. Your closeness to Selena has been noticed, and it has unsettled them. Superstition, nonsense or not, they think you'll bring them bad luck.'

'They're still going to accompany us to collect the supplies after the drop, I hope?'

'Don't worry, Stathis will see to it. I thought I'd let you know, that's all.'

'Good. Do you think I should talk to them before we go?'

'You could, but it wouldn't change anything.'

They crept through a narrow ravine as the sun set in hues of amber and gold, the only sounds were their footfalls on loose stone and the occasional clink of canteens against rifle stocks.

'We should be able to rest soon,' Fanis said, his voice low. 'We'll reach the supply drop in about an hour.'

'It's a clear night; the pilot should see our fires,' Thomas said confidently, adjusting his revolver in its worn leather holster.

Stathis nodded. 'There's a shepherd's hut near the dropping point. We can rest there. Selena has arranged for two mules to be waiting for us.'

James adjusted the wireless radio pack on his shoulders.

'With this height, we should have a decent chance of getting a signal.'

'Dimitri,' Stathis called to the *andarte* leading the group, 'How much further—'

The crack of a rifle shot echoed through the ravine, cutting his words short. Dimitri crumpled to the ground.

And then, the world exploded into chaos.

'Ambush! Take cover!' Thomas bellowed, diving behind a rock as the staccato rattle of machine guns tore through the evening air, echoing like a jackhammer. A deafening roar filled the ravine as bullets ricocheted around them, their high-pitched whine amplified by the stone.

'Get down! Get down!' Stathis shouted, his voice nearly lost in the cacophony.

Fanis spotted the muzzle flash of the German machine gun on the ridge above them, perhaps seventy yards away. 'Machine gun, two o'clock-high!' he called out, pulling his rifle to his shoulder.

The acrid smell of cordite hung in the air as the *andartes* returned fire. A desperate ferocity filled the air as the narrow ravine echoed with the crack of old hunting rifles alongside captured Italian and German rifles and the metallic ping of ejected cartridges striking stone.

'Grenades!' Fanis screamed, covering his head.

A starburst of dirt erupted ten feet from Thomas, showering him with debris and stunning him. His ears rang as he struggled to regain his bearings through the smoke and dust.

A second machine gun opened up from their left flank. 'Fuck!' James screamed. They were caught in the crossfire.

Thomas raised his binoculars, trying to see through the swirling dust. He caught sight of movement advancing down the slope. 'They're flanking us from the north! Stathis!'

As he turned to James, a hot searing pain tore through his left shoulder, and a sledgehammer of an impact spun him around. He stumbled, his breath caught in his throat as his binoculars flew from his grasp, and he collapsed against a rock face.

'Thomas!' It was James, scrambling low toward him, his face streaked with dirt, his eyes wide with concern. 'How bad?' he asked, adjusting the wireless radio pack on his back.

'Left shoulder,' Thomas gasped, clutching the wound, fresh blood seeping between his fingers, warm and sticky, a horrifying contrast to the cold sweat breaking out across his forehead. Each second sent waves of agony radiating from his shoulder, as though someone was twisting a red-hot poker through his flesh.

James pulled a handkerchief from his pocket and ripped open Thomas's jacket. Thomas grimaced, the pain becoming sharper, more focused, like shards of glass grinding inside his joint with every slight movement. He was fighting to stay conscious, the edges of his vision darkening. The coppery taste of blood filled his mouth. 'I think I've bitten my cheek.'

'That's the least of your worries,' James said bluntly, covering the wound as Thomas winced. 'You're lucky,' he said, pressing the cloth against the entry wound. 'An inch more to the right...' He didn't finish the sentence.

The thud to James's chest propelled him backwards, and he lay motionless on the ground.

Stathis had reorganised. Three *andartes* worked their way onto a ledge and were providing covering fire while others retreated to better positions.

Someone lobbed a grenade toward the advancing Germans. Unearthly screams followed the explosion.

'We can't stay here,' Fanis called through gritted teeth. 'We're outgunned.'

Stathis agreed. 'Break contact! Nikos, Andreas – suppressing fire! The rest, fall back. Move!'

Thomas tried to stand but fell back, his vision blurring as his head swam. Fanis grabbed his uninjured arm.

'I can walk,' Thomas protested.

'Not today,' Fanis said with gruff affection, slinging Thomas's good arm over his shoulder.

'What about James?'

Fanis's voice rose above the gunfire. 'Leave him! He's gone! Nikos, retrieve the radio!'

They began retreating up a narrow goat path that snaked away from the main ravine, bullets kicking the dirt at their heels.

Behind them, Stathis and three *andartes* provided covering fire. One of them screamed as a bullet struck him.

They scrambled up through a goat trail, onto a narrow ridge of shale and bramble. Thomas's wounded shoulder was a white-hot coal of pain with each jarring step. Blood had soaked through the makeshift bandage, running down his arm in warm rivulets. He focused on breathing, on keeping his feet moving.

'Almost there,' Fanis grunted, half-carrying him now.

They crested a rise and found themselves in a small clearing surrounded by a dense pine forest. The others were already there, reloading weapons. Through his haze, Thomas counted eight. They'd lost four men.

Stathis was the last to arrive, his face grim as he joined them.

'Where's the radio?' Thomas slurred, sweat beading on

his forehead, his shoulder on fire as each movement sent fresh waves of sharp, stabbing pain and a deeper, more insidious throbbing.

'It's here,' Fanis said.

'Why is James not with us? Why did we leave him?'

Fanis's weathered face was expressionless as he secured the bandage. 'Your shoulder's swelling. The bullet may have nicked bone. Infection could set in…'

'That's not good,' Stathis sighed.

'Neither is this,' Nikos said, holding the wireless set.

The wireless showed a gaping bullet hole where it had passed through James's body.

'How did the Germans know we'd be here?' Stathis said, his voice low but intense. 'Our movements are only known to a few. Even the men don't know what the operation will be, or where they're going until a few hours before.'

'You suspect our own people?' Yannis asked, shocked.

'Everyone is suspect when their family is threatened,' Stathis replied grimly. 'The Germans will torture hostages to gain information.'

Thomas's shoulder throbbed, but the threat of an informer posed an even more immediate danger. He drew himself up into a sitting position and took a deep wheezing breath. 'Who knew of today's route?' he asked.

'Me, Kapralos, and you,' Stathis answered. 'And Selena.'

It made little sense. 'Has anything changed?' Thomas pressed, wincing as a stab of pain shot down his arm.

The *andartes* exchanged looks. 'We took on new recruits,' Andreas said slowly.

'The new recruits were vouched for by Kapralos himself after one of his tours,' Stathis said.

An uncomfortable silence fell over the group.

'We need proof, not accusations,' Thomas said finally. 'The Germans create enough widows without you executing innocents on suspicion.'

'So, we do nothing?' Alexis demanded. 'Wait for another ambush? We'll be like sitting ducks.'

'No,' Thomas said firmly. 'We feed different information to different sources. See which one leads the Germans to us.'

'A trap,' Stathis nodded approvingly. 'But dangerous.'

'Less dangerous than having an informer amongst you,' Thomas countered. It was becoming an effort to talk.

Nikos spat on the ground. 'The mountains have eyes, and some of them are paid in Reichsmarks. I know it,' he insisted. 'The Germans knew exactly where we would be. This was not random.'

Stathis raised his hand, silencing the growing murmurs. 'This is not the time or place.'

'When is the time?' Alexis's grip tightened around his rifle. 'When more of us are dead? The Germans knew our route, our numbers.'

Thomas winced as he shifted position. 'The ambush was well-planned,' he acknowledged. 'But jumping to conclusions isn't the answer. We need evidence, not suspicion.'

'You British always want evidence.' Nikos scoffed. 'While we Greeks bleed.'

'Enough, Nikos,' Stathis said sharply. 'Thomas has bled beside us today and James has given his life.'

'We can't just leave him.' It was an effort for Thomas just to look at Stathis.

'We can't carry our dead out of here either, Thomas. We'll need mules for that. We'll recover the bodies when we can. We need to get you back to the village and get that wound seen to.'

'What about the drop, the supplies?'

'We've lost too many men; we've no means of communication. We need to head back now!'

They arrived back in Porta at dawn. On hearing of the ambush, Kapralos arranged for a doctor to attend to Thomas. The doctor arrived at the house in the late afternoon and set about assessing Thomas's wound.

Selena was waiting with Fanis when the doctor appeared from Thomas's bedroom.

'How is he?' Selena asked.

'It doesn't matter which part of the body is shot; the damage it does is the same, to bones, joints, muscles, soft tissues, blood vessels, or nerves. It was critical to rule out the presence of bullet fragments in the wound and remove them quickly if necessary. Which I've done. He's lucky. As long as infection doesn't set in, the wound will heal in time.'

'Thank you, doctor.' Fanis said.

'He'll sleep now. When he wakes, it will be painful. The wound will need to be dressed daily. I'd be grateful if you could take me to see Kapralos. As well as wanting an update, he promised me wine and some dinner for my troubles.'

For several weeks, the days passed in a succession of routines, forming a predictable rhythm. She would arrive just before dawn and leave late into the night. She shared her meals with Fanis. He spoke of his life before he became an *andarte* and speculated what he would do after the war – his hopes, his plans, probably all just dreams, he told her.

She immediately rebuked him, reminding him there will be a life after all this was done.

Each day, she sat beside Thomas's bed. She filled a basin of hot water and washed him with a cloth and combed his dishevelled hair. Fanis was polite when insisting he would deal with '*The embarrassing things the body will do.*'

Meticulously, she cleaned his wound and changed the dressing, fearing infection given their lack of medicine.

In the confines of the room, she witnessed his most vulnerable moments, yet felt neither surprise nor unease; stunned nor disturbed, she knew how she felt for him.

Between fleeting moments of consciousness, he begged her to leave, confessing his guilt at endangering her. She persevered, reminding herself that each event, each task, brought them closer to the day Thomas could leave his bed and walk downstairs.

One morning, as she opened the window, a rush of air dispelled the closeness of the room, and Thomas woke for the first time with a smile.

After that, he was awake more than he slept, and even though his appetite had not returned completely, he ate, and in both relief and prayer, she took this as an omen of the beginnings to recovery.

'How long has it been that I've been dead to the world?'

She put his half-empty bowl of soup on the table next to the bed and straightened herself. 'Over two weeks, now.'

He asked her, 'Why have you stayed? I wouldn't have thought any less of you if you had left me.'

'And do what? Let you bleed to death?'

He tried to move and winced. 'If the Germans were to

walk into this room right now, they would kill you. Without hesitation.'

'But they're not here. There are over a hundred *andartes* in this town. And anyway, it wouldn't be the first time I've faced death.'

'Every moment I'm here, I'm dangerous to you, to the entire village.'

'Don't you think I know this? Do you think I don't understand danger – that everyone in this village doesn't understand? We take a risk just breathing.'

'I'm not worth risking anything for.'

'I think I'll be the judge of that.'

'Why would you do it?'

'It's not about why; it's about knowing who's worth risking everything for.'

His breath caught at the weight of her words.

CHAPTER TWENTY-SIX

BRINGING HER HOME

Skiathos 2007

The next day, when Carissa finishes teaching a yoga class, she returns to the office to catch up on some admin.

'You're back,' Athena bursts out, inexplicably concerned.

'Is everything alright?'

'Thank goodness you're here. There was a man asking about you. He said he was from Scotland, on holiday, heard you were working here and since you had both been out of touch, thought he'd come by. I told him you were taking a class, but didn't give him any details. He seemed genuinely disappointed.'

Like a fairground ride, Carissa's stomach drops.

'What did he look like?'

'Tall, short brown hair, nice dress sense. He looked a lot like the man in the photograph Dimitrios showed me. He seemed very concerned about you. He said your phone wasn't working properly and asked when you would be back,' Athena adds quickly. 'I didn't tell him anything.'

Carissa grips the edge of her desk. 'You did the right thing.'

'Is everything okay, Carissa? Dimitrios never explained about the man in the photo, just that if we saw him, to tell him right away. Should I have told Dimitrios?'

'It's alright. You've told me. I'll let Dimitrios know.'

That evening, her phone buzzed with a message from her mother:

Sweetheart, a nice man called saying he had some bad news to give you about a former colleague. Something about a sudden death, and he wanted to give you the details and arrangements of the funeral in case you wanted to go. He was very insistent. He said you were very close to the girl that had passed, and he didn't want you to hear about it from someone else. I gave him your new phone number. Hope that was okay? He appeared to care for you very much. Mum.

Carissa frantically typed.

A stupid question, but did he sound like Stuart?

She hits, *send*. Her mother responds instantly.

'No, dear. He had an English accent. It sounded nothing like Stuart. Why? What's going on? Have I just given Stuart your new phone number? How stupid of me. I'm sorry, darling.'

Stuart has my number! He played on mum's naïvety. What was I thinking? I should have warned her he might do something like this. She would be devastated if she knew the truth. Carissa waits several minutes before replying.

It's alright, Mum. Don't worry. The guy you gave my new number to has just phoned. It was Mark. We used to work together. Panic is over. Lots of love, Carissa. XX.'

Her blood runs cold as the implications hit her. *Jesus! He has my number!* She struggles to breathe. Her phone is in her hand, feeling like hot coal burning her skin.

Then, it almost slips from her fingers as it lights up with a buzz that seems obscenely loud in the silence.

The message notification shows an unknown number. Her heart hammers against her ribs. She stares at the screen, hoping the words will rearrange themselves into something innocent, something that makes sense. But they don't change. They sit there glowing, verifying her worst fears.

I've been patient. I've given you time. I miss you. I miss us. We belong together. I'm bringing you home, where you belong. S

She creeps towards the window, her bare feet silent on the cool tiled floor. Her hands shake as she reaches for the edge of the curtain, pulling it back just enough to peer through the gap in the shutters. The path below stretches empty in both directions.

Her phone buzzes again, and she jerks back from the window as if it has burned her.

Her hands are shaking, and she can barely hold the phone, but she forces herself to type a response.

Stop. Leave me alone.

The reply comes so fast it is as if he's been waiting, fingers poised over his keyboard.

I'm not trying to scare you. I just worry.

A pause.

You looked tired today walking with your group. What was it, ten people, you set off at 9.30 a.m. and returned at 12.10 p.m. I believe it's called The Olive Tree Trail. Quite app as it involves mainly olive groves and farmlands. I noticed you started from the town and the Ganoti stream and then led us through the stream of Agalianou to Nikotsara beach; it was too craggy for my liking, and I wasn't keen on the pebbles. I thought it was going to be a sandy beach where you returned to the town. That couple from Sunderland weren't impressed either. Although, I thought you handled them well, especially when the woman got an insect bite. It was a shame we didn't visit the Monastery of Evangelistria, I'm told it's worth a visit, and the taverna next to it serves a lovely lunch. I know you visit there on another of your trails. Next time then, love. By the way, the views were spectacular. I particularly enjoyed the Church of Agios Spyridon and the watermill.
I can see why you chose this place – it's peaceful and safe. Everything is going to be fine. We'll work this out together. Speak to you soon, darling.

The specificity is devastating. 9.30 a.m. The accuracy of the route. The couple from Sunderland. She remembers them now. Had she looked tired? She'd been working since seven that morning.

She stands frozen, holding the phone as if it might explode. He was on the trail with her that morning. She remembers now. A man had been behind them, not part of their group, always keeping his distance. He was there. It was Stuart. He had followed her. *Oh my God!*

She wants to throw the phone across the room, to smash it against the wall and stop the invasion of words from pouring in. But she can't. She needs to see what he is saying; she needs to understand the scope of what she is dealing with. Each message is evidence, proof of his surveillance, documentation of her violation.

The endearment hits her like a physical blow. Love. Darling. Words that once made her feel cherished, now make her skin crawl. The casual intimacy of his tone, as if the months of separation had never happened, as if her flight to another country was just a minor misunderstanding between partners.

She types back with shaking fingers.

'Where are you? How long have you been watching me? Why are you doing this?'

Silence.

Finally, she turns off the lamp, plunging the apartment into darkness. But she doesn't go to bed. Instead, she sits on the floor beside her window, back against the wall. In the darkness, she clutches her phone and tries to think.

He was there. He was watching.

Outside, the night sounds of Skiathos continue unchanged: waves against stone, cats calling to each other, the distant hum of a scooter. But the peace she found in such sounds is gone.

At 2.43 a.m. her phone buzzes, jolting her out of a shallow sleep:

I miss you, Carissa. I miss us. The distance between us is killing me. I know you think you need space, but we belong together. I've been patient, I've given you time to think, but I can't wait forever. This has gone on long enough. We can work this out. We always do. I love you too much to let you throw us away. This is where it ends. It's time to come home. S

Another buzz:

Sweet dreams, darling.

The threat is chilling and implicit in – *This is where it ends.*

This time, she turns the phone off. But sleep is impossible, listening to every sound, watching every shadow, knowing he may be somewhere nearby, watching, waiting, planning the reunion she dreads more than anything in the world.

CHAPTER TWENTY-SEVEN

A TIME OF DISCLOSURE

Mainland Greece 1942

One morning, she asked him after changing his dressing, 'Who is Aliki?' Her voice is sharp, demanding.

Thomas shifted his position in the bed and took a long breath.

'Is she someone special to you? It's a Greek name.'

He heard the accusation in her voice. 'No, she's not,' he said, though the strain in his voice gave him away, and Selena's look confirmed she'd heard it too.

'You speak her name in your sleep.'

Thomas nodded. 'She's someone I met when I was in Crete.'

'This woman, what is she to you?'

His mouth had gone dry. 'She's a young girl; a child, not a woman. Something happened.' He searched for the words. 'She never leaves me. The smallest thing can trigger it – I see the images, hear the sounds, and smell everything.

I relive it day and night. It haunts me.' He turned his head away. 'I've never spoken to anyone about it.'

'Then, maybe you should. It can't be easy keeping something like that to yourself. Closing it off to others.'

'It's how I've coped with it.'

'You don't look like you've been coping.'

'There are places for people like me.'

'What do you mean, places?'

'Institutions, hospitals for the mentally ill. If I told you what goes on in my mind, you would think I was a madman.'

'I would never have known if I hadn't heard you talking in your sleep. You're not mad.'

His face grew hard. 'You don't understand.'

'Well, help me understand. I'm a good listener. I've two ears and one mouth, so I can listen twice as much as I speak. That's all I'll do – just listen. Think about it like being wounded; you can't heal if it stays buried.'

His gaze searched hers. 'I've never thought about it like that. If that's what it is, if my mind is wounded, then it can heal again…'

'You need to give it time. Talking about it and giving it time can be your medicine.'

His jaw set, but as she reached out and touched his hand, pressing against him, it loosened.

Her touch astounded him. He felt his blood race through his veins. She possessed courage, kindness, and always spoke with common sense. If he could not find it in himself to open up to her, then there was no hope for him. How extraordinary was the effect this woman had on him. She was a marvel. He pressed his lips together and closed his eyes, and as his heart skipped a beat inside his chest, he let the memories wash over him.

'When I first arrived here, as in most of the villages I've passed through or stayed in, the layout of the villages is like…' He forced himself to say it. 'They look and smell like a village in Crete. They trigger flashbacks. It could be the church square, the arrangement of houses clinging to the hillside, even the smell of the olive groves – they all remind me of that village.

'It's worse at night. There's a voice in my head, the little girl. Each night, her words reaffirm the simplicity of childhood and my shame. *You are a soldier; you will keep us safe.'*– trusting words confidently spoken with a naïve innocence, untainted by the harshness of life and brutality of war. The mother had flour on her cheek. She'd been baking bread. I can still smell the yeast and olive oil. The girl had a missing front tooth. She whistled slightly when she spoke. Her little brother, he'd been learning to write his name when…' There was a silence and then he opened his eyes. 'And then, my world unexpectedly turned on its head…'

They had arrived on foot early morning. The village was a resting point before their journey into the mountains to rendezvous with a band of Cretan resistance fighters.

The fall of Crete and subsequent Allied occupation found Thomas assisting in the evacuation of British and Commonwealth troops to the safety of Egypt and helping the Crete resistance with sabotage work against the German occupation.

The villagers had welcomed them, even though they knew British soldiers placed them in danger of reprisals from the Germans.

Thomas, in his excellent Greek, informed the president of the village that they were just passing through but needed food and drink.

'We will be here for as short a time as possible. If you can spare

us a little food, we will eat and be on our way. I don't want to place you in any danger.'

'As soon as the first German boot landed on Cretan soil, the resistance began. We don't have much, but what we have we can share with you. I will arrange it,' the president said. 'You and your men can sit outside the kafenion. I'll see that you are given water and some coffee. I will organise the food.'

Thomas thanked him.

Thomas and his men sat outside the Kafenion, enjoying the opportunity to rest, while the owner, an old man with a bulbous nose and weathered complexion, set the tables with coffee and glasses of water.

Soon, from the modest whitewashed houses, people appeared with bread, olives and cheese. They distributed the food among the soldiers, who thanked them.

The little girl, no more than seven, Thomas thought, wore a faded red dress with tiny white flowers, patched at the knee. She shuffled beside her mother, her hands cupped around a small bowl of olives, and tucked under her arm nestled a worn cloth doll with button eyes. She followed her mother, her head bowed, her eyes staring at her bare feet. Occasionally, she lifted her head, a wary glance in the soldiers' direction.

Her mother looked to be in her early twenties, Thomas assumed. She wore a blue headscarf with white edges, and her dark hair swayed along her back as she approached the Kafenion.

As she moved closer to Thomas's table, he slid from his chair and stood up. Then, he spotted flour on her cheeks and apron, where she had wiped her hands. She gave a twitchy smile.

'I'm sorry if we've interrupted your morning. Thank you for sharing your food with us.'

The young woman's eyes widened in surprise. 'I'm happy to help. You speak Greek… very well.' She placed the bread and cheese on the table. 'It's not much.'

'It's better than going with nothing all day. I can't thank you enough.'

'I was making bread. I'll give you a loaf to take with you once it's ready.'

'That's kind of you. Thank you.' Thomas smiled gratefully. He bent toward the little girl. 'Hello, and what's your name?'

The little girl bent her head, tucking her chin in with pursed lips.

'This is Aliki. Say hello, Aliki.'

Aliki took a hesitant step backwards.

'Be careful,' her mother warned, and she took the bowl of olives from her.

'Well, it's nice to meet you, Aliki, and thank you for bringing me some olives.'

Aliki eyed Thomas with unease.

'My name is Thomas.' Thomas pointed to the doll and said gently. 'And what is the name of this little one?' Thomas then spotted a tiny blue ribbon, its edges unravelling in the doll's yarn hair.

Aliki tugged on her mother's apron.

'Is she called… Zoe?' Thomas tilted his head, drawing the name out like a guessing game.

Aliki shook her head, her eyes hooded. 'Angelos,' she said timidly. Thomas noticed a missing front tooth.

'That's a beautiful name. Did you choose it?'

Aliki nodded, her eyes brightening, as her caution melted.

'Well, thank you for bringing me breakfast, Aliki.' He turned to the woman. 'I'll return the plates when we've finished.'

'There's no need for that.'

'We'll return them all to each house that gave us food. It's the least we can do to show our gratitude.'

He walked towards the house with empty plates in hand and thought, in another life, he would have cleaned the dust from his boots. It was a *white-walled house with faded blue shutters and terracotta pots of basil by the front door and a jasmine vine in bloom climbing the wall.*

As he neared the house, the smell of freshly baked bread drifted from the open door.

Thomas caught sight of a boy sitting at a table a year or two younger than the girl, Aliki. Dark curls fell across his eyes, framed by a cap. He clutched a pencil between his fingers and was writing on a sheet of paper. He turned towards Thomas and, holding the sheet in his hand, flaunted it with a smile stretched across his boyish face.

The woman appeared in front of him, and her dark eyes fell to the dishes Thomas was carrying.

'I've brought your plates back,' Thomas said awkwardly.

'Thank you.' She passed her hand through her hair. 'The house gets warm when I'm making bread. I'll wrap some for you and your men.' She nodded towards her son. 'Antonis has been learning to write his name. I think he wants to show it to you but is too embarrassed to bring it over.'

It was an invitation of sorts, permission to enter the house. At that moment, Thomas noticed a wedding ring she kept turning around her finger as she spoke.

Thomas lingered outside. He turned his gaze to the woman. 'I don't think I should enter your house; it wouldn't be seen as the right thing to do.'

The boy's smile faded.

The bracelets around her wrist jingled as she took the plates from Thomas. 'My husband is with the resistance. I don't know whether he is alive or dead. My children have not seen their father in months. Children don't understand or care about the rights and wrongs of civility; they live in simplicity and for the moment. If anyone has anything to say about my inviting you into my home, they can go to hell.'

Thomas hesitated, then, rubbing the dust from his scuffed boots, he entered the house. The comforting aroma of bread, fresh from the oven, enveloped him as light from the opened shutters flooded the house. The smile returned to the boy's face as Thomas gazed at the sheet of paper and the wobbly but determined letters. 'Well done. You're good at writing.'

'Do you know what it says?' the boy asked with wide, eager eyes.

Thomas leaned closer. 'Let me see. It says, Antonis. That must be your name.'

'I've been practising, haven't I, Mum?' Antonis said, bursting with delight.

The woman raised her gaze from wrapping the bread. 'You certainly have. You have been busy all morning writing your name, and you've done a wonderful job.'

'I'm going to write some more.' And with that, he picked up his pencil and wrote, the tip of his tongue protruding from his lips with firm concentration.

She handed Thomas the bread and, smiling, said, 'Thank you.'

'For what?'

'For risking your life for people you don't know. I hope you return to your home soon and to the people who love you.'

Thomas swallowed. Her words conveyed heartfelt selflessness, and even though she must have been troubled not knowing if her husband was alive or dead, she had given him unreserved kindness, a gift of food, and words conveying gratitude that, at that moment, he felt he did not deserve.

They were preparing to leave the village when a message came over the wireless set that two German aircraft had been terrorising neighbouring villages and were heading in their direction. The plumes of smoke that rose ominously into the sky confirmed their worst fears.

'They're heading this way!' the radio operator yelled, exchanging an alarmed glance with Thomas.

Thomas spun around and saw Aliki and Antonis playing outside *their house. He rushed towards them. 'Get in the house! Get in the house! Quickly!'*

Their mother appeared at the door. 'What's going on? What's happening?'

'They'll be here any minute now. Get the children inside.'

'Who'll be here?'

'German planes. They've already hit other villages.'

The mother hurried the children into the house, Thomas following her. She turned to him. 'Are you sure we will be safe?' her hesitant smile grateful but anxious.

Thomas scanned the house. 'Is there a basement?' he answered her question with his own.

She shook her head, her eyes fearful, desperate for reassurance.

'Stay away from the windows,' he warned.

Aliki looked up to him. 'You are a soldier; you will keep us safe from the planes,' she said softly, almost a whisper.

He felt drawn into her innocent eyes. 'I'll stay with you.'

'No. You can help us by shooting the planes out of the sky.' The mother was forceful and insistent.

Thomas hesitated. 'I'll come back to make sure you're okay.' The words stuck in his throat.

She gave him an understanding look.

Aliki waved him goodbye, her doll's arm swaying limply.

He was twenty metres away when the bomb struck. It's blast propelling him forward and he landed with a thud. He spluttered and coughed with a mouthful of dust. It wasn't the sound that haunted him, but the sudden silence in his head. Time dislocated around him. He felt detached, suspended above his prone body. Then, a tsunami of chaos crashed over him. A shockwave sent blue shutters still intact, contorted fragments, and shards of what had, just seconds before, been a family home, plummeting over and scattering around him in a devastating surge of carnage. Machine-gun fire lacerated the air, then it ceased. Thomas caught sight of two aircraft disappearing over the ridge of a hill, leaving the disposition of hell below them, where screams and wails impaled the air.

He moved an arm, and then a leg. Miraculously, he felt little pain. Dirt and dust infiltrated his hair, eyes, nose, and mouth. He felt particles crunch and rub on his teeth. Thomas hauled himself to his knees, coughing and spluttering with dust-filled lungs. He turned towards the house and, through a screen of smoke and dust, saw that the roof was no longer intact. A tremor of numb disbelief rose through him. He scrambled to his feet, stumbling forward as he attempted to coordinate one foot in front of the other, his mind bombarded with unthinkable images, his eyes full of pain, his heart wrecked with guilt. He should have been with them.

He reached the house and walked through the space where the door had been. Thomas stood transfixed, unable to move. He knew no one could have survived such a hit, and a part of him prayed the mother had moved them all out of the house when Thomas left. It was a desperate thought, offering the slimmest of threads. He pleaded for it to be true. His throat clenched and burned like a burst of fire. He squeezed his eyes shut. When he opened them, they floated over the room, his hands sweating, his heart pounding. He could no longer distinguish the stone floor from the rubble. Beams lay at peculiar angles, glass and crockery crunched underfoot, stone had blown from walls, indiscriminate projectiles scattered in every direction. The whole second floor of the house had collapsed onto the ground floor: mattresses, buckled beds and shreds of clothing spilled from a shattered wardrobe. The table had cracked in two and lay prone against the only intact wall of the house, where flames licked across its surface and crackled in defiant conquest.

At first, his eye snagged on the red of Aliki's dress, and then, he realised it was not that at all, but her blood that soaked and spread along the fabric. Miraculously, her face was untouched, her closed eyes *giving the impression she could have been sleeping, if it were not for the abnormal aligning of both her arms and legs. In a blood-stained hand, she still held onto her doll, the blue ribbon in its yarn hair still intact and fraying at the edges. Thomas knelt beside her, and unfurling the ribbon, he pressed it to his mouth and wept, his vision blurring in tears, his heart heaving in his chest.*

His eyes inflamed in despair, another wave hit him hard, as he found the mother on the other side of the house, her arms still wrapped around the broken body of Antonis, both unrecognisable, but joined and inseparable in death, as they had been in life.

It had astonished him that he had eventually told someone.

'I never knew the mother's name. I never asked. I've lived all this time without knowing her name. The thought of it suffocates me. They died because of me. Every day, I wish it had been me that had died instead of them. I'd gratefully trade my life for theirs. In a way, I'm dead already. The person I was died that day.'

Selena looked down into her lap. She tried to breathe and steady her composure, a concealment from the horror and shock his words had unfolded.

She lifted her head and looked at him. He returned her gaze with searching eyes.

'It's not what happens to us that's important; it's how we react to it that matters. Maybe not right now, but one day you'll be able to step away from these thoughts. You'll never forget them; you'll just have a sense of how it was.'

He had kept his eyes on her face, but now Thomas glanced away. He had detailed the most private part of himself, the most intimate moments, and her response had left him hollow and deflated. It had belittled him.

He narrowed his eyes. 'How could you ever know how

I'd feel? My thoughts, my mind are filled with anger and shame. I can get agitated at the smallest thing.'

'Because it was how I felt too,' she answered Thomas simply.

Thomas looked at her, taken aback. He pressed his lips together, shame flushing his chest.

Selena cleared her throat. 'You see, Thomas, bad things happen all the time; very few of us are spared such things. There's not a family I know who hasn't lost a close or distant family member. Some still don't know what has happened to a husband or a son. None of us are immune. We're all casualties in our own way.'

'What happened?'

Selena composed herself. 'I watched as my father was taken from his bed and led outside by a German officer. He was placed against the wall of the house, and without a word spoken, he was shot in the head. I watched as my mother, hysterical with fear and confusion, tried to get to him, but she was held back and forced to watch. The officer shouted at her to stop screaming, but she couldn't hear him; all she could hear was the crack of the pistol that stole my father from her. To quieten her, the German officer shot her too. So you see, Thomas, I know how it feels. I screamed for days until my throat was raw, and when I eventually spoke, I could only whisper my words of grief and pain.'

She glanced into his eyes. 'What happiness can there ever be after such a loss?' she asked with a flick of an upturned hand, as if she had held the question in her palm and was now releasing it to be answered.

It was a question he contemplated many times but never had to answer from the lips of another.

There was a tickle in his throat. 'Can there be?'

'I'm happy just to be alive. There was a time I didn't

think like that. I was so consumed with my grief, my loss, that I wanted to end it all. I tried, but there was something stronger in me that wouldn't let me go through with it. The only way to stop what happened to me from happening to another was to become involved in the fight against the enemy. So, that's what I did. I'm a different person now than I was back then.'

'It's how we react to it that matters,' Thomas said, repeating Selena's words.

She smiled. 'You can't go on like this, Thomas. You must find the strength within yourself to put it behind you and move forward. That doesn't mean you stop grieving; you just carry it differently.'

A twinge of shame slipped across his face. 'Like you?'

'Like me. I still carry my grief, but it doesn't feel like I'm drowning in it anymore. Now, it grounds me by honouring my parents through what I do amongst the living.'

'By being part of the resistance.'

'I'd like to think so. It wasn't enough just to assist the *andartes* in any way I could; I needed a purpose. My father farmed, and he had dealings with many of the shepherds who he bought and sold sheep through. He developed a network where information was passed onto him of troop movements, garrison towns or German raids that the shepherds, his eyes and ears in the countryside, would share. He would then relay this information to the *andarte* bands. He gave a safe house to those that needed it, and was trusted and respected by the resistance. I just carried on his work. I found food and a safe shelter for those that needed it, but that wasn't enough for me. I had to play an active part in the fight to free our country. I had been brought up around guns. I knew how to use them, so I went on raids with the *andartes*. I dressed like them and shared the rigours of the guerrilla life as an equal. I was respected by my fellow fighters because I had proven myself to be fearless in battle. So, Thomas, I honour my parents by what I do amongst the living.'

'I'm so sorry, Selena, for…'

'I know,' she cut him short. 'You don't have to say anything. I've told you, and that's all that matters. We're equal now.'

He saw her sadness as she spoke, but an understanding somehow eased her loss, and she shared it without being uncertain, without being afraid. She had shown him a glimmer of possibility by moving through her grief. She had won her battle; could he do the same and win his?

'Tell me about your family,' he asked.

'What is there to tell? My brother was one of the first to join Kazakos's band of *andartes* and the first to be killed. The Italians shot him. You know about my parents. I'm alone. Now, I do what I can,' she said simply. 'Everything I do, it's for them. Not just revenge, but for them. I have a purpose that keeps me going. It keeps me sane.'

The words of the old woman in the garden echoed in Selena's voice.

'Lying in this bed has given me a lot of time to think,' Thomas sighed. 'The Germans knew we would pass through that ravine.'

'There's an informer?'

'They were definitely waiting for us. It was an ambush. I don't doubt that.'

'I can't believe it. Do you have any thoughts about who it might be?'

'Not yet. I'm hoping Stathis might have progressed matters.'

Outside, a dog barked.

Selena rose from the side of the bed towards the window and glanced outside.

Thomas considered her. 'Are you okay?' he asked, his mouth suddenly dry.

She returned to the bed and pursed her lips. 'Your wound needs redressing,' she said, breaking the intensity. She turned away to gather the bowl of water and cloth, but not before he glimpsed something troubling in her eyes.

As she redressed his wound, a fleeting moment of vulnerability crossed her.

He would not press the matter; she would tell him in her own time – that much he had learnt about her.

As she finished the dressing, he said, 'I still can't believe James is dead.' His heart jolted, struck by the image of James being shot.

'Fanis and some others retrieved the bodies,' Selena explained.

'Thank God. At least that's something.'

She knew from his look what he was thinking. 'Don't worry, he hadn't been touched by animals.'

'Where is he now?'

'They buried him along with the others in the graveyard.'

'I see.'

'There was a service and hymns.'

'I'd like to visit the grave.'

'When you're strong enough.'

'James was a decent man, a good soldier. He didn't deserve to die like that.'

'No one does, but they still do.'

'Why him and not me? He deserved to live.'

'You got lucky. It wasn't your time to die.'

A thought crossed his mind. 'Where's the wireless set?'

'It got damaged beyond repair.'

He moved himself onto his elbows. 'I need to contact Eddie. He needs to know what's happened.'

She placed her hands on him. 'Lie back. You're going nowhere.'

He sank back into the pillow with a sigh and then cursed under his breath. 'Where's Fanis?'

'He's gone for a few days. He went with Kapralos and about fifty of his men to Prodromos, on the edge of the Plain. Another recruitment tour and some business about settling an old score. Fanis told me he is with you so he can keep an eye on Kapralos's activities.'

'He is. Aris sent him. Kapralos is ruffling the feathers of his seniors.'

'To give him his due, Kapralos sent a runner to the British with news of what happened and to return with the equipment you need. I was told this morning, Kapralos's runner has returned.'

'With good news, I hope?'

'He was told the British have moved their headquarters further north in the Pindus Mountains.'

'Why?'

'With summer approaching and the snow melting, the Italians can now bypass the mountain passes west of Avlaki, threatening your headquarters from many directions. They're no longer confined to the traditional routes. The British have moved to Theodhoriana. Unfortunately, Thomas, the runner failed to make contact with them.'

Thomas's stomach twisted. 'So, I'm stranded, without radio contact or support. I'm alone.'

'I'm sorry.'

The look on his face changed. 'I don't trust Kapralos, especially after his humiliation at the hands of Karayioryis.

He blames me; I'm sure of it. I need to get out of this bed. I'm no good to anyone. My shoulder will feel the same, whether I'm in this bed or out of it.' His face tightened. 'I need to get on my feet.'

Selena folded her arms. 'You cannot quicken time. It will take as long as it takes for your shoulder to heal. Until then, you're not leaving this house!'

He looked at her.

She narrowed her eyes at him.

'Very well,' he said gracefully.

A week later, he felt strong enough to sit on the edge of the bed and, with Selena's arm around him, he pushed himself to his feet. He felt lightheaded, but with each step he took, it gradually receded.

He dressed in the clean clothes Selena had washed, and together, under her watchful eye, he navigated each stair with a cautious step. Reaching the last step and placing his foot on the ground was exhilarating, but it had also been an effort, and as Selena's smile confirmed her happiness and relief, he didn't have the heart to wipe it from her face.

In the weeks that followed, he moved through a spectrum of pain and frustration, healing and impatience. Gradually his strength returned, and his body began to feel more like his own.

One day, he went to the window and peered outside into the bright, glaring sunshine. 'I want to feel the sun on my face.'

He stepped out into the warm light and shaded his eyes with a hand.

It felt good to be free of the still-musky air of the house and breathe in the freshness of the morning. He began to take walks. At first, he didn't venture far from the house, but with each completed outing his confidence grew and his body felt like his own once more.

One evening, after his walk, he eased himself onto the wooden bench in the small garden. Selena sat beside him.

'When we first met, you asked me what it was like living in the mountains. Do you remember?' he asked.

'I do.'

'I evaded your question because I couldn't speak freely to you about such things, but now, I can. I want to.'

'You trust me?'

'How else can I thank you for what you've done for me, but with my trust?' He took her hand in his. 'There's something else I need to tell you. Amidst all of this devastation and ruin, being surrounded by suffering and death, I've found something astonishing and wonderful. It's beyond my wildest expectations and unexpected, to say the least.'

'What are you going on about? You're talking in riddles. Just tell me, Thomas,' she said exasperated.

'When I saw you at the square, amongst all those men, and then when I was with you in that room with Kapralos, and you left, remember?'

'I do.'

'I looked out of the window and you looked up at me, I loved you even then. I don't know how that's possible, but I know I did.'

A hot rush of emotion filled her. 'I felt it too.'

She leaned in close to him, so close he could see the pores of her skin. She opened her mouth, and her lips caressed his, the taste of her tongue astonishing as he felt a shiver of unexplained emotion pass through him. 'I can't feel any other way about you,' he said boldly. 'I can't deny what my heart feels.' Then, startled by a sudden panic that squeezed his chest, he asked, 'Is it wrong to feel like this?'

'I feel it too, but we don't have a lifetime together.'

The muscles tightened on his face. 'How do you know we won't? This war won't last forever.'

'And then what?'

'I don't know, we'll leave this place or we'll stay, that's the choice we face.'

'We might not have a choice; it could be taken out of our hands. You might have to leave. If the Germans move further into the Plain, which they will do, you'll have to go where circumstance sends you.'

'Then, I'd return when I could.' He took her hand. 'Whatever happens, I want to be with you. When I was shot, I can't remember returning to this house, but when I woke up that first morning and saw your face, everything in my world felt right. You were a light that dispelled my darkness.'

Selena smiled and rested her head on his shoulder. 'So, tell me, what was it like when you were first dropped into the mountains?'

He squeezed her hand. 'The weather was harsh. I'd never seen snow like it – it was that bad. The pine trees bent heavily under the weight of snow. It was difficult to travel with mules laden with stores. The Italians were happy to wait until spring. They had little appetite to venture into such inhospitable terrain, so there was little movement on their part, or fighting. We were basically free to travel. This worked to our advantage when we planned and blew up the Gorgopotamos viaduct. We lived amongst the *andartes*, and grew to respect them, these bearded mountain men who gave up comfortable lives in the cities, with jobs and salaries, or those who left their families and the village they had lived in all their lives, their wives, brothers and sisters.

'We travelled together, sat around fires together, fought together and became a band of brothers. A bond grew between us, as it often does in war. We drank together, ate together, laid our explosive charges on the Gorgopotamos viaduct and fired upon the enemy and mourned our dead together. Such regard was dented when we came across a burnt-out village or heard of the reprisals, the innocent murdered because of our actions.

'It was difficult to witness the harsh reality of life in the mountains and the casual way in which human life was viewed. The *andartes* told us about executions carried out, men condemned to death who were accused of collaborating with the enemy. I couldn't get out of my head the spectacle of whole villages – women and children observing the death of these men, often known to them, neighbours, or even relatives – as if it were natural. Then, without hesitation, they returned to whatever they had been doing, as if it was normal and commonplace, with no ill effect on their demeanour.

'It was because of the goat tracks, the snow and the inhospitable terrain that we could wander undetected at will, for days at a time, where the Italians seldom ventured.

'Supplies were scarce. We waited for planes through long, snowy, rainy nights. We would head for higher ground. We lit fires, both so the pilots could see us and also for warmth, if we couldn't shelter in a shepherd's hut. *Andartes* often joined us, sharing stories and complaining about the dreadful weather. Poorly equipped, their boots leaked, and their clothes offered little protection. Despite their hardships, they were cheerful and laughed easily.' The thought made Thomas smile. 'They kept their spirits up by dreaming of new uniforms, waterproof boots, endless coffee, and English cigarettes   all to be enjoyed once the planes arrived.

'The planes wouldn't always come, and when they did, they wouldn't always see the fires we lit because of the bad weather.'

Thomas leaned back and stared into the distance. 'Often, the planes would circle several times when the clouds were dense and blotted out the light from the moon. The mist, wind and rain whipped around us, threatening to extinguish our fires. The drone of the plane overhead was a reminder that we weren't forgotten. Sometimes, our elation was short-lived. As the plane moved off in the distance, its engines resounded in the black sky. We knew they wouldn't leave, if they could help it, until they were sure they couldn't detect us. We willed a break in the clouds, so our fires could be seen. Then, like magic, it would appear; usually it was a Halifax. They often circled twice before releasing their load. Each time felt like Christmas. Sometimes we would wait for weeks, every night on top of a hill, in rain, wind, and snow...

'I used to think a lot about those pilots. Their work was hazardous, even more so than ours. It demanded skill in navigation and circling low, in and out of mountains, and at times, in terrible weather. Constantly searching for the pinpoint of a flare below and dodging night fighters or flak returning over the coast defences. It was routine, running to a schedule and not always discerning the dropping points. How many times would they return home disappointed? Still with a full load, knowing they had left behind men desperate for supplies that often-meant life or death.'

'Thank you for sharing this with me. You didn't have to, but it helps me understand.'

'Understand what?'

'Who you are, what's important to you, how you think. It helps me to know you better.' She lifted her head from his shoulder and looked at him. 'Does it scare you? This. You and me?'

'I've never felt this way about anyone. *Us* doesn't scare me; it's what may lie ahead that does.'

'I know. I've just found you; I don't want to lose you.'

Her mouth sought his in a long kiss. She took his hand. 'We should go back into the house. I want to know more than your mind; I want to explore every part of you.'

As she slept, he stared for a long moment, seized by her, like an imprint, forever overwhelming his senses.

He could still feel her hand stroking the nape of his neck, and the rapturous touch of intimacies shared that brought him to the edge of delirious pleasure, luxuriated in its release.

The light had softened along the wall to a delicate suffuse as he listened to her breathing, watched the slight rise and fall of her chest, and glimpsed the slight flutter of her eyes.

An impression, like a hand pushing against his chest, engulfed him. *I've just found you; I don't want to lose you.* He felt the ache of her words, which haunted him in their intimations. He couldn't imagine his life without her. Such a thought did not seem absurd to him, even given the short time they had spent together. He had discovered something that no words could explain, something they gave and shared, embodying a wonder that both astonished and shocked him.

CHAPTER TWENTY-EIGHT

THE PHOTOGRAPH

Skiathos 2007

They arrive at the apartment late. The breeze off the sea brushes Carissa's skin like whispered breath. As she pushes the door open, Dimitrios follows her inside, brushing his hand against the back of her shoulder.

'It's stuffy in here,' she says, moving towards the window. I'll open it a little. Do you want a drink?'

'I'll get it,' he says, already heading to the kitchen. 'Just water. I'm thirsty; that moussaka must've been loaded with salt.'

'I'm glad I had the souvlaki, then.' Carissa unlatches the window and pushes it open an inch. 'Fresh air or mosquitoes,' she murmurs. 'It's a fine balance.'

'You should have screens,' Dimitrios calls out. 'I'll make a point of seeing to that tomorrow. It was supposed to be part of the apartment upgrade, but the company never got around to it. *An oversight,* they said.'

He reappears with two glasses of water and hands one to her.

'You can get those plug-in things at the pharmacy. They release a scent that keeps the devils with wings away.'

Carissa gives a small, distracted nod, but her eyes have fixed on the coffee table.

'That's odd,' she says.

Dimitrios follows her gaze. 'What is?'

'The book I'm reading. It's lying open, face down.'

'So?'

'I didn't leave it like that,' she says slowly, stepping closer. 'I'd never do that. I always close a book.'

'Maybe this time you didn't,' he offers gently.

'No,' she says adamantly. 'No, I remember. I finished the chapter, marked the page, and closed it, right-side up.'

Her chest tightens.

She turns and freezes. She always closes the bedroom door, yet it is open like a mouth.

On the bed, something glistens in the low light. The glass in her hand trembles. She sets it down with a soft clink on the table before it can fall from her hand.

She steps toward the bedroom.

It is a photograph.

A printed glossy image.

Her own body, nude, backlit in warm amber light, smiling. Captured in a moment of intimate trust.

One photo Stuart had taken years ago, when they were younger, before she knew who he truly was.

She backs away from it, as if it might burn her fingers, bile rising in her throat as her hand goes to her mouth.

Dimitrios crosses the room and glances down at the photograph, picking it up with caution, his brow tightening as he examines it.

'What the hell is this?' A fresh, deeper furrow spreads its way across his brow. His voice is no longer casual. It is weighted with an unaccustomed edge. Disbelief. Alarm.

They stand there for an awkward moment. Carissa doesn't answer right away. The thought of explaining fills her with exhaustion, with dread. Her gaze shifts rapidly – to the door, to the window, to the hallway. No signs of forced entry. No broken lock. Everything just as she left it… except it wasn't.

'Dimitrios…' Her voice is quiet now, a tight whisper. 'He's been in here. How?'

'He has a key. Or he knows someone who does.'

Dimitrios's expression darkens, and he gently sets the photo back down, as though it were contaminated. 'And he's left his calling card.'

Carissa stared at the floor. 'The photograph was taken a long time ago, meant only for us. I suppose I did it for the thrill, never thinking beyond that to how it might turn out. I'd forgotten about them, assuming he'd deleted them years ago — I even asked him to.'

'How many are there?'

'A few. I can't remember. The bastard. What does it mean?

'He wants you to know he can get to you even here.'

She can feel the veneer she has built around herself: her apartment, her sanctuary – crack and shatter like glass under pressure.

'He was in my bedroom. He touched my pillow. My sheets. He stood where I sleep and put this… this thing where I would see it. What do we do, call the police?'

'There's no evidence of forced entry. He hasn't broken anything. As far as we know, nothing is missing. He's just turned your book upside down and left a photo that you can't prove you didn't put there yourself. It's all calculated. He knows what he's doing.'

'How can I sleep here now, after this, after him being here?'

'That's what he wants. That's how he will get to you. He knows how you'll react. Don't give him the satisfaction. Don't let him win.'

She lets out a shaky breath. 'Then make love to me. Here. Now.'

CHAPTER TWENTY-NINE

DAYS OF TRIBULATION

Mainland Greece 1943

Fanis hurried through the door of the cottage. He bent forward, clasping his knees and gasping for breath, the door still wide open behind him.

'Jesus, Fanis, you scared me half to death,' Thomas cried, brushing spilled coffee from his lap.

'You haven't heard, then,' Fanis blurted, his eyes huge in his head. 'Selena has been arrested.'

'What?! Arrested!' Thomas looked gaunt with shock.

'This morning.'

'Why in God's name would she be arrested?'

'Collaborating with the enemy was the charge.'

'That's ludicrous. She'd never do that.'

'Seemingly, she was seen.'

'By whom?'

'I don't know. I've just returned with Kapralos from his tour of the villages. He was told the moment we arrived back. She's being held at his headquarters.'

'And Kapralos is allowing this?'

'At the moment, he doesn't have much of a choice. He's being briefed as we speak.'

'Then I'll see him right now.'

'You should know, Thomas. Two days ago, we were in a village called Rendina. One man was brought before Kapralos accused of stealing goats, another of rape. Kapralos presided over the cases and found both guilty. One was shot; the other hung from a tree in the village square while the entire village watched. I've written the whole sordid affair down and will present it to Aris. The man is a law unto himself. He's ignored EAM guidance and policies on many matters. It doesn't look good for Selena.'

'We'll see about that.'

Kapralos welcomed Thomas with a forced smile. 'Thomas, I heard you were on your feet and walking, it's good to see you again, but I wish it was under better circumstances.'

Thomas didn't sit. His boots still dusty from the road, his eyes fierce. 'What the hell is this nonsense about Selena? You can't possibly be taking it seriously.'

Kapralos's jaw tightened. 'I can't hide from the evidence. I don't want to believe it myself, but it's pretty damning. I had a soft spot for Selena, as you know. Whatever I felt for her, the situation has changed that.'

Thomas took a step forward. 'She would never betray Greece, you know that—'

Kapralos raised a hand, cutting him off. 'I can only go on the evidence that's in front of me. I don't have a choice in the matter.'

'You're damn right, *you* don't. This matter is not your choice; it's a matter for senior EAM officials. Karayioryis is the senior representative for EAM in the region, so he should be made aware of this and shown the evidence. It's his choice and his alone that will determine if a trial is called.'

Kapralos's face darkened. 'That won't be necessary. Karayioryis is occupied with the Saraphis situation. It would take days, if not a week, to get the evidence to him so he can give this unfortunate affair his full attention, and then for a decision to be made. Given the circumstances, we don't have the luxury of waiting that long. No, a decision is expected, and it will be delivered. The trial begins tomorrow. There'll be no delay.'

Thomas stood in a daze, stunned at what he had just heard. 'You don't have the authority to preside over such matters.'

'It's the people's will that I answer to, and they demand a verdict, so I'll give them one.'

Thomas's blood pounded in his ears; his fear for Selena tore at his heart. The prospect that death awaited her showed no signs of abating.

Thomas's chest heaved in anger, and it took disciplined control to retrieve a sense of diplomacy.

'Then have the decency to allow me to speak with her.'

Kapralos gave an impatient sigh. His voice dropped, cold and sharp. 'You come in here and demand the trial should not go ahead, you insult me by insinuating I'm not fit to oversee the proceedings, and now you want to see and talk with the prisoner disregarding the protocol on such matters…'

'Don't talk to me about protocols; you've never followed a single one in your life.'

Kapralos scowled at him. 'It's no secret the two of you have, how shall I say this… become close. Given the circumstances, it would be seen as unusual to allow such a request.'

'I'm a British officer; my motives are solely professional. I've given you the courtesy of requesting to see her because of your rank as the leader of the *andartes* in this area. If you push me any further, I'll see her with or without your permission. Do I make myself clear?'

'I understand you well enough,' Kapralos responded irritably. 'You are in my town, in my headquarters and surrounded by my men. You are a guest, enjoying my hospitality and my protection in my country, but one word from me can change all of that. Do I make myself clear?'

Thomas's brow tightened. 'Is that a threat?'

'You can take it any way you like.'

Thomas glared at Kapralos, curbing his annoyance. He understood the point well enough, and given the situation, it didn't have Selena's best interests at heart.

'Very well.' He backed down in frustration.

Kapralos nodded in satisfaction, his authority intact. He pressed his position further. 'I'm not an unreasonable man. You can see Selena for a few minutes…' He let his words sink in before continuing, 'With one of my men in earshot.'

The cramped, windowless room held only a chair, a bed, and a stained mattress without sheets.

Once he unlocked the door, Thomas's escort stood in the corridor and lit a cigarette. Selena was sitting on the chair. She looked up, her large eyes blinking, confused at first, then glinting in astonishment, as Thomas put out his hands and took hers.

'What are you doing here?'

'The second I heard, I had to come and see you.' He

put his lips to hers in a long and deep kiss. His relief was immense as she pressed into him, her heart pulsing with life.

Reluctantly, he pulled away. 'I don't have long.' He couldn't believe what was happening.

'I'm sorry, Thomas.'

'There's nothing to be sorry about. This is a mistake. As soon as it's rectified, you'll be out of here.'

'In their eyes, I'm guilty. And tomorrow they'll make others believe it too.'

'Never! I won't let it happen.'

She wouldn't meet his eyes. 'At the trial, it will look that way.'

'From the evidence they have?'

She lowered her head. Gently, Thomas tilted her chin and kissed her again.

'Tell me you're innocent and I'll believe it.'

She took a deep breath. She caught sight of the *andarte* guard's shadow and grasped Thomas's hand. 'There were things I wanted to tell you. I didn't want there to be secrets between us. Tomorrow, don't see my silence as an admission of guilt; it's the only choice I have to protect those that need it.'

'Who are you protecting? Tell me, Selena.'

She hesitated, looking at him with her large brown eyes. 'In another life, you would have made me happy, Thomas.'

'Don't say that. Don't you dare say that. You'll be happy in this life.'

'It's too late for that now. This is goodbye.' She dropped his hand. He fumbled for hers, clutching at them.

'I don't want to hear you speak like that. This has been a mistake, and it will be sorted.'

'It will be, but not in the way we'd hoped.'

The guard leaned into the room. 'It's time,' he grunted, an undertone of impatience noticeable in his voice.

Thomas kissed Selena's forehead. 'I'll go straight to Kapralos and demand your release. I'll put my revolver to his head and put a bullet in it if he refuses.'

Selena put a finger to his lips. 'No, you won't. There will only be one of us on trial tomorrow.' She kissed him, then lifted her mouth from his. Her voice sank to a whisper, the words carving themselves into his heart. 'I love you, Thomas. Whatever happens tomorrow, always remember that.'

There was a knock at the door.

Thomas put his ear to the wooden surface.

'Who is it?'

'Thomas, it's Stathis.'

Thomas unlocked the door and invited Stathis in.

'Would you like a coffee, or something stronger?'

'I wouldn't say no to a real drink.'

Thomas poured two glasses of cognac and handed one to Stathis, who smiled. 'So, it's not just guns and ammunition that drop from the sky. You get top-shelf drink, too.'

'It helped to keep us warm on the chilly nights in the mountains. It's the last bottle.'

'I'm honoured. I'd better savour it.'

'What brings you here, Stathis?'

'Kapralos would like you to attend the trial tomorrow.'

'What trial? It's a fiasco. I don't believe for one minute there will be any justice served. It's illegal. You know that as well as I do.'

'I feel sorry for you.'

'I don't need your sympathy.'

'She played you as a fool. She was probably priming you for information too,' Stathis said with an amused click of his tongue.

Thomas ignored him. 'How long will it last?' He refused to call it a trial.

'It won't last long, although I suspect Kazakos will want to prolong the inevitable and give the townsfolk some entertainment,' he concluded.

Thomas glared at him. He could see that Stathis was enjoying this.

'I heard that Kapralos's runner returned without a wireless. That's a shame. You're on your own now.'

'Is there anything else?'

Stathis drained the last of his drink. 'Now that you mention it, there is.' He leaned forward. 'She hasn't told you, has she?'

'Told me what?'

'About the two of us. We were together.'

'You and Selena!'

Stathis grinned. 'That shocks you?'

'When was this?'

'Before the war. Her father had given me his blessing.'

'You were to be married?'

'I was going to ask her. Everyone expected it. Then, her mother and father were killed by the Germans.'

'I know.'

'She wasn't herself after that. I told her I'd give her time, that she'd come back to me after she had dealt with her grief.'

'But she didn't.'

'I would have waited for her.'

'I don't think she sees it that way.'

Stathis snorted. 'Why? Because of you?'

'I think she felt like that before she knew me.'

Stathis leaned forward with an intent look in his eyes.

'What do you know about it, Englishman? You come here and speak our language and think you can tell us how to organise ourselves, how to fight, what to think and how to run our affairs. You think you can tell me how to feel? You think you can take our women whenever you please. What gives you the right to come to my country and tell me how to live? You're on your own now. Your position is weak.'

'You need to calm down, Stathis,' Thomas demanded.

'You think you can tell me what to do, well fuck you! We took your advice, Thomas, in identifying the informer for the ambush. We made sure we were loose with our tongues. There was to be an operation to blow up a section of railway line. We had our suspicions who was to blame for the ambush. We put out feelers, and what came back was quite interesting. Just before the ambush, one of the new recruits had been seen in a café frequented by the Germans in a garrison town called Rendina. We made sure that when he was around, he'd hear of the false operation, and where and when it was to happen.

'Obviously, the Germans turned up, but we weren't there. When confronted, guilt was written all over him. He was promised money. The fool.' Stathis gave a sly smile. 'It pleased Kapralos. He now had even more evidence to show Selena's guilt as an informer.'

Thomas shot him a look of disbelief. 'She had nothing to do with it!'

'That's not how it will be told at her trial.'

Thomas glared at him. 'And the real informer?'

'Oh! He doesn't have much to say for himself, not anymore. A bullet to the back of the head saw to that.'

'By you?'

Stathis leaned forward so that Thomas could see him clearly. 'We got one of the new recruits to do it, to prove his loyalty and courage and to show in front of the other new recruits just what it takes to be an *andarte*.'

'To falsify the truth, kill an innocent man and fabricate evidence. Is that what it takes? Is that what being an *andarte* is, Stathis?'

'You're going to wish you'd died in that ambush.'

Thomas's heart pounded. 'What are you talking about?'

Stathis grunted. 'You'll not make a fool of me any longer. It's no secret what you and the informer have been getting up to. It disgusts me. To think I loved her once. She's a traitor to Greece!'

Thomas sucked in his breath. 'You know Selena. She would never do that.'

Stathis rubbed his forehead. 'She's not the Selena I knew. If I'm asked, it will give me pleasure to be part of the firing squad that deals out justice for Greece.'

'You're mistaken, Stathis. Kapralos is taking advantage of you. He's using you. He wants me out of the way, and he knows he can rely on you to do that. He knows your weakness. Selena is innocent. She had no part in it.'

'It doesn't look like that, now, does it? Just before the ambush took place, she was seen handing information to a well-known informer, Apostolis Raptis, who has the German's protection.'

'You don't know that.'

'What else could there be in the envelope? She's guilty. There's always been suspicion about this Apostolis's affairs and how his businesses continue to thrive despite the occupation. I knew he was a German puppet, profiting while his countrymen suffered. It's worked out well, don't you think?'

'The evidence is circumstantial. Kapralos has no

authority to pass judgment. His seniors will not look on this favourably for him; you of all people should know that.'

'What do those in Athens know about the mountains, about our suffering and what it takes to fight the enemy?'

'You would see Selena shot?'

'That's the punishment for traitors.'

The flash of steel alarmed Thomas in Stathis's hand.

'A gun is too noisy; it would bring unwanted attention. A knife is a lot cleaner and quieter. It's time to reclaim my honour.'

Stathis had crossed a boundary, and Thomas understood, judging by the anger within his gaze, that this was irreversible.

The house that was once a sanctuary, where he and Selena shared precious time, now trapped him. The room was too small, too cluttered; a table, two chairs, a cabinet, and the low ceiling made every movement feel claustrophobic.

Thomas steadied himself. 'Whatever you think of me, you know Selena is innocent; she had nothing to do with the ambush.'

'She does now.' Stathis took a step forward, teeth gritted.

'You bastard!'

Thomas lunged.

Stathis dodged him, the knife slashing across Thomas, inches from his face. Thomas stepped backwards again as the knife sliced in front of him. This time, he grabbed Stathis's wrist, but the pain in his shoulder weakened his grip.

Stathis wrenched free, pivoted and slashed again. Thomas caught the arm, redirecting the blade downward. It scraped along the side of the table. Thomas sidestepped, slamming his good shoulder into Stathis's chest, knocking him into the table.

Pain lanced through Thomas's shoulder, threatening to overwhelm him. That was enough for Stathis to steady himself. Thomas grabbed a chair and hurled it. Stathis raised an arm, deflecting the blow but stumbled back against a cabinet.

Thomas charged forward, driving his good shoulder into Stathis's chest. They collided with the cabinet, ornaments and crockery shattering around them, as the knife clattered across the floor.

They grappled in the confined space, slamming into the furniture. The table tipped, crashing to the floor. A chair shattered beneath them. Thomas gasped as Stathis elbowed him hard and drove a knee into his side. Thomas hit the floor hard, his shoulder taking the impact. A strangled cry escaped his lips as white-hot agony flared through his body, threatening to overwhelm him.

He pushed himself upwards, his limbs leaden. Stathis had the knife in his hand again, grunting, breathing hard. Thomas pushed himself to his feet. With a growl, he drove his forehead into Stathis's nose. The crack was wet and sudden. Stathis screamed, the knife clattering to the ground between them.

They both dived for it.

Thomas's hand closed over the hilt, but Stathis was on him, punching wildly. The blade skittered across the floor, lost in the shadows.

They rolled. Thomas's back hit the wall. Stathis clawed for Thomas's throat, pressing tightly, heavily, his eyes wide and wild.

Thomas groped. His fingers swept the floor and closed around something solid – a broken leg of the chair, jagged and heavy. He gripped it, choking, eyes swimming, as the world narrowed.

Selena's face swam behind his eyes, as Stathis's demented face blurred at the edges. The room tilted, and Thomas's grip loosened around the leg of the chair.

The door burst open.

'Thomas!' Fanis's voice thundered through the small room.

Fanis charged with the fury of a storm, his hard frame barrelling into Stathis, sending both men crashing into the wall. Stathis roared in rage, driving his elbow into Fanis's ribs.

Fanis grabbed the broken chair leg and brought it down hard across Stathis's back, who howled in pain, rolling away.

Thomas struggled to his feet, using the wall for support, and watched helplessly as the two men circled each other. Fanis was panting, blood trickling from a cut on his cheek. Stathis moved like a predator, confident despite the cramped quarters.

Stathis threw a punch, which Fanis blocked, grabbing Stathis's wrist. With a roar, Stathis head-butted Fanis, sending him staggering backward. As Stathis moved to press his advantage, his foot caught. He stumbled.

It was all Fanis needed. He seized Stathis by the throat and shirt, and with the momentum, slammed him headfirst into the corner of the stone hearth. A sickening crack of bone echoed in the small room, and Stathis slid to the floor, eyes wide and unseeing, a dark pool spreading beneath his head.

Fanis stood over him, chest heaving. He turned to Thomas, who was staring at Stathis's body. 'He's dead!'

Thomas heard the words as if someone else had spoken

them. He struggled to his feet. 'You did what had to be done. He would've killed both of us. What are we going to do with him?'

'Leave it to me. I'll get rid of him,' Fanis said.

The square heaved with inquisitive townsfolk, of the air thick with anger that swelled like a boil threatening to explode.

A table and three chairs sat ominously in front of the building that was Kapralos's headquarters.

In front of the assembled crowd, the *andartes* stood with rifles slung over their shoulders, a human barrier to remind onlookers who was in control of proceedings.

As Thomas and Fanis jostled for a position that offered an unobstructed view, Thomas found the scene chilling and unnerving.

Kapralos, with two others, took seats at the table. Before sitting, Kapralos acknowledged the crowd, then sat between the two. Kapralos placed a sheet of paper in front of him, covered it with his hands, and continued to smile at the crowd.

'Who are those men with Kapralos?' Thomas asked, forming a peak with his hand to shield his eyes and get a better look.

'The older one, I believe, is a member of the village council.'

'So, he's just for show… and the other?'

'That's Kapralos's brother,' Fanis replied. 'I heard he studied law at Athens University before joining his brother.'

'His knowledge of the law is irrelevant today.'

The guards brought Selena out next, her eyes squinting in the sunlight, her hands bound with rope, a bruise prominent on her cheekbone, and she seemed to lean on the guard's arm for support. The crowd fell silent as Thomas caught sight of her and stepped forward, but Fanis's tight grip pulled him back.

'What have the bastards done to her?' Thomas hissed.

They led Selena to the table, where she faced her accusers with her head bowed.

Thomas reached for the ribbon inside his pocket, feeling it through the fabric.

'Selena Castellanos,' Kapralos began, 'you have been brought before this people's court charged with the serious crime of spying for and colluding with the enemy. It's our duty to examine the evidence before us and come to an informed conclusion about the facts.

'Were you in the village of Rendina on Monday afternoon?'

Selena continued to stare at the ground in front of her.

Kapralos grunted. 'I'll remind you of your activities, shall I? On that day, you met with Apostolis Raptis, an affluent merchant whose wealth was considerable before the occupation but who has grown much wealthier during it. Along with several other business ventures, he runs a taverna in Rendina, and it's no secret that it is often frequented by German officers. Apostolis must be on good terms with these enemies of Greece, as his goods trucks are rarely searched at German checkpoints. To all of us gathered here, he looks like he represents everything that is contemptible – a Greek profiting from his countrymen's suffering.'

Several cries of abuse rose from the crowd.

Kapralos raised his hand, silencing the outburst.

'The accused was seen slipping into the back entrance of Apostolis's taverna. Then, through a window, she and

Apostolis were observed to be engaged in what can only be described as an intense and intimate conversation. An exchange of sealed envelopes took place. Selena was seen tucking her envelope inside her jacket before they embraced.

'Upon returning to Porta, her house was searched, and inside the envelope, this sheet of paper was found. Written on this sheet there is a long message in code. Unfortunately, we don't have the expertise to decipher the code, but I remind the good people of Porta, such messages are only written in this manner because of the secrecy and importance that the information holds. A code is written for a specific reason and for a select few, and that reason is to hide acts of treason and murderous intent against you and your families and Greece's sons and daughters. You were also seen at the same taverna a few days before a German ambush, where several of my men were killed, along with a British officer.'

The crowd was now baying for blood.

'Say something,' Thomas pleaded, squinting in the sun.

Kapralos's voice hardened. 'Your silence is an admission of guilt.'

Selena raised her head and stared at Kapralos. 'I'm not a traitor to my people, and not to my beloved Greece. Those who are, stand amongst us and will be revealed when the time is right and wiped out like all the evildoers until none are standing. Their time is short; their end is near.'

He slid his chair backwards and stood up. He walked towards Selena and bent his mouth to her ear. She flinched at the touch of his breath.

'You think you can threaten me with your words. I'm not the one with my hands bound. I'm not on trial here. I decide if you live or die.'

Her eyes burned into him. 'Some secrets are worth dying for.'

Kapralos stepped away from her with a gratifying smile.

He turned to the crowd and addressed them. 'It is our duty to report subversion. It is a serious matter and involves each and every one of us. We must be vigilant at all times. If there is a traitor, a spy, a subversive, or infiltrator, we must reveal them and expose them.

'They sell themselves for gold and money. They betray Greece to the enemy. It is our duty to report even the most insignificant words spoken by these spies and traitors of the people and our motherland, holy Greece.'

He struck his fist on the table, and the older man jumped in fright. 'We cannot afford to be sentimental, or weak, or naïve; these are states of being that harm vigilance. Let me remind you, the enemy is among us; the enemy prowls amongst us. If we look hard enough, we will find them and expose their heinous deeds and crimes. They will be crushed without mercy.'

The crowd roared its approval.

Kapralos was enjoying the moment and acknowledged the crowd's endorsement with a wide grin and a satisfactory nod.

He raised his hand, and they fell silent.

'According to ELAS, someone can be tried for subversion and treason for one of the following: possessing undisclosed firearms, communicating information to the occupation forces, and, I quote, *defaming the armed forces of the nation and spreading upsetting rumours that could entice panic and harm the people's struggle and the people themselves.*' His voice picked up, sharp and loud. 'It is our duty to strike down such tyranny, such filthy maggots and snakes by drenching our fields with their poisonous and infected blood. We must wipe them out.'

Selena glanced up and recoiled at the bitterness in his voice.

Loud cheering and shouting, denouncing Selena, erupted over the square.

'The court is entrusted with a monumental decision. There is a question we have to answer.'

Kapralos turned and stared at the older man, who hesitated, then said, 'Guilty!'

Kapralos's brother nodded approvingly. 'Guilty!'

Kapralos faced the crowd, now fevered and wild. 'Selena – I find you guilty and sentence you to death by firing squad.'

Selena slumped forward, her legs crumbling under her, and she fell to the ground.

When Thomas knocked on the door, a slight gap appeared.

'Who is it?' asked a nervous voice.

'Thimios, it's Thomas.'

The door opened a fraction more. 'Thomas, it is you. Come inside.'

As he entered, Thomas asked. 'Have you heard what happened?'

'I was there.'

'Then you know.'

Thimios ran his hand through his hair. 'There was only ever going to be one outcome. He used her as an example, the bastard.'

'This isn't how it's going to end for her.'

Thimios had already resigned himself to the fact that Selena would die. 'What can you do? It's been decided.

She'll be shot tomorrow, just like her mother and father were, except this time, it's her own countrymen doing the murdering.'

'Why didn't she speak when she had the chance? Her silence condemned her in the eyes of the crowd.'

Thimios could hear the sharp edge of anger in Thomas's voice. He paused before answering. 'She had no choice.'

'What do you mean?' A heavy weight of dread pushed down on him.

'You know Selena has access to details of German movements because of the information the network of shepherds gives her. She's part of Kapralos's network for gathering information. What Kapralos doesn't know is, she has been drip feeding him information, but the detailed intelligence she was given was for Apostolis's eyes only, written in code that tracked German/Italian train movements, and mapping German troop positions, their movements and fortifications.

'Apostolis is an undercover intelligence agent for EAM. She gave Apostolis an envelope, the contents of which detailed Kapralos's illegal trials, extortion, money laundering, and the execution of villagers – all verified through written eyewitness accounts. Kapralos's time is up; he just doesn't know it yet. Selena couldn't jeopardise that.

'Apostolis is double-crossing the Germans. It's risky, but so far, he's got away with it. While appearing to collaborate, he's deliberately feeding mixed intelligence and misinformation to the Germans. Apostolis's position as a "collaborator" is an elaborate cover that allows him to gather crucial intelligence from German officers who speak freely in his taverna. They think it's a safe space.

'Selena serves as his courier, passing him information

while maintaining absolute secrecy about their relationship to protect his cover.

'She cannot reveal Apostolis's identity without compromising his work. You can imagine the dangerous position that would put him in.'

The expression in Thomas's eyes turned from desperate to astounded to incredulous. 'So, she's sacrificed herself.'

'Selena will never risk his life.'

'Not even to save herself?'

'Apostolis is her brother.'

Thomas's heart felt like it had been wrenched from him.

Thimios continued. 'Years before her parents were married, Selena's mother had relations with a wealthy merchant. Apostolis is Selena's half-brother. He is ten years older. Throughout their adult lives, they have maintained a secret relationship, despite their different circumstances. Only close family members know about this.'

'He has to come forward.' It was a slim thread for Thomas to hang on to. 'Only he can save her. By refusing to explain her actions, Selena's silence worked against her, and she knew it. Each unanswered question increased the crowd's suspicion. The evidence, though circumstantial, was damning – the intercepted messages, the suspicious meeting, and the operation that seemed compromised.'

'Selena knew the risks. Apostolis can't be exposed. This is bigger than Selena. She knows she'll be saving the lives of many innocent people.'

His shoulders sagged. 'Why didn't she expose Kapralos at the trial?'

'How would that have looked? A desperate woman with accusations but no evidence. This way, now that Apostolis has the evidence, once it is given to EAM, Kapralos will be like a rabbit caught in a trap. He doesn't know it yet, but he

is about to get what he deserves. Selena is prepared to die if
it means Kapralos's tyranny is ended and Apostolis's undercover operation remains intact. She is saving lives. If her
acts make the smallest impact on the Germans' grip on
Greece, she'll see that as a victory. She knew this day would
come; it was just a matter of time.'

'She should have told me.'

'She wanted to. Believe me, she really did. It wasn't that
she didn't trust you; she loves you, Thomas, she told me so.
And because of that very fact, she was never going to put
you in any danger. You were wounded; you had no means
of communicating with the British. She didn't want to
compromise your recovery by putting you in an impossible
position. What could you have done?'

Thomas felt his heart swell with hope as he headed for
the door. 'I can do something about it now. I can stop this
from happening. She cannot die. I won't allow it.'

'Then, whatever it is you have in mind; I want to be part
of it.'

After seeing Thimios, Thomas returned to the house, where
Fanis was waiting.

'Even if I leave now and return to Aris and tell him
everything we know about Kapralos, it would be too late; it
still will not save Selena. So, I've been thinking,' Fanis said.
'I'll confront Kapralos, and tell him if he doesn't let Selena
free, I'll report all his sordid dealings to Aris.'

Thomas glanced out of the window, his face blank and
expressionless. A few seconds passed, and Thomas said
nothing. Then, continuing to gaze outside, he finally said,
'When I was in Crete, I met a family – a mother and her
two children. They put their trust in me. I couldn't keep

them safe. Instead, they all died, bombed by a German plane in the very building I told them they would be safe in – their home. It's haunted me ever since. That's not going to happen again. This time, I have a chance to do something and lay their ghosts to rest.' He turned to Fanis. 'Will the execution be in public?'

'Normally, after giving the sentence, Kapralos usually shoots the accused himself.'

'But not this time. Why?' Thomas tapped his bottom lip with a finger.

'Kapralos knows a firing squad will give the execution legitimacy, and that it will look like he is following legal procedures. He can't be seen to be a common murderer in the provincial towns. This is not some rundown village in the back of beyond.'

'He's already pulled the trigger. Do you know where it will take place?'

'I heard a group of drunk *andartes* mention it was going to take place in a small gully not far from here at sunrise tomorrow.'

Thomas nodded. 'Thimios will know where it is, and the quickest route of escape.'

'What are you planning, Thomas?'

'There's going to be an execution tomorrow morning, but not the kind Kapralos wants or expects.'

Selena sat in the confinement of the small room staring at the wall, Kapralos's words and the sentence of death reverberating in her head. She would not see her uncle Thimios, her auntie, Marina, her niece and nephew; she could not continue her work against the Axis occupation. She would no longer hear the voice of Apostolis, or feel the warmth of his brotherly love. Her name would always be uttered with the scorn of scandal; she would be held up as an example to others, the recipient of hatred pouring from their hearts. Her memory will be tarnished with that most despicable of labels – collaborator and traitor. All of this unendurable, yet necessary.

Selena could not bear knowing how distraught Thomas would be. She left without saying goodbye. It had to be that way. She could not bear such an ending, failing to give him explanations. Such was the utter impossibility. She knew that, at the trial, Thomas would feel the charges against her like a blow. Her eyes filled with tears of remorse and guilt, the force of it pummelling her like a raging storm. She would never feel his mouth on hers, or his hands igniting the fires of passion that only he could summon; she would never again know that all absorbing, encompassing universe only they had shared; she would never feel his physical presence and the manifestation of complete surrender that only he could awaken in her. It was the worst punishment.

She lay on the ground and curled into a ball. The love she held for Thomas was her only companion, her only solace.

Thomas believed it was possible. They had arranged it. Trees covered each side of the gully, leaving a clearing between them. Selena would arrive there by truck. The clearing was only accessible on foot, a distance of around fifty feet from where the truck would stop. She was to be shot in the clearing and her body buried amongst the trees.

Thomas would position himself on one side of the clearing, while Fanis and Thimios would be on the opposite side. The firing squad would make easy targets with nowhere to run, like toppling dominoes, Thomas said. They would use the truck as a quick means of escape.

Outside, it was still dark when they set off. Thomas felt the weight of the rucksack, laden with clothes and food, shift on his back. It was the first time he had asked questions of his body since being shot. A pain niggled his shoulder, like a mild toothache, but he pushed on, as Thimios led the way through narrow lanes that the full moon illuminated in its soft lunar glow. Once clear of the buildings, they kept to the cover of the trees and out of sight of the main road.

There came a crunch of gears and the groan of a laboured engine that emitted somewhere to their left. 'If that's them, then they're early. How far, Thimios?' A knot tightened in his stomach.

'Another ten minutes,' he replied, the alarm in his voice clear for all to hear.

By now, Thomas was panting, rivulets of sweat glistening on his forehead. Underfoot, his boots crunched and disturbed dry pine needles with each frantic, leg-burning and gruelling step. His grip tightened, his knuckles white around the rifle, a reminder of what was about to unfold.

He went over on his ankle and stumbled off balance; the pain was searing and hot, but he pressed on with gritted determination.

Eventually, Thimios raised his hand and put a finger to his lips. They halted, Thomas's eyes darted off every shadow, peering beyond the trees, where he heard voices and movement.

No! No! We can't be too late! A hot panic ripped through Thomas's chest.

To their right, the truck stood still; the driver had his

back to them, smoking a cigarette. He would become a problem when the shooting began.

Thomas motioned to Fanis, who nodded his understanding and within seconds had slipped unseen from the cover of the trees and crept along the body of the truck, knife in hand. Fanis approached the driver with silent stealth, and in one swift motion, clasped his hand around the driver's mouth and sliced the knife along his throat. The driver's legs buckled, and with a curdled, blood-filled groan, he slumped to the ground, lifeless and still, a dark flow staining the ground around him.

The coarse hemp of the blindfold had dug into her skin, just as it had from the moment they'd bundled her onto the truck. They had bound her hands in coarse rope, the pain unforgiving and tight. Selena's world was black, interspersed with the sharp tang of diesel, the creak of the wooden bench, and the lurch of the truck and its discordant rhythm, as it drove over every rut and hole on the narrow, winding track.

Each jolt had thrown her sideways, shouldering her into the two *andartes* she sat in between. One reeked of stale sweat, and with every sway of the truck, the sour musk had caught in her nose. She swallowed hard as her stomach churned. The taste of bile had risen in her throat, and she clenched her jaw against it, keeping at bay its acid bite.

She had strained her ears and caught four distinct voices, perhaps more.

Then, with the crunch of gravel, the truck slowed before screeching to a halt, its engine dying with a final, shuddering gasp. Selena's pulse hammered in her throat as she strained to make sense of sound and movement, then her darkened world began to erupt.

The tailgate dropped, hands grabbed her, impatient and rough. They yanked her up and flung her from the wooden bench, and she crashed into the hard-packed earth, first with her shoulder, then her head. A thud. A crack. Air exploded from her lungs, and her body roared with pain.

'Get up, you bitch. You filthy whore.'

The words hit her hard, like the boot that followed. It drove into her side, and she curled, wincing in pain, sharp and raw as it tore through her ribs. A hand wrenched her arm, dragging her, scraping over grit for what seemed an eternity, all sense of direction lost, only motion and the searing burn of pain remained. Then they released her, and she collapsed onto her back, gasping. Dust clogged her throat; grit scraped her teeth. Her side screamed in agony, and she begged it to stop.

She clung to a memory, precious and sustaining. A cloudless sky, vast and blue and endless, where the sun kissed her face. She inhaled its warmth, its touch, but it wasn't enough. Her skin prickled with panic. Suddenly, overwhelmed with chilling certainty, an immense thought struck her: she was going to be shot. Here. Now. And it gripped her like a vice.

Again, a hand hauled at her, and she was standing, swaying, a warm wet sensation seeping down her legs.

It was the knowing that tortured her, the waiting for the final moment. Every sound, every intake of breath, every smell was her last. Her eyes screwed shut, and through clenched teeth her last thoughts came fast: *What will it feel like? Will I hear the shot first? Will there be pain? Will I know the moment before it comes – or will everything just… stop?*

A violent shiver ran through her, every nerve screaming

as her world narrowed to this one, final second. And she waited. Fear and despair pressed down on her. She didn't want to die, not here, not like this. There were too many things unsaid, not enough done. She had a life to live; she yearned to live.

She heard their feet scrape the dry ground, the crack of pinecones underfoot; she sensed a nervousness about them and could even put a face to some voices that travelled towards her. She flinched at the unmistakable sound of rifles being readied, the click of hammers being cocked, then clutched against shoulders, and then, the order to take aim.

CHAPTER THIRTY

DANGER

Skiathos 2007

Dimitrios steps outside the office and spots something tucked under the wiper blade of his scooter. Another flyer, he frowns, as he pulls it free, and then, he instantly knows what it is. His stomach drops as he scans the immediate area for any sign of him. He unfolds the piece of paper and can see the neat deliberative handwriting. His jaw clenches as he reads.

I've watched the way you look at her, the way you touch her. You think it's love, don't you? It's not. I'm the only one who is allowed to love her, no one else.

You think you know her, but you don't. You only know the Carissa she wants you to see. But you don't know her like I do, no one does. I know her better than she knows herself.

Did she tell you about the miscarriage? I stood by her when she was at her worst. I held her together while she screamed at walls. I stayed when anyone else would've walked.

So forgive me if I don't respect your little holiday romance. This isn't love to her. It's an escape. An escape from herself. She's lost, but I've found her, and she can only be happy with me.

P.S.
Did you like the photograph?

He is electrified with worry and concern. He rushes back into the office. Startled, Evangelia lifts her head from the computer screen.

'Where's Carissa?' Dimitrios's voice is so loud and insistent that Evangelia jumps.

'She's finished for the day.'

'Did she say where she was going?'

Evangelia shrugs. 'I don't know. Should she have? She's probably gone home. She did say she was dying for a shower.'

Just then, Athena enters the office door and slides past Dimitrios, she glances at him and sees his frustration boiling like hot water. 'What's going on?'

Evangelia looks up at her. 'I was just telling Dimitrios that Carissa has gone home.'

'That's not what you said, you said she's *probably gone home.*'

'Did I?'

Dimitrios can't think straight; his mind is still consumed by the note.

'She could have gone shopping, I suppose,' Evangelina reconsiders.

Athena wipes a flake of croissant from her top lip, a

trace left from her recent snack. 'I've just been to the bakers; I didn't see her.'

'I'll phone her.' Dimitrios pulls his phone from his pocket.

'Ah! Just before she left, she was annoyed because her phone needed to be charged,' Evangelia recalls.

Dimitrios sighs heavily. 'It's just ringing out.'

'What's the rush, anyway?' Athena asks.

His stomach lurched. 'I think she's in danger!'

CHAPTER THIRTY-ONE

A FLIGHT OF EVASION

Mainland Greece 1943

It came without warning, the crack so loud it tore the air in front of her. Then another. And another. Short, rapid bursts, ricocheting around her.

Selena flinched, curling her arms over her head. Her ears rang as dust, shots, and cries exploded in front of her. She felt no pain, no thudding bullet, only blind, confused, and disoriented panic. She trembled as the blindfold, choking her sight, reduced her world to sound, to chaos, to the brutal percussion of violence.

Her knees buckled under the weight of it. She pressed herself flat to the ground, trying to process what had just happened. Then, as quickly as it began, an abrupt and eerie silence fell around her.

She heard his voice then. 'Selena!' His urgent footsteps pounded closer until he was with her. The blindfold tugged loose. She flinched, blinking, and his face swam before her. Thomas gasped, 'You're alive. I thought I'd lost you.'

Behind Thomas, Selena gazed at the bodies of her executioners – lying motionless, limbs contorted, rifles scattered where they'd fallen from dying hands.

She saw Fanis and Thimios emerge from a covering of trees and felt her eyes moisten with tears, the situation clear to her.

Thomas eased her to her feet, and she fell into his arms sobbing in relief. When Thimios and Fanis reached them, Selena felt a tremendous surge of gratitude.

She wiped her eyes. 'You could've been killed.'

'You're alive, and that's all that matters,' Thimios said, kissing her forehead.

'These men all died because of me.'

Thimios cradled her head in his hands. 'And they would have killed you because Kapralos commanded it so. Never forget that.'

Thomas was acting on instinct now. 'We need to leave.

When this lot fail to return, the entire area will crawl with Kapralos's men.'

With the truck, they covered a lot of ground. When the sun sat fully in the sky, the road offered little protection, so they abandoned the vehicle at a pre-planned location and scrambled up through a goat trail into a narrow ridge of shale and bramble, invisible from the road. They headed towards an old shepherd's hut, only a single-room shelter of dry-stacked stone and smoke-blackened rafters. A tarpaulin patched the roof, a cracked oil lamp hung from a hook, the door leaned crooked on one hinge, and a small ancient brazier stood under a hole in the ceiling. With no chairs available, they sat on the ground, and Selena nestled against Thomas; the press of her body against his side demonstrated the enormity of their accomplishment.

'It's not much, but it's out of the way,' Thimios said. 'I

used to use it when I went on hunting trips when I was younger.'

'It'll do. I'm grateful for everything you've done. I'll always be in your debt,' Thomas said, knowing that killing in such a way had been a first for himself and even Fanis.

'It was necessary, and even if it haunts me to my last day, knowing Selena is safe, is all that matters. Her father, my brother, would've done the same for my daughter.'

Fanis sat quietly, ashen-faced, staring at the ground. He fiddled with the chain around his neck, a crucifix dangling from it.

'That can't have been easy for you,' Thomas said.

'I never thought I'd kill my own.'

Thomas drew a breath. 'I'm grateful.'

Their eyes met, then Fanis veered his gaze away.

'What does it make me?' Irony coloured the timbre of his voice.

'It was necessary…' Thomas struggled to finish the sentence.

'They were just following orders.' Fanis's fingers curled around the crucifix.

'That's why it was wrong, because what they were about to do didn't make it right. They would have shot Selena. Where is the honour in that?'

Fanis rubbed his hand against his jaw. 'There is none.'

'Is that what you really think?'

Fanis's hand fell from the crucifix. He looked at Selena, who could feel the blaze of his eyes as if it scorched her skin.

'It was necessary,' he finally said, repeating Thomas's words. As if to draw a line under it, Fanis handed out cigarettes and lit his own. 'What are you thinking, Thomas? There wasn't time to plan beyond this.'

'I could take Selena to the new headquarters, explain the situation to Eddie, although the part about killing eight *andartes* won't go down well. When Kapralos finds out we're gone, he'll know what we did and he'll turn it to his advantage, a British officer sent to help the resistance kills eight of his men, he'll put a spin on it that makes me look the guilty party.'

Fanis wrinkled his forehead, thinking. 'I can go to Aris and explain it all to him, along with Selena's evidence regarding Kapralos's crimes.'

Selena fiddled with the sleeve of her jacket. 'All of this compromises Apostolis. Even my silence might not have been enough to save him from Kapralos. He has no idea how significant Apostolis is to EAM. Apostolis's close association with the Germans has saved many Greek lives. We've spoken about what we'd do if a situation like this ever occurred.'

'Apostolis's cover as a friend to the German hierarchy in Thessaly has to remain intact,' Thomas added.

'That's the one thing that can't change, not even to save my life. That's why the information I gave Apostolis concerning Kapralos's crimes will already be known to EAM. He's one of the few in this area with a telephone link to Athens.

'The noose is tightening around Kapralos's neck,' Thomas said with satisfaction.

'The problem is, he doesn't know it yet, and that still makes him dangerous,' Fanis grunted.

'We don't have the luxury of time. None of it changes your situation, Selena,' Thomas said.

'Apostolis has contingency plans; if his operation is threatened, he'll disappear or, if time permits, escape to EAM headquarters in Athens. Kapralos's men are dead, and I live, which in the eyes of his men diminishes Kapralos's authority. Knowing the man he is, he'll react to this the only way he knows how – with violence. Kapralos has two suspects responsible for my escape, Apostolis and Thomas. Apostolis is still very much in danger unless he's already acted.' She held her head in her hands. 'I should have died. It would have been the best outcome for everyone.' She looked up at Thomas, the blood draining from her pained face. 'What have you done, Thomas?'

Her words stung him. 'I did the right thing.'

She lifted her gaze. 'Where can I go? I can't go back home. In their eyes, I'm a traitor. The only safe traitor is a dead one,' she said in a sudden gloom of helplessness.

Thimios placed his hand on Thomas's shoulder. 'We need to make a decision, Thomas.'

Thomas thought for a moment. Thimios was right; this was not the time. Even though Selena's accusation cut deep, it would have to wait. Then he said to Thimios. 'You need to go back to your family. You can't be implicated in any of this.'

He turned to Fanis. 'You need to let Aris know what's happened. Tell him everything you've learned about Kapralos, everything you've seen. It'll take at least two days to reach him. If he asks who was involved in rescuing Selena, tell him it was my call. I acted alone, and no one else.'

Fanis stubbed out his cigarette. 'Is that wise?'

'Just tell him,' Thomas said simply.

'The British, your unit – they'll charge you with killing their allies. You could be shot.'

'Not if you tell them I'm already dead. I died of my wounds.'

'Are you sure about this? You know what it means?' His eyes flickered with doubt and fear, entwined into a single look, but his protest fell silent with the brief nod of Thomas's head.

Thomas's resolve was unyielding, no matter the cost. Selena stared at him. She wanted to say, *'No; you are mad. This is madness.'* But she knew she could not change his mind; she saw it in his eyes.

'And what about Selena?' Thimios asked.

'That's her decision to make.' Thomas reached out and touched her arm. 'But you'll be safer in Athens. It's better to take your chances there. Follow Apostolis if that's where he's gone. You're not a traitor to EAM. They'll keep you safe.'

'And you, Thomas?' Thimios asked.

'I'm staying with Selena, whatever she decides and wherever that takes me.'

Selena gazed at him, trying to take in this new revelation. 'You would do all this for me?'

Thomas watched the play of light on her cheekbones. 'And more.' He held her gaze, his words firm and without hesitation.

'Thomas is right,' Fanis said. 'Athens is the only way. If you stay, Kapralos will not stop, not while you're still alive. You're now a living insult to his integrity, his authority.'

Selena slumped a little, pulling at her sleeve, her hair falling over her face in a tangle. 'A second death sentence in a matter of days.' She didn't know whether to laugh or cry, but she nodded, and in that instant, her fate was settled.

'I've a brother who lives in Athens. Your Uncle Theodore, Selena,' Thimios reminded her.

Selena nodded. 'I haven't seen him since I was a child.'

'He runs a safe house in the Plaka district. The street is called Patroou. He stays at number five. It's close to Syntagma Square.'

Thomas tried to smile. 'We'll leave at night; it will be safer and easier to travel without being seen.'

Even in daylight, light failed to permeate the hut. Fanis lit a candle. Its hardened wax spread like lava from its holder, and it mustered a meagre glow, throwing shadows long against the scraggly stone walls, while they ate some bread and cheese that Thimios brought with him.

Thomas stripped out of his uniform and dressed in the clothes he had brought: a shirt, trousers tied with a belt, a jacket patched at the elbows, and a flat cap that sagged over his eyes. Selena watched him. Even in these clothes, he was still Thomas: taut in posture, carrying himself with the practised detachment of an outsider, with that certain English reserve. And yet, even with everything stripped to bone, he was still the man who had lifted the blindfold from her face.

Thimios pulled a flask from his jacket pocket, and they all took turns drinking, passing it between themselves, hoping the ouzo would quell the horror of their actions, shake off their dread, and strip the tremor from their nerves.

Selena huddled closer to Thomas. She took his hand and pressed it to her cheek, luxuriating in its touch. Her guilt sat heavily in her chest, and she braced herself against it, knowing his future was now tied to her own.

She sat watching him, searching his face for doubt, for any trace of the recklessness that had so often soured the promises of men in her life. She found only a stubborn kindness; it was so incongruous amidst the day's killing that she almost laughed.

'I don't know what happens next.' It was almost a question rather than a statement, her voice barely above a whisper. 'I don't even know who I am anymore. What if this is the end?' Her hands braced against her knees.

He reached across and tucked a loose tangle of hair behind her ear. 'It isn't. From now on, you get to choose what's next.'

For the first time since the *andartes* had thrown her into the back of the truck, Selena let herself believe it.

The hours passed with only the sound of birdsong and the distant bleat of goats. They made final arrangements as the landscape blued with the pressing dusk; the sky deepened into indigo, and the sun melted into a smudge on the horizon. Selena wondered if its touch would ever feel like warmth again.

They wrapped themselves in their coats. Fanis left first. They said their goodbyes with firm handshakes, and then Thomas pulled Fanis towards him in a warm hug and wished him a safe journey. 'Thank you, Fanis, for everything. You've been like an angel sent from God.'

'Let's hope my wings don't get clipped, then. Goodbye, Thomas, and God be with you.' Fanis smiled, slipping away, the butt of his rifle clutched close against his jacket. Thomas watched him with awe. It was the stare of a soldier who'd braced for the worst but had found a kindred spirit.

Selena struggled to contain herself as Thimios left.

'I'll make for home and hopefully get there before sunrise,' he said, keeping his voice low, as though afraid even the hut's bare stones might betray them.

Selena rested her head on Thimios's chest, and he embraced her. 'Since your mother and father died, you have been a daughter to me.'

'And you have been a father to me.'

'It breaks my heart to let you go, but I must. Go with my

love and God's protection.' He turned towards Thomas. 'Keep her safe.'

Tears filled Selena's eyes. 'This is not goodbye. I'll return to you, I promise.'

'I don't doubt it.' He bent towards her and kissed her forehead.

He turned to Thomas. 'My house will always be open to you, and there will always be a place for you at my table, even if you are a ghost.'

Thomas and Selena watched him go; each lost in their thoughts. By the time the last echo of his boots had faded, Thomas took Selena's hand. 'Are you ready?'

She nodded, a thin line of tears welled and dried, streaking salt over her cheeks.

CHAPTER THIRTY-TWO

FOUND

Skiathos 2007

Carissa is sitting with Thomas under the shade of the pergola, as has become their custom. Thomas has set the table with a pot of tea and two cups and saucers. This morning, there is an addition. Carissa bought a *Portokalopita*, a traditional Greek orange cake with syrup, at the bakery just on the corner of the small square next to her apartment.

She feels herself sinking further into the wicker chair. 'I don't know what I would have done if it hadn't been for Dimitrios.'

'Ah, yes. Your chap. He sounds nice. Is it serious between you two?'

'I like him a lot. Well, if I'm honest,' she tries to catch her breath, 'more than a lot.'

'And I take it he feels the same?'

'He does.'

Thomas takes a sip of tea. 'That makes me happy, but it

could also complicate things, if it hasn't already. You're in a tricky situation. You're in a relationship, and your ex-partner has decided to follow you to Skiathos. Stalk you by all accounts. Does he know about Dimitrios?'

Carissa nods.

Thomas taps his hand on his knee. 'I really think you should have gone to the police.'

Carissa sighs in exasperation. 'And tell them what, exactly? Dimitrios and I have spoken about this. My ex is sending me notes and text messages that on the surface look like he's just looking out for me.'

A brief frown pulls at Thomas's eyebrows. 'You need to persuade the police that's how it looks but not his intention.'

'And how am I going to do that without coming across as paranoid?' She looks down at her hands. 'Although the tone of his last text was different,' she mumbles.

'In what way? Is he dangerous? Has he threatened you?'

Shit! She's said too much. She doesn't want to worry Thomas more than she has to. She's definitely not telling him about the photograph. 'Oh, nothing like that. He's becoming more insistent, that's all.' To her frustration, her voice cracks a little. 'I think he wants me to go back to Edinburgh with him.'

'Is the man delusional? What a nerve!'

'You haven't tried the cake yet,' Carissa says, trying to distract Thomas's attention away from the direction their conversation is taking.

He takes a slice and pops it in his mouth. 'It's delicious.'

He breaks off a piece, offering it to Daisy, who is hovering at the table. She swallows it whole, then eagerly cleans up the crumbs around Thomas's feet.

'Someone else thinks so too,' Carissa says, intentionally returning her attention to the cake.

Thomas considers her, and sensing her reluctance to speak about Stuart further, he rubs his head. 'Very well then,' he sighs. 'Given the recent unpleasantries, are you still enjoying your job?'

She nods. 'Apart from Dimitrios, and present company included, it's the only thing that's keeping me going.' She mustered a smile. 'I'm living and breathing it. It's been an education, that's for sure. I've had to learn so much. I've got scripts I have to learn by heart that detail the various areas we walk through, places of interest, the landscape, the history of the sites, the monasteries and churches.

'I never knew there were so many wildflowers, plants and trees on Skiathos. I know them all by appearance now. My mum would never believe it; she tried for years to get me interested in gardening.'

'Come on then, let me hear that encyclopaedic knowledge.'

'Let me see now.' She thinks for a moment. 'There's cistus rose, wild carrot, eagle fern, oriental bull's eye, spurge…'

Thomas smiles. 'I like the sound of that one.'

Carissa shakes her head and gives a small smile. She carries on. 'Common lilac, common plantain and male orchid. Now, for the wildflowers. My favourite are the poppies, there's also crowned goose flowers and star anemones. Oh! I nearly forgot – hawkweed, barberry and morning star.'

'That's very impressive.'

'I'm not finished yet. The trees. Obviously, there's pine and olive trees, then maple…' She screws her eyes. 'Ah! I remember now; I keep forgetting this one – Phoenician juniper. There's also the strawberry tree, mastic tree, tree holly and, last but not least, the oak tree.

'I've become an amateur horticulturist and historian, and I get to walk the trails, meet new people, teach fitness and wellbeing. I love it.'

'I can see that. Your face is virtually glowing just telling me about it, and your voice is practically singing. It's nice to see.'

He takes a sip of tea. Carissa notices what looks like an old tape recorder she hasn't seen before.

'What's that on the table?'

'Ah! I almost forgot, I was going to tell you, I took your advice.'

'My advice?'

'Yes. Writing about my time in Greece during the war.' He points towards the table. 'That's a Dictaphone. It's easier than typing, quicker and more natural for me to get my thoughts down.'

'That's wonderful. Will you publish it?'

'Thomas laughs. 'Good God, it's a long way off from that, but one day, yes, I'd like that.'

Something, or rather someone, catches her eye. He is standing by the garden gate, a baseball hat and sunglasses shielding his face, but Carissa recognises that gait, the way he holds himself; the body language is unmistakably familiar.

Thomas turns to follow Carissa's gaze.

Her mouth drops open, and she covers it with her hand. 'My God! It's him.'

'You mean Stuart?'

She nods disbelievingly.

'What does he want?'

She gasps. 'Me!'

CHAPTER THIRTY-THREE

ARRIVING

Mainland Greece, Athens 1943

For the first few miles, they walked in silence, quiet as falling snow. Scrub and bramble gave way to olive trunks, and then to thick and dense forests, where the sloping hills loomed menacingly and the mountains rose, brushed with the luminous sheen of the full moon. When morning came, they slept under the shade of pine trees for several hours, and then, continued on their way, Thomas sure they had put enough distance between themselves and Kapralos's reach.

They skirted many villages, only entering them to buy food and water. They slept in crudely made shelters of branches and ferns and washed in streams. Once, they came across a waterfall that fell into a deep pool. They shed their clothes, their inhibitions long having deserted them. He took her hand and together, naked; they waded into the water up to their waists and then their chests. She let her body drift into the water, and she swam from him, and then turned onto her back, as he watched the water slosh over her belly and breasts, glistening in the sunshine.

They lay on the bank together, her hair loose and falling around her shoulders in tangles and waves, watching a cloudless sky, the sun drying their skin, as they clasped each other's hands.

The longing inside him was so intense and so confined, he could feel his heart pump against his breastbone. It was an inexplicable desire, so unfathomable, he struggled to put it into words. He ached for her, so much so that he felt dazed, disoriented. His mouth slid along her skin, tracing the dip between her breasts, and the length of her flat belly as a sensation, hot and striking, bubbled deep inside him. Delicately, he touched her, and she pressed herself against him, and moved his head gently towards her. She called his name, and it was the most entrancing sound he had ever heard.

When at last they reached the worn dirt road that arced towards Athens, Selena felt both lighter and more exposed. The early hours would be safest, with the streets empty and the city's pulse still to waken from its sleep.

They crossed a deserted small square, where a pack of dogs fought over something dead. The streets were so empty that each footstep bounced back at them. They ducked through shadows, weaving along alleys and walls pocked with bullet holes. They passed a bakery and a school. Thomas urged her onwards, down the close-walled street, past closed doors and drooping laundry lines.

In the early morning light, every footstep seemed to echo, and Selena longed for a crowd, for the anonymity of jostling bodies, of noise, of safe invisibility. Her skin crawled with the thought that every eye could see her, through the open slit of window shutters and behind every lace curtain.

They turned a corner and nearly collided with a girl hauling water in a battered tin pail. She stared at Thomas first, then Selena, who braced herself for the cry, the dart of running feet, but the girl said nothing. She glanced away and disappeared down a lane. A dog barked somewhere. Thomas tensed, pressing a gentle hand to Selena's shoulder as he reassured her, 'We're almost there.'

The windows of a bakery glowed, spilling ribbons of yeasty warmth. A man in a battered apron swept the front of the shop, he looked up, his lips pressed to a thin line, his eyes flicking from Selena's face to Thomas, but instead of freezing at the sight of them, he continued working his broom.

Thomas took her by the arm. 'It's okay. We're not drawing attention; no one knows us here.'

They reached the first houses on Patroou, the air thundering with the early morning silence. Here and there a shutter banged lazily, as if the city couldn't quite decide when to wake from its slumber. For a breathless moment, when Selina knocked on the door of her uncle's house, she imagined someone from another life might open it. She prayed he recognised her.

CHAPTER THIRTY-FOUR

A SUPERFICIAL ENDING

Skiathos 2007

Carissa rises to her feet, sweat beginning to bead on her upper lip. She can't believe it. He has followed her. She feels like the ground has slid beneath her. 'This can't be happening,' she mutters, horrified, as Stuart saunters along the path towards them, his stony expression burning right through her.

'Well then, tea for two, I see. And cake. How civilised.'

'Stuart. What are you doing here?'

His face darkens. 'That's not the welcome I was hoping for, sweetheart.'

She tries to gather her thoughts, but they tumble and melt in her head. To her surprise, the shock at seeing Stuart is slowly beginning to erode with an anger that is nudging at her, and all she can think to say is, 'This has to stop!'

'Only you can make that happen.'

'By going back to Edinburgh with you?'

'Actually, yes. It's that simple.' There is a hint of a grin as he says it.

'You're deluded. It's over, Stuart.'

'Do you think so?'

'I refuse to be defined by your actions. You're sick, Stuart. You can't control me any longer, I won't allow it.'

'I know I made mistakes,' he says. 'I was intense. As you said, controlling, even. But that's not the whole picture, is it? We had something. Something – *real*. You told me that. Remember. You used those exact words.'

'That was a long time ago. That isn't now. Stop the mind games.'

He looks away. For a second, he seems smaller.

'I lost everything when you left,' he says. 'I thought… if I could just find you, if we could talk face to face, you'd remember what we were, what we had.'

His gaze lifts. 'I never stopped loving you, Carissa.'

'That's not love. I was just a thing you wanted to possess, to own. Your idea of love is warped. You don't know what love is.'

'And you do?' Stuart takes a step forward.

'I've found someone worth a hundred times more than you. You see, Stuart, understanding me isn't the same as owning me.'

He laughs. 'No, but it means we belong together. You and me – we were right for each other; you don't just walk away from something like that.'

She takes a step back.

Stuart's eyes narrow. 'He won't last,' he says. 'Dimitrios. He won't.'

Carissa's skin chills.

'You're sick.'

'No. I'm loyal. You think I came here to ruin your life? No, Carissa. I came to save it.'

'Why are you doing this?'

He grins. 'Did you find the little present I left for you?

'How did you get into the apartment?'

'Your colleague was very helpful. Evangelia.'

'What do you mean, she was helpful?'

Stuart smiles, and Carissa notices the genuine pleasure in his expression. 'You want to know how I got in? It was beautiful how it all worked out, but you'll have to ask Evangelia.'

As the words fall from his lips, Carissa's stomach drops. 'What?'

'Yes, Evangelia. She's been so helpful.'

'How could she? Why would she?' Carissa stammers.

Stuart's smile widens. 'Oh, the reasons are delicious. Shall I tell you what your dear colleague really thinks of you?'

'You're lying.'

'It's fascinating. She was able to tell me your daily routines, where you like to eat, and who you talk to. But here's where it gets interesting,' Stuart continues. 'She blames you for Dimitrios choosing you over her. Apparently, she has feelings for him too, and she's convinced you drove him away from her.

'I couldn't believe my luck, how easily she fell into my lap. She thinks that since you came here, everything has been handed to you. You didn't appreciate what you had, and if you suffered a little, you'd understand what she was going through. She really has a deeply ingrained resentment about her own inadequacies and romantic failures... fortunately for me.'

He pulls out his phone and scrolls through it. 'Ah!

Here we are. She believes she's helping us get back together, and you're making a terrible mistake. Listen to this: *I can see you love her so much; you can't hide that when you talk about her. Why is she being so cruel to you and punishing you for some imagined wrong? Every couple has their quarrels, but the best part is getting back together again. You've shown how much you love her by coming here. What more have you to do? What you have together is worth fighting for. There is nothing for her to forgive you for. She should go home with you, where she belongs. How can she not see that?*

'It's beautiful, isn't it? She wants to facilitate our romantic reunion.'

Carissa feels the shock of his words like a blow to the stomach.

'Of course, the money helps,' Stuart adds casually. 'Evangelia's mother needs medical treatment. Cancer. She has to visit the hospital on the mainland for treatment. My financial contribution has helped ease her financial worries, which she is obviously grateful for, as she's shown her appreciation in several ways.'

'How do I know you're telling the truth? After all you've put me through.'

'She told me something fascinating about her childhood,' Stuart continues. 'Always a bridesmaid, never the bride. Always the friend, never the girlfriend. Always watching other women live the life she wanted. When I offered her a chance to be important, to be needed, to be the one with power over someone else's fate... well, how could she resist?

'I started small. Just asked her to tell me if you seemed upset after I left the notes, sent the text messages. Then, to mention if you were dating anyone. Then to let me know your work schedule. Each request seemed reasonable, caring. By the time I asked for keys, I'd caught her hook, line and sinker.

'Don't think badly of her, Carissa, she really thinks she's helping you by helping someone who loves you find their way back to you.'

Carissa feels physically sick. The woman who greeted her every morning, who listened to her worries, who seemed like her closest friend on the island – had been documenting her life for her stalker.

'She even suggested the best times to enter your apartment,' Stuart adds. 'When you'd be teaching, when you'd be on a walking trail, when you'd be with Dimitrios. She knows your routine better than you do.

'The photos were inspired, weren't they? A nice touch, I thought. I've been saving them for the right moment. Did you show them to Dimitrios? Or were you too proud, too embarrassed?

'Within seconds, with just a few clicks, they could be all over social media: Twitter, Facebook. You can call it black-mail, whatever you want. Frankly, I don't give a fuck.'

It feels like a hand is constricting Carissa's heart. 'You wouldn't. It was just a bit of fun. I was younger. You wouldn't do that to me, Stuart?'

'Try me.' He opens the screen again and clicks on the Facebook icon. 'You humiliated me, Carissa. You left me. What must people have thought? Your friends, your family, my friends, my family, people at work. It's not me who's the failure; it's you. You were the one who had the miscarriage. You were the one who ran away. You couldn't even get that right. Could you?'

'Stuart, you need help.'

'Shut the fuck up! I'll decide what I need, not you, not anyone.'

Her hands shake. 'You're frightening me.' In the distance, she can hear the drone of an engine.

'How naïve you were. Did you really believe there would be no consequences? Do you think I would start a sword fight with a plastic ruler? No, I'd use a fucking huge machete. And that is what this is. Do you see this phone, the photos of you naked?' He waves the phone in the air. 'This is my machete, and I'm going to slice you into pieces with it. Soon, everyone is going to see you for what you really are. A whore.'

Thomas digs his hand into his shirt pocket and extracts a dictating machine. 'Everything that has just come out of that nasty hole in your head is now on this tape. You've just incriminated yourself.'

Stuart stares at Thomas. 'You can't prove anything on there.'

'I think the police will be interested in hearing it.'

'They'll never get the chance too.'

'Your attitude is beginning to tire me.'

Stuart disregards Thomas and turns to Carissa, grinning. 'Do you hear this? Who does he think he is?'

Thomas takes a sip of tea and replaces his teacup on the saucer with a click. 'I think it's time you left.'

Stuart glances over at Thomas. He aggressively massages the back of his neck. He takes a few steps forward menacingly; he brings his face down to Thomas's face. 'And who's going to make me? *You*, old man?' Stuart cocks an eyebrow. 'I'll leave when I've done what I came here to do.' Stuart holds out his hand. 'I'll only ask you this once. Give it to me before I take it from you. If not, I'll hurt you.'

'I think not,' Dimitrios says as he rounds the corner. Stuart runs his eyes over the table and in one motion, he swipes the kitchen knife, used to cut the cake, from the table and in a full arc, swivels on his heels, slicing the air towards Dimitrios. Carissa screams and Daisy's ears prick upwards. For a split second, the momentum forces Stuart off balance and Dimitrios's foot slams into Stuart's groin. He buckles over, hot flushing pain spreading through his lower abdomen, gasping as he tries to suck in air to quell the sudden nausea clawing at his throat. Then, his head jerks backwards as Dimitrios's fist crunches bone, and blood gushes from his nose.

Stuart stumbles backwards, screaming in pain. The knife clatters to the ground, as his hands cover his nose, blood dripping dramatically through his fingers.

Wide-eyed, with her mouth hanging open, Carissa can't keep her stare from Stuart's moaning and swaying body in front of her.

Dimitrios's foot slams into the back of Stuart's knee and as it buckles, the motion forcing him to fall with another painful scream.

Carissa glances at Dimitrios and then back to Stuart. Her breath stalls in her chest. 'Dimitrios, what have you done?' she gasps. 'I think you've broken his nose.'

Thomas takes a deep breath. 'He'll live. Its only superficial. God. He's dripping all over my floor. I'll call the police.'

'They'll arrest Dimitrios,' Carissa says alarmed.

Thomas shakes his head. 'They won't,'

Unable to suppress her worry, she asks, 'How can you be so sure?'

'This piece of shit entered my property without my permission. He lunged towards Dimitrios and threatened him. Under Greek law, in such circumstances, a person is not punishable when they act to repel an unjust attack, provided the defence is necessary and proportional. His injury isn't fatal; he'll live, unfortunately. It'll be viewed as an act of legitimate self-defence,' he assured her.

'Are you sure?'

Thomas nods, a momentarily look of satisfaction crossing his face. 'I'm good friends with the commander of the police station; we go back a long way. I think it's Stuart who needs to be worrying. Stalking, harassment, threatening violence – and all recorded in his own words. I wouldn't want to be in his shoes.'

Carissa stares at Stuart slumped forward on his knees, his forehead inches from the ground, clutching his nose. He looks like he is supplicating God, yet the sounds that emanate from his lips are not prayers but painful and muffled moans.

He has invaded her life, robbing it of all promise, safety, and happiness, and filling it instead with vile threats, toxic mind games, and constant attempts to shame, humiliate, and demean her.

Now, she realises, she is seeing him for what he is, pathetic, weak, and a coward.

Everything about her feels different now. She has crossed a defining line.

She crouches down so her mouth hovers next to Stuart's ears, and, like a draft of icy cold air, she tells him, 'You're nothing to me. I despise you, and now I'm free of you.'

As she pulls herself to her feet, Carissa fights back the tears. Dimitrios puts his arms around her, and releasing a deep breath, she buries her head into his chest.

'It's over,' he tells her simply.

CHAPTER THIRTY-FIVE

THE SAFE HOUSE

Mainland Greece, Athens 1943

To Selena's relief, Theodore welcomed them into his house, as if he had been expecting them to visit.

'Selena, how you have grown! My God, you were just a child when I saw you last.'

'Of course she has grown, she's a woman now,' Maria, his wife, said, shaking her head.

Theodore poured thick, viscous coffee from a battered pot, his movements quick and noiseless, the gesture so familiar and practised that Selena felt a scrape of nostalgia in her chest. They sat at the table, the drawn curtains muting sunlight to a faint dusty haze, while outside, the city made its slow, cautious start to the day. She saw the resemblance. Theodore was definitely Thimios's brother, but older looking, his hair receding, with a thinner face, where his cheeks sagged with deep-set lines.

Selena sipped the coffee from the chipped cup

Theodore pressed into her hands, and she explained the events that led them to Athens and finally to his house. Theodore was insistent that they stay under his roof until they contacted EAM headquarters.

Maria watched Selena with a nervous sympathy. 'You're safe now,' she said and set a small bowl of three boiled eggs onto the table. 'Eat, you must be starving. I'm afraid it's not much.'

'It's enough, thank you.'

Maria smiled and nodded. She seemed pleased.

'I need to get word to an agent of ours. He goes under the name of Prometheus,' Thomas said.

Theodore looked at Thomas and smiled sadly. 'I know this name. I'm afraid you're too late. He's been arrested. The news of his arrest travelled through Athens like wildfire. He was a big catch for the Germans.'

Thomas allowed this news to sink in. 'Damn!' He was grasping the gravity of their predicament. 'This is a safe house, right?'

'I do what I can.'

'Then you must have connections, people you're in touch with. People inside EAM.'

'I know a man. Not his name. He contacts me when they want someone to be invisible for a while, before they move them on.'

'This man, can you get a message to him?'

'If I need to. There is a way.'

'Then, get him to come here. Selena needs to speak with him. Can you do this?'

Theodore nodded.

'It's important we see him. Can this be arranged?'

'I will try.'

Thomas took off his jacket, and Theodore's eyes caught

the holster and revolver. Theodore glanced towards Maria. She, too, had seen it, but she couldn't hide the tremor of shock that passed through her. She wiped her hands on her apron and turned to Selena. 'I'll show you the room you're sleeping in. You can wash. There is a basin with water and a towel.'

Two days later, Theodore returned from the market.

'I heard some interesting news when I was out. The Asopos viaduct has been blown up. Operations led by British officers and *andarte* bands have blown up railway lines and roads between Larissa and Salonika, and the Tempe valley beneath Olympus. In Thessaly, bridges have been blown up, and closer to home, east of Agrinion on the coastal road that leads to Athens, a large road bridge was also blown up. It looks like the Allies are stepping up their operations. That can only be a good thing, right?'

Thomas knew Eddie and Chris had now been instructed to begin widespread sabotage throughout Greece. He smiled to himself. This could mean one thing: the Allies were going to invade Sicily, not Greece. These operations were a decoy to make the Germans think it was Greece the Allies intended to invade. Thomas thought of Denys Hamson and Tom Barnes, and the other British Liaison Officers he had spent so much time with since arriving in Greece and how he wished he could share in their success. He sighed. His war was different now.

'I thought this would make you happy, Thomas. You look like you've just attended your mother's funeral,' Theodore said.

'I'm happy. Of course, I am.'

'Then you're sad you missed all the fun?'

'Yes, something like that.'

'I also heard something else. Given the recent upsurge in the Allies' operations, the Germans are desperate for information and intelligence that can help them counter these operations. A British officer like yourself, who is already in Athens, would be a valuable prize and a major coup for them if captured. They're searching the city as we speak. It's no secret that there are British officers operating in Athens.'

Maria handed Theodore a cup of coffee. 'Thank you, dear.'

'The streets will be a dangerous place. Patrols will be increased. The police and the Germans will view everyone with suspicion. Everyone is a suspect. There'll be roundups, many arrests, most not warranted,' Thomas warned.

'It's worse than that,' Theodore said.

'What do you mean?'

'The Germans have put up a reward if it leads to the capture of British officers. It's a small fortune. Priests would turn in their own children for so much money.'

Selena's hands curled reflexively, her nails biting into her palms. 'Even in Athens there's no escape. We're not safe. Wherever we go, people will bargain for our heads.' The realisation rattled her nerves.

Theodore set his cup down, both hands folded around it. 'War rots everything it touches; nothing remains sweet for long, not even loyalty.'

Maria set her knife down with a brittle clunk. 'People are afraid. Already at the baker's and the grocer's, food is running short. People are paranoid that their houses are being watched,' she said, and let it hang in the air, as her hands worried the edge of her apron.

'What about Apostolis?' Thomas thought out loud. 'Do you think he's in Athens?'

Selena shook her head. 'If he knows what's happening, he won't risk coming here, not now.'

Theodore gazed at Selena. 'You can't trust anyone. Not even EAM.'

'What do you mean?'

'Even within their ranks, there're shadows within shadows, if you know what I mean.'

'How do you know this?' Thomas asked.

'My contact, he's told me. No one is safe, not even me, if it suits the interests of his superiors. It's like swatting a fly to them.'

'And yet, you still do this,' Selena said.

'If I'm betrayed, it'll be with the eyes of a neighbour, the voice of a friend.' He fixed Selena with a stare, hard and cold, and she flinched from its certainty.

'We can't stay here,' Selena said, 'Not even another night.'

'I'm meeting my contact this evening. He has reassured me, he will set up a meeting with important people high in EAM's apparatus. Be patient, Selena. You can't keep running. Eventually, there'll be nowhere for you to run to.'

No one pretended this prospective meeting was enough. But it was something. It is always something, Selena thought, until the little somethings are all that's left.

The rest of the day stretched and coiled like a snake between the shabby walls. Selena fought the urge to pace. She wanted desperately to move, to act, to be the Selena she used to be, not this trapped bird in a cage.

Maria had called in on a neighbour, recently fallen ill,

and left them a pot of stew for their evening meal. When darkness fell, Theodore left the house, promising to return with his contact.

He had reminded them to stay in their room as he switched all the lights off in the house. 'If I am seen leaving, the house needs to look like there is no one home.'

They sat in the dark murkiness of the room. Thomas rubbed his hand against his jaw. 'Theodore is right; we need to be patient. It's a delicate situation and one we have no control over.'

'I'm getting used to that,' her voice withered.

'Whatever happens, we'll do this together,' he reassured her.

In the dimness, he saw a thought pass across her face.

She moved her weight against him. 'Do you love me?'

This surprised Thomas. 'Why do you have to ask?'

'Just answer me.'

'What's this, the inquisition?'

'I'm being serious. Do you love me?'

'You know I do.'

'It's the only thing in my life I still have, the only thing that still feels real.'

He saw a shaft of light, heard a murmur, a rattle, and then a shuffle. He inclined his head, his mind now alert. Their eyes fixed on one another. He couldn't see the details of her face, and later, the lack of such intimacy would crush him. She took his hand and whispered, 'I love you.' He squeezed it in return and said her name; a final pleading summons.

He hesitated just once, then he was crouched by the door, head pressed to its surface, his grip tight around his revolver. A thud of boots preceded the rush of air. Thomas stood then, arms raised in front, the revolver poised. He thought then he should turn around to see her one last time, and then it began. Thomas couldn't remember how many shots he fired or how many hit their intended targets, but when the door cracked from its hinges, the world exploded in front of him. He heard her fractured voice, shrieking his name, again and again, before it broke into a muffled sound, then darkness – and finally nothing.

CHAPTER THIRTY-SIX

RESOLUTION

Skiathos 2007

Two days later

'What happened?' Carissa's brain is in turmoil as she sits in the porch's shade, along with Dimitrios and Thomas. The customary pot of tea takes centre stage in the middle of the table as Daisy snores softly at Thomas's feet.

After a deep breath, Thomas says, 'Somehow, not one bullet hit me. The Germans wanted to take me alive.'

'So, who were they firing at, Selena?'

'It was too dark to see anything. I fired first, and obviously they returned fire. It was confusing mayhem. The thing is, I don't know what happened. I just remember bodies rushing at me, knocking me over, blows to my arms, legs and head, then nothing. The next thing I knew, I was in a cell. Somewhere in Athens.'

Her heart clenches. 'And Selena?'

'I prayed she had been taken as well, otherwise…'

'She was dead?'

He nods.

'The Gestapo interrogated me for days. They were civil at first, but then, when I refused to answer any of their questions, they employed more severe tactics. Eventually, I was taken to Haidari prison.'

'It was a harsh place; even today, people know about it.' Dimitrios points out.

'It was hell on earth — an expression that can't be overstated for a place like that. The British were placed in the same block. Which helped keep us sane. We were fed one meal a day, if you could call it that — soup that was little more than cloudy water, with a taste so foul it lingered in your mouth like something rotten. A scrap of bread came with it, dry and stale, but you learned to savour it as though it were a feast. Still, it wasn't the food that kept us going. It was each other.

'There's something about hearing your own language; it reminded us that we weren't alone. There were Englishmen, Irish lads, Scots and Welshmen too. Each of us brought a piece of home.

'We swapped stories. We even sang, sometimes just to drown out the screams from another part of the prison. It forged an unspoken bond. Without that camaraderie, I think many of us would've gone mad. The Gestapo could strip us of everything else — our freedom, our dignity, even our health, but they couldn't take that from us.

'I became friendly with a chap from Edinburgh; we were about the same age. Both Frank and I bonded through our shared affection for two Greek women and similar experiences of separation. His story was a fascinating one. He wasn't a soldier; he was a war artist.'

'He drew pictures of the war?' Carissa asks, not sure what that really meant.

'Before the war he was an artist. Being a war artist was important work, as much a part of the war effort as ours was in the mountains of Greece. It built morale among the troops. It stirred the nation's conscience and patriotism too.

'I often wonder what became of him, if he eventually made it back to Corfu and the woman he loved. He was adamant he was going back there, back to find her.'

'And you?' Carissa asks hopefully.

'I didn't have that choice.' Thomas looks down at his untouched teacup. 'When it was certain the Allies were winning and pressing the Germans back further into Europe, they abandoned the prison and Athens in retreat. By then, my old demons had returned with a vengeance. My body was broken, as was my mind. The little girl continued her visitations, this time with more vengeance, reminding me it was not just her family I couldn't save, but Selena too.'

Carissa stirs her tea. 'And now?'

'We've grown into a married old couple. Now, she's just a noise in my head, that I've learned to switch off… most of the time.'

'I see.' She looks intently at him. 'Did you ever return to Greece after the war once you had recovered?

Thomas clears his throat. 'Back in England, I spent months in hospital, waiting and willing my body and mind to heal.

'Eventually, the army had little use for a man in my condition,' he states flatly. 'So, I returned to what I knew, academia. I was fortunate to secure a lecturing post at my old college at Eton. The Dean was an old army colleague; otherwise, I doubt I would have been offered such a position

given my medical records. He arranged for me to get counselling. And after a long, protracted two years of weekly,
then monthly sessions, the nightmare receded, but was not
entirely conquered. The years passed, and on the whole, I
was happy with my lot.'

'Did you meet anyone?' Carissa asks, eager to know.

'I did. We married and we divorced.'

'Oh, I'm sorry.'

'Don't be; it was for the best. Luckily, there were no children involved, just material wrangling. And then, an opportunity came my way, which I grabbed with both hands. A
post at Athens University, Greek classics and Greek studies.
It was perfect. I spent fifteen happy years there.'

Carissa regards him in surprise. 'On your own?'

'Not exactly. I'd been stung by my failed marriage, and I
enjoyed the bachelor life too much. I suppose in a way, I
became selfish. I couldn't commit to anything serious.'

'Did you ever think about Selena? Did you find out what
happened to her?'

'The war changed everything. Back in England, I wasn't
the man I'd been back then. Life has a habit of continuing.
If she were still alive, if she had survived that night, she
could have married, had children, moved away from
Greece. As time passed, my life changed. She has never
been far from my thoughts… never.'

'You still love her.'

'I never stopped.'

'How did you end up living in Skiathos?' Dimitrios asks.

Thomas smiles. 'Ah! Now that was rather unconventional for someone who likes to know what's two feet in
front of him. I loved my work, but there comes a time when
even the things we love become a burden. Well, that's not
entirely true. Athens had changed. It was noisy, too busy,

with too much traffic, and it had got too big. I took the decision by the horns and retired. I had a map of Greece on my study wall. I picked up a pen, closed my eyes, hovered the pen and placed it on the map. When I opened my eyes, the ballpoint lay over Skiathos. It's been a good choice. After all these years, it's been my home. It's the only place I've ever felt grounded in. It's where I belong.'

'Any regrets?' Carissa asks.

'Only one. And at my age, I think it's time I resolved it.'

CHAPTER THIRTY-SEVEN

A BEAUTIFUL THING

Skiathos 2007

Dimitrios wraps his fingers around her hand. It is the first time he has displayed his affection in public. It feels liberating, reaffirming. He can no longer carry on with the pretence.

'It doesn't matter to me that we're colleagues and what people might think,' he tells her. 'I want the world to know what you mean to me and just how much I love you.'

Carissa looks into his face and can see his eyes smiling back at her.

'I want to take you somewhere.'

'But we're going to visit Thomas, he's expecting us,' she reminds him.

'I know. It won't take long. It's just up here,' he says, as they turn off Papadiamanti Street, along a narrow lane and ascend white stone steps that lead to Agios Nikolaos Church.

It's a steep and narrow climb that takes her past white-

washed houses blooming in striking colours that cascade
from walls and wrought-iron balconies like floral water-
falls. A black cat eyes them suspiciously before disappearing through a wooden gate. They climb, hand in
hand, a few more steep steps before reaching Agios Nikolaos Church and the unfolding panoramic view of
Skiathos Town.

'It's wonderful. What a view!' Carissa enthuses as she
catches her breath.

'I thought you'd like it.'

'I can't believe I've been here all this time and never
knew about this place, this view.'

'If you look over there,' Dimitrios points. 'There's the
old port and just beyond it, Plakes, where your apartment
is.'

Carissa's eyes gaze out over terracotta tiled roofs that
incline towards a headland, then gently slope into the glass-
like sea. She is smiling.

'And do you know what else you see?'

She looks more carefully. 'What?'

'Down there, amongst the houses, the lanes, the shops
and restaurants, along the old port and up to Plakes, you
can now walk and live without ever having to wonder if he's
watching you.'

She remembers the rage and the fear, the waves of
nausea, her body forever tensing and the paranoid sense of
being watched every time she set foot out of her apartment.
It felt an indulgence to feel free, to feel normal again. She
felt the strangest sensation, as if the darkness was lifting and
her world was finally transforming and beginning to shine
in a glorious and wonderful light.

'Did you scream at walls?' a half-smile stretches his lips.

Carissa gives a small, humourless laugh. 'Only once. No,

maybe twice. After the miscarriage. And when I realised how small he'd made my life.'

She looks at him and lets out her breath. 'I wasn't perfect by any means, but I was scared. I'd started to believe what he said about me – that I was difficult. Overreacting. Selfish for wanting to be with my friends and not him. And the worst part? I stayed. I stayed even when I knew something was *wrong with him*, not me.'

She reaches out and takes his hand, curling her fingers around his. 'I thought if I told you about the ugly parts, the weak parts, maybe you'd see me like he does. A mess to manage. A fire that will burn you. And despite it all, I still have you and this life together.' She brings his hand to her lips and kisses it. 'It's a beautiful thing to finally know who I am.'

CHAPTER THIRTY-EIGHT

RETURNING

Thessaly 2007

He wonders whether the village, now grown into a small town, will bear any resemblance to how he recalls it. The olive groves have changed little, and the road is now smoother than the dirt track he remembers. A ferry, then a bus, has brought him this far, and now he walks the final stretch, the afternoon sun warming the back of his neck.

A narrow path opens to the square where the old café still stands, now a thriving restaurant, its shutters freshly painted. To his amazement, the same tree remains from all those years ago, its silver leaves still rustling in the breeze and casting shadows over wicker chairs and tables.

He stands, leaning on his walking stick as the swirl of voices and the clatter of cutlery wash over him. It is a bustle of activity and serenity all at the same time. Children dash between tables, women gossip with flailing hands, old men drink coffee, and day trippers sample with gusto the authentic Greek menu.

He takes in the sign, *Selena*, and his heart jumps in his chest.

He watches the woman at the heart of it all. She is walking amongst the diners, placing a gentle, encouraging hand on a waiter, stopping and talking at each table, her back stooped, her hair pinned up in a loose bun and her hands quick and expressive. The melody of her voice tumbles over the laughter of children, and her smile, genuine and warm, spreads beneath the slope of her cheeks. She is the centre of attention, and even from where he stands; the resemblance is enough to make his pulse race.

His eyes remain locked on her, unable to look away, his gaze fixated, captivated.

Her gaze lifts, and Thomas sees a strange expression steal across her face, and then, a subtle glimpse of recognition. She presses a hand to the base of her back and straightens herself. As Thomas's hand tightens on the handle of his walking stick, he can hardly breathe, barely move. Around him, the sun's light is dazzling and jarring.

It is her, and it is not. The realisation folds around him, like a clamp, squeezing the years of hope from his heart.

She is standing beside him. 'Are you alright?'

Thomas nods. 'I thought I saw someone I knew, but I was mistaken. You look remarkably like her.'

'I'm sorry to disappoint you. I'm Sofia. This is my restaurant.'

'But the name, it says, Selena.'

'I know; I named it after my sister, in her honour.'

The taverna swirls around him.

'I didn't know she had a sister. She never spoke about you. I'm sorry, this won't be making any sense to you.'

Sofia smiles at him; it is a look that reaches across the years. Gently, she places her hand on his arm. 'Before the war, I was married, and my husband found work in Salonika. I followed him. Before I left, Selena and I had a falling out. The reason is not important, but we never spoke from that day on, and when the war came, it was impossible to visit. I heard of my parents' death at the hands of the Germans three months after their funeral. Before then, my relationship with Selena was, how can I say, fractious. Only a miracle was ever going to repair it. I never got my miracle.'

'She could be stubborn. I felt her bite a few times too,' a smile creeps slowly across Thomas's face.

'You were the one who saved her from the firing squad, the soldier she was with in Athens.'

He nods his head.

'I saw you standing just now. I thought it was you. I've been waiting for this day. I knew you'd come.'

'That night when it happened, it was just the two of us. When I think back, it was as if she knew. She asked me whether I loved her. She knew I did, but it was like the final confirmation. She was getting ready.' The brim of his eyes glistened with tears. He attempts a smile; it proves difficult. 'How can she be dead, when she has been alive in my heart all these years?'

Sofia waves a waiter over, a young girl, who pulls up a chair.

'Please sit down,' she says to Thomas and turns to the girl. 'Clara, could you fetch us some water? Thank you, my dear.'

Once they are seated, Thomas apologises. 'I'm sorry. I didn't expect that to happen.'

'It's been a shock.'

'For a second, when I saw you, I thought it was her. I thought you were Selena.'

Clara places a jug of water and two glasses on the table. Sofia flashes a smile at her.

'I have to ask you. What happened to her?' Thomas asks.

For the first time, sadness clouds Sofia's face. 'We don't know. I'm sorry. Her body was never recovered. Thimios tried his best to find out, but his efforts were fruitless. All we know is she died that night at Theodore's house.'

Thomas knows this. He has known it since his incarceration in Haidari, since convalescing in England after the war, every single day during his marriage, his years in Athens, and latterly in Skiathos. Was it too painful to confront the truth? Was the hope she may still be alive enough for him to hold on to – a hope that helped him to keep going, and that, in the end, allowed him to pursue a life of possibilities?

Sofia's usual smile returns. 'There is a memorial to her in the cemetery here in the town.'

This news is unexpected yet pleasing. 'I'd like to see it.'

'I could show you, or if you prefer, you can go on your own.'

'If you don't mind, I'd like to go on my own.'

She nods, 'I thought you would. There's another thing I should tell you. Theodore and Maria never collected the reward for your capture. In the end, there was no reward. They were both tried and shot by the Germans for keeping a safe house and harbouring Allied soldiers and enemies of the Third Reich. Their greed was their downfall, but unfortunately, it sealed your fate and Selena's death.'

Thomas feels nothing towards Theodore and Maria at this news.

. . .

The cemetery is bigger than Thomas imagined, where cypress trees gently sway below a blue canopy of sky. He walks under an ornate arched entrance, crowned by a cross and flanked by weathered stone pillars. The first thing that strikes him is the profusion of colour from bouquets of roses and lilies interspersed amongst the many brilliant white crosses, some new and polished, others crumbling and aged, all stretched out in rows.

The air is fragrant with incense and candles burning amongst the white-marble headstones, each etched with names that once echoed through the lanes and village square, now immortalised in stone. Many bear icons: the tender face of Christ or the visages of saints whose names have been passed from grandfather to grandson.

The gravel path crunches softly beneath his feet. It leads him past small lamps that stand over graves framed in low, whitewashed walls, or small, roofed shrines with clouded glass doors, where oil lamps glow dimly beside curved photographs, their edges faded with time. Every grave, old or new, shares the same truth: all have been lovingly cared for, holding the dead in their gentle embrace.

Eventually, he finds it − a square marble plaque, bordered by freshly laid flowers and a flickering oil lamp. He places his glasses on the bridge of his nose and bends forward to read the inscription.

Selena Castellanos, daughter of Greece.
Who, in the struggle against tyranny, chose honour over fear.
A partisan of freedom, a flame in the dark years, her struggle lit the
path to liberty.
She gave her life for her homeland − a martyr for the people.

Those who live in every free breath of Greece will remember her name.
May Greece never forget her.
In eternal memory.
Selena Castellanos
1920 – 1943

His hand presses on the handle of his walking stick, the knuckles white and taut. He remembers what she said when they rescued her from the firing squad. *'Where can I go? I can't go back home. In their eyes, I'm a traitor. The only safe traitor is a dead one.'*

His eyes water with tears. He recalls her blind panic, her distress, deep and instant, her dark eyes fearful of the accusations that would stain her memory. It tore at her, the thought that she would be known as a traitor to her country, while all her heart ever did was beat for Greece.

'You have been admonished, my darling. You have been written into Greece's history. The truth will forever be spoken, and your name will be honoured forever.'

There were a million things he wanted to say, but they fell into insignificance around him. There was only one thing she needed to hear.

'It's been a lifetime, lost years that feel like yesterday. I have always felt you around me; your closeness saved me. I never stopped loving you, my darling, Selena.'

Something inside him flutters, and for a moment, Selena is reaching out across the years; he feels her around him, that familiar density he knows so well. In the still, fused air, he breathes in the scent of her and knows the intimate touch of her hand upon his face, the brush of her hair on his cheek.

He has not said goodbye. This is not a place of endings,

but of returning families, returning husbands, wives, friends, and lovers.

His past breathes softly.

He has found her.

ALSO IN THE HELLENIC COLLECTION

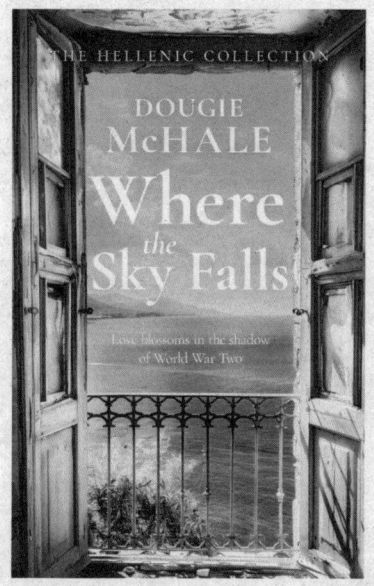

vinci-books.com/skyfalls

In the shadow of World War Two, love blossoms—but at a devastating cost.

Turn the page for a free preview…

WHERE THE SKY FALLS PREVIEW
CALTON HILL

Edinburgh 2010

He feels it instantly, plummeting through him, a surge of regret, a spasm of unfaithfulness. In the slanting light, her sapphire eyes sparkle like the gliding seawater of the River Forth that carves the shoreline behind them. It was an immediate reaction; he felt it the moment Zoe looked at him, a definite attraction. Admitting his desire felt a betrayal to his past.

'We were on holiday in St Monans, staying at a caravan park,' Rob tells Zoe, whose gaze is fastened to her shoes as they stroll.

'I was fishing with my dad on the pier and caught a flounder, or a plaice. I'm not sure which. It was a flat fish, anyway. Mum gutted it in the sink, cooked it and we ate it for dinner. Before that, I had my photograph taken with it. It was the late 70s, and I had on these jeans with massive flares, so wide they looked like sails. I couldn't tell you what my shoes looked like. And my haircut, God, it was a typical bowl cut. Horrendous now, but back then, it was your mum that cut your hair and there wasn't a menu of styles on offer.'

Zoe laughs and lifts her head. She glances at Rob. 'I'd love to see that photograph.'

'I'll need to dig it out. It's still at Mum's, in the cupboard under the stairs. She's got hundreds of photographs. Not that long ago, she said she was going to throw most of them out. There were too many of them, she said. Luckily, I persuaded her not to. I told her it would be like throwing away your history. They're not just photographs, they're time capsules, captured moments of family and friends, past generations who live forever in images that are precious, that tell the story of where we've come from and who we are. She said she'd never thought about it like that.' Rob smiles. 'A few weeks later, when I visited Mum again, she couldn't wait to show me what she'd done.'

'And what was that?'

'She'd put them in albums, catalogued them, recorded who was in a particular photograph, where it had been taken, and all in chronological order. I couldn't believe it.'

'You must have made a big impression on her. She went from one extreme to the other.'

'She did, but that was her nature.' He smiles at the memory. 'There was never any middle ground with Mum.'

'How is she?' Zoe asks.

Rob thinks for a second. He scratches his head. 'She looks like Mum, but Mum has gone. The person she was no longer exists. She's been erased. I don't know how else to describe it.'

'It's a terrible disease… devastating.'

'I try to visit as often as I can. I know she's in the best place. The staff are amazing. I can't fault them. It doesn't make it any easier, though.'

'You had no choice. She was a danger to herself, wandering outside in the middle of the night.'

'I know. I just thought I'd have more time with her. I didn't expect the dementia to take her from us as quickly as it did. It's not just that. I feel like her whole life has disappeared. The house is going on the market, the furniture is being sold or going to charity shops. I'm sifting through everything just now. It's going to take a while. She never threw anything out. I've found receipts from years ago.'

'What about Sue? Is she helping you?'

'She keeps promising to come up from London, but there's always an excuse, usually work related.'

'She's her mother, too. Has she visited her?'

'Not much. The last time was about two months ago.'

'That's bad. You'd think she'd want to spend time with her.'

'She hardly visited Mum at the best of times. Mum would never hear a bad word against her, always made excuses for her. She'd say, *"A job like that comes with a lot of responsibility."* It was her default for Sue's constant absence. It came with a big salary. It would be nothing for her to jump on a plane and be up here within an hour.'

'I don't understand that. Why wouldn't she want to visit her mum, especially now? And what about her children? It's their gran. When did she last see them?'

'It must be about a year ago.'

'That's dreadful,' Zoe snorts incredulously.

'I know. The thing is, Mum never did get on with Gary, Sue's husband, and the feeling was mutual. Sue was oblivious to it. I'm sure half the time she wasn't even in the room. It was like her head was in a bubble.'

'Maybe that was intentional. Easier to just ignore it.'

'The things Gary used to say to Mum were dreadful at times. He treated Mum like she was beneath him. I'm sure that's what he thought, anyway. You could tell he hated having to visit. He made no attempt to hide his disdain. *"The house was too small, the neighbours were too noisy, and why did Mum still live in a council estate?"* He seems to forget that's where Sue grew up, too. I'd hate to think about what he used to tell his kids; it would be all lies. It's a shame. They have never really got to know their gran. Gary made sure of that.'

'And it's too late now.'

There is a silence as Zoe's words seep into him.

'They think Mum won't last the month.'

'That's just two weeks.'

A resigned smile crosses his face. They look out over the panoramic cityscape. A slight breeze licks at their clothes; Zoe's hair blows over her face and she flicks the strands from her eyes. The light is fading as a bank of clouds rolls above the River Forth and silver pin prick lights twinkle over the coastline of Fife.

'How did your mum end up living in Elie?'

'My mum's sister, Auntie Betty, moved there when she got married to my uncle Max. He was a lawyer and had just become a partner in a practice in St Andrews. Mum loved to visit them in their little mansion, as she called it. It wasn't, it was just a big house, but I suppose it felt like a mansion to Mum back then. Anyway, Betty and Max never had children and when Max died, Mum stayed every week-end. She even went to the church on a Sunday with Betty and, as a result, met a lot of people who became friends.

When Betty died, to Mum's disbelief, Betty had gifted the house to her. By then, Dad had passed away, so Mum left her little council house and moved into her little mansion, where she lived for several years blissfully.'

'That's so lovely and I bet it stuck in Gary's throat. I'd have loved to have seen his face.'

'Oh, he never visited Mum. Sue came a few times with the kids, but always had an excuse about why Gary wasn't with her.'

'God, I hate that man and I haven't even met him.'

Rob laughs. 'I wouldn't worry about it. He has that effect on most people.'

They strolled for several minutes until the imposing clock tower of The Balmoral Hotel came into view and the Gothic spires of Scott Monument and St Mary's Cathedral rose above Princes Street towards the early evening sky.

'There's something empowering and calming at the same time when you see Edinburgh on this hill. Don't you think?' Zoe asks.

'She's full of contradictions, but isn't that her charm?'

Zoe's eyes fasten on him. 'Your eyes seem to brighten when you speak about this place. Your face lights up. If Edinburgh were a woman, you'd be madly in love with her.'

'There's only one woman I've ever been madly in love with.'

'Oh, Rob. I'm sorry. I still miss Soph every day.' Zoe touches Rob's arm. 'I can't imagine how it must be for you.'

'If I said it gets easier as time passes, I'd be lying. I think I've just got used to living this way, but there isn't a day that goes by that the loss of Soph doesn't stab my heart.'

They walk a little further and then Rob turns to Zoe. 'I'm going to Mum's tomorrow. There're a few documents I need to pick up for the solicitor. Would you like to come?'

'I've nothing planned. I'd like that.'

'I'll show you that photograph if you promise not to laugh.'

She smiles. 'I'll try.'

Rob was married to Sophie for two years when a routine trip to the doctor changed their lives. Sophie had been feeling tired and lost weight and thought she might be iron deficient. Being vegetarian, and ironically, not liking many vegetables, she thought the supplement tablets she took were enough to balance what she otherwise lacked.

The resulting blood test highlighted something more sinister. Sophie was referred to a specialist and after further investigations involving an ultrasound scan and CT scan, they diagnosed her with ovarian cancer. She underwent surgery to remove the cancer, but they discovered the cancer had spread.

Zoe was Sophie's best friend, and they both enjoyed the same social group. They went to the same university and trained as primary teachers, securing their first job, and starting on the same day in the same primary school. Zoe was the chief bridesmaid at Rob and Sophie's wedding.

Rob had been married for 857 days when his wife was taken from him, and for the next six months, he too felt like he was dead.

WHERE THE SKY FALLS PREVIEW
THE PHOTOGRAPH

Elie

'I've never been to this part of Fife,' Zoe says as she scans the fields that gently descend into a thicket of trees and the wide River Forth and in the distance, she can make out the familiar shape of the Bass Rock.

He turns to look at her, his hands set flat against the steering wheel. 'Really!'

'Yeah. I wasn't expecting it to be...' she pauses, searching for the word.

'So nice.' It is a weak attempt to hide his sarcasm.

'I can't think of the word, but sometimes the simplest expression is best... just beautiful.'

He smiles. 'We're almost there.'

Soon, the flat fields, farm buildings and narrow road are left behind as the wider road and stone and brick houses of Elie engulf Zoe's view. She catches sight of a church with a dominant steeple and when they turn into the High Street with its quaint shop fronts, she notices a small deli and café and imagines Rob's mum shopping and meeting friends for lunch. To her surprise, around them, the sky fills with large black birds, gliding and landing in several small trees that populate the ground amongst picnic tables. She cranes her neck to get a better look.

'They're crows. Look up into the trees. You'll see their nests.'

Zoe sucks in her breath. 'My God! I've never seen so many nests. They're huge and so close to people.'

'I know. I had the same reaction when I first saw them. Here we are, just in here.'

Rob turns right, and the car enters a gate between a garden wall draped with foliage. They stop in front of a red brick house where the bricks around the windows are painted white, as is the prodigious entrance door. They step out of the car and Zoe is delighted to see an apple orchard.

'Mum was famous for her apple pies. She had an endless supply of apples here,' Rob says, smiling at the memory.

'I can't believe you're selling this place.' Zoe takes in the house and garden.

'Sue wants to sell it.'

'And you don't?'

Rob manages a smile. 'What do you think?'

'I think I know who's behind it.'

He puts the key in the lock and opens the door. They step into a black and white tiled mosaic hallway with a dark wooden staircase.

'Wow! This is incredible.'

'It's all original features.'

His expression is hard to read, but she can hear a sadness in his voice.

After a tour of the house, they sit in the kitchen. Rob hands Zoe a coffee and settles into a chair opposite her.

Zoe cradles her cup in both hands and looks around the kitchen. 'There's no way I'd sell this house. It has far too much potential.'

'House prices have gone through the roof, especially for property like this. There's a high demand for this area. There's a lot of city types who'd pay well over the price to have a house in the East Neuk.'

'A holiday home, you mean?'

'It would make an ideal family home.'

'It would.'

'Mum was happy here. She loved it. I'd hate for it to be empty half of the year.'

'It doesn't have to be.'

Rob tilts his head. 'What do you mean?'

'Buy her out.'

'Sue?' His voice rises.

'Yeah.'

'I couldn't afford to. You're talking about four hundred and fifty thousand pounds, maybe half a million.'

He gazes out of the window at the sunshine shafting through the branches of the trees in the orchard.

'I thought you were going to show me that photograph,' she says, attempting to lift his mood.

'They're stored in the cupboard under the stairs. I'll just be a sec.'

He returns with a large box and places it on the kitchen table. The dates 1980 to 1985 are written in a felt-tip pen on the lid.

'There're hundreds of photographs in here. Luckily, since Mum catalogued them, it should be easy to find.'

'I love looking at old photos. There's just something special about holding one in your hand. It's handy being able to store them on your phone, but I just feel you're closer to the subject, the person... That sounds weird,' she says dismissively.

'I don't think it does. I'd agree with you.'

Rob opens the box and peers inside. He runs his finger along the spines of the photo albums where specific dates are written. 'This is the one.'

He pulls out a photo album and sits down, grinning to himself. 'Promise you won't laugh.'

'I'll try not to.' Zoe smiles and shuffles to the edge of her chair.

He locates the photo and turns the album so that Zoe can get a better look.

She leans in. 'You look so cute, and your hair is blonde... Wow! Now that's what I call flares and that must be Sue standing next to you.'

'She must be about six.'

'And you. How old were you?'

'I'd be ten.'

Zoe raises her eyebrows. 'The fish isn't the biggest I've seen.'

'No, it's not. It looked big to me at the time. It was probably the first fish I caught.'

'And were there more... fish?'

'I can't remember ever enjoying fishing. It was the only thing Dad and I did together. I was playing football for the school team by then, so the fishing took a back step.'

Zoe flicks through the photographs that sit smugly in

their protective sheets. 'Here's one of your mum and dad. He was a handsome man, and your mum looks so young.'

'Let me see.' Rob thinks for a second. 'That was Sue's First Holy Communion. There's a photo of her on the next page looking saintly.'

Zoe moves on to the next page and tilts her head to the side in mild bemusement. Sue is wearing a white top and skirt and a blue sash with a silver pendant pinned to it. Zoe notices Sue's shoes encased in a tidemark of mud, and she grins. 'She looks like she's hating every minute of it.'

'She got grounded for a week. Mum was furious, said she had never been so embarrassed. Before the mass took place, Sue tried to run away right through a field covered in mud. She was caught by a man walking his dog and seeing how Sue was dressed, he brought her right back to the church. That's the last photograph taken of my dad before the accident.'

'It must have been hard for your mum, two young kids to look after on her own and she was so young herself.'

'I don't know how she would have coped if it weren't for Gran and Grandad. Mum had to work, so Sue and I spent a lot of time at their house. My grandad was like a father to me. He filled a massive hole. He was always there for me. He brought me up like I was a son to him, and when he died, it was like I'd lost my dad. I miss him. In a way, it brings it all back. Grandad, Soph, and... Well, Mum hasn't got long.'

Zoe looks in the box and tries to sound upbeat. 'There must be hundreds of photographs in here.'

'There's another three boxes under the stairs.'

Zoe hands Rob the photo album, and just as he is about to replace it in the box, a small envelope drops onto the table. He picks it up and turns it on his fingers, studying its yellow edges. 'I've never seen this before.'

'It must have been tucked in between the pages.'

'How intriguing.'

'It's an old envelope.'

'Well, aren't you going to see what's inside it?' Her voice is louder than she expects.

A small frown creases the side of his mouth and Zoe wonders what he is thinking. Rob runs his finger along the length of the envelope before opening it. He sits back in his chair and pulls out a photograph.

Zoe waits for him to speak. His silence seems an eternity. He gazes at Zoe. 'It's an old photograph of a family I don't recognise,' he says, mystified.

'Can I see it?' Zoe stretches out her hand.

Rob hands the black-and-white photograph to her. It is old and not what she is expecting. A couple, in their late twenties, are sitting together on two separate chairs, their postures stiff and formal. The woman is wearing a hat and a nondescript, long dress that almost covers her boots. She is in her twenties, her hair is long, her stare unswerving, her cheekbones prominent. She sets her mouth firm. The man's dark suit, waistcoat and white shirt seem worn and aged. And, at his side, a young girl of about three years of age stands, her hand resting on the adult's shoulder. It is the portrait of a family anticipating the flash of the camera.

There is something odd about the composition, and then it dawns on her. None of them are smiling. It was maybe the thing in those days, she thinks.

'Do you know who they are?'

Rob shifts in his chair. 'No. I've not got a clue. It was taken a long time ago.'

'The photograph must mean something to your mum, otherwise why would she have kept it?'

Rob thinks about this. 'I wish I knew.'

WHERE THE SKY FALLS PREVIEW
REMEMBRANCE

I t feels like a bright light has flooded his mind. It is uplifting, important. It feels worthwhile. To do nothing is not an option, this much he knows.

Rob has studied the photograph countless times that his eyes could have, by now, bored a hole in it. He peers into the eyes of the young man and wonders about the man that stares back at him through the grainy image. And his thoughts are always framed with a question - Who are you?

Set in an expanse of farmland and forest, the Georgian country house that is now Leyway Care Home comes into view. Rob's stomach always drops when he turns off the country road and swings onto the long driveway that curves through manicured lawns, tall hedges, and mature trees. He feels he has given up on his mum. He has handed her over to strangers, the caring professional. He knows his guilt is a normal reaction, and that she is now in a place with people that can care for his mum in a way that he, or others, could not. But whenever this building comes into view, he cannot help thinking he has abandoned her, and the dreadful feeling in the pit of his stomach is a constant reminder of this.

Rob parks his car. There are another six cars in the visitor's section of the car park. He checks his watch. It is almost two o'clock. It's always busy on a Saturday, more so on a Sunday, so he always visits his mum on a Saturday afternoon. Not that she is aware of what day it is, or the month. Most days now, she does not even acknowledge him. He often wonders if she is aware of who he is. On the few days that she is lucid, she will call him by his name and if he is lucky, she will say a few words in context before the darkness falls behind her eyes and she is gone from him again.

There are two nurses at the nurse's station. Both are familiar to him, although their names are not.

'Hello, Mr Webster.' A nurse stands to meet him. She is squarely built, in her thirties, he supposes, and he notices the skin at the edges of her lips crease as she smiles. 'How are you today?'

'I'm fine, thanks. And you?'

'I'm good.'

The other nurse, a younger woman, is studying a computer screen. 'It looks like Bill is with your mum. If they're not in the dayroom, he's probably taken her out into the garden. It's a nice day for it.'

'Thanks. I'll take a look.'

The dayroom is off a wide corridor with yellow and brown patterned swirls in the carpeting. Rob has always thought it a depressing floor covering that adds nothing to the ambience of the care home.

There are only a few people sitting in the dayroom, two women drinking tea, and a man, his chin resting on his chest, sleeping in front of a television. One woman appears to be listening intently. She nods and smiles, but the other is not talking to her at all, instead she is staring into her lap. A nursing assistant is standing with his back to the room and looking out of the window.

In the garden, Rob can smell freshly cut grass. The sun has broken through the clouds and is already warming the air. He sees his mum sitting on a bench looking over a fish-pond. Bill is sitting beside her. She looks shrunken, a tiny version of the woman she has been, and he feels a sudden ache in his throat.

When he reaches them, Bill stands, as if now it is not his place to sit beside Rob's mum.

Bill smiles. 'Jeanie, look who's come to see you.'

Rob bends towards his mum and kisses her forehead.

'Hello, Mum.'

A flash of recognition brightens her eyes.

Bill turns to walk away. 'I'll leave you to it.'

Rob nods in appreciation and sits beside his mum, taking her hand in his. Jeanie returns her stare to the fish-pond, retreating from the world around her.

It is enough just to sit with her, to feel her close to him. The familiarity of it sustains him in the absence of conversation.

The air seems heavy; the silence hanging thickly around them. It still catches his breath.

There were always words. His mum was an enthusiastic communicator. If she was not talking to someone, she was absentmindedly talking to herself. She was a tremendous presence that filled the space between people with her infectious personality.

Her eyes flick open and close again.

'Hello, Mum.' Rob tries to sound cheery.

She is not here, but she is. The contradiction, the bitter reality, torments him.

'Mum. I've got something to show you. It's a photograph I found in your house. An old photograph.'

'The fish have all gone.'

Jeanie's words startle him. They are unexpected.

'I liked to watch them swimming in the pond. Did you take the fish?' Jeanie's eyes skim the water.

Rob holds her hand. 'No, Mum. I didn't take the fish.'

'Well, someone did. Are you sure it wasn't you?'

'Maybe whoever took the fish will put them back again.'

'Yes, I would like that. Did you take the fish?'

Rob squeezes his mum's hand. 'No, Mum, I didn't take the fish.'

'Oh.' Jeanie looks at him. 'My son Rob is visiting today. Maybe he knows who took the fish.'

A heaviness bore into him. It feels like grief, the bereavement of a loved one. Rob takes an envelope from his pocket and takes out the small photograph. He shows it to his mum.

'Look, Mum, I've got a photograph.'

Jeanie stares at the pond.

'Do you know who these people are, Mum?'

She looks, but her eyes glaze, and her expression remains set.

'What about the woman? Do you know who she is?'

Jeanie leans in closer.

'I've never seen them before. Do you know who they are, Mum? I found the photograph in your house amongst all the others?' In his desperation, he is asking her too many questions. He knows this. It only confuses her. It is a gamble he thinks is worth taking.

Jeanie screws her face up.

'Try to remember, Mum.'

'He wasn't supposed to be there.'

'The man in the photograph?'

Jeanie stares at the pond.

'Where? Where was he not supposed to be?'

Jeanie leans a hand on the bench, and with an effort, she takes her weight until she is standing. She struggles to keep her balance and sways. Rob stands and takes her by the elbow.

'Careful.'

'I want to see the fish. I always look at the fish.'

They walk the short distance to the pond. Jeanie stares into the murky water. After a while, she looks up and turns to Rob with a questioning look in her eyes. 'The fish have disappeared, just like he did.'

Rob forces a smile. 'Where did he go?'

Jeanie runs her fingers along her forehead. 'An island.'

Rob seizes on the opportunity. 'Try to remember, Mum. I know it's difficult, but it's important.'

He can see she is growing tired. A few seconds pass. He must proceed with patience, yet he is unable to refrain from one more attempt. 'What was the island called?'

Jeanie touches his arm. 'I'd like a cup of tea and some biscuits. Chocolate biscuits would be nice.'

He is aware his mum is slightly swaying. A slight breeze has lifted, cold against his face. 'Come on, let's get you back to your room.'

She looks at him then and smiles. 'Corfu. That's what it was called.'

Get your copy:
vinci-books.com/skyfalls

ABOUT THE AUTHOR

Dougie lives in Dunfermline, Fife, with his wife, daughter, son and golden retriever.

Thank you so much for taking the time to read my novel. It really does mean everything to me. My novels are inspired by my favourite city, Edinburgh and my passion for Greece, her islands, people, landscapes, sea, light and ambience, all of which are important themes and symbols in my writing.

My books encapsulate themes such as love, loss, hope, coming of age and the uncovering of secrets. They are character-driven stories with twists and turns set against the backdrop of Edinburgh and Greece.

I never intended to, but seemingly I write women's contemporary fiction and since ninety-five percent of my readers are women, I suppose that is a good fit.

Since all my books are set in Edinburgh and Greece, you will not be surprised to know that I identify with a physical place and the feeling of belonging, which are prominent in my writing.

Edinburgh is one of the most beautiful cities in the world, it is rich in history, has amazing classical buildings, (the new town of Edinburgh is a world heritage site) and it also has vibrant restaurants and café bars.

Greece occupies my heart. Her history, culture, religion, people, landscape, light, colours and sea inspire me every day. There is almost a spiritual quality to it. I want my novels to have a sense of time and place, drawing the reader into the social and cultural complexities of the characters. I want my characters to speak from the page, where you can identify with them, their hopes, fears, conflicts, loves and emotion. I hope the characters become like real people to you, and it is at that point, you will want to know what is going to happen to the characters, where is their life taking them in the story.

The common denominator is, I want my novels to be about what it means to be human through our relationship with our world, our environment and with each other. Most of all, I want them to be good stories that you, as a reader, can identify with and enjoy.

ACKNOWLEDGMENTS

Heartfelt thanks to Sheona, my wife, for her continued support and constant encouragement. A special thanks to all my advanced readers. They know who they are. I couldn't do this without them, as they have given me invaluable feedback on all my novels. Also, immense gratitude to Debra Newhouse for her editing skills and suggestions that have made this a better novel.

Also, thank you to Vinci Books and to the whole team who support me, especially Stuart Bache for his gorgeous covers and Jane Harris for always being there.

AUTHOR'S NOTE

Eddie Myers, Chris Woodhouse, Themie Marinos, Denys Hamson, Nat Barker, John Cook, Tom Barnes, Barba Niko's, Colonel Zervas, Karalivanos and Aris Veloukhiotis are real-life characters, who were involved in the extraordinary times and events before, during and after the Harling Operation in occupied Greece during World War Two.

My interpretation of Eddie Myers, Chris Woodhouse, the other British Service men involved in the Harling Operation and the major key Greek players of the Greek resistance is my own in accordance with the known facts. All the other characters, including Thomas, are fictitious, and any resemblance to persons dead or living is purely coincidental.

I have tried to be scrupulous in my interpretation of the historical pattern of events in the novel. In order to meet the demands of the plot, I have altered these slightly in the novel's sections where, instead of Eddie Myers, Thomas undertakes the reconnaissance of the three Roumeli viaducts and also, when Thomas is sent to Thessaly, where the sequence and the events are driven and influenced solely by my imagination.

Many online resources and reference books cover the complexity of Greece's history before, during, and after World War Two. I found two to be exceptional in their portrayal of the political, historical and cultural intricacies of Greece during World War Two. C.M. Woodhouse's *The*

Struggle for Greece 1941-1949 and Spyros Tsoutsoumpis' *A History of the Greek Resistance in The Second World War, The People's Armies*.

Eddie Myers' book *Greek Entrapment* is an exceptional account for those wishing to know more about one of the more daring and successful episodes in Greece's history during World War Two. I used this book as a historical reference and tried to remain true to the facts as much as possible.

Greece is more than a backdrop or setting in my novels. It is a significant character. Its history, culture, religion, people, landscape, light, colours and sea inspire the narrative themes such as setting, plot, structure and characters.

As an author, I want my novels to have a sense of time and place, drawing the reader into the social and cultural complexities of the characters. I want my characters to speak from the page, where you, the reader, can identify with their hopes, fears, conflicts, loves and emotions. I hope that you, as a reader, become invested in my characters and want to know where their lives are taking them in the story.

The common denominator is I want my novels to be about what it means to be human through our relationship with our world, our environment and with each other. Most of all, I want them to be good stories that you, as a reader, can connect with.

I wrote The Island Between Us to try and depict the strength, foritude and courage that the men and women both British and Greek showed in abundance during the events of the Greek resistance during World War II. I hope my portrayal does justice to and reflects their bravery and resilience.